T0243184

The Disabled Tyrant's Beloved Pet Fish

Canji Baojun De Zhangxin Yu Chong

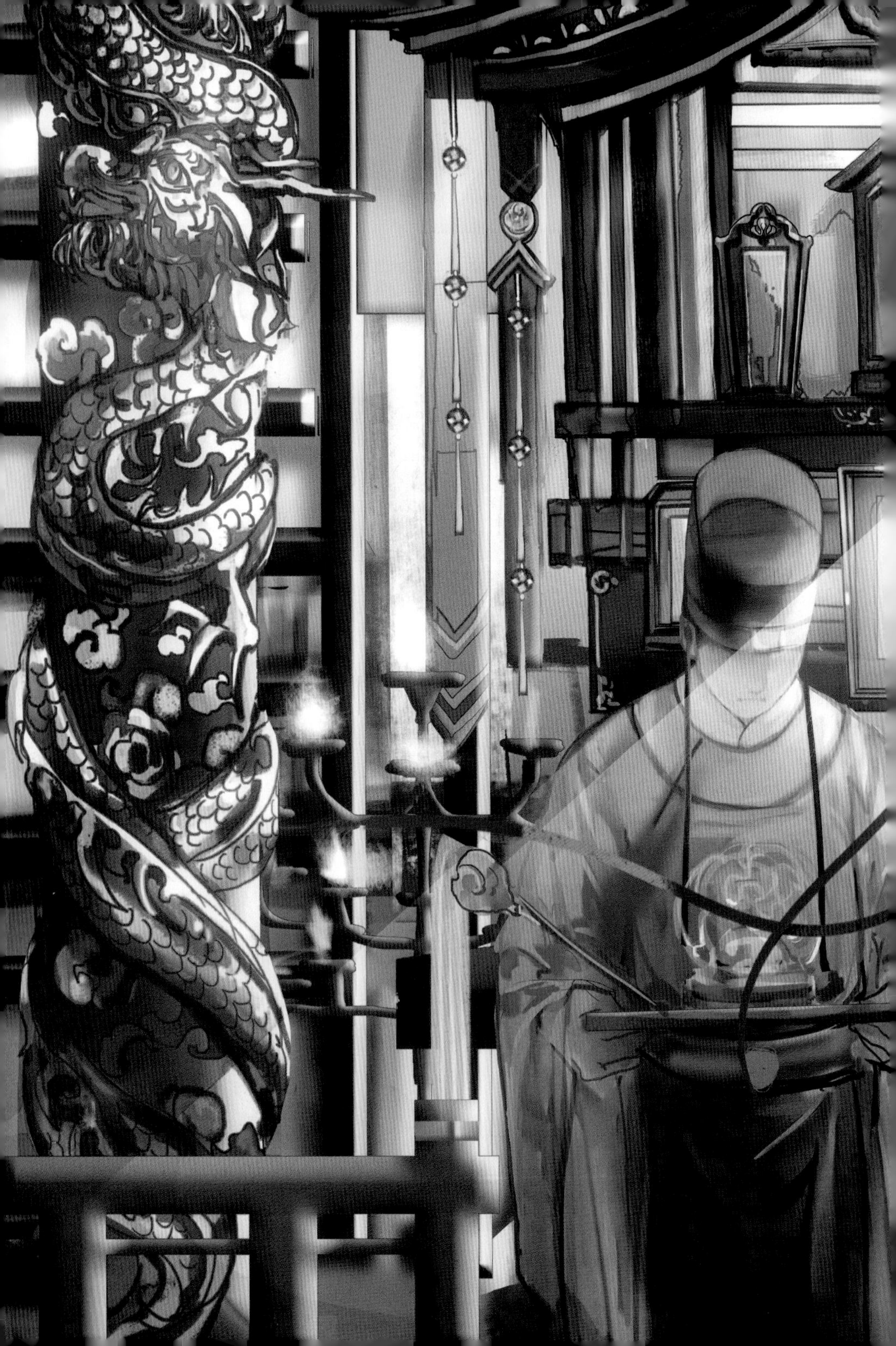

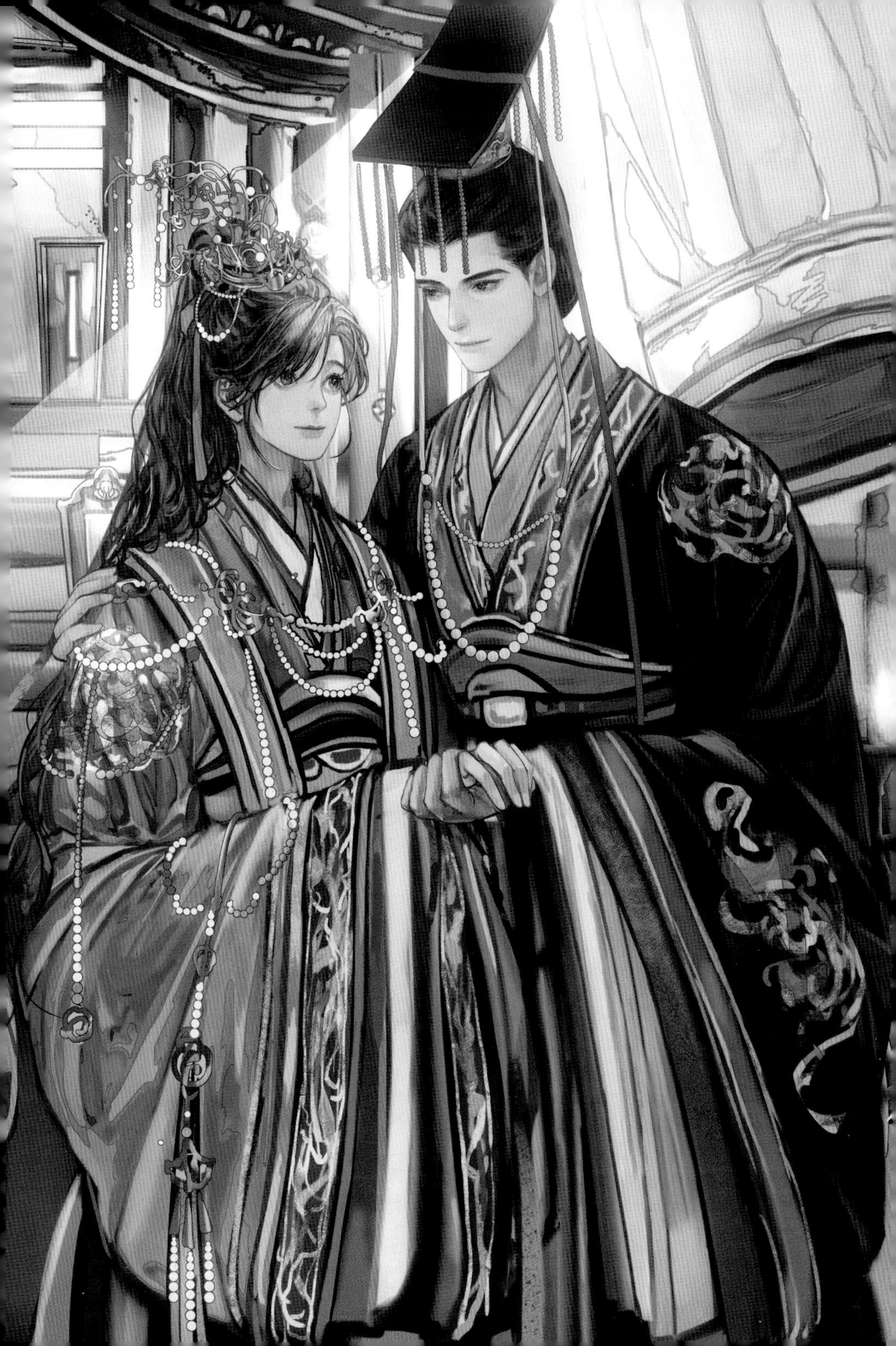

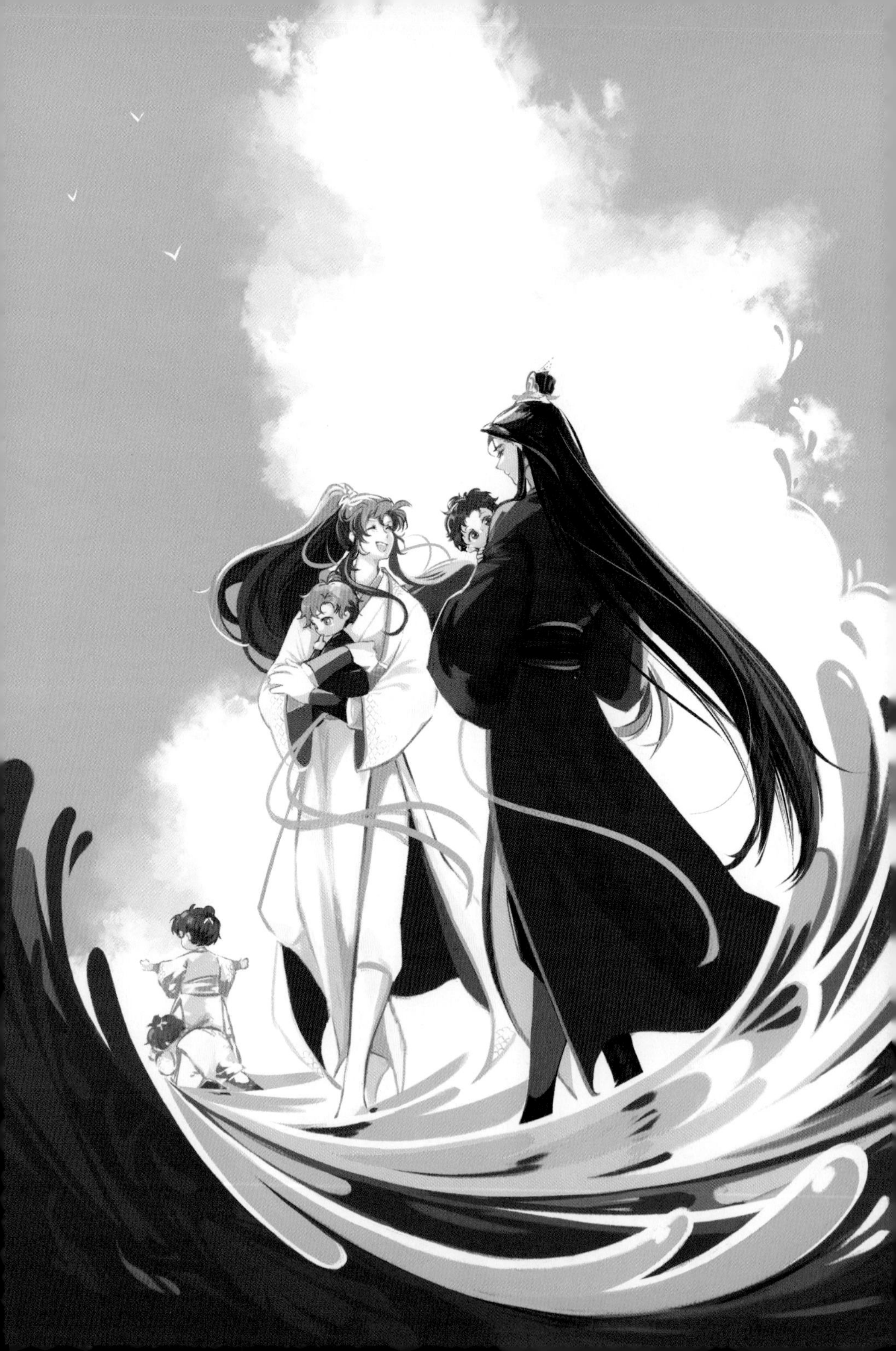

The Disabled Tyrant's Beloved Pet Fish

Canji Baojun De Zhangxin Yu Chong

WRITTEN BY
Xue Shan Fei Hu

TRANSLATED BY
Mimi, Yuka

ILLUSTRATED BY
Ryoplica

BONUS ILLUSTRATION BY
Kura

COVER ILLUSTRATION BY
Changle

Seven Seas

Seven Seas Entertainment

The Disabled Tyrant's Beloved Pet Fish:
Canji Baojun De Zhangxin Yu Chong (Novel) Vol. 3

Published originally under the title of 残疾暴君的掌心鱼宠[穿书]
(Canji Baojun De Zhangxin Yu Chong [Chuan Shu])
Author©雪山肥狐 (Xue Shan Fei Hu)
US English edition rights under license granted by 北京晋江原创网络科技有限公司
(Beijing Jinjiang Original Network Technology Co., Ltd.)
US English edition copyright © 2024 Seven Seas Entertainment, Inc
Arranged through JS Agency Co., Ltd
All rights reserved

Cover artwork made by 長樂 (Changle)
Original Cover by Fin Publishing Part., Ltd. (Thai edition, Thailand)
Arranged and licensed through JS Agency Co., Ltd., Taiwan
Interior illustrations: Ryoplica
Bonus color illustration: Kura

No portion of this book may be reproduced or transmitted in any form without written
permission from the copyright holders. This is a work of fiction. Names, characters, places,
and incidents are the products of the author's imagination or are used fictitiously.
Any resemblance to actual events, locales, or persons, living or dead, is entirely coincidental.
Any information or opinions expressed by the creators of this book belong to those individual
creators and do not necessarily reflect the views of Seven Seas Entertainment or its employees.

Seven Seas press and purchase enquiries can be sent
to Marketing Manager Lauren Hill at press@gomanga.com.
Information regarding the distribution and purchase of digital editions is available
from Digital Manager CK Russell at digital@gomanga.com.

Seven Seas and the Seven Seas logo are trademarks of
Seven Seas Entertainment. All rights reserved.

Follow Seven Seas Entertainment online at
sevenseasentertainment.com.

TRANSLATION: Mimi, Yuka
ADAPTATION: Leah Masterson
COVER DESIGN: M. A. Lewife
INTERIOR DESIGN: Clay Gardner
INTERIOR LAYOUT: Karis Page
COPY EDITOR: Leighanna DeRouen
PROOFREADER: Jade Gardner, Kate Kishi
EDITOR: Harry Catlin
PREPRESS TECHNICIAN: Salvador Chan Jr., April Malig, Jules Valera
MANAGING EDITOR: Alyssa Scavetta
EDITOR-IN-CHIEF: Julie Davis
PUBLISHER: Lianne Sentar
VICE PRESIDENT: Adam Arnold
PRESIDENT: Jason DeAngelis

ISBN: 979-8-88843-311-9
Printed in Canada
First Printing: December 2024
10 9 8 7 6 5 4 3 2 1

TABLE OF
CONTENTS

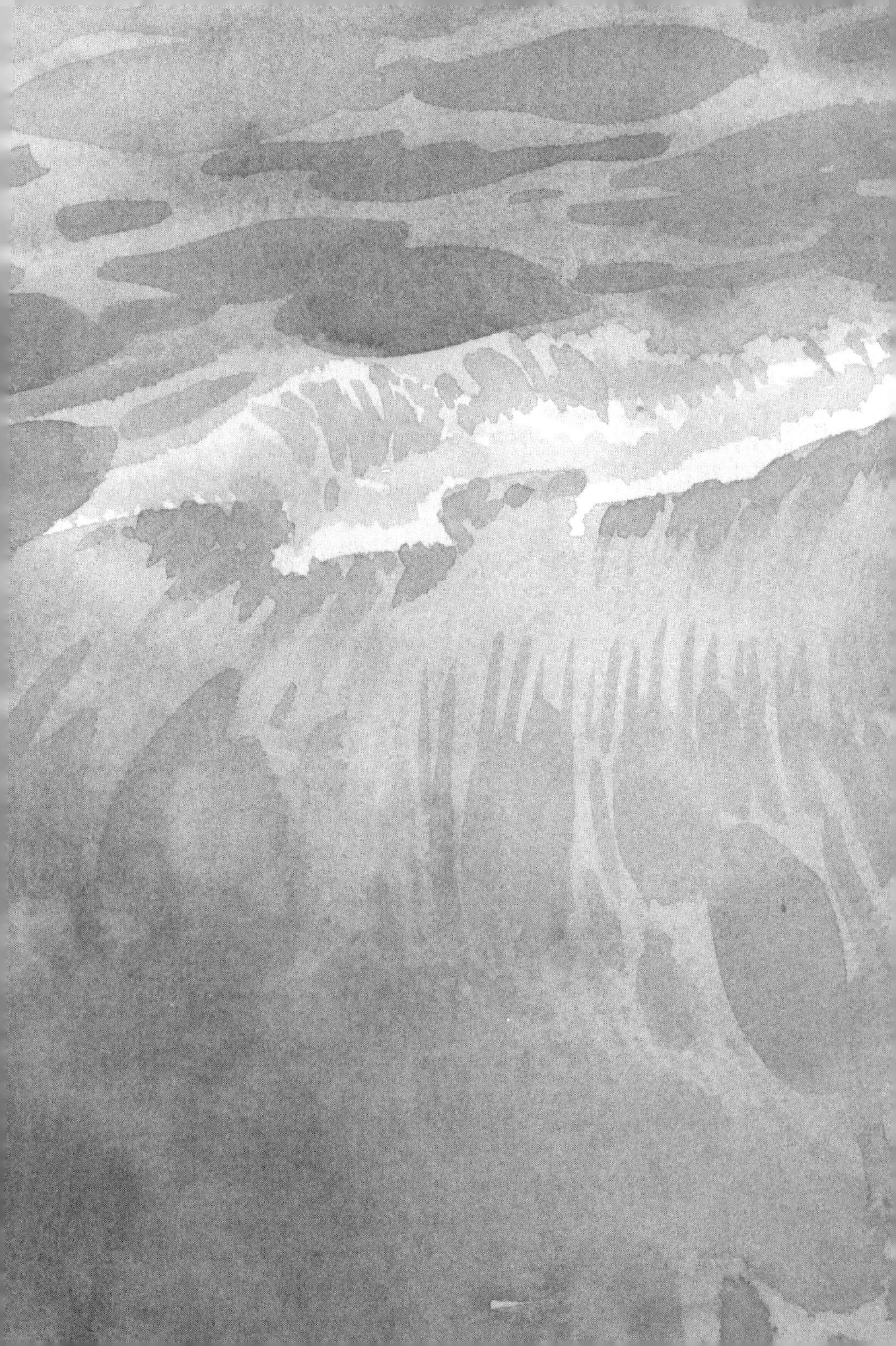

Fish Wants to Do It

L I YU'S DAYS PASSED chaotically as he did his best to protect his secret fish identity. He had never spent such a long time traveling before, so whenever they passed by a village, Prince Jing always stopped a few days at the local inn and took Li Yu out to shop and eat a couple of hot meals. After Li Yu was rested, they would continue their journey.

Because they were on the road, they carried a lot of travel rations with them. At first, Wang-gonggong was able to prepare a lot of side dishes and meat-filled pancakes, but they were gone within a few days. Li Yu quickly grew tired of the rations, but luckily for him, he could transform back to a fish. He had no problem eating fish food every day. Sometimes Prince Jing would take him out to eat meat too, and he'd order Wang Xi to purchase snacks for Li Yu in the villages they passed. Li Yu was being taken care of so well, he felt like traveling was barely a hardship.

Once they were truly in the middle of nowhere, they camped out a few times. Li Yu gave up his comfortable carriage to sleep in the thick furs together with Prince Jing. The moment Li Yu got over his own mental block, he became absolutely shameless and even started begging for intimacy, insisting that being out in the wild had its own sort of charm. Unable to convince him otherwise, Prince Jing always ended up giving in. The two of them would hold each other, listening to the howling winds outside the tent as they felt each other's racing heartbeats. If only Li-gongzi didn't have to end each encounter by rushing back to the carriage, half-dressed and panicking.

Several parts of their journey took them through the isolated wilderness. In his boredom, Li Yu discovered a new skill.

When he tried hunting for wild vegetables on the mountainside, he found his success rate was one hundred percent. He'd even tried digging up sweet potatoes, a task he completed with equal perfection. Wang Xi returned empty-handed, but Li Yu's arms were piled so full he could barely hold all the vegetables. Wang Xi couldn't be more envious.

When they passed by a river, Li Yu proved to be just as lucky at fishing. He just stood by the shore where the water wasn't too rapid and gently patted the rocks there, and shrimp, crabs, and loaches would come teeming out, occasionally joined by other fish. Li Yu didn't eat fish anymore, so he'd return all the fish to the water, but the shellfish could all be eaten with just a little boiling, retaining their natural flavor.

Wang Xi was pleased and excited, but still insisted on boiling it for him, refusing to allow Li Yu to get involved. Li Yu was confused. He'd cooked back at the manor and Wang Xi never stopped him then, so why was he stopping him now?

Quick-witted Wang-gonggong suddenly had nothing to say. It was actually because he was afraid Li-gongzi's cooking skills would ruin all the food. But His Highness had ordered them not to comment on the gongzi's cooking skills, so no matter how many times Li Yu asked, Wang Xi's mouth was shut tight and he never let anything slip.

But it wasn't a big deal. Li Yu quickly pushed those thoughts to the back of his mind. To him, being able to find ingredients to cook with was more useful than being able to cook. He'd finally noticed that his luck was unbelievable when it came to finding food.

This was when Li Yu finally understood that the "Well-Fed and Well-Clothed" stat that he'd been given a buff on wasn't about his cooking skills, it was about his ability to find food. Perhaps in the future, it would affect clothing too! Thinking back on it now, other than the time he'd purposefully starved himself, he'd really never gone hungry. Li Yu was torn between complaining that the fish-scamming system picked such weird places to give him good luck and celebrating that he'd never starve as a koi.

Two months later, they finally arrived at a small village on the western border: Luofeng Village. This was the temporary home the emperor had handpicked for Prince Jing.

The village head had received the secret order a while ago and had a dwelling already prepared for Prince Jing. It was apparently the best manor in the village and had been cleaned from top to bottom. However, when Prince Jing took Li Yu to see it, although the village head had referred to it as a "manor," it was just a two-courtyard home[1]—compared to what they were used to, this was practically cramped.

Of course, Li Yu usually stayed in his tank, so he didn't care much about the size of the house. Prince Jing rubbed the fish's head silently. As far as he was concerned, anywhere smaller than his manor was a downgrade for Xiaoyu. Due to the distance, they also hadn't been able to bring the crystal fish tank along, so Prince Jing was forced to make do with a few of the smaller ones. He thought this was a downgrade too, even though Xiaoyu didn't care at all.

---

1 *Standard dwellings (四合院) at the time usually had three courtyards, while princes' manors (王府) might consist of several standard homes linked together with additional gardens and ponds.*

Prince Jing had brought along plenty of guards, as well as a few servants, but they wouldn't all fit in the two-courtyard dwelling. Thinking quickly, Wang Xi bought the properties on either side. Now there was enough space for everyone.

Though the residence had been cleaned, it was a little outdated. Wang Xi wanted to renovate it slightly and expand the main courtyard, but Prince Jing shook his head—they were here on the emperor's orders. It would be best not to act outside those orders.

As soon as Li Yu arrived at his new house, he took a look around, strolling along until he spotted his tank in Prince Jing's room. This room was a lot smaller than the one in the prince's manor, and all the furnishings were quite ordinary. There was barely even enough space to turn around. Li Yu had the feeling it would be a hassle to transform here. He was just about to protest when Prince Jing asked Wang Xi to prepare the room next door for Li-gongzi.

"Is Li-gongzi not staying with Your Highness?" To Wang Xi, this was unbelievable. During the whole trip, his master had never ridden in the carriage, riding on horseback so that Li-gongzi could have the carriage to himself. Wasn't that enough? Now he was living apart from Li-gongzi? Was he that into the idea of Li-gongzi being pregnant?

Prince Jing leveled Wang Xi with a look. It was too small here. Li-gongzi wouldn't be able to sleep well.

Originally, the room next door had been reserved for Prince Jing's study. Since Prince Jing was adamant, though, Wang Xi could hardly protest, so he quickly had it cleaned up for Li Yu.

Li Yu was very embarrassed, but he felt he couldn't say anything either. It was his fault for keeping such an unspeakable secret!

Because their new home was so small, Prince Jing laid down some new rules. There was no need for the servants who came with him to wait on him at night. The guards were still obliged to continue with their jobs as normal, but everyone else was only tasked with taking care of themselves.

"Li-gongzi, I'm leaving His Highness to you!" Wang Xi kept going over reminders with Li Yu. Prince Jing was sending Wang-gonggong away too, so he had to ask Li Yu to handle it in his stead.

Li Yu agreed, blushing, but his heart was beating wildly.

After Wang Xi and the others left, Li Yu poured some hot water into a clean copper basin, a little clumsily. After he thought it over, he added a bit of cold water to make it a mild temperature and brought it over to Prince Jing.

"Your Highness, wh-why don't you wash your hands and face first?"

Li Yu didn't really know how to take care of other people, so he just followed his own habits. He'd already combed out his hair and taken out his hairpiece. His hair was now longer than ever, and he'd gathered it into a casual ponytail at the back of his head to stop it from falling in his eyes.

Prince Jing loved seeing him in such a relaxed, domestic state. Grabbing Li Yu's hands, he put them into the warm water and rubbed his palms gently. Li Yu couldn't be any more familiar with water. He scooped some up and poured it over the back of Prince Jing's hand. The prince smiled, and the two of them played with the water for a while.

Li Yu cursed inwardly as he realized he had lost track of time. He furtively glanced at the hourglass he'd brought from the manor, which kept track of the time he could spend as a human. Making a quick estimation, Li Yu figured he had more than enough time to take a bath.

"Your Highness, do you want to take a bath? I-I can help you wash your back," Li Yu blurted out. As soon as the words left his mouth, he felt like an idiot. Prince Jing had just cleaned his hands and face, and now he was talking about a bath?

He was a fish, so he spent most of his time in the water and he never got too dirty. But while they'd been on the road for two months, Prince Jing had only been able to take a bath when the inns they stayed at allowed for it. Li Yu was just worried Prince Jing was uncomfortable.

Prince Jing understood his intentions and nodded, smiling. He didn't want to overwork Li Yu, though, so he walked to the bathtub himself. Wang Xi had prepared plenty of hot water. After seeing how awkwardly Li Yu poured water into the copper basin, there was no way Prince Jing was going to let him pick up the water jug again. Prince Jing tested the water temperature and poured the water himself.

"Your Highness, I can help wash your back!" Li Yu's eyes were bright as he draped a towel over his arm.

Prince Jing took a secret glance at the hourglass. They seemed to still have enough time, so Prince Jing suddenly pulled Li Yu into the tub.

"Your Highness, what are you doing?!" Li Yu exclaimed in shock as he toppled headfirst into the water.

Prince Jing smiled and pressed Li Yu into the side of the tub. His Highness didn't just want a back scrub. He wanted a full fish meal.

Li Yu was completely red after the bath, and there was still a bit of...something lurking in his eyes. Sitting on the chair, he kicked his feet aimlessly while Prince Jing helped him change into a snowy-white silk top and dry his hair.

Li Yu suddenly realized who was taking care of whom... Whatever! This fish wasn't fussed with the details! He shook off the towel and, smiling, stepped onto Prince Jing's feet, one foot after the other. He wasn't wearing socks or shoes, and his feet were still a little wet.

Prince Jing went very still.

Li Yu knew he was fanning the flames. They had been dating for nearly half a year, and their feelings were steadily growing deeper. He had followed Prince Jing from the manor all the way to this dilapidated dwelling, but everything still felt sweet. Did this mean they could push things a little bit further?

He'd only laid down those rules in the beginning because he was afraid he'd turn into a fish in the middle, after all—not because he didn't want to.

Actually, the transformation problem wasn't impossible to overcome. He had an accurate way to measure time now. He could totally split the bed activities into two halves. For example, he could transform on the night of the first day. When it was close to midnight and his time was almost up, he could find an excuse to go to the other room—such as going to the bathroom—and turn back into a fish. He just had to wait a moment until the next day and then transform again.

In simpler terms, he just had to minimize the time between transformations, and night was the best time for such activities. Hard work always paid off: the fish had finally managed to come up with an ingenious plan, and he definitely wanted to try it. Over the last few months, Prince Jing had practically become a monk. Li Yu had tried to seduce him over and over, but Prince Jing followed the rules to a T, refusing to even enter the room. Li Yu suspected that if this continued, he might become a monk as well.

Seriously, why did he lay down those rules in the beginning?! Now he was facing the consequences. Sob sob sob, he really wanted to do it!

With Li Yu's legs shifting restlessly, Prince Jing was also uncomfortable. He took a step, wanting to find out the fish's intentions. Li Yu's feet were on Prince Jing's, and he was zoned out. Losing his balance, he was about to fall over when Prince Jing quickly caught him.

Li Yu seized the opportunity: he fell onto Prince Jing and rubbed his eyes, pretending he could no longer keep them open.

Prince Jing picked up the fidgeting fish and set him down lightly on the bed. Li Yu quickly clung onto him, not letting him go. Although they had taken a bath together, he knew Prince Jing was holding himself back and was currently in a bit of a state.

Despite all the time they'd spent abiding by the rules, Li Yu still knew how to get his boyfriend worked up. Prince Jing was clearly affected. In unison, the two of them glanced at the hourglass out of the corners of their eyes.

Now that they were cuddling together, Li Yu thought he was about to succeed. Prince Jing let go of him as usual, but Li Yu didn't say goodbye. Instead, he hinted in a small voice, "Your Highness, wait for me."

Prince Jing froze. Li Yu fluttered his lashes at him playfully and gave him a sultry glance, about to rush to the other room to prepare.

At that moment, the unexpected happened. There was a yell from outside: "Your Highness, watch out!"

Li Yu and Prince Jing heard the sounds of knives and swords outside. They glanced at each other. Who could have guessed assassins would appear in this tiny town thousands of miles away from the capital?!

Li Yu was not at all prepared. It was almost time for him to transform. For a moment, he was frozen in place, at a loss for what to do. Prince Jing, on the other hand, reacted much more quickly.

He rushed forward, grabbing Li Yu, who was nearly out the door, and shoved him behind a wardrobe. He nodded at Li Yu: *Hide here, don't move!*

Prince Jing waited until the noises grew louder, then rushed out with his sword drawn.

The western border was rife with conflict, but this had been an empty dwelling. As soon as they arrived, so did the assassins. What a coincidence!

Naturally, Prince Jing assumed they were here for him—but he still had to confront them. There were only so many rooms in this residence. If he didn't face them now, the assassins might make their way inside, and Xiaoyu would be in danger. If he went out to challenge them, at least Xiaoyu would be safe.

He closed the door behind him and took a moment to calm himself. The guards were engaged in a brawl with a group of masked people in dark clothes. It was unclear who had the upper hand.

One of the assassins broke away to head for him, but Prince Jing kicked them away and entered the fray. As expected, the assassins were in the midst of searching through the rooms, but as soon as Prince Jing showed up, they stopped their search, with more than half of the assassins concentrating their attacks on Prince Jing.

Inside, Li Yu paced around worriedly, listening to the sounds of shouting and fighting from outside. He couldn't bear to hide by himself, so he cracked the window open a bit to see Prince Jing battling alongside the guards. He suddenly felt much better.

He scanned the scene just in case—and happened to spot someone drawing a bow in the distance.

His heart raced. He didn't know if Prince Jing would be able to avoid it. Beside himself with worry, he glanced around inside the room. His eyes brightened as they landed on the copper basin, but then he quickly glanced at the hourglass. He gritted his teeth—he still had a little bit of time. As long as he was decisive and moved quickly, it would work!

Li Yu grabbed the copper basin, hiding behind it like a shield, then pushed open the door and ran out wildly.

"Your Highness, watch out for the archer!"

No sooner had the words left his mouth than an arrow sped toward Prince Jing. Li Yu screamed in alarm, but Prince Jing calmly tilted his head to the side and avoided it.

Li Yu rushed forward and shielded Prince Jing with the copper basin. His fear only lasted a short second. The hand holding the copper basin was shaking but very quickly steadied.

He was a man too. He knew Prince Jing had rushed out in order to protect him, but he wasn't afraid of death! He wanted to protect Prince Jing!

Meanwhile, Wang Xi arrived with even more guards, and others rushed over from nearby. The dark-clothed intruders were gradually surrounded. Seeing that the situation was not in their favor, they started to retreat. Prince Jing grabbed a bow from Wang Xi and, without taking the time to aim, shot down the archer from before.

Very quickly, the archer was surrounded by the guards. With the danger over, Li Yu clung tightly to Prince Jing. He used to be afraid of blood, but now that Prince Jing was covered in it, he didn't seem to care anymore. Not only did he not care, he straight up burst into laughter.

Just now, a thought had flashed through his mind: What if Prince Jing had been shot by the arrow? He was afraid of the assassins, sure, but he was much more afraid of losing Prince Jing. He wanted them to live peacefully together.

As Li Yu made this realization, there was an announcement from the system: "Through Thick and Thin" was now completed.

Li Yu smiled smugly. He was just about to praise himself when his smile suddenly froze.

...Fuck, his time was up!

Li Yu had no time to say anything to Prince Jing. He ran back to the room. The moment he pushed open the door, Li Yu heard the chilling sound of a bow being pulled back.

"Gongzi, be careful!" Wang Xi yelled in a panic, but he was too far away to help.

Li Yu's eyes widened. He didn't even have time to look back. Seeing that the arrow was about to reach Li Yu, Prince Jing threw himself at him, toppling both of them into the room. They fell to the ground, narrowly avoiding the arrow.

Li Yu was held protectively in Prince Jing's arms, but the corner of his eye was a little damp.

"Your Highness..." Li Yu choked up, but before he could voice any of his gratitude, he turned into a lively, jumping fish before Prince Jing's very eyes.

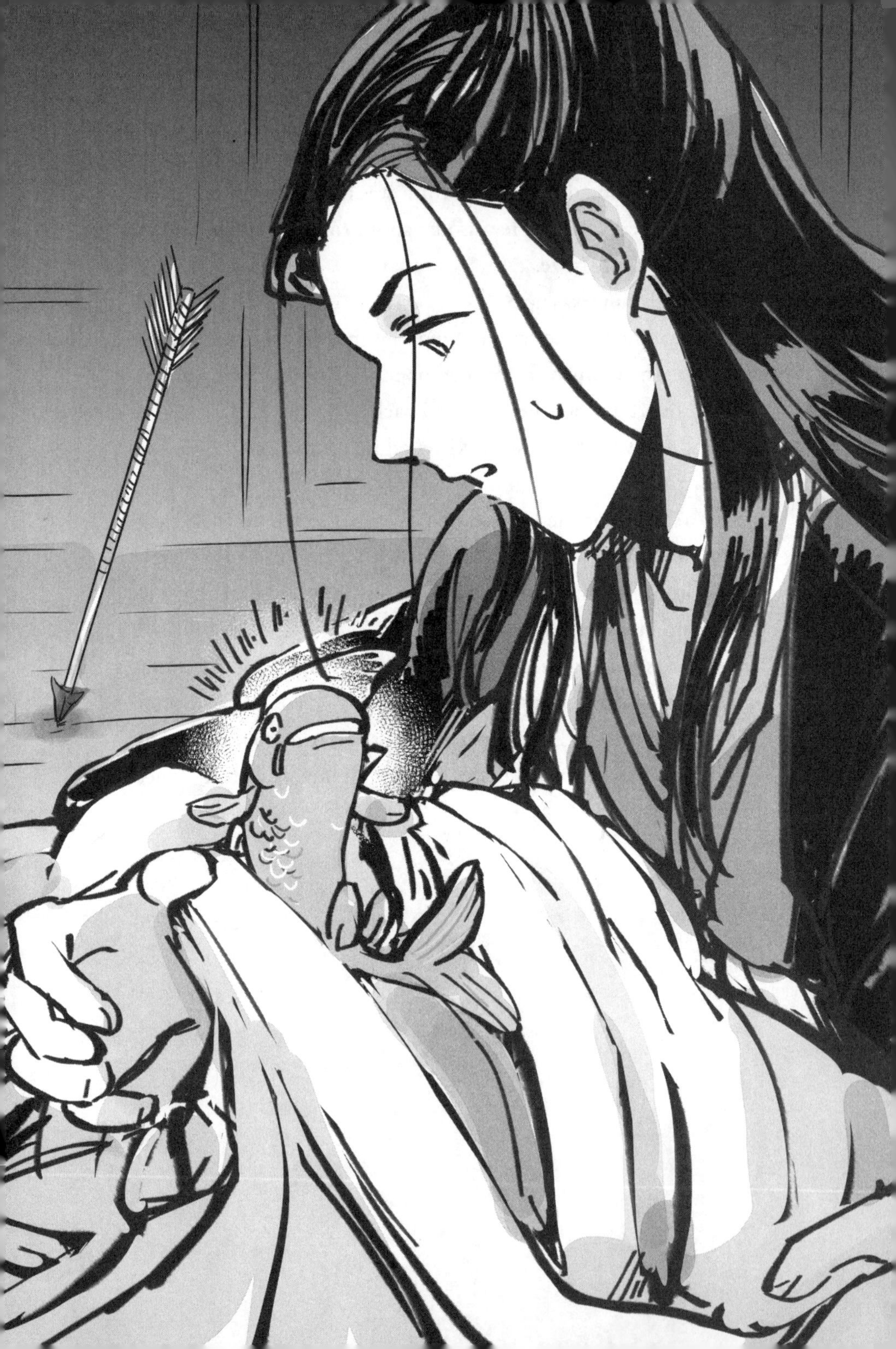

Bossy Fish Spirit

L I YU'S MIND went blank. He...had just transformed right in front of Prince Jing.

How was he going to cover this up now? Slap Prince Jing into unconsciousness, then tell him it was all a dream? How absurd. Fish or human, his strength was no match for Prince Jing's. His cover hadn't just fallen off, it had shattered to pieces! He couldn't just put it back on!

Struggling wildly inside his clothes, Li Yu almost forgot to jump back into the tank. What would happen now that Prince Jing knew Li-gongzi was a fish? He'd think Li-gongzi was a carp spirit, right? Li Yu had heard that in ancient times, people burned yao. He didn't want to become a grilled fish!

Preoccupied with his internal screaming, Li Yu completely forgot there was a third person here. The assassin who'd shot at him had escaped into the room because he was injured—and he'd just witnessed a human transforming into a fish. He was so shocked he couldn't even speak.

Prince Jing quickly got up, kicking the door closed. He had to keep Wang Xi and the others outside before they could rush over. Then he approached the assassin menacingly and knocked him out. With the assassin taken care of, Prince Jing glanced back at the carp spirit.

Xiaoyu was still struggling, lost...as though his mind had gone completely blank.

Prince Jing sighed inwardly. He'd done his best. Now that the situation had come to this, he didn't know how to deal with it either. His most pressing concern was that the fish lacked water, so he immediately put him into the tank. He'd find out what the carp spirit's intentions were before making any other moves.

Li Yu's brain was complete mush at this point. Watching Prince Jing rush here and there, he didn't know what to do with himself. It wasn't until Prince Jing stopped in front of him that the fish snapped out of it.

Was Prince Jing going to capture him?

Li Yu was too afraid to move. It wasn't a big room. Now that he'd been spotted, there was nowhere he could hide. Besides, he couldn't go without water for long. Even if he managed to escape...the only place he could run to was the fish tank.

What was he supposed to do? He was about to become a dead fish!

Li Yu's body went stiff, allowing Prince Jing to pick him up. Li Yu resisted the urge to take a swipe with his tail. Even now, he couldn't bear to slap his boyfriend in the face!

Sob, no, his boyfriend was definitely about to dump him. Now that Prince Jing knew he was a fish, it was hard to say whether he'd even want to keep him anymore. Yesterday, he was his beloved pet fish; today, he might just sauté him!

The more Li Yu thought about it, the less confidence he had. Prince Jing held him in his hands, but Li Yu didn't wrap his tail around his finger like normal. Instead, his tail was straight and stiff. He'd have to lay flat later anyway, when it was time to get skewered for barbecue...

Li Yu's thoughts dissolved into shock as Prince Jing stabbed—no, put him in a crystal bottle.

Wait, didn't Prince Jing want to kill him?

After Prince Jing dropped him into the water, Li Yu observed quietly. Prince Jing was just looking at him intently. It didn't seem like he wanted to arrest him.

Li Yu swam a careful lap, and Prince Jing didn't have any other reaction.

"Your Highness, how are you and Li-gongzi doing? Are you hurt?" Wang Xi yelled loudly from outside. There was still an assassin inside and Li-gongzi might even be injured, but his master had closed the door. Why?

At the moment, Li Yu was very sensitive to sound. Wang Xi banging on the door gave him quite a fright, and he sank to the bottom of the bottle. Ah, was it too late to pretend to be dead?!

Prince Jing glanced helplessly at the fish's attempt to play dead. He couldn't speak, so it was hard to communicate... He thought about it for a moment, then reached into the water with a finger and patted Xiaoyu's head comfortingly, confusing the fish even more.

If Wang Xi didn't get an answer soon, he was going to knock down the door. Prince Jing grabbed the unconscious assassin, walked out, and then immediately closed the door behind him, not letting anyone see inside.

As soon as he left the room, Prince Jing's handsome face darkened. He took care of the assassin with a single stab of his sword and threw him onto the floor. Thanks to Xiaoyu's fear of seeing him kill someone, this assassin, who had dared to harm his beloved, had been allowed to live a few moments longer. But Xiaoyu's identity had to remain a secret.

Wang Xi quickly ordered someone to move the corpse. "Your Highness, what about Li-gongzi?"

Prince Jing glanced back at the room.

Wang Xi immediately understood. "As long as he's all right... Your Highness, do we need to summon a physician?" The attack had been so chaotic. Wang Xi was afraid his master or Li-gongzi was hurt.

Prince Jing wanted to refuse, thinking about how scared Xiaoyu was. But after a moment's consideration, he gestured with his hands.

Wang Xi nodded. "This old servant understands. We'll leave Li-gongzi to rest for a few days. I'll call for a physician another time."

Li Yu was listening from just the other side of the wall. Every time Wang Xi mentioned him, he'd tremble with anxiety. He couldn't see what was happening and he didn't know how Prince Jing would explain things to Wang Xi, so he could only guess from Wang Xi's responses.

He listened for a while, but it didn't seem like Wang Xi knew he was a fish. Did Prince Jing not tell him...? He'd seen him transform, so why didn't he tell Wang Xi? Even if it was unbelievable that a human could turn into a fish, Wang Xi of all people would believe Prince Jing, so why didn't he...

Li Yu's scrambled brain finally started to catch up with what had happened. Prince Jing's expression when he left, as well as the gentle way he touched his head—it really didn't seem like he was angry! Li Yu couldn't help the pitiful hope blooming at the bottom of his heart. Was it really possible that even though he'd discovered his secret, Prince Jing wasn't angry and was instead helping him cover it up?

How else could he explain the prince refusing to let Wang Xi into the room, and carefully putting him in the crystal bottle?

...Didn't His Highness think he was a monster?

While Li Yu floated in his tank, feeling uneasy, Prince Jing took care of all the things that needed his attention right away. First, he had to make sure no one else had noticed anything when Li Yu transformed back into a fish. Luckily, he had thrown himself on top of Li Yu, and other than the assassin who had already been taken care of, no one else had been close enough to see anything.

There were no high-ranking officials in Luofeng Village. Now that Prince Jing was here, he was naturally the highest authority. There was no need to take the assassins anywhere else; they were handed over to the guards for questioning.

The reinforcements Wang Xi had brought consisted of two squads of imperial guards. The captain came over to bow to Prince Jing in greeting and said he was under the emperor's orders to protect him. Rubbing his brow, Prince Jing ordered Wang Xi to first thank them on his behalf and then to begin a draft of the message he was going to send to the emperor. Now that Prince Jing had decided to fight for the throne, he had to let the emperor know when anything serious took place.

Prince Jing picked the most important things to relay. After taking care of all these tasks at top speed, he went to look for Xiaoyu. Before entering the room, he once again signaled to the servants that they should not enter. Then he stepped quietly over the threshold and went to look for the fish in the tank.

The difference was obvious as soon as he entered the room. Xiaoyu no longer seemed dejected and swam to him willingly, his tail wagging eagerly.

...The carp spirit had thought it through? The corner of Prince Jing's lips quirked up as he affectionately patted the fish's back. But Li Yu responded by diving behind an underwater plant and peeking out at him.

Prince Jing knew Xiaoyu was testing him because he was afraid, so he didn't make a big deal out of it. He took out the note he had just prepared and spread it open where the fish could see.

Li Yu saw what was written on the paper clearly: *Don't be afraid.*

Oh...

Prince Jing had written many notes to the fish. He'd gotten hurt for him, and just now, he'd saved him. Li Yu suddenly felt a little teary-eyed.

Sorry, Your Highness. Perhaps I should've told you...

The fish and human faced each other. Earlier, in his quest to get intimate, Li Yu had delayed his transformation until the night. Now that it was past midnight, Li Yu knew he could transform back into a human.

In the end, the plan he'd put so much thought into was going to be used to come clean.

Before, afraid that Prince Jing would hate him, Li Yu would never have dared to transform rashly. Now, he let it all go. That note had given him endless courage. Without hiding anything, Li Yu poked his transformation scale, and right before Prince Jing's eyes, he turned into a human again.

Wrapping himself messily in his clothes, he said, "Your Highness, I have something to tell you. About me, about why I can turn into a fish, I—"

Ah... How was he supposed to explain?

Belatedly, Li Yu realized he didn't know how to start. Was he supposed to tell Prince Jing that he was originally human, and for some reason had transmigrated into a fish with a system, and Prince Jing was a character in a novel he'd read?

Even if Prince Jing could accept his transformation, there's no way he could accept that he was a character in a book. After all, it would change his entire worldview. What if he told the truth, but Prince Jing thought he was talking nonsense?

It was best not to mention the system or his transmigration. But if he didn't, how was he going to explain this?

Li Yu had never expected his identity to be exposed so suddenly. And he definitely hadn't expected that explaining afterward would be so hard. He had to come up with a reason that would be acceptable to Prince Jing...

Aha!

As he desperately searched for an explanation, a light bulb went off in Li Yu's head. Prince Jing had personally witnessed him turn into a fish, so he definitely must have presumed he was a yao. But Prince Jing had chosen to protect him regardless. That meant that there was still room in Prince Jing's heart for Li-gongzi even if he was a yao.

Prince Jing had read all those novels about cultivation and yao recently—that was probably why he could accept that Li Yu was a yao so fast! That and the fact that he wanted to protect Li Yu. Prince Jing wasn't a man who lost his cool easily. If he was the sort to be panicked and at a loss the way Li Yu had been when his identity was exposed, Wang Xi and the others would've found out on the spot.

As Li Yu came to this realization, he wanted to weep. How could this man be so good? He always knew how good Prince Jing was to him, but somehow, every time, he found a way to treat him even better.

Since Prince Jing could accept that he was a carp spirit, he might as well stop trying to look for an excuse. He'd just pretend to be a carp spirit. What was the difference between a fish with a system and a cultivating fish? They could both go back and forth between human and fish, it was...basically the same thing, right? If he was a carp spirit, then couldn't the system be categorized as the immortal guiding him and the tasks as—a kind of cultivation?

It all matched up. Then why did he transmigrate? It was to... endure a tribulation?

He could only transform for two hours a day because...he hadn't cultivated enough?

Li Yu suddenly felt much better. He almost started waving his arms around in his excitement, but Prince Jing patted his arm, encouraging him to calm down. Li Yu thought everything through in his head hastily before finally stammering, "Your Highness, I-I want to tell you, I'm actually...a carp spirit."

Prince Jing nodded cooperatively. He'd known for a long time.

Li Yu spun a fantastical tale. Once he was done, he looked at Prince Jing worriedly, afraid that Prince Jing would spot his lies— or that he would suddenly go back on his decision and decide it was off-putting that he was a fish.

Fortunately, Prince Jing didn't show a hint of disgust. He even spread his arms in response after Li Yu's tale. This meant he was willing to accept him, to support him, and to continue being his boyfriend.

Li Yu's nose prickled with emotion. Not even he believed his own shoddy explanation, but this person chose to believe him... He choked on a sob. "Your Highness, I would never harm you. Let's continue just like before, okay?"

Prince Jing nodded. Their situation had never changed.

Li Yu approached him slowly, leaning carefully and gradually into him. Occasionally, he'd glance up at Prince Jing's expression, but he could see that he really didn't mind... Li Yu was eventually completely relieved. He couldn't believe he'd managed to safely make it through exposing his identity. He let out a few muffled shouts, unwilling to let go of Prince Jing's arm.

When he remembered to check, the hourglass was once again almost empty. He couldn't continue with his original plan to finally consummate their relationship, but Li Yu still didn't want to leave. He had a boyfriend who didn't care that he was a yao!

"Your Highness, I'm a little sleepy. Let me sleep for a while."

The bossy carp spirit found a warm, comfortable position in Prince Jing's arms and fell asleep, at peace.

Prince Jing kissed his forehead, wrapped him up in the blankets, and lay down with him. He waited until the hourglass was empty and the person sleeping in his arms turned back into a fish, and then got up and put his fish into the tank.

He hadn't been able to bring the crystal fish tank, but the bed of silver rocks and the gold-embroidered blanket were here. Prince Jing put the fish on the rocks and wrapped him up in the blanket.

The fish remained comfortably in dreamland. In his sleep, he reached out with his tail and wrapped it lovingly around Prince Jing's finger.

Fishy Probing
the Secret

L I YU SLEPT for an entire day. This was the most peaceful sleep he'd gotten since he'd transmigrated. When he woke up, he thought he was still dreaming.

Luckily, the note and food that Prince Jing had placed next to the tank reminded him that he already knew and accepted his identity. He'd even gotten him plenty of local snacks. Li Yu happily turned into a human to eat them. When he wasn't worried about anything, he had a big appetite.

Prince Jing was in the next room working. When he heard the fish moving around next door, his lips twitched and he ordered Wang Xi to summon the physician.

He had brought along a few skilled physicians from the capital all the way to the western border just in case. After Li Yu was done eating, he was asked to come out so the physician could check his pulse.

Li Yu was confused. He ate and slept well, so why did he need to see a physician? But Prince Jing's presence reassured him, and he walked over obediently. He sat down right next to Prince Jing and extended an arm toward the physician.

The physicians kept their surprise to themselves. They were all curious what kind of background this Li-gongzi had, and were worried they'd say something to offend him. But looking at the two of them together, they were sure they couldn't go wrong with treating him like Prince Jing's family.

After checking him over, the physicians declared that Li-gongzi was fine. Prince Jing had even ordered Wang Xi to ask if Li Yu had suffered any shock. Li Yu had indeed been scared in the beginning, but after his biggest worry was resolved, he had slept extremely peacefully, without a single bad dream. But seeing how concerned his boyfriend was for him made Li Yu smile. He was just about to tell Prince Jing not to worry when the prince reached for his hand under his sleeve and rubbed it slightly.

Li Yu recognized this as a signal from Prince Jing. Li-gongzi, after sleeping well and eating heartily, paused for a second, and lied, "I can't really fall asleep, and I have a hard time eating."

The physicians discussed this amongst themselves for a while, deciding Li-gongzi might've really suffered a fright. After all, shock wasn't an illness one could easily see. The physicians all asked Li-gongzi to rest easy for a while. Prince Jing gave Wang Xi a look, and Wang Xi immediately understood. Since Li-gongzi was suffering from shock, they should probably tell the imperial guards, as well as mention it in the note they were sending back to the palace. And of course, there was no need to mention Li-gongzi directly. Li-gongzi was deeply precious to His Highness! If Li-gongzi suffered a shock, didn't that mean His Highness had also suffered a shock?

Courtesy of Wang Xi's secret signals, the news successfully reached the capital: Prince Jing had encountered a huge group of assassins as soon as he arrived at Luofeng Village, suffering a huge shock, and was now unable to get up from bed.

When he received the news, the emperor was beside himself with worry. He sent a number of reinforcements to the western border and ordered the imperial guards stationed there to thoroughly investigate the backgrounds of the assassins. He wanted to test Prince Jing, not kill him. Prince Jing was his only di son, and as soon as he'd arrived at the border, he was attacked. It was hard not to be suspicious. The emperor also ordered the guards to investigate any recent letters going from the capital to the western border— he suspected this incident had something to do with the fight for the throne.

It was so quiet in Qianqing Palace that one could hear a pin drop. The emperor's gaze landed on a list of the princes' names.

The second prince was in no mental state to assassinate anybody. Who could have done this to Prince Jing?

"Your Highness, you must be careful of the sixth prince." Using the excuse of his newly revealed carp spirit identity, Li Yu once again started lecturing.

He couldn't not. They had already been attacked by assassins. Prince Jing never went to the western border in the original story, so Li Yu had no way of knowing who had sent the assassins, but, as the final boss, the sixth prince was the most suspicious. Li Yu was afraid of Prince Jing underestimating him.

Prince Jing could finally ask: *Why?*

They were all princes, but Xiaoyu rarely mentioned the second or third princes. The idea of the sixth prince presenting a major obstacle seemed rather far-fetched.

Li Yu had already thought of an excuse. His identity as a carp spirit was indeed useful. He cleverly spun his transmigrator's golden finger into the ability to foresee things due to his cultivation. "I am able to see into the future a little bit, so I know the sixth prince will become Your Highness's greatest enemy. Your Highness has suffered at his hand many times already."

Prince Jing thought to himself, perhaps not just in the future. When the sixth prince had tried to one-up him at the emperor's birthday, he had realized the sixth prince was quite ambitious.

Now that he wasn't in the capital anymore, the sixth prince should gain the emperor's attention and favor—at least on the surface. His future life seemed set. But if anything happened at the western border, the sixth prince would be first on the list of the emperor's suspects. Besides, Prince Jing wasn't inclined to let the sixth prince get too comfortable: the sixth prince had tried to hurt him through Xiaoyu multiple times. Prince Jing would never let this go. He hadn't even gotten back at him for the emperor's birthday yet.

Seeing Prince Jing getting serious, Li Yu smiled. "But don't worry, Your Highness," he said. "There's no way he'll win against you. I'm just bringing it up because I don't want you to suffer through any unnecessary hardship."

Prince Jing nodded. So, the sixth prince was nothing but a paper tiger.

Prince Jing asked, *What sort of technique is your foresight? Is it the same as the time with Ye Qinghuan?*

"It was a prediction last time with Ye-shizi as well," said Li Yu. "This technique...uh, it's called the Golden Finger."

Prince Jing thought for a moment. *Did your Golden Finger predict you and me?*

Li Yu shook his head hurriedly. "No. The Golden Finger isn't always accurate. It's just a possibility."

The plot had long since gone awry.

In a roundabout way, Li Yu told Prince Jing everything the sixth prince had done in the book. But he didn't mention Prince Jing ascending to the throne, because that might affect Prince Jing's evaluation of the situation. Though the ending wouldn't change, what if it made the process too tragic? The best course of action was what they were doing already, taking things slowly and cautiously.

Prince Jing then asked, *Can I learn this technique?*

Li Yu was exasperated. Why didn't Prince Jing care more about the sixth prince? Why was he only asking about cultivation? *Hello, wake up! You are the male protagonist of a palace drama, you know!* Why couldn't they move past Prince Jing's interest in cultivation?

Li Yu suppressed his urge to shout and did his best to persuade him. "Your Highness is of the royal family. Cultivation is not for you. Please reconsider, and stop thinking about this."

Prince Jing looked down, expression growing sad. *After your tribulation is over, how long will you stay?*

Li Yu squeaked, then remembered that the tribulation was his excuse for showing up in Prince Jing's life in the first place. The prince was asking Li Yu how long he would stay in this ancient world.

The fish-scamming system had never mentioned this before, and Li Yu hadn't thought about it either. At first, he'd just wanted to get back as quickly as possible. Now that he had attachments in this time period, Li Yu thought, if he could choose, he would want to stay with Prince Jing for a long time. At the end of the book, Prince Jing was still healthy at forty years old. That was still a long way away from now. To Li Yu, who was only eighteen, it seemed like a lifetime.

But he hadn't transmigrated of his own accord. Would it be up to him how long he stayed?

Li Yu thought about it carefully for a while, then said honestly, "I'm not sure." He found he didn't want to lie to Prince Jing about this.

When he heard his response, Prince Jing's expression turned furious, and he grabbed Li Yu's hand tightly in his, so tightly that it hurt a little.

"Your Highness, what's wrong?" Li Yu asked, surprised. He didn't know why Prince Jing was suddenly so emotional.

Prince Jing pulled him roughly into his arms and repeated silently, over and over, *Don't leave me.*

"Your Highness?" Li Yu didn't understand what was going on. He tried to wrap his arms around the other man's shoulders to calm him.

The two of them fell into silence while in each other's arms.

After a while, Wang Xi came to get Prince Jing, saying the assassins had confessed, so Prince Jing had to go deal with them. This wasn't something he could put off, so Prince Jing let go of Li Yu, looking much calmer.

He glanced at Wang Xi. *Take care of him.*

Wang Xi nodded enthusiastically. There was one good thing about the assassins: they made Li-gongzi and Prince Jing more affectionate with each other!

Soon after, Li Yu managed to get Wang Xi to leave, and immediately headed into the mental world of the system.

He recalled that the quest "Through Thick and Thin" had been completed when the assassins showed up. Because his cover was blown, he hadn't been able to check until now, but he could claim his reward now, right?

Li Yu entered the system, immediately checking the main quest line. As expected, "Through Thick and Thin" was now completed. The reward was another one of Prince Jing's secrets.

Li Yu let his mind wander as he looked at the four options, then suddenly asked, <*System, can I go back and look at the secrets I've viewed before?*>

That secret with the tiger doll, the one that had to do with Changchun Palace, kept popping into his mind. He'd never worked it out, and so he couldn't let it go.

The system was silent for a while, as though it was thinking it over. Just as Li Yu thought there was no hope, one of the four choices became a dark palace.

...Changchun Palace! Yes!

‹The user is allowed to swap his reward,› the system said. *‹Please choose.›*

Li Yu understood that the system meant he had to pick from the three secrets he didn't know yet, or Changchun Palace. There was no hurry, he decided. He could check out Prince Jing's other secrets as he completed future quests. He wanted to figure this one out first.

Li Yu chose Changchun Palace and immediately arrived at the location of the secret: a room in Changchun Palace.

This time he was ready, and he observed everything very carefully: the woman's appearance, as well as the melody she hummed quietly as she waited for the servant. He also noticed that there was a bundle of cloth on the bed behind the woman. Li Yu hadn't really noticed last time, but this time, he took a closer look. It looked a bit like swaddling clothes. When the woman and the servant began to struggle, he noticed that the swaddling moved slightly, and a pair of dark, grape-like eyes peered out, observing everything curiously.

So, there was a baby in the room. At first, the baby had been hidden behind the woman, and then the conflict started between the woman and the servant—so the first time, Li Yu's focus had been on the fight. He hadn't noticed the baby, but the child had always been there...

Wait. This child made Li Yu suddenly come to a realization!

Why was this Prince Jing's secret? When he'd asked Prince Jing about it, he hadn't seemed to remember it at all. And since this was Prince Jing's secret, why was there no sign of Prince Jing himself?

Actually...Prince Jing was here; he just hadn't noticed before. Because Prince Jing was this baby. No wonder he had no memories of this. But these memories existed!

Li Yu had seen Prince Jing as a chubby little boy. Faced with the baby version of the chubby boy, he was able to recognize him quickly. Now that he had confirmed his suspicions, he already had more questions. Since Prince Jing was a baby, and Li Yu hadn't spotted any cloth hangings used for mourning inside Changchun Palace, that meant that in the memory, Empress Xiaohui was still alive. Why would Empress Xiaohui allow a woman to be with the little prince alone? Judging by the woman's age, she wasn't a normal servant...

Li Yu noticed that the woman was a bit on the plumper side, and suddenly paused. Was this Prince Jing's wet nurse? Age, body type, and being alone with the little prince... It all added up.

So, was the secret that when Prince Jing was a baby, he had unknowingly witnessed his wet nurse being murdered by a servant? But there were plenty of people that Prince Jing had dealt with. Why was this a secret?

He'd had a small breakthrough but was now stuck in another bottleneck.

When he emerged from the flashback, the system reminded him: *<User, the "Revitalizing" quest line has been updated. Please confirm the information before proceeding with the next step.>*

Li Yu made a noise in response. His thoughts were interrupted again. Might as well continue with his quests.

A notification immediately popped up in the system.

<User, please confirm your relationship with the tyrant.>

The fish-scamming system was asking him to confirm, but it was actually just another multiple choice: pet fish or lover. He had leveled up from pet fish now. Li Yu naturally chose 'lover,' unable to keep the smile off his face.

The system said: <*User, please complete the next quest according to what you have selected: as Prince Jing's lover.*>

The system updated the next step of the "Revitalizing" quest: Burn with Passion with the Tyrant.

Seriously?!

System, come out here, I promise to beat you to death!

They had to be willing to give up their lives for each other to complete the "Through Thick and Thin" quest. What was required for "Burn with Passion"?

It could be a problem if one's feelings developed too deeply too quickly.

Li Yu gave a lewd smile. Didn't this mean the system wanted them to hook up too? Was spring here? He'd eaten and drunk his fill, and now, more and more, he was craving the other man's body.

Fishy Masterpiece

THIS WAS THE TASK Li Yu was most excited for. After everything had been taken care of, he secretly started to plan.

The room had to be neat and clean. He even ceremoniously switched to a set of bright red bedding. He placed a pair of jade pillows on the bed and stuffed a few boxes of different kinds of ointment behind one of the pillows—a friendly suggestion from Wang-gonggong. Li Yu didn't know what would be most useful, so he just made sure to have one of each kind.

All that was left was to use his silver hourglass, time his transformation, and wrap himself in the blankets to wait excitedly. He figured he was being obvious enough. If his boyfriend still didn't get it, he was dumb as a block of wood.

Li Yu asked Wang Xi to help pass along the word, requesting that Prince Jing come back early. Although they were now at the western border, it didn't feel any different from Prince Jing's manor—he always felt safe and secure wherever Prince Jing was.

Li Yu waited and waited, until eventually he fell asleep. When he woke up again, the hourglass was almost halfway finished, but there was still no sign of Prince Jing. He rubbed his eyes and sat up. Why wasn't Prince Jing back yet? Had he gotten caught up in something?

Li Yu recalled that the prince was probably dealing with the assassins—of course, he couldn't take him along, Li Yu himself being very willing to avoid such situations. Prince Jing was, after all, a prince from ancient times. He had his own means of dealing with things. In the future, he would have to fight for the throne; Li Yu couldn't force him to see things from a modern perspective. As long as he didn't carelessly harm innocents, Li Yu could understand.

Li Yu waited a little longer, his concern for the prince sweeping the filth out of his mind. He decided to go look for Prince Jing himself. He was just about to get dressed when he spotted the faint light coming from the window next door. A light bulb went off in his head: he knew where Prince Jing probably was.

Wrapped in the blanket, Li Yu pushed open the door to the next room. Sitting at the table with a bunch of secret reports spread out in front of him, the tall youth had his brows furrowed, deep in thought.

In that instant, Li Yu desperately wanted to chase away all his worries.

"Your Highness, you're still busy?" Li Yu called out in a soft voice.

Prince Jing looked up, spotting Li Yu standing in the doorway wrapped up in a red blanket. He looked very cute with the way he was shaking his head, and Prince Jing couldn't help the upward quirk of his lips. He waved Li Yu over. Eagerly, Li Yu approached and sat down next to him.

There were many maps laid out on the table. Li Yu had accompanied Prince Jing to his job at the Ministry of Works, and he immediately recognized them as topographic maps. Clearly, the prince was studying the terrain.

As soon as he sat down, Prince Jing swept him into his arms, blanket and all. When he touched Li Yu's hand that stuck out of the blanket, his palm was a little cold. Prince Jing gave him a slightly accusatory side-eye, and warmed Li Yu's hand in his.

Li Yu felt warm and comfortable. "Your Highness, what are you looking at?" he asked quietly, pointing at one of the maps. They had just arrived at Luofeng Village. Was Prince Jing planning on building another house?

Prince Jing grabbed a brush, circled an area on the map, and wrote: *One man can hold out against ten thousand.*

"You're preparing for battle, Your Highness?" Li Yu asked curiously.

The border lay just outside Luofeng Village. The constant risk of battle left the area in chaos. Li Yu had known coming here that it was very possible that battle would break out, but wasn't it rash to start one as soon as they arrived? Why were they fighting?

Prince Jing understood his worry. He handed a secret report to him.

Li Yu asked hesitantly, "Can I?"

Prince Jing nodded, and Li Yu opened the report. It turned out to be the assassins' confessions. The assassins had admitted they were under the orders of a local gentleman[2] by the name of Wu, who had paid a hefty sum for this assassination attempt.

It was a little shocking to read. Li Yu had assumed the assassins had been sent by the sixth prince. But it was a random member of the gentry instead? Li Yu was confused. This Squire Wu had never met Prince Jing, and men like him might not have much influence outside their jurisdiction, but they were all rich. Why did he try to kill the prince?

Seeing Li Yu's confusion, Prince Jing slowly handed Li Yu the other reports.

---

2 Squire Wu is a "country gentleman" (乡绅), a class of lower-rank, non-hereditary nobles who owned land in rural areas.

Prince Jing found it just as suspicious as Li Yu did that such a minor noble would dare hire assassins, so he'd ordered the guards to investigate the man's background. In just one short day, the guards had already completed the background check. It was no secret in Luofeng Village: the reason Squire Wu was able to wield such power and accumulate such a fortune in a remote, impoverished village was that he was secretly colluding with the bandits that the western border was overrun with.

Prince Jing had done his research before setting off.

So far, two great threats existed on the western border. The bandits were one of them, and they had the emperor constantly on edge. The border was rife with war, and so bandits often took the opportunity to harass people, going against the imperial government. The emperor had sent troops to deal with the issue before, but with little success. The bandits colluded with enemy countries, and they had the terrain advantage, so the army had never been successful in wiping them out. As a result, the bandit issue was a sore spot for the emperor.

Amidst all this, Luofeng Village was a choke point at the western border. The emperor had tried to appoint several officials there, but none lasted more than half a year before they invariably either quit or died, and the village head had run out of candidates. Currently, an interim official was taking over temporarily. The emperor had sent Prince Jing for two reasons: first, to give the prince a chance to test his skills, and second, because he had made up his mind to solve the situation at the western border.

Before Prince Jing had left the palace, the emperor had given him a secret decree that he was to look at only when he arrived at the border. Now that he was here, he took it out to read it. The emperor had ordered him to strike when the opportunity was right, and to bring the western border under control. With this decree, Prince Jing was free to do as he saw fit.

He first ordered the guards to arrest Squire Wu. When he was brought before Prince Jing, he denied everything and refused to admit guilt. He behaved arrogantly, so Prince Jing skipped the pleasantries and had him beaten half to death.

When the guards searched and seized Squire Wu's property, aside from money and gold, they found countless rare treasures and plenty of weapons. It turned out he wasn't a gentleman at all: he was just a bandit playing pretend, lurking within Luofeng Village. He had been planted there by the bandits to help them transport things in and out.

When Prince Jing arrived, the bandits didn't take the mute prince from the capital seriously. They saw him as just another official, no different from all the ones they had bullied before. The bandit chief decided to prepare a special welcome for him and had Squire Wu send the assassins.

Since Prince Jing had discovered Squire Wu's true identity, he wanted to bring him to justice and crack down on the bandits immediately. But that would anger the bandits, who'd been running rampant for such a long time. Prince Jing had considered dealing with them before, but the people he had initially brought with him were just a handful of elites. They were highly skilled, but there weren't many of them. Now that the imperial guards had arrived, he had a greater chance at success, and he could finally attempt the fight.

Although Prince Jing had read many military books, it was still his first time actually going to battle. After selecting the optimal position to face the bandits, he still had to think of a comprehensive strategy. Unfortunately, the bandits had strong soldiers and horses. It was difficult to come up with a plan.

All these secret reports were making Li Yu go cross-eyed. He felt renewed admiration for his boyfriend. The fish's brain was full to the brim with filth. His boyfriend was preoccupied with sticking it to the bandits instead of sticking it in him—this is what was called putting the interests of the whole before the individual.

It seemed that if the bandits weren't dealt with, there'd be no action for the fish to look forward to.

"Is Your Highness worried about strategy? I have an idea." Li Yu stroked his chin, giving Prince Jing a very meaningful smile.

He had seen the emperor and the Duke of Cheng'en stroke their chins like this, and he wanted to try it too. But their chins had majestic-looking beards while Li Yu's was still the smooth, hairless chin of a young man. If he kept rubbing, it would look extremely out of place.

Prince Jing held in his laugh. His gaze was expectant, as though asking, *What idea?*

Prince Jing's dark, reflective eyes were undoubtedly his most beautiful feature. When he looked at others, they were cold as frost, but when he looked at Li Yu, they were full of emotion. With this pair of shining, sparkly eyes on him, Li Yu could feel his heart beating hard in his chest. He felt like ever since he'd admitted to being a carp spirit, Prince Jing's trust in him had only grown...

He snapped himself out of it, trying his best to keep his thoughts out of the gutter. "Look, Your Highness," he said, pointing at the map, "many families in Luofeng Village have cellars in their homes. These can be expanded. Once we really start fighting, we can prepare some food and water and have the people stay in the cellars. They'll be safe, and it will prevent the bandits from attacking fleeing villagers." Li Yu didn't want any harm to come to the villagers, so he'd thought of using the cellars as something like air-raid shelters.

Prince Jing nodded in agreement: *Not bad.*

"Once the villagers are all hidden, you won't have anything to worry about. You can lure the bandits into the village. Then they'll be out in the open, and we'll be hidden. If Your Highness can dig some underground tunnels as well, you'll be able to attack from those too." Li Yu batted his eyes mysteriously and drew a few traps on the map. The fish hadn't ever read books on war before, but he knew about mine and tunnel warfare!

Prince Jing gave careful consideration to Li Yu's words and gained quite a lot of inspiration. He was about to ask for more when he realized...Li-gongzi had turned back into a fish. He was currently waving his tail, flap flap flap. He scooped up the fish and the blanket with practiced ease, put the fish in the tank, and put the blanket back on the bed.

After all this, Prince Jing suddenly noticed the pair of jade pillows on the bed.

This must be Xiaoyu's masterpiece.

Prince Jing chuckled, putting the bright red blanket away. A little box was peeking out from the jade pillow. Reaching out to grab it, he discovered a few more. Prince Jing opened one and found a milky, smooth ointment inside. He finally realized exactly what he had just missed out on.

After he was captured, Squire Wu remained calm at first, assuming Prince Jing would use him to negotiate with the bandits. But once Prince Jing found out his true identity, he didn't bother keeping him alive. Instead, he had him hanged from a large tree at the entrance of the village and confiscated all his illegal wealth.

If the bandits were going to try to scare Prince Jing, then Prince Jing would slap them right back.

The village head was very worried about this. Prince Jing was a prince from the faraway capital. The village head wasn't hoping for much, but a son of the emperor definitely couldn't be allowed to be hurt in any way while visiting his village. When he found out there had been an attempt on Prince Jing's life, the village head nearly fainted. But Prince Jing had ordered the bandit to be hanged in retaliation. The village head laughed helplessly—never mind being hurt, now it would be a miracle if Prince Jing wasn't murdered.

Killing Squire Wu was as good as declaring war on the bandits. The army had tried many times before and had never been successful. How many people did Prince Jing have? How did he think he was going to defeat the bandits so soon after arriving at Luofeng Village? His Royal Highness Prince Jing would be fine after initiating the chaos; he could just leave and wash his hands of Luofeng Village. But what about its people? Suddenly, everyone in the village was in a panic. The village head asked to see Prince Jing many times, but Prince Jing never agreed.

Eventually, one night, the furious bandits launched their attack.

But when they invaded the village, they discovered it was empty. The next thing they knew, their opponents seemed to appear out of nowhere and had them completely confounded. Realizing something was wrong, they tried to escape but were brought up short by traps set at the village exit.

This was the first time the bandits had been defeated so effectively. They had been caught by Prince Jing, who had been waiting patiently for his prey.

Fishy Burning
with Passion

L I YU WAS WALKING along the small streets of Luofeng Village, accompanied by Wang Xi and a couple of guards. After the battle with the bandits, the villagers should have been exhausted, but all the people he saw along the way were full of energy and excitedly discussing what had happened.

"Gongzi, this was the result of a victorious battle from His Highness!" Wang Xi praised his master enthusiastically. "He's given them so much confidence!"

This had been Prince Jing's first battle against the bandits, and it was also Luofeng Village's first victory against them in all these years. The villagers had received a huge burst of encouragement. The bandits weren't as invincible as they had imagined, and they now knew that the emperor, who might as well have been on the other side of the world, hadn't given up on them.

They were especially heartened by Prince Jing leading the battle against the bandits himself. Several villagers had witnessed Prince Jing's tactics in person and were vividly reenacting them for everyone else. When the bandits had been tricked into the village, the guards following the prince kept appearing silently where the bandits least expected it, striking them where it hurt. Prince Jing, though only a single person, seemed to be possessed by the god of war himself, slaying three bandits all on his own. As a result, Prince Jing had gained the reputation of a skilled warrior.

Before Prince Jing had arrived at the border, the villagers had heard this prince was a mute with a brutal personality, so they didn't have a very good impression of him. Later, when Prince Jing hanged Squire Wu in front of an audience, the villagers were somewhat gratified, but not so gratified that they weren't terrified of the inevitable consequences. They all hoped that this prince would hurry up and leave. But it turned out this prince was hiding his true plans extremely well. He had managed to defeat the bandits that had been plaguing them for so many years! All the villagers now saw Prince Jing in a new light. Right now, they saw Prince Jing as their guardian angel. As long as Prince Jing was there, Luofeng Village was safe!

The person whose opinion had changed the most was the village head. Before Prince Jing fought the bandits, he was filled with worry. Now that the battle was over, the village head wanted to spend all day gushing about Prince Jing. He thought Prince Jing was much better than the useless officials they'd been assigned in the past.

Hearing the villagers praise Prince Jing made Li Yu happier than if they'd been praising him. Although he had given Prince Jing some ideas by mentioning the underground passageways and traps, he didn't understand war. He had only talked about those concepts briefly, and Prince Jing immediately understood what to do with them.

Their luck was also pretty good. Luofeng Village just so happened to already have a few very short passageways in place, which the villagers had originally dug out because they were afraid of the bandits making their way into the village. Prince Jing took advantage of them and had ordered the guards to create more overnight.

He had also planted many traps where the bandits were sure to pass by, leaving them to suffer miserably.

Prince Jing had fought in the battle himself too, boosting the morale of the soldiers. With Prince Jing in the lead, they responded flexibly to the battle. Prince Jing's contribution to the victory was undeniable, and Li Yu felt very lucky to witness an ancient version of mine and tunnel warfare.

Before he left for the battle, Prince Jing told Li Yu he had to hide with the villagers and that he would have someone stand guard over him, but Li Yu refused. He wanted to watch the battle from somewhere hidden. Prince Jing acquiesced. The entire time, Li Yu's eyes were locked onto the mute prince. He fought so bravely, it seemed he was invincible. Li Yu was no longer so afraid of such bloody scenes—at least, not in the way he had once been.

Every moment, he was gripped by the fear of losing Prince Jing, but he knew Prince Jing had to participate in this battle in order to establish himself. This was his first official step on his journey to the throne. Although he didn't hold the same deep hatred in his heart that drove him in the original book, some people were just born with certain qualities—and Prince Jing possessed the invincibility of someone destined for the throne.

"Gongzi, please hold on a moment." An old woman holding a child called out to Li Yu.

"Are you with His Highness?"

Many bandits had been captured after the battle, and all the villagers had been checked by the village head. None of them were suspicious, and Li Yu had the guards and Wang Xi with him, so he stopped without hesitating.

"Grandma, I'm Prince Jing's attendant, is there something you need?" Li Yu asked in a gentle voice.

After confirming she'd found the right person, the old woman shakily pulled out a flower crown from her sleeve. She handed it to him and said, "Please pass this on to Prince Jing for me. I made this flower crown myself. Please, thank him for saving my grandson and me."

Li Yu didn't know how to react. "What???"

The old woman explained that most of the villagers had been moved to a safe place during the battle, but her grandson was mischievous and had disappeared somewhere. The old woman had missed her opportunity to be transferred to the safe area because she was trying to find him and hadn't known where to go. She was left sobbing on the side of the road, which was how Prince Jing had found her.

"...He ordered the guards to help me find my grandson, and took us somewhere safe. That's how we remained unharmed." She knew that if it had been anyone else, they might not have cared about an elderly person like her, especially one with a child. She was extremely grateful and wanted to thank Prince Jing.

Li Yu really didn't know the tyrant could do good deeds such as this. Was the tyrant turning into a benevolent ruler due to the wing-flaps of the little butterfly that was him? He smiled. "Grandma, don't worry, I'll definitely pass it along."

The old woman thanked him profusely, and Li Yu asked Wang Xi to hand a red envelope to her grandson. Li Yu puffed up his chest proudly. His heart felt sweeter than honey.

After seeing all he wanted on his stroll, Li Yu returned to the residence with the old woman's flower crown.

Prince Jing was in the middle of taking off his armor. Li Yu's eyes lit up as he rushed up to him. "Your Highness, hold on! I want to touch it!"

It wasn't clear exactly what Prince Jing was thinking of, because his face suddenly went slightly red, and he lowered his hands.

Li Yu carefully smoothed a hand over his shining armor. He knew Prince Jing had already wiped it down to minimize the amount of blood Li Yu would have to see.

Sometimes Li Yu thought he was being unreasonable. When you liked someone, shouldn't you accept every part of them? Like how Prince Jing couldn't speak, how Li Yu was able to transform into a fish, and the blood that once stained this armor. All of that was part of them.

Not bringing up the topic was a way to show that he cared, but wasn't acceptance also a way to show it?

"Your Highness, in the future I...will do my best to get used to it," Li Yu said gently, helping him remove his armor. "It will be okay."

At first, Prince Jing didn't know what he was talking about. Halfway through taking off his armor, he suddenly understood and wrapped Li Yu in his arms, kissing him aggressively. The armor was too hard and it hurt Li Yu a little, but he still hugged the prince back tightly.

After removing the armor, Li Yu wanted to help him change into a set of casual robes. Prince Jing often helped him change, so Li Yu didn't think it was a big deal to help the prince now and then. But as soon as he moved to do so, Prince Jing shook his head.

Huh? I'm already helping you change, is there something you're not happy with?!

Prince Jing wasn't unhappy. He pulled out a red robe edged in gold and handed it to Li Yu with a smile. It wasn't that Prince Jing didn't want Xiaoyu to help him, it was that the casual robes weren't quite suitable.

Li Yu was bewildered, but he helped the prince change. This was probably Prince Jing's most eye-catching robe. It was red, patterned with gold, and the jade belt was encrusted with pearls. If he tied a red ribbon in his hair, he'd look like he was getting married.

Li Yu was just thinking it was an amusing coincidence when Prince Jing really did pull out a red ribbon and a jade comb, handing both to him.

Li Yu kind of understood. "I'm really bad at tying hair," he chuckled. "Are you sure you don't mind?"

Prince Jing nodded again and again. Li Yu used all the skill he had and tied Prince Jing's hair up in a way that was almost competent.

Having taken care of his boyfriend, Li Yu said excitedly, "I want to change too!"

There was a new set of robes Prince Jing had made for him in his inventory. Prince Jing thought, on principle, no matter where they were, his wife had to have enough clothes. Before leaving the capital, he had made a rush order for Li Yu. Added to the clothes Li Yu had from before, he could wear a different set each day and never have to repeat an outfit.

Li Yu liked the one he pulled out now the best.

For once, Prince Jing hadn't had a lot of gems added to this one. Instead, it was made of heavy, bright red silk, embroidered with fish playing amongst peonies. The peonies, woven with gold thread, were many layered, blooming from the hem of the robes all the way to the waist. A lifelike carp wrapped around the waist, as if smelling the peonies. The embroidery on this robe was exceptional. Each flower petal seemed delicate and charming. The fish was silver with flecks of gold, and its scales shone.

Li Yu already had a set of silver robes quite similar to the color of his fish form. This embroidery was even closer, as though it had perfectly captured him as a fish. Even the size was accurate. Li Yu fell in love immediately.

Since Prince Jing was wearing red robes, Li Yu wanted to wear red too. They had worn matching outfits at Ye-shizi's wedding as well.

After he was finished changing, Prince Jing put his hair up for him too, and tied a sash around his waist that was embroidered with a pair of fish.

Now dressed, the two looked at one another, each stunned by the other's appearance.

"N-now what?" Li Yu couldn't help but stutter.

Prince Jing smiled and reached into his sleeve.

Li Yu was screaming in his heart, *Here it comes, here it comes! This man's about to do something again!* What was it going to be this time? A nauseating love note or a little golden fish?

It was neither.

Prince Jing pulled out a rock and placed it on Li Yu's palm.

Li Yu looked at it. This rock was shaped like a fish, and it was very familiar.

It was the fish-shaped rock he'd put next to Prince Jing's jade figure in the huge fishpond in Prince Jing's manor!

He remembered that after the fit he'd thrown while he was sick, both the rock and the figure had gone missing. He assumed they'd been swept to some random corner in the pond, and thought it was a shame. But after Li Yu got a boyfriend, he didn't pay it too much attention. Had it really been with Prince Jing all this time?

"Your Highness, how did you find it?" Li Yu played with the rock, pleasantly surprised. He hadn't played with it in his human form before.

But Prince Jing just wanted to give him this rock. He didn't want to explain how he'd found it. It'd take forever.

Li Yu rubbed the carvings on the stone, then suddenly looked up at Prince Jing with bright eyes. "Then did Your Highness have the jade figure as well?"

Jade figure...? Very quickly, Prince Jing realized what he was talking about. He had wanted to keep it to himself originally, but since Li Yu wanted it, he took it out as well and placed it in Li Yu's hand.

Li Yu held the jade figure in one hand, the fish-shaped rock in the other, and placed them both together. His eyes were curved from smiling. Prince Jing watched on silently as the fish played. After Li Yu put them away, Prince Jing pulled out a jar of wine from a sealed box.

Through the lid, Li Yu could already smell the fragrance of green plum wine. He didn't know Prince Jing had brought such a thing from the capital, and he burst out laughing. "Your Highness, did you bring the entire manor with you?"

Prince Jing shook his head and opened the jar with a silver blade.

This was a previously unopened jar of wine. The moment it was open, a strong fragrance spread through the room, making Li Yu's mouth water. Prince Jing, who normally didn't let him touch alcohol, suddenly changed his ways and fetched two jade cups.

The cups were special too. There was a fish etched onto each one. One on the left, one on the right. When they were put together, they were a perfect pair.

Prince Jing filled the two cups and handed one to Li Yu.

Li Yu was just about to bring it to his lips when he snuck a glance at Prince Jing.

Prince Jing was also holding the cup, but he wasn't moving. He just had his arm extended. Li Yu immediately realized what he wanted. He reached his arm over as well.

The two intertwined their arms and drank the wine together.[3]

"...This wine has such a nice smell." Li Yu thought it tasted even better than the first time he tried it.

Prince Jing smiled, deciding he would tell the fish later. He'd grabbed it from the old Duke of Cheng'en before they left the capital. It was their wedding wine.

Now that they'd changed and drunk the wine, there was still...

...He'd almost forgotten the old lady's flower crown! Li Yu handed it to Prince Jing and gave a simple account of the old woman's story.

"...Did Your Highness really do that?" Although he was sure it was true, Li Yu was still shocked. After all, Prince Jing had never done anything like that, aside from saving the fish.

Prince Jing nodded a little awkwardly. It was true, but there was a slight misunderstanding.

Prince Jing didn't care how the people on the western border viewed him. He hadn't saved the old woman because he pitied her. He was used to being alone, ever since he was young, and rarely cared for others. His heart was still cold even now. But Xiaoyu cared about the villagers and didn't want them to come to harm—he just wanted to grant Xiaoyu's wish.

Prince Jing didn't want to explain. He smiled and placed the flower crown on Li Yu's head. Xiaoyu should be the one receiving this reward.

With the flower crown on his head, Li Yu suddenly felt playful. He smiled as he picked a red bloom from the flower crown and placed it against Prince Jing's chest. Wearing red, drinking wine, and wearing a flower: he was a real groom now!

Li Yu couldn't help but think of the "Burn with Passion" quest, and his mouth suddenly went dry.

---

3   Jiaobeijiu (交杯酒) is a part of a traditional Chinese wedding when the couple will drink their wine with their arms intertwined.

"Your Highness, are you tired?" he asked, face red.

Prince Jing was afraid of missing this fish again. He had enough energy to fight the bandits ten times over. He shook his head fiercely.

"Huh? You're not tired... Then...let's talk some more?"

Prince Jing thought they were getting further and further away from the main event. Opportunities were hard to come by. Prince Jing grabbed Li Yu's hand and pulled him in.

When their lips approached, they were saturated with the wine's fragrance, gentle and romantic. Li Yu lost himself in the kiss, and Prince Jing scooped him up into his arms. Seeming to sense that something was coming, Li Yu couldn't help but fidget restlessly.

Prince Jing brought him to the bed that was covered in red. The very bed Li Yu had prepared secretly before. Li Yu's gaze swept across the bed, both shy and pleased. Prince Jing patiently unfastened the bun he himself had helped Li Yu put up.

On this night where he was destined to lose something, Li Yu thought he should say something sweet to initiate it.

He'd thought about this scene thousands of times. It should be playful, yet lure Prince Jing in so that he couldn't resist. Something Prince Jing would never be able to forget.

Remembering Prince Jing's whole deal with "absorbing essence," Li Yu found his inspiration. Imitating the characters in the novels, he teased, "Husband, we yao need to absorb essence..."

Before he could finish speaking, something blocked his view and he was pushed down.

Fishy Aftermath

LI YU HAD BEEN a fish for a long time. It was a terrible feeling to be away from water for too long. But he enjoyed his current state of breathlessness. He cried and screamed, leaving mark after mark behind on the other man's shoulders. Prince Jing's overwhelming love shone through the pain of metamorphosis, and very quickly, he was lost within it.

The system's notifications went off inside his head, one after another, almost like explosions. Obviously the "Burn with Passion" quest was complete, but Li Yu was practically an inferno by now and had no attention to spare for the system. Not that he needed to pay attention—all he had to do was collect his reward and figure out the next step. He'd take care of that when he had time.

Li Yu screamed internally for the system to shut up and that he accepted everything, and the stupid thing finally quieted down. Now he could focus his attention on the sport of love.

But the hourglass was almost up. Prince Jing stopped and kissed his bright red face, and though he looked at him with restraint in his eyes, his meaning was clear: *Is it time to leave?*

Li Yu thought he was like Cinderella in the fairy tales, sitting in his pumpkin carriage. As soon as the clock struck twelve, he would have to leave. But his prince, Prince Jing, knew that he would turn into a fish. And even though he knew, he still loved him.

"Your Highness, I don't want to leave." Li Yu loved this man before him more and more. He smiled while hugging him, and his voice was now hoarse from overuse. "Because I know...Your Highness would never judge me." Li Yu giggled as he hugged Prince Jing again.

Prince Jing stilled for a moment before he figured out what Li Yu meant. He felt both emotional and exasperated. The fish had thrown all caution to the wind and begun to act recklessly. He...he had to grit his teeth and bear with it. Prince Jing took a few deep breaths so he wouldn't be led astray by the fish. This truly was a huge test for him.

As the final grains of sand were falling in the hourglass, Prince Jing laid Li Yu down and ruffled his hair. His lover's soft, sparkling eyes peered up at him, tears of pleasure still glistening in his eyelashes.

"Your Highness, wait for me," Li Yu said quietly. His fingers touched Prince Jing's fingertips longingly, like a small promise.

Prince Jing held back all the passion he felt in his chest and waited quietly. In the next second, he watched as the youth turned back into a fish.

Prince Jing had witnessed Li Yu transform many times by now, and he rushed to get to the fish tank—but the fish stopped him. He jumped up to his shoulder, rubbing against his face affectionately. Then, using his hair as a slide, Li Yu slipped into his palm.

Prince Jing was confused at first. The fish was too big now to be held in just one hand, so he cupped both hands, holding the fish within them. All of a sudden, his palms felt cold, and out of nowhere they were filled with clear water. The fish was looking up at him from inside it.

Prince Jing immediately understood that this was the carp spirit's magic. He'd conjured water.

He waited, just like he had been asked, until the sound of the dageng⁴ woodblock could be heard outside. When the hour was struck, it was as if the fish in his hands felt something, and he happily jumped out of Prince Jing's palms.

Li Yu flipped over, making a beautiful arc in the air, and once again returned to human form, flying into his arms.

Prince Jing caught him with a smile. Li Yu pouted, panting slightly. "Your Highness, when carps absorb essence, it happens in two acts. Now that the first act is over, the second act is about to start." His hoarse voice contained a sliver of sweet charm as he continued to stoke the passion in his heart: "You'd better be careful, Your Highness, or I might drain you dry."

He wanted to drain him dry in just one night? It wouldn't be that easy. Prince Jing smiled, no longer suppressing the desire within his eyes.

They'd had no choice but to extinguish the raging fire before, but now, without hesitation, they both added more and more kindling, letting the flames roar higher and higher...

Li Yu slept late into the morning. When he woke, he realized he was laying on his silver rock bed with the leaf blanket wrapped around him.

It was a shame he couldn't wake up pillowed on his boyfriend's chest, but with his fishy circumstances, being able to successfully absorb essence was already a great achievement.

Li Yu was very satisfied with the whole process. He was just about to swim away from his bed when he realized his entire body felt as

---

4   Dageng (打更) is a traditional method of time-telling at night. A night watchman would walk around town with a gong or woodblock, striking five times throughout the night, roughly once every 2.4 hours.

heavy as lead, and his fins felt like they had rusted over. Meanwhile, his tail...

It hurt whenever he tried to move it.

When he'd been secretly looking forward to it before, Li Yu had known there would be some discomfort afterward. He was familiar with human discomforts, but how would that pain feel in fish form? He felt better as a fish when he was sick, but what about after doing the deed?

Now he knew. It wasn't much better in his fish form. It felt like the spot beneath his tail fin had been punctured by a hard, merciless steel fork; it burned. He understood now why fish mating was called "intertwining tails"... He might be the first fish to survive being skewered by a steel fork.

Last time, when he'd asked Prince Jing how long he could last, Prince Jing held up one finger. Li Yu assumed he meant ten minutes, or maybe even just one minute if he was unlucky...

But now he realized the asshole had probably meant an entire hour! Oh right, and last night he'd been skewered twice: the first half and the second half. He'd suffered through the fear (pleasure) of being skewered both times.

Sob, it felt great when they were doing it, but he was suffering from the aftermath now.

He couldn't just lay here not moving forever. Li Yu couldn't even flip over, and he was hungry. Fortunately, his boyfriend, Prince Jing, was not far. Li Yu hadn't been hungry for long before Prince Jing was already walking over.

Noticing that the fish was awake, Prince Jing felt boundless gentleness well up within his heart. He took out a piece of fish food to play with him. In the past, the fish would happily swim over and play around with him. Prince Jing liked to pet the fish...but now, despite his attempts, the fish just stared at him pitifully. After a while, he lifted his fish head, struggled for a bit, and then rolled off the silver rock bed. He continued to stare pitifully at him from the bottom of the tank. Prince Jing was shocked and rushed to pick him up.

The fish was entirely limp in his hands. Last night, Prince Jing had tossed around the human Xiaoyu, but now he didn't know what to do when it came to this seemingly boneless fish. He brought the food to the fish's mouth, and the poor fish moved his mouth as quick as lightning and took the food.

He could still eat, so it probably wasn't a serious issue. Prince Jing felt somewhat relieved. Before Li Yu had turned back into a fish, he had carefully examined him and made sure he was uninjured. As for his fish form, the physicians and servants who had experience with fish had all come to take a look before the fish had woken up. The physician couldn't check the fish's pulse, while the servants' faces turned worried and ashen, hemming and hawing without being able to give a definitive answer. Prince Jing just had to figure it out for himself.

He knew at least a little. If he was uncomfortable, then they needed to apply medicine. But he couldn't apply it while Xiaoyu was still a fish. If he left it until the fish turned back into a human, they'd have to wait until the next day. Prince Jing was conflicted on how to take care of an...injured fish for this period of time.

Li Yu rubbed against his finger, wanting him to relax. His recovery speed had been buffed by the system, so perhaps he'd be fine soon. It was just a metal fork. He was a strong fish. Besides, he wanted more in the future.

With the help of Prince Jing, Li Yu ate plenty of fish food and felt a lot more comfortable. He rewarded Prince Jing with a fishy kiss, then remembered he had to go claim his rewards and entered the system.

The system's notifications had come one after another last night, like fierce waves. But at the time, he was so thoroughly preoccupied by the waves of passion he had no time to worry about it. Now he could look at his reward.

He could receive another one of Prince Jing's secrets, heh heh...

Li Yu entered the system and was immediately greeted with an influx of notification windows. They nearly smothered him to death.

What was going on? Didn't he just complete a quest? Shouldn't he be ready for the next? Why were there so many notifications? Li Yu wasn't in the mood to check them all. He checked the main quest progress first.

Last night's raging fire had completed the "Burn with Passion" quest. The next step, "Spread Your Seeds with the Tyrant," was in progress.

...Spread Your Seeds???

Surely that wasn't quite right. Spreading seeds meant continuing the family line, which meant having children, right? Li Yu was shocked and a little put off, and he hurried to read the description. Perhaps he misunderstood. Perhaps he and Prince Jing simply had to plant crops?

Fortunately, the quest had a description this time, though it was only one line.

Give birth to the tyrant's children.

Li Yu was freaked out. *Holy shit!!!!*

This description might as well not exist. What did it mean, give birth to the tyrant's children? He was a man! Even if he was a fish, he was a male fish! What was he supposed to give birth with? The system was asking him to go against the laws of nature!

...No, why did the system even have such outrageous quests?!

Li Yu was so shocked his voice shook. *<System, what's going on?! Why do I need to have children?!>*

The system responded in a low voice, *<User, please check last night's notifications.>*

Li Yu no longer dared to ignore them. He hurriedly opened them all up.

The notifications were actually all warnings.

The one on the very bottom, which meant the one that came up first was: *The "Burn with Passion" quest is now complete. Warning: the user is about to enter the highest level of intimacy with the tyrant. This will affect the subsequent missions. Please consider carefully.*

Li Yu thought back to when the first notification had popped up. It was when Prince Jing had pressed him into the red bedding and kissed him with mouthfuls of green plum wine.

Wait, so that also counted? He didn't have to actually do it?

But he wanted to. Who would stop at a time like that? Who *could* stop at a time like that?

The second from the bottom: *The next step, "Spread Your Seeds with the Tyrant" has begun. User, please confirm whether or not you consent to having children.*

The third from the bottom: *User, please confirm whether or not you consent to having children.*

The fourth from the bottom: *User, please confirm whether or not you consent to having children.*

The fifth from the bottom: *User, please confirm...*

The long string of notifications all contained the same line. It was clear how persistent the system was. But that wasn't right. If he had to consent, it wouldn't just make him give birth casually, right? So how...did it advance to the next step?!

What had he done?

Li Yu suddenly recalled that last night, he was frustrated by the system's constant notifications, so he had accepted everything blindly. That seemed to be when the system had quieted down too.

So...he'd done this to himself??

Holy fucking shit!!

This was way too much information at once. He was the one who had done this to himself?

Realizing this, Li Yu went to look at the second most recent notification. It now read: *The next step, "Spreading Your Seeds with the Tyrant" has now been started. Please select the form you would like to complete this mission in: 1. Fish 2. Human.*

Nani?!?

The "Burn with Passion" quest had asked him to select a form too. What did this mean?

Li Yu had a bad feeling. He immediately opened the most recent notification.

The user has accepted the quest without making a selection. The default choice has been selected: fish. User, please complete this quest in fish form.

Li Yu finished reading the whole message, shaking. Complete the quest in fish form. Which meant giving birth as a fish. Ok, at least he didn't have to have a swollen belly as a human...

...No, no, he couldn't have a swollen belly as a fish either!

Li Yu was vexed, feeling like he'd gone in circles. *‹System, how am I supposed to give birth as a male...fish?!›*

‹User, don't worry. The Moe Pet System can change the genes of the fish. Some male fish can get pregnant.›

...

The system certainly had no problem defying nature! It could give him secret special genes that'd make a male fish pregnant? A-all of this was making him dizzy!

In this world, the system was god, the golden finger. He couldn't go against it.

Li Yu made a last attempt. *‹Even if some male fish could give birth, can humans and fish breed cross species? Even if a fish can give birth, will it give birth to a fish or a human?›*

‹Don't worry, user, just complete your mission. As your reward this time, transformation time will double, and you will gain the ability to cancel your transformation.›

Sob... It was so over. Every time the system told him not to worry, it was definitely scamming him... What kind of bullshit quest was this?! And the reward was exactly what he wanted! Couldn't he just get the reward without doing the quest?!

‹The reward can only be claimed after finishing the quest.›

Li Yu kept trying to comfort himself. The quest was already in progress, sure, but how could he get pregnant after just one time?

‹Once is enough.› The system seemed determined not to let him live and announced loudly, *‹User, don't worry. You have the One-Shot-and-Done skill. The first time will definitely be enough.›*

What?!

He had always wondered what the One-Shot-and-Done skill was. So this was what it meant!

The world spun before Li Yu's eyes. *‹System, come out here!›* he yelled. *‹I promise to beat you up until you give birth!›*

He was ejected by the system before he could even claim his rewards from the last quest.

Li Yu had experience now, and he knew protesting was useless. Nothing could stop the fish-scamming system's quests...

Wait. Did this mean. He. Was. Already. Pregnant?

Li Yu couldn't hold back his gasp. He looked down fearfully at his slightly distended stomach. W-was it fish food in there or fish roe?!

Prince Jing had been watching over the fish this whole time, and noticed that after the fish came out of meditation, it had become a little agitated. He touched the fish's back. *What's wrong?*

Li Yu stared up at his handsome face. Before, he thought Prince Jing was handsome no matter how he looked at him, but now, all he could think about was the pregnancy.

Sob, help, I just want to do it, I don't want to give birth!

The Fate of a Fish

L I YU WAS UNHAPPY and didn't want to move, but it wasn't because of his skewering anymore. His fish form really was fast at recovering. Before very long, the dull pain he had felt had abated quite a lot and he could now swim around freely. His true reason for languishing was because he couldn't accept his fate of giving birth. And he had to do it as a fish! He'd seen fish give birth before transmigrating. Was he going to lay a bunch of eggs?

Sob, it was...a little too scary. He was a boy who had just lost his virginity. He hadn't even lost it many times yet and he already had to give birth? God no, the system had scammed him way too hard. The fish was down in the dumps, his spirits low. He was so put off by the specter of pregnancy that he didn't seem at all like a coy little fish who had just had his first time.

Prince Jing could sense the fish's dejection and put aside his work to spend time with him. As soon as the fish made any sort of movement, Prince Jing was at his beck and call.

Eating the red fish food Prince Jing gave him, the tiny bit of resentment Li Yu felt toward him disappeared. Never mind, it's not like Prince Jing knew he would...get pregnant. He couldn't have possibly predicted that himself, so how could he blame the prince?

Prince Jing had always respected him and kept himself in check. Between the two of them, Li Yu had been the one who desperately wanted to do it. Prince Jing was just giving him what he wanted. If it wasn't for the sudden pregnancy, they'd both be doing great.

He was avoiding Prince Jing, but the prince still took such good care of him. Li Yu felt a little guilty.

The system was so cold. Only his boyfriend's embrace was warm.

The fish, who had been avoiding Prince Jing for less than a second, started warming up to him again.

Prince Jing didn't know what the fish was thinking. He tried to rub him a bit. While Li Yu enjoyed the attention, he was also unconsciously protective of his belly. Sob, it was just because he was afraid his boyfriend would notice what had happened...

In order to please the fish, as well as show his happiness, Prince Jing had ordered a new stone rocking chair and placed it in the tank. As soon as Li Yu saw there was a new toy, he couldn't contain his fishy instincts, and he immediately went to rock on it for a while.

Soon, though, he realized something wasn't right: Ahhhh, nooo, he shouldn't be playing! Li Yu hurriedly swam away from the rocking chair. A pregnant fish couldn't do such vigorous activities, right?

He knew almost nothing about human pregnancies. He knew even less when it came to fish. What was he going to do?

He wanted to rub his tummy, but his fins weren't long enough. It wasn't fair. Should he tell Prince Jing? But being a carp spirit was already absurd on its own. Would Prince Jing accept his sudden pregnancy?

What was he pregnant with? He didn't know. How long would he be pregnant? He also didn't know. He couldn't even produce any evidence.

Would Prince Jing believe him? Would he think he was joking again? Why had he said he was pregnant before? Did he have nothing better to do?!

It seemed that when the boy cried wolf too much, he really would suffer the consequences.

Perhaps he should wait until his tummy grew larger...

Li Yu rolled around, frustrated. He couldn't make a decision. He considered many options, but not once did he consider getting rid of the life inside of him. Li Yu knew almost nothing about pregnancies, but he knew at least one thing: this was a little life that he and his beloved created together. Although he hated that the system had scammed him, he just couldn't muster any hatred toward this little life.

If they were blameless, then what about this life?

Li Yu sighed. His heart softened so much whenever he thought about this future child. He was probably going to have to keep it.

When he was able to transform again, Li Yu didn't rush to turn into a human to get intimate with his boyfriend. His fish belly was a little bloated. He didn't know if it was because he'd eaten too much or because he was pregnant. He was worried that if he turned into a human, his belly would be huge.

But if he didn't transform, Prince Jing would be confused.

They had just gone through a momentous, once-in-a-lifetime occasion, and Prince Jing was expecting kissing, cuddling, and hugs. But he received nothing. The carp spirit who had sworn an oath with him didn't even want to speak to him.

Prince Jing didn't want to accept that he was being rejected after having his essence absorbed for the very first time. Was it a skill issue?

But apart from not transforming, the fish seemed fine; he still ate and slept, and Prince Jing couldn't see anything wrong. If his fish refused to transform, there was nothing he could do about it. He could only stay silently by the fish's side until he changed his mind.

Again and again, Li Yu felt like Prince Jing was trying to suck his soul out with his eyes.

Ah ah ah, he missed his deeply affectionate boyfriend!!!

Sob sob sob, he had a baby in his belly now, so he didn't dare.

Li Yu pretended not to notice for a few days, but at last it was too much. He couldn't do it anymore. When he found the right time, he transformed.

Once he'd transformed, he didn't rush to get dressed. First, he looked down at his stomach.

Still flat.

He patted it, unconvinced. But it continued to be flat. Thank goodness—he really had been worried that after he transformed into a human, he'd have a huge pregnant stomach.

Prince Jing had been keeping watch over him the entire time, but he had left for a little bit just now. When he came back, he suddenly ran into Xiaoyu in his human form staring at his belly...

Why wouldn't he see him? Why had he been hiding?

Prince Jing walked over to Li Yu quietly, with infinite questions in his heart. But he was also afraid of scaring Xiaoyu. As he hesitated, Li Yu finished examining his stomach and suddenly spotted the person behind him. Li Yu was easily caught and found himself pushed up against a folding screen, his lips trapped against Prince Jing's. Prince Jing wasn't mad at him, but he felt the need to assert his dominance.

Li Yu had missed him deeply. Although they were together every day, it was different when he was a fish. Now that he had tasted ultimate joy, peaceful coexistence seemed to be missing a little something. Surrounded by warmth, Li Yu immediately let down his guard.

As Prince Jing lavished him with affection, Li Yu thought vaguely, it'd be fine if it was just a few kisses, right?

He knew how Prince Jing had been these last few days. He'd been able to feel his unease. He wanted to respond just as enthusiastically. He didn't want the prince to think there was any chance he disliked any of it...

In the afterglow, Li Yu, whose brain was finally returning to him, felt a wash of belated regret.

Another One-and-Done. It was so, so, so over.

He could control his human transformation, but he couldn't control the passion he felt toward Prince Jing. If this kind of thing happened once then it would happen again and again and again. Besides, his boyfriend had just fallen in love: he was full of energy and drive. It was completely normal for him to want to absorb essence at the drop of a hat.

If Li Yu was pregnant after this, he'd just have to accept it. He couldn't get pregnant *every* time, right?

Since this had to do with his future happiness and possible children, Li Yu felt obligated to go talk to the system.

The system said, <*After One-and-Done is activated, it will disappear. The user's fertility rate will return to normal.*>

That was better. He had just gotten unlucky the first time and had to get pregnant...

Actually! It wasn't better! He didn't even want children! Why was the system so persistent about this?

In response, the system showed Li Yu a vision.

In the vision, Prince Jing was a lot older. He was wearing the emperor's robes, sitting all alone on the throne.

What was this? Li Yu's heart jumped inside his chest. He didn't like this feeling.

The system didn't explain anything. Continuing to watch, Li Yu saw Chu Yanyu walk out wearing a set of imperial robes.

Huh? Prince Jing had stopped paying Chu Yanyu any attention a long time ago, why would he—

Wait. A thought flashed in Li Yu's mind. Why did it seem like Prince Jing and Chu Yanyu had aged several years... This was—this was a middle-aged Prince Jing and Chu Yanyu, it was—

Li Yu immediately realized this must be the end of the original book, when Prince Jing was around forty years old.

Chu Yanyu, whose life was nearly half over, had finally started falling for Prince Jing.

Li Yu watched as Imperial Noble Consort Chu talked cheerfully by himself, but Prince Jing remained expressionless on the throne.

The original book hadn't gone into detail about the end of their relationship, but the system had shown him. In the end, Prince Jing no longer cared for Chu Yanyu and had become a complete coldhearted tyrant.

Although he knew his boyfriend wouldn't meet the same end, Li Yu couldn't help the pang in his heart.

But why had the system shown him this?

The scene changed. Li Yu saw a few young princes bowing in greeting to the Prince Jing wearing emperor's robes.

This was—!!

Li Yu was shocked. So, Prince Jing had children in the original book. After all, the person Prince Jing was willing to give up having children for had no qualms with acquiring concubines for him to "solve the issue." Realizing that Chu Yanyu wasn't worth his affection, Prince Jing had grown to no longer love him. He was just completing his duty as emperor.

<The tyrant possesses the protagonist halo, which means he must have children,> the system said. *<But because of the user, he will be prevented from having them unless the user is the one to provide them.>*

This was even more shocking than when he found out he was pregnant. It was all because of him? The system spoke vaguely, so it took Li Yu a moment to understand. Was the system saying Prince Jing was ready to give up on children because of him?

Honestly, he had known the answer to this question for a while. When he had pretended to be pregnant, Prince Jing was delighted— but after he found out Li Yu was just pretending, while Prince Jing was disappointed, he had never blamed him.

Children and heirs were very important in ancient times. It wasn't something to joke about. But Prince Jing held him in higher regard than the promise of heirs and had agreed to never take on any concubines. Then...what about Li Yu?

Li Yu admitted that he was moved by Prince Jing's actions, but regardless, he was still afraid of giving birth. He lowered his head. *<Let me...think about it.>*

He almost exited out of the system, but that vision from the original story reminded him that he hadn't claimed the reward for the last quest. It was, as usual, another one of Prince Jing's secrets.

He might as well claim it.

Looking at the four options, he wanted to know exactly how important he was to Prince Jing, so for the first time, he chose the option that involved himself. He saw the scene where he'd helped Prince Jing clean his eyes at Jingtai Hall.

Huh?

Li Yu couldn't figure out why he was being shown this until he saw Prince Jing noticing a fish scale on the fabric he had dropped. Prince Jing asked Ye Qinghuan if he'd taken care of a yao before.

...Holy shit, how did I miss something so important?!

Prince Jing...had known since then.

Understanding dawned on him. Details that he'd thought were odd before suddenly made sense.

Prince Jing always gave him gifts that involved fish. Li Yu had assumed it was just because he had "fish" in his name, but it was actually because Prince Jing had known the entire time that he was his pet fish.

He had done so much for Li Yu without his knowledge.

Helping him take care of the situation when he'd broken the crystal bottle for a moment of satisfaction, covering for him in front of everyone so his identity would remain hidden, turning the entire manor into a fish tank...

Even Li Yu had been jealous of Prince Jing's fish before. But it had all been for him all along.

Li Yu's heart felt heavy. He didn't know if he wanted to laugh or cry.

He thought he had done a lot, but in the end, he was the one being taken care of, the one being loved. He was moved by this love, and he already felt soft and fuzzy on the inside. But so what?

<System,> Li Yu asked, sniffling, *<does it hurt to give birth as a fish?>*

Li Yu exited from the system, feeling refreshed.

It should be in him already. Since the system had said it wouldn't hurt, he'd go through with it. When he'd had no idea what was going to happen, everything felt wrong. But now that he'd thought it through and calmed down, he wanted to know what kind of children he would have.

The system said that this was the beginning for these small, new lives, and of the fate between him and the tyrant.

Weeks one and two, his human stomach remained flat, and as a fish there wasn't much of a change either.

One day during the third week, Li Yu suddenly noticed that he no longer fit in the ornamental mountain.

Every day, when he thought there was nothing left to look at, his stomach would visibly grow a little bit more. Prince Jing felt like the fish had gotten somewhat fatter. Had he been eating too much every day?

I'm not! I haven't! Li Yu complained. *Stop randomly touching my stomach!*

Fishy Pregnancy

No matter whether it was happening to a fish or a human, male pregnancy was completely absurd. Li Yu had even specifically clarified before that he couldn't get pregnant. He'd inadvertently shot himself in the foot. It was too humiliating.

He hadn't figured out how he was going to tell Prince Jing. But he assumed fish pregnancies lasted approximately nine months, just like humans. At the very least, it would definitely be a few months away. He didn't need to rush and could take his time coming up with a plan.

In human form, his stomach started to change ever so slightly. Compared to his fish form, it wasn't obvious. Because he didn't like to use jade belts and always just wore a length of silk or string of beads tied casually around his waist, it was fine even if he kept his robes a little looser. But Li Yu was worried Prince Jing would notice eventually, so he asked Prince Jing for "maternity leave," saying he needed to focus on his cultivation for a few months and couldn't turn back into a human. Prince Jing stared at him questioningly. He could tell this fish was hiding something. But Li Yu made up some excuse and managed to avoid answering.

Prince Jing felt like after they'd become one, there still always seemed to be something separating them. But no matter how much he thought about it, he couldn't figure out what it was. He had always spoiled this fish. If the fish wanted to focus on his cultivation, then Prince Jing would not deny him.

He wasn't afraid of spending time apart temporarily, but he *was* afraid that when the carp spirit finished going through his tribulation, he would leave. Prince Jing had worried about this ever since Li Yu had come clean about his "identity." And now, due to his need to hide his stomach, Li Yu was constantly avoiding him. Unknowingly, he had added to Prince Jing's fears.

Xiaoyu must be hiding something that he didn't want him to know, Prince Jing thought.

In the past, he used to pretend he'd never seen through the fish, always silently protecting him, so there was no reason for that to change. As long as the fish stayed in the tank by his side, somewhere he could see him every day, Prince Jing could accept it.

In the fourth week of his fish pregnancy, Li Yu felt his entire body growing sluggish. He didn't want to move at all. He'd told Prince Jing he'd be cultivating—and occasionally he'd make a couple of moves to keep up the appearance—but he got tired quickly when he swam, and using his brain was even more exhausting.

Maybe he should just lay down and try again tomorrow.

Li Yu thought this every time he was wrapped in his leaf blanket, just before falling asleep. But each day he woke up, he still felt the same.

There was nothing wrong aside from that.

One night, just as he was resigning himself to remaining in this state for several more months, Li Yu suddenly awoke to his stomach feeling a little heavy and bloated.

Li Yu got up in a hurry and glanced at his stomach. The view shocked him deeply. His stomach had shrunk.

No way???

He hurriedly looked below the rock bed, but the bottom of the fish tank hadn't changed. He searched all the corners and still couldn't find anything.

Then he remembered. Nudging away the gold embroidered blanket on the silver rock bed, he saw four round, glowing white "beads," each around the size of a thumb.

...He couldn't have possibly laid these, right?

No, he must have. Otherwise, why did his stomach shrink so much?

The fish-scamming system had finally decided not to scam him for once. He hadn't expected it to be this easy; laying eggs as a fish was actually pretty painless. It only took four weeks, and...it happened while he was asleep.

These things that looked like beads were probably roe.

Li Yu no longer felt sleepy or lazy. He swam over carefully and poked one egg gently with a fin, then stared closely at it.

Of course, there was nothing to see.

He still hadn't thought about how to tell Prince Jing, and now he'd already given birth. And he'd laid not one but four eggs. That was even more awkward.

Could Prince Jing accept that his kids were four small orbs?

This was going to be difficult. They might even float away when he wasn't looking.

Then again, laying eggs was what fish did. The tiny Merman or tiny human that Li Yu had originally been hoping for was impossible. But although fish eggs were a little disappointing, they were still his and Prince Jing's children. Li Yu didn't mind.

How was he going to take care of them now that he'd laid them, though?

Li Yu didn't know what to do. After circling his egg children a couple of times, he suddenly remembered that he had the system! Li Yu wrapped the four eggs snugly back in the blanket and entered the system.

The system was already prepared with a notification: *‹Congratulations, user, for completing the "Spreading Your Seeds" quest. The main quest line "Revitalize the Family" is now finished! Please accept your reward...›*

Li Yu didn't have time to celebrate completing another quest line. He didn't even have time to look at the reward. He hurriedly asked, "Wh-wh-wh-wh-wh-what do I do with the fish eggs?"

‹The side quest "Growing Up" has been unlocked,› the system told him. *‹Please select whether you'd like to proceed.›*

This quest clearly had to do with child-rearing... Ah, of course he had to start it! Besides, this quest made it sound like the fish eggs could grow into humans? That would be the best-case scenario.

‹The fish eggs will hatch after four to five days of incubation. Please protect them. After you have fed them for nine months, they can complete their own quests and become human.›

...Seriously? Why did the little Xiaoyus have to do quests too?! Were the fish born from a system fish also system fish???

Li Yu was almost impressed. The fish-scamming system sure was unbelievable, going so far as setting something like this up! It made him pretty worried, though, when he thought about the quests he'd completed. The little Xiaoyus were so tiny, and they had to worry about quests just like he did?

The system could read Li Yu's thoughts and helpfully added: *‹User, don't worry. They will be very ordinary, simple tasks. They are usually completed without any issue.›*

‹Fine, I'll trust you for now!›

He had no other choice.

After learning about taking care of the eggs and young hatchlings, Li Yu exited the system and stealthily peered around. No one had noticed that he'd secretly laid four round fish eggs. Incubating them over the next four days should be easy enough.

The system had told him he had to choose somewhere quiet to incubate the eggs; the warmer the better. It hadn't told him he had to incubate them himself, but Li Yu had seen birds do that: they usually sat on their eggs, keeping them warm with their feathers. Li Yu thought that made sense, and fish eggs were probably similar. He didn't have feathers, but he did have scales, so he decided to do the same.

He arranged the four round eggs into a small circle, laying on top of them to cover them completely, then draped the blanket over himself.

It should be very warm.

From a distance, you couldn't even tell he was incubating eggs.

Prince Jing never let him go hungry, so he didn't ever have to worry about food. If someone came to change the water, he'd temporarily hide the eggs in the cave of the ornamental mountain. Four days passed just like that; it was all quite easy.

When these round little balls became children, he wouldn't be able to keep it a secret anymore. It would be easier to explain then as well. He could just show Prince Jing directly that he'd given birth to four kids and how many of them were girls or boys, instead of confusing him trying to guess at what exactly was in his fish stomach.

Li Yu had never been so focused, concentrating entirely on his eggs. Gradually, he forgot about everything around him.

Prince Jing noticed that Xiaoyu hadn't been moving much lately. Xiaoyu had warned him ahead of time, so he hadn't asked anyone to come take a look, in case he disturbed Xiaoyu. Xiaoyu still swam a little bit every day at first, but recently, he'd been mostly just sleeping and eating. His stomach seemed to have grown a bit bigger. Perhaps because he was busy cultivating, he didn't move much.

Prince Jing didn't consider any other possibilities, nor could he ask about the fish's cultivation. He just made sure to pay particular attention to Xiaoyu.

It was fine if he didn't want to move much, but the fish seemed to get worse. He was always wrapped in the blanket and wouldn't get off his bed. He wouldn't even move when it was time to eat, only eating the few pieces that drifted to the silver rock bed. Prince Jing was incredibly worried. Desperate times, he decided, called for desperate measures.

Prince Jing lifted the blanket, wanting to take the fish out and take a good look—and in doing so startled Li Yu, who was busy incubating his eggs.

What was going on?! Li Yu desperately held on to the silver rock bed with his fins, making it clear he did not want to leave this bed.

Prince Jing paused. The fish was clearly unhappy, so he had to change his tactics. He couldn't just pull him out by force. Just then, Wang Xi arrived with something to report. Prince Jing turned to listen, and Li Yu took the chance to grab each of the round eggs with his mouth and hide them in the cave.

Wang Xi didn't stay for long. When Prince Jing turned back around, he saw that the fish who refused to leave his bed just a second ago had now slid off the bed and was waiting obediently by his hand.

Prince Jing smiled, petting the fish's head. Li Yu rubbed his mouth against his palm.

Prince Jing remembered that this fish had always really liked to take walks. Afraid that he was bored in the tank, Prince Jing took out the crystal bottle, ready to take Xiaoyu out for a change of scenery.

Oh no...Li Yu liked being alone together, but he was still incubating his eggs!

What if he couldn't get back soon? What if they decided to go for another round? What about his fish babies? Li Yu was torn between his husband and his children. Making up his mind, he thought, *Your Highness, I'm sorry!*

In the past, Li Yu had always jumped into the bottle himself. This time, he refused to do it. Prince Jing brought the fish to the mouth of the bottle, but Li Yu turned around with a swish of his tail and fell back into the tank. He paddled his fins and blew some bubbles: *Your Highness, go on a walk for me!*

Prince Jing didn't know what to do with this fish. He pet Xiaoyu fondly. If he didn't want to go this time, there was always next time.

Now that Prince Jing was stationed here at the western border, he was in charge of all the military and political business. Soon, he had something he needed to take care of and left.

Li Yu let out a sigh of relief. Once he was sure Prince Jing had left and he could no longer hear any footsteps, he took the eggs out of the cave again.

It was too much hassle to carry each egg by itself, so Li Yu came up with an easier way. He grabbed one with his mouth and put the other three on his back. Like that, he swam slowly back to the silver rock bed.

He'd only just reached the bed when Prince Jing returned. He stood before the fish tank silently. Li Yu was shocked at his sudden reappearance. Was this a surprise attack? Li Yu rushed to cover the eggs with the blanket but forgot there was still one in his mouth.

Prince Jing couldn't see what was hidden under the blanket, but when the fish opened his mouth, something rolled out, and he managed to get a good look at that.

This was…

Prince Jing didn't recognize what Xiaoyu was hiding.

But his expression didn't show it.

Li Yu saw that Prince Jing was completely calm and assumed he had figured it out. Now he had no choice but to come clean. Li Yu transformed, then moved the blanket away. Prince Jing saw the three other…round things.

Face red, Li Yu said, "Your Highness, there are four f-fish eggs in total."

The first thing Prince Jing registered from Li Yu's words was that these were fish eggs. He tried to figure out how fish eggs had appeared in his fish tank.

Li Yu looked at him nervously. "I-if I tell you I-I laid them," he said tentatively, "would you believe me?"

Prince Jing felt his eyebrow twitch as he looked at Li Yu.

"Your Highness, these are the eggs I laid," Li Yu repeated shyly. "I'm sorry I told you I couldn't have children before. I only found out recently that I…I'm a fish that can give birth."

Prince Jing felt like his entire world had exploded in a flash of lightning.

Slowly, carefully, he contemplated Li Yu's words.

So Xiaoyu could give birth.

So Xiaoyu had laid four eggs.

So…

He knew that fish eggs became the children of fish, which meant this was—

Prince Jing suddenly felt dizzy. These were his and Xiaoyu's children!

Looking at Prince Jing's expression, Li Yu could see this information was a huge shock even to someone as calm as Prince Jing. Li Yu figured since he already had to tell Prince Jing all this, he might as well explain the rest of it too and shakily informed him of his plan to raise the fish babies.

Apparently, their children had to be incubated—that's what Xiaoyu had been hiding from him. Prince Jing's gaze was warm as he looked at Xiaoyu, who was standing before him. *I won't let you be too tired. Let me help,* he said with a determined gaze that left no room for argument.

The Fish and His Young

L I YU COULD TELL Prince Jing wanted to help. He laughed. "What can you help me with, Your Highness?" he teased him. "It's actually not hard; I can do it myself." He'd already done the hardest, most unbelievable part: giving birth. Now he just had to quietly incubate the eggs: easy!

Prince Jing pursed his lips before shaking his head lightly. He asked Li Yu to repeat the instructions, then reached into the water with one hand to hold the eggs.

They were still tiny. An adult could easily fit all four in the palm of their hand. Prince Jing maintained this position, unmoving. After a while, he very carefully switched to the other hand, keeping the eggs underwater.

When he took his hand out, it had already gone a little pale from soaking in the water too long. He wrapped it in a towel, then switched to the other hand. Rinse and repeat.

Li Yu didn't understand what he was doing at first, but after Prince Jing had repeated the action several times, Li Yu let out a soft exclamation. He got it. Prince Jing was using the warmth from his palms to help warm the eggs. Not only was he willing to believe everything he said, he was even willing to help him incubate the eggs... How could there be such a caring person in this world? Li Yu was overwhelmed by emotion.

Prince Jing smiled at him, not at all angry or upset, and glanced at the empty chair next to him. *You're tired. Rest.*

"Your Highness!!" Li Yu threw himself forward, but he didn't sit down in the chair. Instead, he landed on Prince Jing's back and latched on to him tightly.

Prince Jing was knocked forward slightly by the force and rushed to protect the eggs in his hand. He wanted to hold Li Yu with his other hand, but it hadn't quite warmed up yet and was still a little cold.

Prince Jing always carried himself with calm confidence, but he was starting to get flustered.

"Your Highness, it's okay, you're the best..." Li Yu pressed his face against Prince Jing's broad back and rubbed against it comfortably, wiping away the slight moisture gathered at the corners of his eyes. Ever since he found out he was pregnant, then laid the eggs and started incubating them, he'd endured a lot of fear and misery. But when he saw the joyous smile blooming on Prince Jing's face, Li Yu felt himself smile as well. He suddenly felt like none of this was a big deal.

No matter if he was a human or a carp spirit, whether or not he could have children, whatever he gave birth to, Prince Jing always believed him. He was Li Yu's safe harbor.

Li Yu ignored the empty chair and squeezed into Prince Jing's lap instead. Prince Jing let him sit right down, giving him a kiss. Then he wrapped an arm around him, all while keeping a hand cupped around the fish eggs.

Prince Jing once again encouraged Li Yu to sleep on his shoulder with a look that said, *Rest.*

"Your Highness, I'm not tired, really!" Li Yu hurried to reply.

He'd hadn't even been incubating the eggs for two hours total, and he'd been lying down on the bed that whole time. He wasn't tired at all. Besides, he was already sitting in Prince Jing's lap. If he leaned back onto his shoulders, Prince Jing would be the one who'd get tired.

But no matter how much he objected, Prince Jing insisted that he lean against him.

In the end, Li Yu had to give in. He leaned against Prince Jing, watching as he incubated the eggs. When he changed hands, Li Yu would help him wipe his hands dry, then hug that hand to his chest to warm it up.

The fish eggs had to be incubated for four days, so Prince Jing watched over them the entire time. If any urgent business came up, he'd ask the servants to leave it outside his door. Once they'd left, he would retrieve it and do all his work with one hand on the fish eggs, before putting the papers back outside.

Li Yu had collected his reward, doubling his transformation time. Now, he could maintain his human form for four hours. He'd wanted to take turns with the eggs, but Prince Jing insisted he could do it alone. Li Yu urged him to rest, but only managed to get Prince Jing to take a brief two-hour nap. When he woke up, he immediately went back to incubating the eggs.

Prince Jing was so dedicated. Li Yu had gotten jealous of himself before—now he felt jealous of the amount of attention Prince Jing paid to the eggs instead, which caused a lot of drama.

Li Yu, who'd insisted he wanted to watch as the little eggs hatched, accidentally fell asleep on the fourth day. In the midst of his dreams, something seemed to be tickling his face. Li Yu rubbed his eyes and sat up.

Prince Jing was standing right in front of him. He had his hands held suspiciously behind his back, with a childlike smugness all over his face.

Li Yu froze. Then—"Have they finally hatched?" he asked ecstatically.

Prince Jing nodded, then coughed lightly. Under Li Yu's eager gaze, he slowly brought his hands in front of him. He uncurled his fingers, and in his palms swam four young fish, each an inch long!

Li Yu yelled in excitement. Prince Jing placed the fish into his hands, letting him watch them swim around.

Although he was their father, Li Yu could not tell the difference between the four. The other father, however, insisted that all four fish looked like him.

...Get it together, Your Highness, how could fish look like a human? If you're going to brag about it at least wait until they've changed into human babies!

Prince Jing got out a tea bowl he had prepared for Li Yu and put the four fish babies inside. Although the fish tank was a little larger, he was afraid he wouldn't be able to find them again if he put them inside.

Li Yu could now cancel his transformation whenever he wanted and change back into a fish. He narrowed his eyes playfully at Prince Jing. Being a fish wasn't completely bad. In an instant, he transformed and jumped into the tea bowl.

Would his children recognize him? C-could they speak?

Li Yu started swimming toward them slowly. The little babies quickly noticed and swam to meet him. Li Yu rubbed his mouth affectionately against each of them.

He was still very young. If he hadn't transmigrated as a fish, he might have never had this experience or learned how to interact with baby fish. But the moment he saw his fish babies, he knew he loved them. No matter if they were fish or human, he'd do anything to protect them.

THE FISH AND HIS YOUNG

The baby fish couldn't communicate yet, and they were nearly transparent, with tiny little black dots for eyes. But they were quite lively as they swam around Li Yu.

Li Yu had gotten information from the system on how to feed the baby fish in advance. Following his instructions, Prince Jing had wrapped a boiled egg yolk in a cheese cloth, and now he shook it gently in the water, splashing a bit of soy milk in with it.

Three of the baby fish were immediately interested, fighting with each other to start eating. The last one was still swimming in circles around Li Yu, confused. After a gentle push from Li Yu, it tipped headfirst into the soy milk.

A notification came from the system: <*Congratulations, user, you are now in Team Mode. Your children, the Baby Fish, have joined your Team.*>

This was a thing? He could lead the baby fish to complete quests?

He remembered that the system had said that the One-and-Done skill was one time use only. In the future, his pregnancies would all be normal. But even so, he had given birth to four babies at once. Did that mean he'd end up having even more children later?

Once the babies grew up, they'd also have their own children. Perhaps he could have an entire tank of grandchildren. He sure was "revitalizing the family."

This Team might turn into a whole Platoon.

When other people had children, they had one or two.

When *he* had children, he had one or two *tanks*.

Prince Jing could afford that many fish babies, right...?!

Now that he'd experienced it once, Li Yu was very used to the idea of having children. He thought it was kind of fun. If he wanted more children in the future, he'd just tell Prince Jing to get busy.

Though fish pregnancies didn't take long, it would take nine months for the baby fish to grow into a baby human. Altogether, it wasn't much different from the gestational period of a human. The next step was for the baby fish to grow into humans; it was going to be a very important time.

Prince Jing had asked someone to check, and they confirmed that all four fish babies were male. Now that their sex was confirmed, Prince Jing decided to name them. The next generation of the Royal Family needed to have names that contained the radical for "heart." Prince Jing chose the four characters Kai, Xin, Wei, and Heng.[5] Li Yu couldn't tell the difference between the four at the moment, but Prince Jing could. He knew the order in which they hatched, which is how he decided their order.

Prince Jing chose their given names, so their nicknames were up to Li Yu. He came up with a few cute ones, but then, considering he might have even more fish babies in the future, he decided to just call them Dabao, Erbao, Sanbao, and Sibao[6] for convenience. These nicknames were enough while they were still baby fish. When they grew into humans, they could use the names Prince Jing decided for them.

Now that their names were set and their order determined, Li Yu thought that would be the end of that. But Prince Jing pulled out a thick stack of papers from his sleeve and stuffed it into Li Yu's arms.

Royal children had to start learning a lot at a young age. They were at the western border now, so the conditions weren't as good as the palace, but Prince Jing would not deprive his children of anything. As soon as they could talk, Prince Jing was planning on asking for two of the best teachers in the capital to come teach them.

---

5   Kai (恺), Xin (忻), Wei (惟), and Heng (恒) all have the radical 忄, meaning "heart."
6   Literally Baby 1 (大宝), Baby 2 (二宝), Baby 3 (三宝), and Baby 4 (四宝).

Prince Jing had thought a lot when he was incubating the eggs, and had written it all down, resulting in this stack of paper. He handed it all over to Li Yu to look over.

Li Yu was taken aback. He had assumed he'd be raising their fish babies like you raised *regular* baby fish. He had to teach them all this?!

Looking at Prince Jing's warlike determination, then looking at the four babies fighting for the egg yolk, Li Yu had a flashback to his painful student days. Would the fish babies be all right with a fish dad who'd never had good grades?

Ahem... Should he tell Prince Jing that the babies couldn't be returned now that they'd already been shipped?

As Li Yu flipped through the stack, he came across a piece of red paper. He wondered why there was a piece of paper here that was completely different from the rest—it was incredibly eye-catching. Was there something he needed to pay special attention to?

Li Yu took a closer look and froze. Prince Jing had written "An Eternal Happy Union" and stamped it with his official stamp.

"Your Highness, what is this?" Li Yu looked at Prince Jing. Prince Jing was looking back at him too, with expectation in his eyes. His gaze was filled with so much emotion, Li Yu felt like he was about to be swept away.

Prince Jing took out the jade figure and fish stone that he'd given Li Yu the day they had completed their union and placed them on the red paper. The jade figure was on the side with the stamp. But the side with the fish was empty.

Li Yu's intuition had always been quite good. Red paper and a pair of keepsakes—this was what he thought it was, right?

"Your Highness, you—" Face completely red, Li Yu asked excitedly, "Are you asking for my hand in marriage?" He'd always thought he had a very sensible view on marriage, but now that it was his turn to be proposed to, he couldn't control the fireworks exploding in his chest.

Prince Jing's handsome face was serious: *Yes, I am.*

Before, he hadn't given Xiaoyu an official status because he was trying to protect him. But the situation developed faster than he'd planned for. He had children now. He could not let Xiaoyu or his children be the target of any criticism.

He had written this marriage contract before they'd even left for the western border. This was his determination as the master of the house. As for the emperor's official approval, he would get it before the fish babies transformed!

Fish School

"T O BE HONEST, I didn't think we'd get married so soon..."
Li Yu chuckled.

Prince Jing was in a glum mood. He'd noticed long ago that Xiaoyu had never mentioned wanting an official title. Yao didn't care about such things. But why didn't Xiaoyu want to get married even after giving birth?

The unease in Prince Jing's heart increased. He looked down at the marriage contract, gripping it so hard his fingers turned white.

Li Yu had never thought about being the prince's consort, or the future empress. That was just the truth. He was still very young, so his hope for the future was just for a happy relationship and living each day to the fullest. He hadn't spared much thought to the idea of fighting for a title or status. Besides, back where he came from, men couldn't get married to each other, so Li Yu didn't see anything wrong with the way things were now.

But when he picked up on the prince's deflated mood, he knew he had misspoken. He grabbed the marriage contract back and hurriedly tried to make up for his mistake. "Although it's unexpected, I didn't say no."

Prince Jing looked up at him with his dark eyes. For some reason, Li Yu detected a hint of a pout. His heart quivered. Was Prince Jing... really pouting at him?

"Your Highness, don't be like this, I-I agree!" Li Yu stuttered.

Prince Jing remained unmoving, seeming even more pitiful.

Li Yu's heart was a complete mushy mess. He hurriedly wrote down his own name in the empty spot on the contract.

Other than his signature, he also needed his stamp. But Li Yu didn't have one. Just as he was looking for an inkpad to stamp his fingerprint, Prince Jing pulled out a small square seal from his sleeve and handed it to Li Yu.

It was made of crystal, and a small, lively golden fish was inlaid at the top. The stamp was Li Yu's name.

"Your Highness even had this prepared?!"

Prince Jing nodded and gave the stamp to Li Yu.

Li Yu immediately put the beautiful stamp to use. Then, he and Prince Jing each pressed a fingerprint down next to their stamps.

The moment the fingerprints were printed onto the page, Li Yu's heart sped up. He thought of Ye Qinghuan and his wife, and of all the couples in the village. Just like them, he now had his own family.

In that moment, he wasn't hesitant or worried for the future. He felt the faint joy of settling down. He finally understood how wonderful it was to be married to your beloved.

Prince Jing looked over the wedding contract. After confirming that everything was in order, he handed it over to Li Yu for safekeeping.

Although the marriage of a prince was ultimately the emperor's decision, a handwritten contract counted on its own. This was enough to show the emperor how serious he was.

Prince Jing handed Li Yu a note. *Don't worry. I will take care of things with my father.*

"I'm not worried. And you don't have to rush, Your Highness."

He really wasn't worried. He'd signed the marriage contract, so in the future he would naturally be Prince Jing's consort and then the empress. He didn't doubt Prince Jing's feelings toward him, but getting the emperor to grant an official title to Li Yu, someone with no background, would not be easy. But Li Yu was optimistic. If the emperor didn't allow it, he could just wait until after Prince Jing ascended to the throne.

"Your Highness, don't force it. If it doesn't work out, then just forget about it for a while. I can wait, it's okay." He was half reassuring him about his efforts and half reminding him that in the future, he'd be allowed to do what he wanted.

But Prince Jing shook his head. He'd always known Xiaoyu didn't care about all that. He would care in Xiaoyu's place.

I have a plan. Prince Jing didn't reveal anything further.

Since he said so, Li Yu was filled with confidence and eagerly awaited his results.

Now that Li Yu had signed the contract, Prince Jing asked Wang Xi to prepare for the wedding. It seemed a little rushed to drink their wedding wine the one time when they consummated, so Prince Jing wanted to give Li Yu an official wedding. He'd already written his letter to the emperor to ask for his blessing, which was rushing to the capital at this very moment. Meanwhile, he was fervently preparing his plan. He was sure that by the time he received the emperor's response, he would be ready.

Prince Jing would take care of everything. All Li Yu had to do was wait and focus on a more important mission: raising the fish babies.

Prince Jing could help him incubate the eggs, but he could not help him educate the fish babies. As the only fish parent, he was the only one who could try to communicate with the little ones.

After spending two whole days with the fish babies, Li Yu finally figured out who was who. Dabao's tail was a little longer, Erbao's stomach was very round even when he didn't eat, Sanbao was the first to grow unusually colored scales, and Sibao was usually the most confused baby. If the four babies were gathered together to eat, then the last one to arrive would definitely be Sibao.

Li Yu started trying to talk to them as well as feed them. Aside from Sibao, the other babies were all quite smart. Very quickly, they learned how to say "eat" and "swim."

When Li Yu said "eat," they would gather together to wait for food. When he said "swim," they would follow behind Li Yu.

Li Yu worried that as they swam, they would get lost, so he shook his tail gently in front of Dabao, then made a biting motion. The smart Dabao immediately bit down on his tail fin. Li Yu then taught Erbao to bite onto Dabao's fin, and so on and so forth. The fish babies formed a line so no one would get lost.

Three of the four babies very quickly formed a string with their dad—only Sibao was still confused. Li Yu noticed that this baby was always a little slow to react, but he didn't say anything about it. He just nudged Sibao gently with his mouth and put him on his head. This way, all the babies could swim with him.

But now Dabao, holding on to his tail, was unhappy Sibao was getting preferential treatment. He and his two brothers let go and swam to face Li Yu.

...Should he be happy that these children already knew how to be jealous?!

He was finally getting to experience the hardships of being a father. He wasn't setting a good example by treating them unequally, so Li Yu nudged all of them onto his head. The fish babies waved their tails excitedly, copying him. It seemed they were all happy now.

Li Yu continued to teach them how to speak. "Daddy!" he demonstrated clearly.

The fish babies stared at him, confused, not knowing what to do.

Li Yu realized he was going about it the wrong way. He thought about it, grabbed a peach blossom pastry, and then ripped it into small pieces. Circling the pastry, he tried again: "Daddy!" Children who could say it for him got a treat!

The sweet, fragrant pastry attracted the babies' attention. Dabao tilted his head a little and tried, "Dad?"

Dabao was so smart! Li Yu wanted to clap for him. Who said fish were stupid? He rewarded Dabao with a piece of pastry. Dabao waved his tail happily and started eating in large bites.

Erbao and Sanbao were both envious of Dabao's snack, so they imitated Dabao. "Da?"

Hmm... Li Yu thought they weren't completely wrong. It was a good first attempt. He rewarded the two of them as well, to encourage them.

The older brothers had all set a good example. Only Sibao was left. Li Yu nodded at Sibao gently. But Sibao looked dazed, as though he didn't understand. Li Yu wondered what was wrong, when the fish baby began sinking.

Li Yu rushed to catch Sibao, who seemed just as frightened as he was. Did he fall asleep? Li Yu was both irritated and amused. Who did this child take after?

"Daddy!" Li Yu once again tried to teach Sibao. But Sibao still didn't know what to do. In response to his fish dad's instruction, he blew two small bubbles.

No, no, he had to teach him how to say "Daddy"!

With Li Yu using the peach blossom pastry to tempt him, Sibao finally ended up just barely getting it right.

Prince Jing came over to see his fish wife and sons. Li Yu was playing with the fish babies, leading them in a circle. "Your Highness, our sons can say 'Daddy' now!" he said excitedly.

Prince Jing couldn't understand fish, so he just watched Li Yu swim around with a smile on his face.

Li Yu wanted to try it again in front of his husband; he grabbed another piece of peach blossom pastry. That way, he could tell the fish babies that this tall, handsome man was their daddy too.

He took out the pastry, but before he'd had a chance to say anything, the fish babies were already yelling out "Dad!" With Dabao in the lead, the four babies rushed happily toward the pastry.

...It seemed like the fish babies had misunderstood.

There had originally only been one fish in Prince Jing's room. Now that there were four more little ones, people would definitely notice, so Prince Jing just told everyone that these were Xiaoyu's babies. That way, the fish babies didn't have to keep hiding.

Prince Jing's fish was very large by now. There was nothing strange about him having children, so no one thought anything of it. Nobody even asked where the "female fish" was—horses and dogs could be bred, after all. Why not fish?

Wang Xi liked Master Xiaoyu a lot. Now, with the addition of these tiny fish, Wang Xi was so happy he couldn't stop grinning. Prince Jing asked Wang Xi to ensure their safety, and told him this was now his top priority. Wang Xi understood immediately.

Wang-gonggong had deduced the following: His Highness cared for Master Xiaoyu a lot, about the same amount as he cared for Li-gongzi. So, the same could be said comparing these fish babies with Li-gongzi's potential son, right? Not to mention, if Li-gongzi really were to have a son, whose would it be?

Ha, wasn't the prince just subtly telling him that he had to treat these tiny fish as tiny masters? Wang Xi desperately wanted some little masters, so he carried out his orders to the letter.

Back in the capital, at Qianqing palace, the emperor had been asking about the situation at the western border every few days, ever since Prince Jing arrived there. He also read all the reports coming from the western border several times each.

There had been an assassination attempt as soon as Prince Jing arrived, and the emperor was worried for his safety. Following the news, he had sent over many guards and imperial physicians, and had secretly ordered the generals at the border to help Prince Jing if he was ever in danger. The emperor was worried he had made a big mistake. It was fine if Prince Jing wasn't up to this test, but what if he couldn't even make it back?

The emperor spent several months living in suspense. But the physicians hadn't even arrived yet when he received a second report from the western border: a battle report.

In his first battle against the bandits, Prince Jing had come out victorious.

The report carefully detailed the reasons Prince Jing had decided to initiate the battle, as well as his specific tactics.

The emperor was first furious over the bandits' wild disregard for order, and then shocked by Prince Jing's cold-blooded decisiveness. The emperor had sent many experienced soldiers in the past, but they had never been able to win. Prince Jing had no experience with real battle, but he still had the guts to challenge the bandits. Not only that, he had won. After being so worried for so long, the emperor felt extreme joy.

Prince Jing didn't disappoint him: he was capable of shouldering this heavy responsibility.

Although the emperor was happy, he wasn't going to reward Prince Jing too lavishly, in case he started getting arrogant. The emperor ordered Head Eunuch Luo to send a set of top-quality armor to the border, intending to continue watching to see what Prince Jing would do next.

Privately, the emperor was very proud of his son and ordered the Ministry of War to analyze the detailed battle report. When they simulated the battle on a miniature battlefield, even the Minister of War praised Prince Jing for his military command. The emperor was extremely satisfied.

Apart from the battle, Prince Jing had also mentioned a youth called Li Yu. Apparently, this youth had a wealth of knowledge and had helped out quite a lot. Prince Jing admitted that it was all thanks to this youth that he was able to win against the bandits. Prince Jing wanted to reward the youth for his contribution and was hoping the emperor would let him.

The emperor was happy. It was such a small thing—did Prince Jing really need to ask him? With a wave of his brush, the emperor allowed it.

The capital was a long way from the western border, so it was incredibly difficult to communicate. It was half a month later when the emperor received Prince Jing's second and third message.

The emperor allowed Prince Jing to reward the youth, so in the next two messages, Prince Jing described exactly how he thought he might reward Li Yu. But at the end of each message, he concluded it still wasn't enough.

The emperor could tell that Prince Jing wanted to keep discussing this, but he had run out of patience. He felt like Prince Jing was being too careful. Since this Li Yu had made a great contribution, he told Prince Jing to consider things carefully and make the decision himself.

A month later, the emperor received Prince Jing's fourth message.

The message said that after some careful consideration, he decided to reward Li Yu with marriage, and the title of Consort.

Fishy Babies
Change Color

THE EMPEROR was shocked. He was only meant to be rewarding a subordinate. How had they reached the idea of marriage?

Prince Jing insisted on calling the marriage a reward, and the emperor *had* told him to figure out the reward by himself. He had several messages as proof. Remembering how Prince Jing had asked several times, the emperor realized Prince Jing had tricked him. He hadn't really been worrying over the reward; he'd wanted to make the marriage happen from the start.

After the initial shock subsided, the emperor was furious. He was angry that Prince Jing dared to trick him, and also that Prince Jing chose a male consort.

There was no ban on homosexuality in this dynasty, and past emperors had taken on male concubines, even showering them with affection. Even the emperor himself, curious about trying something new, had a male Noble Lady—or perhaps he should say Noble Lord—when he was young. Politically, it was no big deal to have a male concubine, because they couldn't have children. But they couldn't be one's official wife. If Prince Jing insisted on taking Li Yu as a concubine, perhaps the emperor would've let him. As a prince, Prince Jing was entitled to have one consort and two concubines.

Merely becoming a concubine would be a great honor for a commoner like Li Yu, and everybody would be happy.

But Prince Jing talked about the position of his consort in his letter, and that was the title he wanted to give Li Yu. Of course the emperor wasn't happy with that.

How could a man, especially a man with no background, become the official consort of a prince? If the emperor allowed this, it would be difficult for Prince Jing to take any young noble woman as concubines. After all, what young lady would be happy being in a lower position than a man who couldn't even bear children? And her own children could only ever be shu children?

Very quickly, the emperor came up with a bunch of reasons to refuse. He didn't agree to this marriage, it was just a clever little trick Prince Jing had played. If the emperor could be convinced that easily, he wouldn't be the emperor.

But he'd already officially given his approval, so he couldn't just take it back. The emperor thought about it and decided to just delay his response. He wouldn't say yes or no.

If he didn't respond, Prince Jing wouldn't be able to proceed with the wedding.

The emperor was quite vexed and disappointed with Prince Jing.

He'd once spent a lot of time worrying about Prince Jing's marriage, but Prince Jing had seemed uninterested. Now that he finally wanted to get married, if it had been a woman who'd caught his eye, the emperor would definitely have given his blessing. But Prince Jing wanted a male consort. He'd only just started being impressed with this son, and now he'd gone and done this!

Livid, the emperor decided to leave Prince Jing hanging so he could reflect on himself. He sent Prince Jing to the western border to test his abilities, not to recklessly seek a male wife.

In a fit of anger, he summoned the former Duke of Cheng'en, Prince Jing's grandfather Ye Qian to the palace to discuss a solution with him.

Ye Qian had received a message from Prince Jing a while ago, and had met Li Yu even earlier. In the face of the emperor's anger, Ye Qian calmly and subtly persuaded him to relax.

Prince Jing wanting a male wife had made the emperor realize it was finally time for Prince Jing to have his own family. It was improper not to have a woman by his side to take care of him. Perhaps he, the emperor, should find a woman to marry Prince Jing. Perhaps then he would stop thinking of this Li Yu. If he still wanted him, Li Yu could be a concubine. Wouldn't that be better than marrying a male consort directly?

Ye Qian understood what the emperor was thinking, so he asked purposefully, "Does Your Majesty already have someone in mind?"

The emperor had no response.

This wasn't the first or even the second time that the emperor had worried about Prince Jing's marriage. It was true that Prince Jing didn't really care, but it was also true there wasn't anyone suitable.

All of the noble young ladies in the capital who were of similar status to Prince Jing had all tactfully communicated that they'd much rather be any other prince's consort. They had no interest in the mute Prince Jing.

There were some of lower status who were willing, but they either had bad reputations, bad appearances, or had some sort of disability, just like Prince Jing. The emperor thought none of them suitable, so he'd never ended up appointing a marriage for Prince Jing.

Was there no way for his son to find a normal wife?

The emperor's temper flared up even more. He would find a suitable wife for Prince Jing no matter what.

"This servant has something to say that may not be appropriate," said Ye Qian. "I've never seen His Highness Prince Jing ask Your Majesty for anything. His Highness isn't a reckless person, so he must have truly fallen in love. His Highness is different from other people. I think perhaps he truly values this person."

But how could the emperor not have already realized this? Prince Jing had subtly praised this Li Yu several times in his messages. The emperor knew he was a good kid with a good character who had contributed a great deal to help Prince Jing. Otherwise, the emperor might've simply gotten rid of him.

That was why the emperor was so vexed. Prince Jing truly wasn't reckless at all. He'd planned this trick far in advance. Thinking about the way the prince had led him here step-by-step made him extremely annoyed. But somehow, each step was perfectly reasonable. He couldn't find any evidence of Prince Jing tricking him. All he could manage to accuse Prince Jing of was not thinking straight and treating marriage like a joke.

How dare this brat anger him like this? Wasn't he afraid he'd leave him at the western border forever and never let him return to the capital?

The emperor knew that probably wouldn't be necessary. Prince Jing had just made a little error in judgment regarding his marriage. It was nothing compared to the second and third princes' mistakes. Besides, Prince Jing was now a prince with achievements under his belt. If he punished Prince Jing over this, his ministers would try to convince him against it. All he could do was scold Prince Jing in front of the old Duke of Cheng'en.

Ye Qian was familiar with the emperor's temperament. If the emperor was angry with the prince, Ye Qian would just listen quietly, occasionally agreeing here and there without trying to convince the emperor of anything. After a while, the emperor grew bored. Empress Xiaohui had passed away many years ago, and the old Duke of Cheng'en was technically his father-in-law, an elder. It wasn't very proper to scold his son in front of his father-in-law.

The emperor finally calmed down a little.

Soon Prince Jing's next letter arrived. It had only been a few days since he decided to ignore Prince Jing's last letter—Prince Jing couldn't know yet that he was avoiding responding, and the emperor assumed this message must be unrelated.

The emperor skimmed over it. It contained another suggestion from Li Yu.

Aside from the bandits, the emperor had another concern. There were a few villages on the western border that suffered from locusts every year or two. The western border was often rife with battle, and there was barely any farmland. If there was a locust infestation, the villagers would have to go hungry and possibly even become homeless.

The emperor was worried that the locust problem would get worse and worse. At first, the locusts only appeared at the very border, but in the past two years, they had begun to spread.

Every year, the emperor allocated a lot of money toward controlling the locusts, but they were never truly eradicated. It seemed unlikely that this youth could prove more useful than the experienced officials in the Ministry of Works...

But it was this youth who had helped Prince Jing defeat the bandits.

The emperor was curious. He knew Prince Jing was just trying to promote Li Yu, but he couldn't help it: he read on.

The babies that Li Yu had given birth to were now a month old. Under Prince Jing's attentive care, their bodies started to change.

They had once all been nearly transparent, but now three out of the four had the colorful scales of a koi.

Dabao was a majestic fish covered in gold scales, Erbao had a gold base with flecks of silver, the opposite of Li Yu, who was silver with flecks of gold. Sanbao was the prettiest: silver from head to toe. From a distance, his scales looked like tiny, dazzling pearls.

Gold and silver were all colors Li Yu had on his body. At first, since the fish babies hadn't grown gold or silver scales, Li Yu thought they wouldn't turn into koi. After all, his own koi status had been achieved through completing quests. He wasn't born with it, so it shouldn't be passed down to the babies.

But unexpectedly, after a month, the fish babies each had their own colors. The koi appearance could be passed down after all; they just needed to grow more.

Of the four baby fish, Dabao, Erbao, and Sanbao had all changed colors. Only Sibao still looked the same. Li Yu was, of course, worried. Sibao often had a hard time keeping up with the others. Would it be the same for growing scales? Could there be such a large difference between fish from the same clutch?

The fish babies still didn't quite know how to talk, only knowing a few simple words, so Li Yu still didn't know what Sibao was thinking. Dabao, Erbao, and Sanbao slowly started to look more and more like koi, and after another half month, Sibao finally started to change too.

Li Yu had waited for this day for so long.

But Sibao's scales were not the gold or silver of his brothers—they were grayish black. He had grown into a regular small black fish, similar to how Li Yu had looked when he first transmigrated.

Why was the difference so huge even though they were part of the same clutch of eggs?

Sibao seemed to realize that he was different and got a little dejected that he wasn't turning into a koi like the rest of his brothers. When Li Yu saw this, he immediately put the little black fish on his head, spinning around in circles to cheer him up.

"No matter if Sibao turns into a koi or not, Daddy loves you!" Before, whenever Li Yu heard people say things like this, it would make him shudder, but now he said it to his fish baby without any hesitation, and Sibao quickly perked up with his father's encouragement.

After that, Li Yu transformed into a human and put the babies into a crystal bottle to visit Prince Jing.

Prince Jing was working at the moment. Every day, Li Yu would take the fish babies with him to visit their other dad. Although they all spent each evening in the same room, Li Yu was still very diligent about developing the relationship between the fish babies and Prince Jing.

As soon as Prince Jing saw them, he set down his brush. Prince Jing was very happy when he realized Sibao had turned into a small, black fish. Sibao's personality was a little like Li Yu's. Now that he looked even more like Li Yu used to, Prince Jing liked him even more.

Li Yu put the crystal bottle on the desk and sat down to keep Prince Jing company while he read some reports.

There was too much useless writing in the reports, and it was all in ancient Chinese. One word was written particularly messily. Li Yu struggled to read it for a while, but he wasn't able to figure it out, and he fell asleep again.

He had a tendency to fall asleep when reading. As he kept nodding off, the fish babies in the crystal bottle started to bob up and down with the movement of his sleepy head.

...Too distracting. Prince Jing glanced at the fish babies in the bottle and made a shushing motion. The fish babies all stopped moving. They pressed against the crystal, staring back at him with wide eyes.

Prince Jing took off his outer robe and wrapped it around the sleeping Li Yu and himself, creating a soft, warm space just for them. Holding Li Yu gently, he kissed him on the lips. He'd already sent the message asking the emperor to give Li Yu an official title. The plan was in motion; now they just had to wait.

After watching the robe covering his dads rustle for a while, Dabao turned around. Without knowing why, Erbao and Sanbao followed his example and turned around too.

Sibao knew he was a little slower, but following Dabao was always the right move, so half a beat later, Sibao also turned around. But he kept looking back curiously at his fathers.

Li Yu had fallen asleep because he couldn't recognize a specific word. After a brief nap, his brain felt a little clearer, and he suddenly remembered what it meant.

It was the word "locust." Followed by the word "disaster."

A locust disaster.

Li Yu was suddenly wide awake. "Your Highness, have locusts appeared somewhere?"

This was a serious situation! Locusts ate a wide variety of crops and had a tendency to start swarming. When a swarm of locusts flew past, all the crops the farmers had carefully taken care of for the whole year would vanish into the mouths of these pests!

Prince Jing told Li Yu about the locusts that had been spotted in a village near the western border.

Li Yu's expression changed.

Prince Jing misunderstood and thought he was afraid. He showed Li Yu a map of the western border and pointed out Luofeng Village. Luofeng Village was still very far from where the locusts appeared. They were definitely safe.

Prince Jing comforted Li Yu: *Don't be afraid.* As long as he was there, he would protect Li Yu and the children.

Li Yu looked up at him. "No, Your Highness, I'm not frightened. I want to help the villagers and try to stop the infestation."

THE DISABLED TYRANT'S BELOVED PET FISH

Duck, Duck, Fish

P RINCE JING TRUSTED Li Yu wholeheartedly, but solving the issue of locusts was no trivial matter. Prince Jing paused, holding Li Yu's hand in his. His gaze was worried, as though asking him, *Are you sure?*

Li Yu giggled, "Of course. But the method isn't very dignified."

Prince Jing didn't care about dignity. When it came to getting rid of the locusts, he was more worried about Li Yu's safety. Usually, people got rid of locusts by burning them with fire. Although it was very effective at getting rid of many locusts at once, being so close to fire was very dangerous. Xiaoyu was a carp spirit—he probably feared fire, right?

Li Yu saw his hesitation. "Don't worry, Your Highness, I won't go myself." There wasn't a chance he'd be doing any of this in person. Sob sob, don't treat him like an all-powerful yao. He was just a fish with a system who was very afraid of bugs!

Prince Jing observed Li Yu. Seeing that he wasn't joking, he finally nodded, letting him give it a go.

Li Yu borrowed a brush and paper, then wrote a few lines down. It just so happened that right before he transmigrated, several countries in Li Yu's previous world had been suffering from locusts, and his country had lent a helping hand. He'd been curious at the time, and so he'd done some cursory research on how to control locusts.

Though he couldn't remember everything, he remembered a few things because he thought it was interesting.

He wrote them down: deep plowing, choosing crops, and a duck army.

Prince Jing had no idea what these phrases meant.

Li Yu tried his best to explain in a way that could be understood by people in ancient times. "Locust eggs are usually laid in the dirt. When plowing, if we dig a little deeper, the eggs will be exposed to the sunlight, and they'll be...scorched by the sun. For the next step, locusts don't eat everything, so if we plant only crops that locusts don't eat, then they will have less food. Then they won't be able to cause as much havoc."

Prince Jing was an intelligent man; he immediately understood. Both these points made sense. His gaze landed on the third point. What was the duck army? Was it...the kind of duck he was thinking of?

"Your Highness, it's exactly what you think." Li Yu blinked. "Everything has a weakness. Ducks eat locusts. The first two methods are too late to use for the areas that have already been infested, but you can gather some ducks to take care of those regions. This is what's called...a duck army."

Prince Jing furrowed his brow. It wouldn't be an exaggeration to say he'd never heard of any of these things that Xiaoyu mentioned— especially not the duck army.

But what he said seemed to make sense. And fire wasn't involved either, so it would be much less dangerous. Prince Jing nodded slowly.

There were a few families who owned ducks in Luofeng Village, but not many. They were either used for selling or eating. Prince Jing ordered Wang Xi to buy a few. They had to try it out and see for themselves whether ducks ate locusts.

Wang Xi volunteered himself for this job. The next day, he left before the sky even lightened. Not even an hour later, he came running back and said in an excited voice, "Your Highness, it really works! This old servant saw with his own eyes that as soon as the ducks showed up, they ate plenty of locusts. They ate the whole time I was there without even stopping!"

He was in such a rush to get back and report this that he nearly lost a shoe on the way.

According to Wang Xi, one duck could eat around a hundred locusts in one shot. Prince Jing did some rough calculations, and his excitement grew uncontrollably.

If he sent a report to the emperor first and waited for the Ministry of Works to give him the funds to buy the ducks, the situation might get a lot worse. Prince Jing needed to strike immediately, so he ordered Wang Xi to use his own money to purchase all the ducks in the western border. If that wasn't enough, they could send someone to the other nearby counties.

Li Yu had another idea. "Your Highness, don't just buy the fully grown ones. Buy some ducklings as well, and we can start a duck farm. Ducks grow fast, so they'll soon be able to help with clearing the locusts too!"

Prince Jing thought about it, decided it was a good idea, and ordered Wang Xi to go ahead.

A single duck wasn't expensive, and Prince Jing had plenty of money. The people of Luofeng Village were all grateful to Prince Jing for defeating the bandits. When they found out he was looking to buy ducks, they all brought their ducks over, and many of them refused to accept money. Several nearby counties heard that Prince Jing was buying ducks to control the locusts, and out of curiosity, they sent flock after flock.

Prince Jing ordered guards to be stationed along the way to ensure the villagers' safety, as well as to prevent any looting bandits. But when the bandits heard that Prince Jing planned on eradicating the locusts, they were eager to see him fail, and they lost interest in stealing ducks for the time being.

In no time at all, Wang Xi was able to gather five thousand live ducks and just over a thousand ducklings.

The ducklings needed to be fed, so the ducks were gathered together into a duck army and sent off loudly to the most affected village.

Prince Jing headed over himself. After just a day, they had made encouraging progress. The duck army could really eat. A small group of ducks was able to clean out nearly all the locusts in an acre of land in just half a day.

What previously frustrated the villagers was that locusts didn't live for very long. Even if they burned all the locusts around them, another wave would quickly replace it, and there was danger of the fire spreading. Now, they didn't have to worry at all. The ducks could keep eating for days on end, and there were no other risks. There was also very little loss. By the time an entire village was taken care of, they had lost less than ten percent of the ducks.

The ducks were truly a fascinating army. Smiling, Prince Jing gave Li Yu a thumbs-up, and continued to order Wang Xi to buy ducks from the surrounding area.

But Wang Xi ran into a problem during his second round of duck purchasing. He noticed that once it had got around that they needed ducks, some merchants had been purchasing them at cheap prices from local farmers in advance and wanted to sell them to him for a higher price.

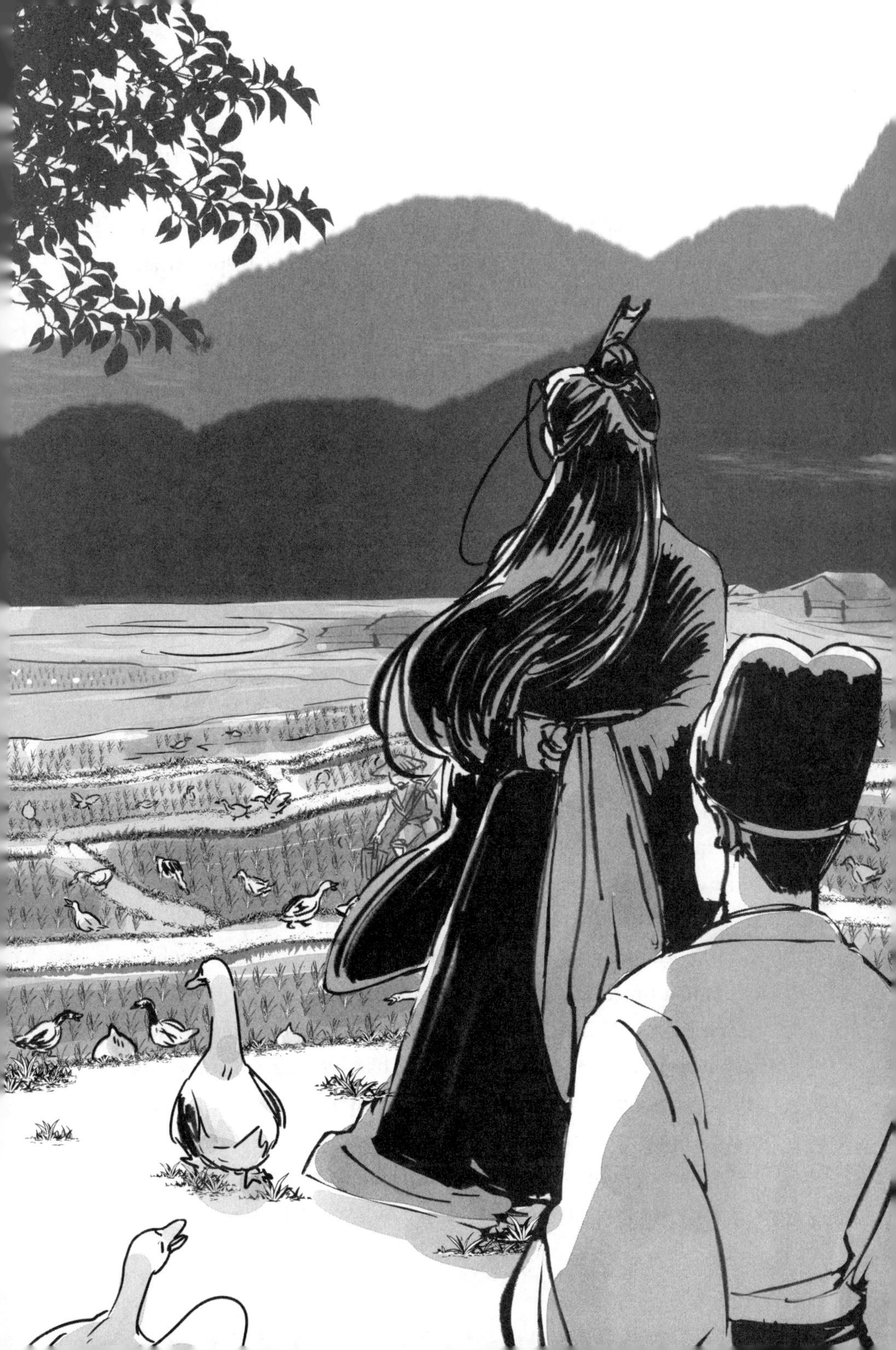

Wang Xi couldn't be more furious. When he reported it to Prince Jing, Li Yu was bewildered. After all, stocking up on food and water was understandable. Who stocked up on ducks? Besides, couldn't they grow a brain? Prince Jing was purchasing ducks to help alleviate the locust situation. How could someone try to make a profit off a plague? If the locusts ate all the crops, where would they get food?

An opportunity to make three times the profit was enough for them to forfeit their life, huh.

Prince Jing was prepared. He gave Wang Xi a glance, ordering him to make a record of who was doing this. Those duck scalpers could keep on stocking up, there was no need to pay them any mind.

This time, Wang Xi wasn't able to get very many ducks and was worried he was causing a delay. Prince Jing, however, was unruffled. He looked at Li Yu. *We could buy chickens too, right?*

"Chickens are fine too! But they don't eat as much as ducks..." Li Yu nodded repeatedly. His Highness knew about this as well!

Prince Jing just wanted anything that would eat locusts, so he ordered Wang Xi to buy some chickens. Meanwhile, the duck farm that Li Yu had asked for was ready. He hired a few brave people to raise the ducks. With locusts as feed, the ducklings grew quickly. Just as the duck army was starting to run short, the ducklings grew up to fill the ranks. Not to mention, the duck army laid plenty of eggs.

Li Yu was delighted. "It's a good thing Your Highness bought a lot the first time. Now we can replenish the ducks!"

These days, Wang Xi, the head eunuch of a prince's manor, was busy buying chickens and ducks, and hatching eggs. Prince Jing smiled confidently and took over. His Highness was very experienced in egg incubation.

As for the people who were hoarding ducks, they never managed to get Prince Jing to purchase them, and eventually they couldn't afford to keep storing them. Ducks were livestock. Unlike grain, they couldn't just be stored in a warehouse. They had to be fed and taken care of. If they weren't careful, the ducks died or escaped.

Seeing as Prince Jing was no longer buying any more ducks, the merchants were dumbfounded. What were they going to do with all these ducks? Who else but Prince Jing could afford such a vast quantity of ducks here at the western border?

These people were afraid of not making their money back, so they personally went to apologize to Wang Xi. With Prince Jing's reminder, Wang Xi stood with his back ramrod straight and haggled the price down again and again, nearly grinding the merchants down to their bones. In the end, he only agreed to buy the ducks at a price way lower than market value.

The duck army and duck farm were both running smoothly now. Li Yu had gone to the duck farm before and taken a look everywhere. With his modern sensibilities, he suggested a lot of improvements. He thought the ducklings in the farm were all adorable too. On a whim, he bought two yellow ducklings and started taking care of them at home.

When the fish babies saw the new and exciting ducklings, they were overcome with excitement, just like their fish dad. The crystal bottle almost couldn't contain them. All four babies—even Sibao, the poor thing—were jumping up and down eagerly.

Li Yu was afraid the ducklings would eat the fish, so he refused to let them get close. He only let the babies look from a distance.

Sibao really liked the beautiful ducklings. Once, when Li Yu was taking his afternoon nap, he snuck out of the crystal bottle to go play with the ducks.

The afternoon nap was a habit Li Yu had picked up after giving birth. Apparently, sleeping a lot as a child led to good development, so Li Yu wanted the fish babies to sleep more. Every day, when the time came, he'd take a nap with the fish babies.

But the fish babies were all lively and liked to move around. Before Li Yu fell asleep, they would get into the fish blanket with him. Once Li Yu had drifted off, though, they'd dart out from the blanket and play on their own.

That was how Sibao came to leap out of the crystal bottle. Luckily, Prince Jing had the foresight to spread a thick carpet on the ground just in case. Sibao wasn't injured from the landing. But he was just a small, palm-sized fish. He completely forgot that it would be hard for him to get anywhere after he left the crystal bottle and fish tank. Soon after landing, he started to feel uncomfortable.

Dabao, Erbao, and Sanbao all swam to the edge of the crystal bottle, worriedly looking down at Sibao as he struggled. Their brother was in danger!

Dabao jumped out without hesitation, and Erbao and Sanbao followed. They all wanted to save Sibao.

But now all four fish babies were flopping around on the ground instead of just Sibao.

Li Yu had only slept for a little while. Every so often, he had to wake up and check on the fish babies. Almost immediately, he realized all four of them had jumped out of the bottle. Li Yu was scared nearly half to death and hurriedly gathered them all back inside.

Sibao was terrified. He stuck closely to Li Yu, who was both angry and worried. It was hard for him to blame this worrisome, confused baby, so he fed Sibao some fish food to distract him. But even while he was eating, Sibao continued to cling to him.

Li Yu wanted to know what was up with Sibao, so he tried to get him to speak. Sibao spoke a little unclearly: "Daddy, want duckies!"

Li Yu figured out that Sibao ended up on the floor because he wanted to see the ducks. Why did Sibao like ducks so much?

Li Yu thought about it a bit, then took Sibao to see the adult ducks with a mischievous smile on his face. After seeing the big ducks—with their bigger beaks and longer and bendier necks, as well as their much larger size—Sibao burst into tears when he thought about the small, fuzzy ducklings.

Now that he'd teased Sibao, Li Yu went to tease Dabao.

Dabao had failed to save his younger brother, and the attempt resulted in him and his brothers all on the floor. Dabao knew he'd made a mistake. As soon as Li Yu approached him, he apologized on his own. "Dad, I'm sorry."

Li Yu, who also liked exploring, asked, "Oh? Can you tell Dad what you did wrong?"

"I...wasn't strong enough to bring my brother back." Dabao was a little downtrodden and embarrassed.

What?! Hello, son, please wake up! Your mistake wasn't that you weren't strong enough!

Dabao, unaware of his father's complaints, said sincerely, "I want to become the strongest fish to protect my brothers and you, Dad!"

Li Yu felt like he could almost see Dabao's determination. Seriously, they were all born from the same clutch, but Sibao couldn't even speak properly while Dabao was already announcing his aspirations!

"Dabao, you're a good kid." Li Yu patted him comfortingly with a fin. "But you have to know your own strength."

Dabao was confused. What did "know your own strength" mean?

Li Yu taught him. "It means Dabao can only protect his fathers and brothers after he grows up."

Dabao nodded, only half understanding. "Then Dabao wants to grow up quickly."

Jeez, it was a bit over the top, but why did he feel warm all over from Dabao's words?!

Thanks to the hard work of the duck army, the locust disaster had been brought under control. Although a few areas were facing repeat infestations, with the duck army at its current power, the locusts would soon be taken care of.

Although they got the locusts under control this year, that didn't mean they'd be able to just relax in the future. Locusts were hard to deal with because they always came back. But now that they knew how to deal with it, it wasn't a big deal if they returned. All the villagers along the western border who could afford a few ducks now kept ducks.

Ducks were quite a valuable thing. Not only could they be sold for money, they could be eaten, and they could get rid of locusts!

But in the end, the issue of where to store the duck army, fat from their locust feast, became a headache.

Li Yu's eyes went bright at all the ducks. Remembering something, he started drooling a little, and said to Prince Jing, "Your Highness, let's eat roasted duck!"

Prince Jing had eaten the smashed cucumbers Li Yu had made himself without batting an eye. Roast duck was nothing.

Prince Jing nodded, and the Quanjude[7] at the western border was opened.

---

7   *Quanjude* (全聚德) *is a famous, long-standing Peking Duck restaurant from Beijing.*

Stuffed Fish

THE LOCUSTS would be completely exterminated any day now. Prince Jing had already presented Li Yu's ideas to the emperor in his letters, and they were on their way to the capital. Now, he wrote a more detailed report on the status of the locusts at each village.

In his last letter, he had mentioned his marriage with Li Yu, but the emperor hadn't responded, so Prince Jing knew he was just letting it sit. Before he made his request clear, he had already revealed plenty of Xiaoyu's good points and had taken advantage of the emperor's good mood. The emperor hadn't denied his request outright, which meant he was still thinking about it. So, if he sent this letter over, the emperor would surely be swayed.

Of course he couldn't reveal Xiaoyu's true identity, but he hoped just this letter would be enough for the emperor to see how good Xiaoyu was. Even if he didn't have a distinguished background, even if he couldn't bear children, he was more than qualified to stand at his side as his consort.

He'd never asked the emperor for anything in his life. He could fight for the spot of crown prince with his own abilities; he didn't need to ask for that. The only thing he wanted was this marriage. He had considered whether this would anger the emperor, whether this would completely put an end to his bid for the throne, but if that were the case...

Prince Jing glanced at Li Yu, who was teaching the babies how to play tug-of-war. Although the western border was desolate, he had already had some of the happiest times of his life here, living together as a family of six.

If the emperor really chose to give up on him, then he would ask to stay at the western border forever. That way, he and Xiaoyu could still be together.

But that was the worst-case scenario. It shouldn't get to that point. He had other tricks up his sleeve.

In the end, Prince Jing sent their marriage contract in the letter to the emperor.

When the emperor received Prince Jing's next letter, he noticed it came with a marriage contract.

The emperor was very unhappy with Prince Jing for deciding on this without consulting him first. But at the same time, the emperor understood that Prince Jing had sent the marriage certificate because he was making his position clear: this was a silent plea.

In his memory, Prince Jing had never asked him for anything. Even when the emperor had sent him to the western border immediately after receiving Prince Jing's birthday gifts, the prince hadn't asked for any leniency. He'd just accepted, bowed in farewell, and left the capital. Prince Jing had a cold personality, and that was how the emperor expected him to behave.

But now, he realized Prince Jing had a stubborn side. To an emperor, stubbornness wasn't a good thing. But who didn't have something they were stubborn about? The emperor wasn't perfect either.

The emperor could tell the words "An Eternal Happy Union" were written in Prince Jing's handwriting. This was a marriage contract

Prince Jing himself had written. It was clear how seriously he took this marriage.

...Prince Jing might really be in love.

He thought back to the true love the old Duke of Cheng'en had jokingly mentioned. The emperor had been on the throne for many years and he could just laugh it off, but now, his heart felt inexplicably heavy.

He put the marriage contract away in his report box, then opened Prince Jing's letter. It was probably full of praise for Li Yu.

Last time, the youth had suggested many unique ideas for controlling the locusts. The emperor had asked officials from the Ministry of Works to take a look. They all said the suggestions made sense and that they should be tried if the chance arose. The emperor didn't say anything, but in his heart, he respected Li Yu. Gaining the approval of the Ministry of Works meant he was capable.

So, what did the letter contain this time?

When the emperor was done reading the letter, he found that Prince Jing had already used Li Yu's suggestions against the locusts in the western border.

If this task was given to any of the officials in the Ministry of Works, they would have to come up with a detailed plan and have the Minister of Works approve it. After discussing it in court, they would have to wait for the Ministry of Revenue to provide the money—but doing so would take months. Only once all that bureaucracy was out of the way could the Ministry of Works send someone to affected areas.

But Prince Jing never mentioned any of this in his reports. He just spent his own money and got it done. Not only that, he'd done a good job. The locusts in the western border had been taken care of.

Damn insolent brat!

The emperor couldn't decide what he was feeling. Was Prince Jing throwing his achievements in his face because he hadn't responded to his last letter?

He was a little angry, but honestly, he couldn't deny that Prince Jing had done a beautiful job. After all, out of all of his sons, the one who was most decisive, the one most to his liking, was Prince Jing. The locust issue at the western border had been bad enough that it caused him unease. If he had followed normal procedure, who knew what the situation would be like by now. The officials strictly followed the rules and regulations, and while they deliberated, the people suffered. In comparison, Prince Jing was a little more rash, but he had controlled the locusts effectively.

The emperor put down the letter, deep in thought. When he looked up again, he noticed there were a few reports from counties around the western border. Skimming through them, the emperor found out that Prince Jing had bought a large number of ducks to control the locusts, causing quite a stir in the counties. But all of them were grateful to Prince Jing. If the locust problem hadn't been solved, it would be their turn to suffer in the future.

One of the reports was quite descriptive. The emperor could almost see the ducks flapping chaotically about in front of him. He smiled.

Somehow, sending Prince Jing to the western border had allowed him to gain power. He hadn't expected it would turn out that way.

He could allow Prince Jing to continue growing due to his achievements, or he could choose to punish him for tricking him. Choosing such an impossible candidate for his wife still made the emperor incredibly displeased.

The emperor suddenly remembered something and flipped to the end of Prince Jing's letter. As expected, Prince Jing credited all the success to Li Yu.

All of this had been to pave the way for Li Yu.

Even though he couldn't just ask, the emperor wanted to know what the prince would choose: the position of crown prince or his consort.

The emperor sighed and once again didn't respond to the letter.

Prince Jing's actions on the western border weren't a secret; news had long since spread through the court.

At first, when they found out Prince Jing had been sent to the western border, many of the officials thought the prince had somehow offended the emperor. But the sixth prince started to worry. Prince Jing had clearly won during the emperor's birthday. If the emperor was truly angry with him, why hadn't he scolded him in front of everyone?!

And the House of Cheng'en, the Duke of Cheng'en, and Ye Qinghuan were all on Prince Jing's side. They were Prince Jing's biggest backers. But Prince Jing had already left the capital, and none of them had tried to ask the emperor for forgiveness. That meant Prince Jing had probably warned them in advance.

Mu Tianxiao still couldn't work out why the emperor had sent Prince Jing to the border.

But soon the unease he felt was smoothed out by the emperor.

Due to the nursery rhymes and fake monks, the emperor had the third and sixth princes beaten and punished. The emperor's punishment for the third prince was truly harsh, but he'd only been angry with the sixth prince by association. Even so, accordingly, he'd taken away the sixth prince's job. In order to regain the emperor's trust, Mu Tianxiao had made many preparations. In the end, his hard work paid off, and after Prince Jing left, the emperor had given him

Prince Jing's job at the Ministry of Works.

Prince Jing had completed most of the job already, so all the sixth prince had to do was to clean up the loose ends. The emperor had even appointed a deputy minister to guide him. There was no way anything could go wrong; he had basically been given a free achievement.

Although the Ministry of Works was the least respected of the Six Ministries and fixing Zhongcui Palace wasn't a very dignified job, at the very least it was clear the emperor held the sixth prince, who was here by his side, in higher regard than Prince Jing, who was thousands of miles away.

Mu Tianxiao made up his mind. Prince Jing was mute, after all, and the western border was full of strife and turmoil. If he did a little something at just the right time, perhaps he could get rid of Prince Jing for good...

But he'd only just regained the emperor's trust—he couldn't act recklessly. He'd simply watch and observe Prince Jing. Maybe he wouldn't have to do anything. Maybe Prince Jing would mess up and die, getting rid of himself.

Then, instead of dying quietly, Prince Jing killed the bandits. Several ministers praised him vocally, and the emperor was in a great mood. Now, whatever achievements the sixth prince had gained through fixing Zhongcui Palace were insignificant. An official who was a secret supporter of the sixth prince mentioned his work during court, but very quickly, he was drowned out by praise for Prince Jing.

That was when Mu Tianxiao fully realized that despite being at the distant border, Prince Jing was still his enemy.

Now he was hearing Prince Jing had managed to eradicate the locusts on the western border. The emperor should have been happy and heavily rewarded Prince Jing, but this time, when the officials

praised Prince Jing, the emperor seemed somewhat displeased. Mu
Tianxiao picked up on this and sent someone to Qianqing Palace
and Prince Jing's manor to see what was going on. That was when
he discovered a great secret.

Prince Jing had fallen in love with a youth at the western border
and dared ask the emperor for permission to marry him!

Prince Jing was mute, and he might pass that along to his children.
If he also got married to a male consort who couldn't bear children...

All of this was great news to the sixth prince. If Mu Tianxiao had
dreamt this, he'd wake himself up laughing. When he found out
how much of a headache this was for the emperor, Mu Tianxiao
decided he had to do everything in his power to make this happen.

He knew the emperor still had regrets about Empress Xiaohui, so
he asked his mother, Consort Zhang, to speak up.

Recently, the emperor had picked the di daughter of a marquis
for the sixth prince to marry. Consort Zhang went to thank the
emperor, and she took the opportunity to start reminiscing about
Empress Xiaohui. Consort Zhang had once been Empress Xiaohui's
servant, so she was deeply grateful to the empress for her current
life. While she spoke about Empress Xiaohui, she "accidentally"
mentioned that the empress had always wished for Prince Jing to
lead a safe and happy life.

She said that on purpose, of course, but it got the emperor thinking. It was rare for Consort Zhang to say such things, considering
her status, and she said it with such sincerity it was quite believable.
Adding this on top of all the praise Prince Jing had heaped onto
Li Yu in his letters... When he returned to Qianqing Palace, the
emperor sat by himself for two hours, deep in thought. In the end,
he finally wrote down his response to Prince Jing.

"Li Yu's character is worthy of the title of Consort, but

unfortunately, due to the fact that he is a man and cannot bear children, he can only be given the position of concubine."

When Li Yu found out about this, he ran to comfort Prince Jing. At least the emperor had agreed to the two of them staying together. They had a long future ahead of them. Perhaps if he acquired more achievements, the emperor would promote him to consort in a fit of joy!

When Prince Jing received the emperor's reply, he smiled. After all his planning, this was the exact response he had been waiting for. As long as the only reason the emperor gave was that Li Yu couldn't bear children, then all his problems would be solved.

Li Yu had already given him four fishy sons. Considering how long it would take them to transform, now was the exact right time to announce the pregnancy.

Originally, Prince Jing had planned to invent a nonexistent concubine and say the children were "hers." Once he had children, it would be far easier to convince the emperor. But firstly, he was afraid this ruse would fall apart as soon as Li Yu had more children, and secondly, he was afraid the emperor would still refuse because Li Yu still couldn't give birth.

Why did he have to invent a whole other person? He could just say Xiaoyu was special and could give birth. Even if no one else had heard of such a thing, it didn't mean it couldn't exist. Although it was a little unbelievable, there would be proof once the fish babies transformed.

As the emperor had clearly said "due to the fact that he is a man and cannot bear children," he wouldn't be able to refute himself.

There were many inconveniences on the western border, but there was one thing that was very convenient indeed: as long as he said Li-gongzi was pregnant, no one would be able to question it. If the emperor sent a gynecological expert, by the time they arrived at the border, the fish babies would have already been "born," turning into human children.

The reason why he hadn't mentioned this at the very beginning was because he was afraid the emperor would choose a different reason to deny him. Prince Jing had taken step after careful step, slowly dispelling any hesitations he might have toward Xiaoyu, just so that only this one reason remained. Although it was a little difficult, he could deal with it.

Prince Jing put a hand on Li Yu's stomach and patted it. It was about time to stuff a little pillow inside.

Fishy Babies
Transform

L I YU COULDN'T BELIEVE that the "cooperation" Prince Jing had mentioned before involved him pretending to be pregnant.

"That's...not appropriate, is it?" Li Yu was a little conflicted. Wasn't this lying to the emperor?

It's fine. Prince Jing found a whole bunch of pillows, all in various sizes, then handed him a note. *Didn't you give birth to Dabao, Erbao, Sanbao, and Sibao? This is just so people think you gave birth to them as a human—what's wrong with that?*

The shock Li Yu felt was like an arrow to the knee. Prince Jing wasn't...wrong. The kids were his either way. He hoped they could officially call him father in the future.

Maybe, then, he could just...pretend to be pregnant?

The moment he agreed, a slightly flat pillow was stuffed into his robes. There were strings on the pillow so he could tie it behind his back. Prince Jing tested the tightness and kept looking at Li Yu with concern, as though asking, *Is it heavy?*

...Okay, he might be the first person to be treated this well despite lying about being pregnant.

Li Yu shook his "stomach" happily and quietly said, "No, it's fine."

Despite his reassurances, Prince Jing still kept worrying. He knew Li Yu's stomach would have to become very big in the future to feasibly fit four children.

Prince Jing had always wanted to keep Xiaoyu at his side and away from the sight of others. Now, he was even more sure of this decision. Even though it wasn't strictly necessary, it was still better if random people didn't show up around Xiaoyu...

Since Prince Jing had to report the news to the emperor, though, Wang Xi, as the head eunuch, obviously also found out. After he was notified that Li-gongzi was pregnant, Wang-gonggong was dazed for a good while. Li Yu was afraid of their ruse being discovered, but to his surprise, after a momentary pause, Wang Xi started to cry.

"This old servant is so happy that His Highness is about to have children." Wang Xi wiped his eyes and said in a trembling voice, "I used to think that if I could one day see His Highness's children, I could die without regrets."

At first, Wang Xi had also doubted the truth of the situation. How could a man get pregnant? But when he saw His Highness guiding Li-gongzi around himself, and that Li-gongzi's stomach was a little raised, he looked very pregnant. Could this be faked?

So what if it was a man who was pregnant! It was still His Highness's children!

After crying, Wang Xi wanted to laugh. He thought Li-gongzi must be very blessed. Master Xiaoyu getting pregnant was an excellent sign; after all, now His Highness was going to have his own children!

Wang Xi was too excited. Prince Jing had no choice but to pat him on the shoulder to calm him down. Wang-gonggong was this thrilled to learn he was pregnant with just one baby. How would he react when he found out there were four?

After Wang Xi calmed down a little, Prince Jing told him he held high hopes for this child and that he would take care of all necessary business himself. Wang Xi nodded to show that he understood. His Highness already held Li-gongzi in extremely high regard. Now that Li-gongzi was pregnant, it made sense His Highness wanted to do everything himself.

If His Highness was taking care of the pregnancy, then what was left for him to do?

Wang Xi slapped himself on the forehead. How could he forget? His Highness had asked him to prepare for the wedding. He felt galvanized to pay even more attention than before, so His Highness and Li-gongzi would be pleased.

After he'd let Wang Xi know, Prince Jing summoned the physicians that had come along with them to the western border. But now that Li-gongzi was officially his family, and would eventually be given an official status, the physicians were not permitted to see Li Yu directly. Instead, they had to do it with a couple of veils between them. "Li-gongzi" sat behind the veil, and all the physicians determined that Li-gongzi had been pregnant for two months. After the initial shock, they congratulated Prince Jing.

Prince Jing just nodded slightly in acknowledgment. Everything was going according to plan. The purpose of having this diagnosis done was so that the distant emperor would be informed. The emperor's trusted physicians wouldn't arrive at the western border for a while yet. The diagnosis would come in handy, as the emperor would definitely ask the physicians around Prince Jing for their opinions first.

Before having the physicians assess Li Yu's pulse through the veil, Prince Jing had secretly found a woman who was two months pregnant to sit behind the veil in Li Yu's place. The physicians had never assessed a pregnant man before to know any differences, so it was enough as long as they could tell "he" was pregnant.

They would do the same thing each time afterward, until the birth. Prince Jing was prepared.

When the news made it back to the capital, the emperor was so shocked his jaw nearly hit the floor and he reread Prince Jing's letter several times. He never expected Prince Jing's response to be "Li Yu is pregnant, please give him the consort position!"

The imperial guards that the emperor had sent to the western border reported the same thing, and came attached with the physicians' diagnosis. The emperor read it several times over, afraid he was misreading the words.

Could men really get pregnant?

Previously, the emperor would've been certain it was impossible. But seeing the physicians' diagnosis now, he wasn't sure.

After all, the reason was that he had a "unique constitution."

The emperor quickly summoned all the imperial physicians overnight and ordered them to analyze the diagnosis. They discussed it for the entire night, but they couldn't reach a conclusion. They didn't know Li Yu's actual condition, so there was no way they could say with one hundred percent certainty that men could not get pregnant.

The emperor sent a gynecological expert to the western border to take Li Yu's pulse. He gave it some thought, then sent a letter to Liao Kong as well. Liao Kong had a wealth of knowledge. He'd be able to give him a straight answer.

There were only two possibilities when it came to Li Yu's pregnancy: it was either real, or Prince Jing was putting on an act. Although Prince Jing kept paving the way for Li Yu, the emperor didn't believe the prince would do such a stupid thing. A faked imperial pregnancy was very easy to expose.

But what if it was real?

Li Yu had no family and came from a poor background. He really wasn't a suitable candidate for consort. However, he had also accomplished a lot in a short period of time and made Prince Jing fall in love with him. The emperor was already being quite generous by granting him the title of concubine. But he couldn't agree to anything further due to the issue of Prince Jing's future heirs.

If Li Yu really could bear children, then there was no reason not to give him the consort position.

Staring at Prince Jing's letters, the emperor finally woke up. Prince Jing had probably waited until now to mention this specifically so that the emperor wouldn't have any reason to say no. He laughed ruefully. Damned brat, he'd actually achieved the impossible...

Soon, Liao Kong's response arrived. As expected of an eminent monk, all he said was, "The world is vast and full of wonders."

The emperor understood that, based on Liao Kong's knowledge, he believed that it was possible for a man to get pregnant. His curiosity was satisfied.

Now he just had to wait for the physician's diagnosis.

First, though, the emperor assured Prince Jing that if the imperial physician confirmed that Li Yu could get pregnant, he would be willing to let Li Yu become consort.

Prince Jing saw hope for victory and would occasionally take Li Yu on walks within the property to show him off in front of the servants. The entire western border hung on to Prince Jing's every word. Everyone was delighted at the news that he was about to have a child.

Due to safety, Prince Jing had not publicized that the one who was pregnant was a man, as he didn't want that to become the topic of discussion. As a result, not many people knew, and all the villagers were full of happy congratulations.

During this time, the bandits tried to use this chance to take revenge, but they ended up being discovered by the guards.

When they'd realized that the bandits were only human and could be defeated, plenty of strong young men had signed up to join the guards. Prince Jing had more and more people under his command, and they grew stronger every day by training with the imperial guards. Meanwhile, Prince Jing had predicted an upcoming attack by the bandits, so he strengthened the defense. When the bandits came, they were once again defeated by tunnels and traps.

From the outside, under Prince Jing's close guard, Luofeng Village seemed impenetrable. And inside the village, he guarded Li Yu with equal care.

Prince Jing never left Li Yu's side. Although it was a fake pregnancy, he kept telling Li Yu to rest and took care of everything for him. Prince Jing seemed almost obsessed, but he was happy. Li Yu thought Prince Jing must be taking this chance to take care of him to make up for all the times he couldn't before. And what else could he do other than to accept all the attention?

Eventually, Prince Jing didn't even want Li Yu to hold the crystal bottle. The responsibility of taking care of the fish babies fell to Wang Xi.

Wang Xi couldn't help but sigh as he stared at the lively fish babies. "Wouldn't it be lovely if Li-gongzi could give birth to four babies too?"

Li Yu felt a bit awkward. Wang-gonggong had accidentally predicted the truth.

The fish babies also started noticing the change between their fathers.

The first to notice was Dabao, but eventually, even Sibao, who was a little slower, could tell something was different.

Daddy Prince Jing was always guiding their fish dad around. They knew Fish Dad could transform into a human just like their prince dad, but now, Fish Dad's stomach was even rounder than Erbao's! Dabao had already guessed what might be going on by listening to their fathers' words, and was eagerly anticipating.

But the innocent Erbao and Sanbao asked, "Is Daddy going to give birth to another brother?"

The even more innocent Sibao said, "Aww...Daddy must've eaten a lot of peach blossom pastries. He never gave them to Sibao! Sibao wants to eat too!"

The imperial physician that the emperor had sent was still on the way, while the "Growing Up" quest kept ticking down. One day, Li Yu had just taken off his belly pillow and was feeding the fish babies when Dabao, who'd always been very attentive, suddenly seemed distant and zoned out.

Li Yu didn't give it much thought. But in the time it took him to turn around, Dabao had disappeared and a chubby, pale baby had appeared on the bed, waving his arms and legs around.

Dabao was the first one to complete the system's quest, he realized. As expected of the smart Dabao...

Wait, no! Dabao must be very afraid!

Li Yu quickly picked Dabao up and wiped away the water on his body. Luckily, the system hadn't transformed Dabao right in the fish tank. That would have been disastrous.

Prince Jing had prepared swaddling clothes in advance, and Li Yu bundled Dabao up haphazardly, holding him to his chest.

Even though it was his first time being human, Dabao was very brave and thought everything was very new. He stared around at everything with grape-like black eyes. Was this what it felt like to grow up?

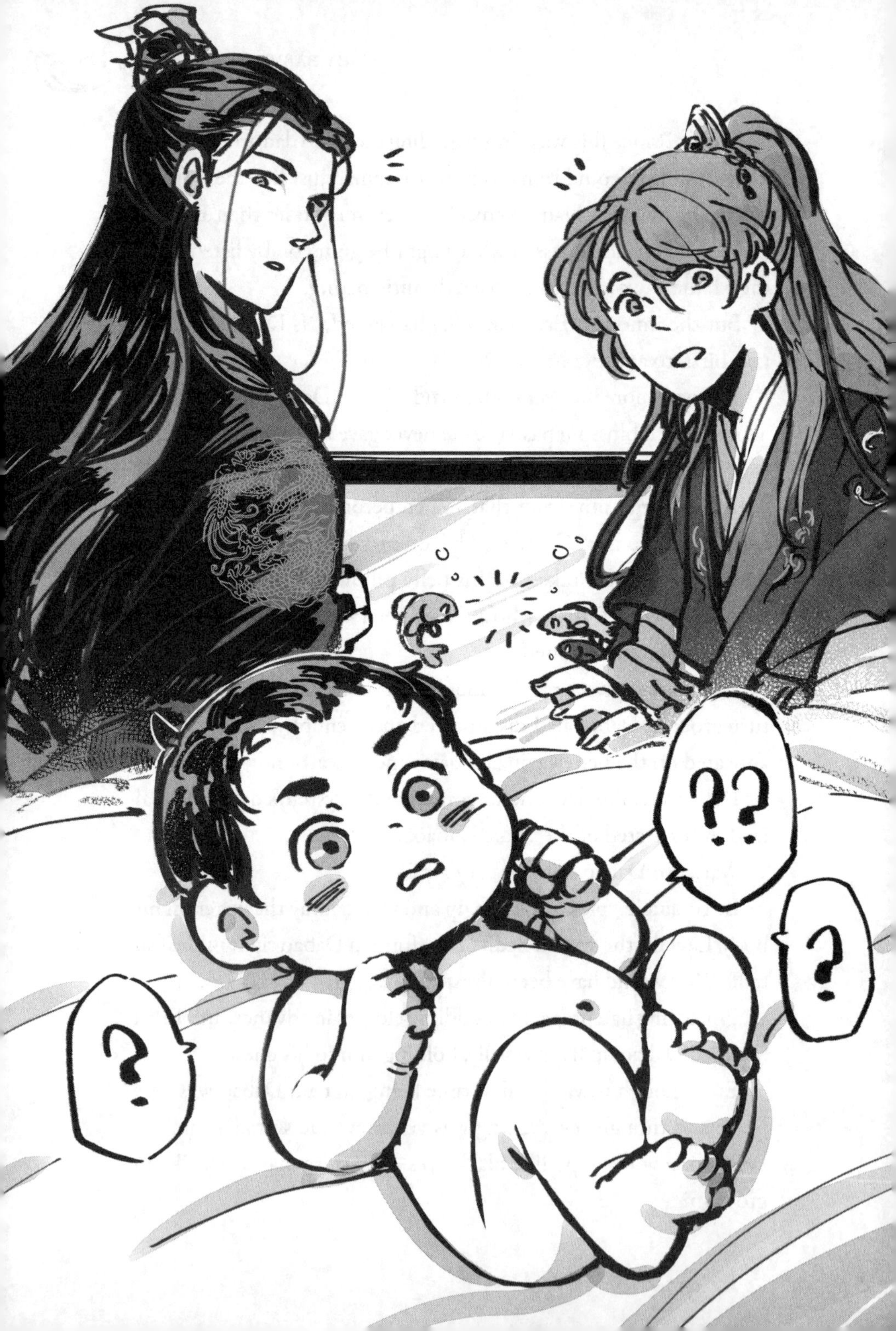
??
?
?

Dabao moved his legs as usual, attempting to swim, but his arms and legs didn't listen to him. He wanted to call out to his fish dad, but when he opened his mouth, only crying came out. The brave Dabao finally felt a little fear. Now that he was human, he couldn't swim or speak. Dabao cried even harder.

Prince Jing heard the crying from outside. As soon as he ran in, he saw Li Yu holding a human baby, doing his best to try to comfort him.

Prince Jing had seen Li Yu and the fish babies holding each other's tails so they formed a line. Although he already knew those babies were his children, they'd all looked like fish. That scene wasn't as shocking as seeing Li Yu try to comfort a real live baby.

Prince Jing's gaze started to blur. He walked over extremely carefully, afraid to startle Xiaoyu.

"Your Highness, come look at Dabao!" Li Yu handed the child over.

It wasn't very clear when he was a fish, but now that Dabao was human, it was very obvious. Prince Jing had also been a chubby little guy when he was young. He and Dabao looked like they came out of the same mold.

Looking at the long-awaited small round child, Li Yu held in his laughter, but his eyes were slightly red. How strange. He was more emotional than when he laid the eggs, or even when they hatched.

Prince Jing accepted the child from his arms, gazing endlessly at him as though it would never be enough. *Don't cry.* He wiped Li Yu's eyes gently. But his own eyes were already wet.

At that moment, Erbao, Sanbao, and Sibao suddenly realized Dabao had turned into a human. The three of them were so afraid that they all held their breath and sank to the bottom of the tank.

Fish Baby Rebellion

BECAUSE DABAO had suddenly turned into a human baby, Prince Jing had no choice but to inform the servants that Li Yu had started giving birth.

The "midwife" they had ready came into the room, and Prince Jing stood guard over the birthing room.

Wang Xi had been extra attentive these last few days. As soon as he heard the sound of an infant crying, he was delighted. But he didn't see the new young master for a long time. He was beside himself with worry when Prince Jing sent the word out that Li Yu had given birth to one child but was still in labor.

Wang Xi was stunned for a moment, then became ecstatic. Li-gongzi's stomach had been a little larger than normal, so he'd guessed there might be more than one. But since Prince Jing hadn't revealed anything, Wang Xi didn't dare spread the news based only on his own predictions.

Now that he knew it really was a pair of twins, he was still happy, but immediately started praying. He had heard giving birth to twins was a very painful, dangerous, and laborious process. Wang Xi hoped Li-gongzi and the young masters would remain safe.

Outside of the room, Wang Xi and the servants waited anxiously. Inside the room, it was a completely different scene.

The "midwife" was actually a trusted confidant of Prince Jing's who had a bit of medical knowledge. As soon as he entered the room, he cleaned Dabao up, checked him over, and rewrapped Li Yu's haphazard swaddle.

"He's crying so hard. Is he uncomfortable somewhere?" Li Yu asked quietly. When Dabao had been a fish, he hadn't shed a single tear. What had happened to make him so upset?

The confidant finished checking and bowed to Li Yu with his hands clasped. "The young Highness is very healthy."

He didn't know where this baby had come from, but he knew this was the young Highness. He disregarded everything else and just answered when he was asked. As for why the young Highness was crying, that was easy. It was normal for babies to cry.

Li Yu had been looking for a specific explanation and felt pretty disappointed. Never mind. Fish Dad decided he'd just ask Dabao himself once he learned how to speak.

Dabao was healthy, and his cries were clear and bright. Prince Jing felt his heart settle back down. Ever since he could remember, the imperial physicians had told him his muteness might be hereditary.

As both he and Xiaoyu were male, he hadn't worried about this before. Then, he had been surprised with some fish babies, and Xiaoyu had told him proudly that all the fish babies could say "Dad." That was when Prince Jing thought that perhaps his muteness wouldn't be passed down to the carp spirit's children. But he'd never managed to hear the fish babies speak himself. Afraid Xiaoyu might be disappointed, he'd never mentioned it to him. But now that Dabao was perfectly fine, Prince Jing could stop worrying.

The confidant reported that all was well, and Dabao was a healthy human baby. Now, it was time for the three other fish babies to follow him.

FISH BABY REBELLION 151

Prince Jing ordered the confidant to leave the room for the time being, leaving only him and Li Yu. The two of them silently waited for the other fish babies to transform.

From "pregnancy" to "birth," Prince Jing had thought of and taken care of everything. But they'd both expected the fish babies to transform all at the same time. Instead, they were transforming one by one. Because Dabao had already transformed, the other fish babies had to follow him quickly so Li Yu could successfully "give birth."

After all, if a pregnant woman gave birth to many children, there wouldn't be too much of a gap between each one. It was easy to explain an hour or even two, but if there was an entire day or longer between each one, that would be way too suspicious and dangerous.

So, the current task was to convince the other three babies to transform as soon as possible. They couldn't let this "birth" drag on for too long.

Li Yu thought that with Dabao as an example, the other babies would transform one by one, but for some reason, the other three fish babies were all crowded together, trembling.

They waited for a while, but Erbao still wasn't moving. They couldn't just keep waiting like this. Li Yu gave Prince Jing a look, then transformed into a fish to ask the fish babies what was going on.

As soon as he returned to fish form and entered the tank, the fish babies all swam over.

"Dad! Dad!" Erbao, Sanbao, and Sibao cried out together. "How scary! Dage turned into a human!!!"

Li Yu asked, amused, "Do you guys not want to be human?"

Erbao, Sanbao, and Sibao shook their heads fiercely, "We don't!"

"...Why not?" Fish Dad thought being a human was much more interesting than being a fish. Why didn't the fish babies agree?

Erbao hesitated. "Dad, I wanted to try it before, but dage couldn't even move after he turned human, so I've changed my mind."

"Yeah, turning human is so scary!" Sanbao agreed. "I wanted to be human before too, but dage stopped being able to speak. I'm afraid of being like dage."

Sibao said decisively, "Dad, I'm not turning into a human!"

Li Yu never would have expected that before the revolution had even succeeded, the wide-eyed fish babies already wanted to rebel.

The three babies huddled tightly together in a scared, fishy ball, and Li Yu couldn't do much about the current situation. He first had to dissolve the three babies' alliance.

Li Yu started by bringing Sibao a large piece of peach blossom pastry. Sibao immediately forgot about his brothers and focused on the pastry instead.

As for Erbao and Sanbao, Li Yu defeated them one by one.

He knew one liked food and one liked beauty, so he persuaded them using their specific preferences.

Li Yu enticed Erbao patiently. "Being a human is fun! You can be just like Dad. Other than peach blossom pastries and fish food, there's plenty of other delicious things. And you can play with the ducklings whenever you want."

Hearing that there was lots of delicious food to eat, his eyes grew wide. He also liked ducklings, but he was never allowed to get near them. If he turned into a human, could he play with them? In the face of food and fun, Erbao was suddenly tempted.

Then Li Yu said to Sanbao, "Once you turn into a human, you can wear clothes just like Dad and have lots of shiny accessories."

Sanbao liked being pretty. "Ah, Dad, I like shiny things! I want to wear Dad's clothes!"

Although Sanbao was a very pretty little silver fish, he couldn't go back and forth between forms. No matter how pretty something was, if someone looked at it for too long, it would become boring. The same applied to fish. But Fish Dad got to wear something different every day! Sanbao wanted that.

Just like Erbao, Sanbao changed his mind.

Without much effort, Li Yu had managed to convince two out of the three members of the rebellion. "So, do you guys want to try being human?" he said, smiling.

Erbao and Sanbao looked at each other, then giggled and nodded. "Yes!"

With that, Erbao and Sanbao simultaneously turned into a pair of infants about as large as their big brother.

Prince Jing was waiting by the side of the tank and quickly scooped both of them up.

Li Yu jumped to Prince Jing's shoulder to see what they looked like. They looked just like Dabao, with chubby little faces.

Li Yu couldn't help but be a little upset. How come they didn't look like him?

Soon Erbao and Sanbao both started to bawl, perhaps because they didn't immediately receive delicious food and pretty clothes.

Li Yu thought guiltily, *You'll have it when you grow older.*

After Erbao and Sanbao transformed, the only stubborn one left was Sibao.

Sibao was still munching on his pastry. When he looked up, he realized his brothers were all gone. Only his fish dad was left, looking at him benevolently.

"Sibao, do you want to become a human?"

Sibao shook away the crumbs on his fins. "Ah! No!"

Li Yu tried to tempt him the same way he had tempted Erbao and Sanbao. "There's delicious food, fun things to play with, and beautiful clothes. Sibao doesn't want any of that?"

"No!" Sibao said loudly, "Sibao has pastries from Dad to eat, and I can play with Dad. Sibao also doesn't like beautiful clothes."

"Then what *does* Sibao like?"

"I like my dads the best!"

Li Yu's heart felt warm. Following Sibao's train of thought, he asked, "Then can Sibao help Daddy out?"

Sibao nodded. If he could help Daddy, the innocent Sibao thought that made him even better than his brothers.

Li Yu was now very good at convincing his children, and said to Sibao, "You'll be helping Daddy out if you transform. Can you do that?"

This time, Sibao didn't even have to think about it. "Yes!"

...

...

Li Yu thought he'd transform as soon as he agreed, but Sibao didn't.

After agreeing, Sibao just kept waving his tail very earnestly.

Li Yu and Sibao stared at each other for a while, waiting. He didn't know what the problem was.

"Sibao, why aren't you transforming?" Li Yu couldn't help but rush him.

Sibao glanced at his own fish body, spread his fins out, and tried very hard, shouting, "Transform!"

But he was still a little fish. Nothing had changed.

They went back to staring at each other, faintly confused.

Li Yu suddenly realized something. "Sibao, you do know how to transform, right?"

"I don't know!" Sibao cried.

If this fish still didn't transform, this was about to turn into a difficult birth!

Li Yu, risking revealing himself as a system fish, reminded the slightly slow Sibao, "Hasn't there been anything called a 'system,' telling you to complete quests?"

"Hm? Yes! He's really annoying, so I ignored him! Dad, aren't I good?" Sibao thought the system was something bad.

"...You can pay attention to him." Li Yu pushed back the urge to face palm and guided Sibao. "If you do what he says, you should be able to transform."

"...Really?" Sibao finally worked it out. He spun in circles on the spot a few times, then mumbled something.

Li Yu thought he still didn't understand, when Sibao suddenly swam over and rubbed his mouth against Li Yu warmly.

"Dad!" Sibao shouted happily. He wanted to tell him that he'd finally figured it out, but before he could get the words out, he disappeared. At the same time, a baby appeared before Li Yu. He had a pair of dark eyes, slightly curly hair, and pale skin. He was quiet like a little angel and smiled at Li Yu toothlessly.

‹Congratulations, user. "Growing Up" has been completed. Please collect your reward.›

After Li Yu had laid the eggs, just like last time, the system had gone into careful calculation and planning. It hadn't given him a new quest in a while. The current quest line he was on was to help the fish babies grow into humans. It took a while to complete this quest. The description said that all the kids had successfully turned into humans: they had become part of that world.

When Li Yu looked around the empty fish tank, with only him inside, he felt a little wistful.

Li Yu had asked the fish-scamming system before about the quest that the fish babies had to complete to transform. The system was quite secretive, though, and it had never told him the details of the quest. All Li Yu knew was that the tasks weren't too hard. After the fish babies completed them, they could turn into human babies, but they wouldn't be able to turn back into fish until they were seven years old.

If at the age of seven they could still remember being a fish, and would like to try being a fish again, the system would give them a new quest. Completing it would give them the ability to transform into a fish. But if they forgot, it wouldn't necessarily be a bad thing for their new life.

Li Yu paused, knowing this was something his children had to go through. But knowing was one thing. He wouldn't be able to see the lively, jumping fish babies for a long time and couldn't help but feel sad.

A hand reached down, gently rubbing his back. As though leaning against driftwood, he pressed himself tightly against this hand. Whether the children remembered this or not, whether they remembered their fish dad or not, he would always have Prince Jing at his side. His Highness would never let him feel lonely.

Very quickly, Li Yu's mood recovered, and he shook his tail, wrapping it around Prince Jing's finger.

The people outside had been waiting for too long. It was time to bring the children out. Li Yu jumped into the crystal bottle so Prince Jing could take him along. That way, he could see the children too.

Everything was all set. Prince Jing rang the jade bell. Hearing his master's summons, Wang Xi shot into the room. Wang-gonggong had heard the cries of three babies and was so happy he couldn't stop smiling. But when he came in, he saw...four young masters??

"My heavens, how amazing!" Wang Xi was stunned for a while, then knelt to the ground to thank all manner of deities.

On the same day Prince Jing gained four sons, the gynecological expert arrived at the western border. Without resting, he came to Prince Jing's residence in Luofeng Village.

Hearing that Li-gongzi had given birth to four babies, the physician couldn't even believe it.

Li-gongzi, who had just "given birth," needed rest. Prince Jing wouldn't let anyone disturb him. Even the imperial physician had to check his pulse through the veil.

After checking "Li-gongzi's" pulse, the physician went to check on the four little newborn gongzi.

Men getting pregnant was completely unheard of. The emperor had given him a secret order to verify the identity of these children. The imperial physician had wanted to take a bit of blood from Li-gongzi to test and asked Prince Jing to understand.

But Prince Jing shook his head. He couldn't let the physician disturb Li Yu. He stopped him and rolled up his own sleeve. The physician was stunned, but after a moment he quickly drew some of Prince Jing's blood. Compared to whether or not Li-gongzi could really give birth, the emperor cared far more about whether or not these children were actually of Prince Jing's blood.

Testing proved that these little gongzi were indeed Prince Jing's. And each child's voice was louder than the next; none were mute like the emperor had worried.

What wonderful news! The imperial physician wrote a letter himself and sent it back to the capital at the fastest speed possible.

.

Gifted Fishy

THE EMPEROR HELD the letter in a shaking hand, afraid that his eyes were playing tricks on him.

The imperial physician had reported that Prince Jing now had four healthy sons, and none of them were mute.

The emperor pressed the letter to his chest, taking deep breaths. He had once believed that his and Empress Xiaohui's line would end with Prince Jing, but...

Prince Jing had healthy children! Four of them!

There was no news better than this.

The emperor laughed out loud, no longer bothered by Prince Jing's slight offense from before. Now that he suddenly had four new grandkids, the emperor couldn't be happier. He immediately ordered Luo Ruisheng to bring the materials so he could write an imperial edict, officially announcing Li Yu as Prince Jing's consort, Prince Jing's oldest di son as shizi, his second di son as standard class, rank five[8] Cloud Cavalry Commandant, his third di son as standard class, rank seven Grace Cavalry Commandant...

The emperor was so overjoyed that he appointed four official titles in one go, muttering the whole time. "I am *appointing* Li Yu

---

8   Government officials in ancient China followed the nine rank system (九品中正制), which classified officials into nine ranks, each having a standard and secondary rank, to make a total of eighteen classifications.

as Prince Jing's consort, so that isn't a reward. Li Yu and Prince Jing both have made great achievements at the western border, so I will grant my grandsons titles instead."

Watching from the side, the corners of Head Eunuch Luo's lips twitched. As he witnessed the emperor grant Prince Jing's youngest son the Grace Cavalry Commandant position as well, he thought, *You were the one who refused to give Li Yu the consort position, and look at you now!*

At least now Head Eunuch Luo knew who he should kiss up to in the future. This was just fate. The emperor had other grandsons, like the ones in the Marquis of An's household, but it had been a long time since they last entered the palace, so the emperor barely remembered them. The third prince also had sons, the oldest now six years old, the youngest three. The third prince made them see the emperor often, but they had been taught too well. The emperor did want to see them, but it wasn't much fun when he did, so he didn't end up seeing them very often. None of them were like Prince Jing's sons, who the emperor hadn't met yet. How exciting! The emperor couldn't stop thinking about them and had even given them titles. This was a rarity indeed.

Head Eunuch Luo was very smart and made sure to only say things that made the emperor happy. "This servant heard the imperial physician say that three of the royal grandsons look like Prince Jing. The youngest one looks more like Li-gongzi."

The emperor had never met Li Yu, but he remembered what Prince Jing looked like when he was young. Thinking back on it, he chuckled, "It could be fun, if that's the case."

The emperor wanted to see his grandsons, and after finding out they looked like Prince Jing, he wanted to see them even more. He knew that under Prince Jing's guidance, the western border was now in a pretty good state, but it still couldn't compare to the capital. It was best if his grandsons didn't continue to suffer there.

Originally, the emperor had planned to make Prince Jing stay at the border for two years to prove himself. Now that his son had given him grandsons, the emperor wanted Prince Jing to rush back immediately. Luckily, Head Eunuch Luo was there to persuade him against being so rash. The royal grandsons had only just been born. How could they withstand such a long journey?

The emperor finally relented, recognizing that the joy had gone to his head. If he wanted to summon them, of course it had to be after they grew up a bit.

Over the past year, the emperor had been very satisfied with Prince Jing's various achievements on the western border. In comparison, the sixth prince, who'd only fixed Zhongcui Palace, seemed incredibly lackluster. Besides, Prince Jing already had a healthy di son, so it no longer mattered whether or not he could speak.

Unconsciously, the scale in the emperor's heart started to tilt toward Prince Jing. Considering that his entire family was on the western border, though, the emperor decided not to spread the news that Prince Jing already had a di son before he returned. The emperor ordered Luo Ruisheng to announce the edict secretly and let the old Duke of Cheng'en in on the secret as well. As Prince Jing's grandfather, Ye Qian should be informed of the good news, but the emperor told him not to spread it around.

When Ye Qian received the news, tears flowed down his wizened cheeks. The emperor's warning, however, made him realize there was something unique about the situation. When he thought it over, he suddenly understood why.

Ye Qian followed instructions and kept it to himself, only ordering the manor doors to be tightly shut. He summoned an opera troupe, and they sang for three days and three nights straight. These days, when he walked, there was a spring in his step, and his health seemed much improved.

The emperor finally agreed to let Li Yu become Prince Jing's consort.

Last time, he'd only written a letter to Prince Jing. This time, he'd written an entire imperial edict about it. Everything was done and settled.

Prince Jing had predicted this result and asked the emperor to allow him to hold the wedding at the western border.

Originally, the emperor wasn't happy with this. How could he, as the father, not be present at his son's wedding? But his grandsons were already born, they couldn't delay the wedding any longer, and the emperor couldn't leave the capital. With all that in mind, he had no choice but to agree to Prince Jing's request.

Next, Prince Jing sent a list of names to the emperor. These were the families who had stocked up on ducks while Prince Jing was taking care of the locusts. The emperor immediately understood that Prince Jing was reporting these people.

And he was smart about it. He just asked the emperor to look into it, avoiding involving himself directly. Ever since the emperor had sent Prince Jing to the western border, he'd ordered someone to keep an eye on the communications between the border and the capital. With this list in hand, the emperor quickly determined that these families who had hoarded ducks had someone supporting them from behind.

While Prince Jing had been dealing with the locusts, the Marquis of Jinyi was the only person who had sent word over to the western border. The family that had first started stocking up on ducks were distant relatives of Vice Director Qin from the Ministry of Rites.

The Marquis of Jinyi and the third prince were in-laws. Vice Director Qin stood on the third prince's side and often did things for the third prince, so it was obvious who was behind all of this. When the imperial guards looked into Vice Director Qin, they also discovered something else. Before Prince Jing reached the border, there had been rumors spreading about Prince Jing having a terrible temper and harming innocent people. These rumors were Vice Director Qin's doing.

The guards had even found incriminating letters in Vice Director Qin's residence. The emperor was shocked at all the evidence. Mu Tianming was right under his nose. These days, he was only allowed to study in the imperial study room, but his influence still reached all the way to the western border? Was he trying to harm Prince Jing?

The emperor had planned on leaving the third prince be, wanting to preserve his dignity—but clearly, the third prince was throwing it away himself.

With a cold expression, the emperor first punished the unappreciative Marquis of Jinyi, demoting him to the lowest rank. Then he gave the third prince the title of the Marquis of Ping. With the second prince, the Marquis of An, they made a pair.[9]

When he found out that he'd been completely abandoned, Mu Tianming ran to the palace, stumbling the whole way. The guards wouldn't let him in, so all he could do was kowtow in the direction of Qianqing Palace, sobbing.

"Royal Father, please let me speak to you! It really wasn't me!"

Every time Mu Tianming's forehead came in contact with the ground, he grew more hopeless.

He really couldn't explain it. The Marquis of Jinyi truly was keeping tabs for him, but that was it. He'd never asked him to do anything.

---

9 Together, the Marquis of Ping (平) and the Marquis of An (安) make the word peace (平安).

He didn't know why Vice Director Qin had done all that, nor did he know how those letters written in his hand had ended up in Vice Director Qin's study.

But the emperor was convinced it was him, and he didn't want to hear any excuses.

The third prince kneeled for an entire day and night. A rainstorm swept in and chilled his heart completely. He was in a daze, but just as he was about to pass out, an oil-paper umbrella was slowly moved over the top of the third prince's head.

Mu Tianming looked up to see Mu Tianxiao, expression full of concern.

Beneath the umbrella, the sixth prince was still elegant and refined.

"Third brother, you're going to catch a cold." Mu Tianxiao reached out to help Mu Tianming up.

Everybody knew the sixth prince followed the third prince, never leaving him behind even when the third prince had fallen into the dust. But at this moment, Mu Tianming's mood was even colder than the rainwater.

"Mu Tianxiao, let me ask you." Mu Tianming slapped away the sixth prince's hand, wiped his face, and asked in a low voice, "Was that Qin guy following your orders?"

Mu Tianming had given his token to Mu Tianxiao. If *he* hadn't sent the orders to Vice Director Qin, then it had to be Mu Tianxiao. He'd even stolen his handwriting. Mu Tianxiao had secretly planned everything behind his back, and now the third prince was the one suffering the emperor's wrath!

"Third brother, have you finally realized?" Mu Tianxiao smiled easily, twirling the umbrella carelessly, watching as the raindrops fell. "I just wanted to create some trouble for Prince Jing. That way, I could gain power faster, and it would be good for you too."

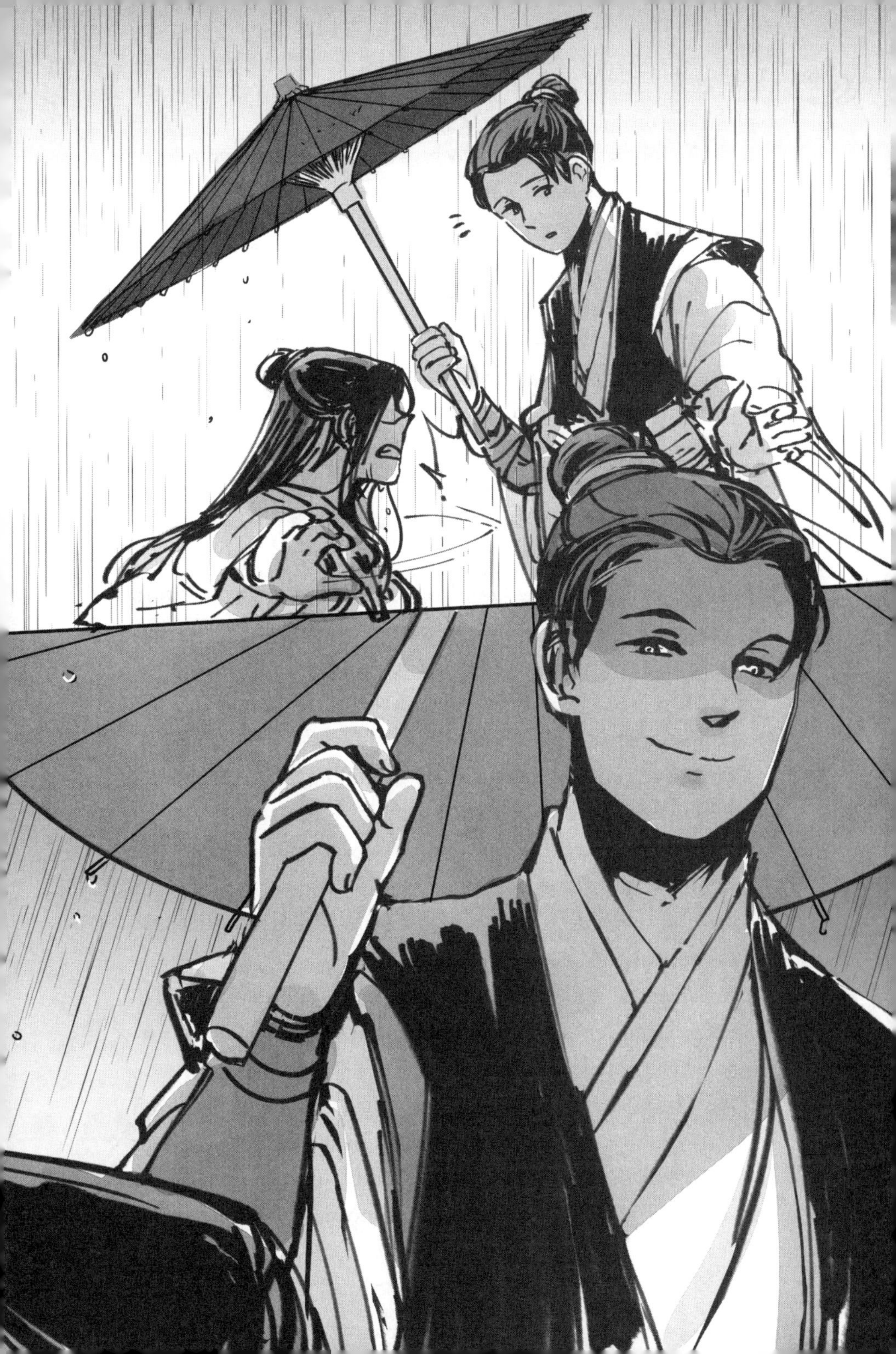

"You're full of shit! You clearly broke my trust and used me as a stepping stone. You—did you forget you used to be nothing? Who was the one who protected you, who was the one who gave you something to do?"

Mu Tianming grabbed on to Mu Tianxiao's collar in a fit of rage, wanting to choke this traitor to death.

Mu Tianxiao didn't struggle. He let Mu Tianming shake him, then smiled as he said, "Third brother, with how things are now, you should really calm down."

Mu Tianxiao peeled Mu Tianming's fingers off him one by one. Mu Tianming realized with a start that the sixth prince was a lot stronger than he seemed.

Mu Tianxiao smoothed out his collar and said slowly, "Third brother, our Royal Father won't bother with you anymore. He won't listen to anything you have to say. If you behave as the Marquis of Ping, when I ascend to the throne, perhaps I will remember the good times we had in the past."

"How dare you—" How could Mu Tianming suffer such humiliation? He lunged for Mu Tianxiao again.

A guard appeared behind Mu Tianxiao and stopped Mu Tianming.

Mu Tianxiao smirked as he turned around. "Third brother, please do as you see fit. I'll be leaving first."

Mu Tianxiao walked into the rain alone with his umbrella. No matter how much Mu Tianming cursed or screamed behind him, he completely ignored him.

Mu Tianxiao's mood soared. He was finally completely free from the third prince. When he returned to his manor, his confidant reported that the emperor had appointed Li Yu to be Prince Jing's consort. Mu Tianxiao couldn't help but snort. Taking a man as his official consort? Prince Jing probably wouldn't be able to achieve much anymore.

He was in the midst of reveling in his victory when his confidant backed up a step and said in a low voice, "Your Highness, news just arrived from the western border that Prince Jing now has four healthy di sons."

"...What??" Mu Tianxiao's expression was panicked. Wasn't Prince Jing about to marry a man? Where had these four di sons come from? And they were all healthy?

Had his confidant made a mistake?

Mu Tianxiao didn't believe his confidant and grabbed the report from him, reading it carefully line by line.

The sixth prince didn't have that many people working for him at the western border, so he didn't have anyone in Prince Jing's residence directly. His reports essentially just contained what the villagers knew.

Prince Jing really did have healthy children. In that case, Prince Jing's muteness was no longer a flaw he couldn't overcome...

The sixth prince didn't understand where the children had come from, but he could already foresee the outcome. If Prince Jing's muteness wasn't a problem, what did he have to compete against Prince Jing with?

The palace he'd spent over half the year repairing at the Ministry of Works? Or his mother who had once been a palace servant?

He'd finally escaped from the third prince's halo to reach this point. He was about to marry an aristocratic lady and receive support from the Yue family. The third prince's power and authority were now his, and he was walking step-by-step toward his goal. Was Prince Jing going to snatch everything out of his hands just because he had a son now?

He would never let such a thing happen!

The sixth prince read the report over and over, searching for some flaw in Prince Jing he could use against him.

Prince Jing, who had no flaws, was currently suffering from a headache.

Wang Xi saw the four children as a symbol of luck, and found the best wet nurses for them. But aside from the day they were "born," these symbols of luck refused to breastfeed at all and cried all day. They had truly become spoiled little princes.

When the imperial physician was summoned, he couldn't find anything wrong with them.

Li Yu was beside himself with worry, but also puzzled. If he held the kids, they immediately cried a lot less. But if he handed the children off to the wet nurse, they would cry until their faces went red, each of them gasping for breath.

It seemed they had grown too used to being fish, and they couldn't live without their fish father.

Li Yu was secretly delighted that his children still thought of him, but babies had to drink milk; they couldn't continue like this. Did that mean he had to be the one to feed them?

Feeding babies was different from feeding fish. It seemed kind of interesting.

Li Yu rubbed his hands together excitedly. "How about I try?"

Prince Jing was stunned. Taking a peek at Li Yu's flat chest, he couldn't help the flurry of thoughts in his head. Were carp spirits that gifted? Not only could they give birth, they could also breastfeed?

Grand Fishy Wedding

LI YU THOUGHT he could feel Prince Jing's gaze burning into him, but the waiting baby was more important, so Li Yu didn't have time to think about it too much.

Baby bottles didn't exist in ancient times, so Li Yu thought of another way. He asked the wet nurse to squeeze the milk into a bowl. Then he picked up Dabao and a tiny silver spoon, and started trying to spoon small amounts into Dabao's mouth. Dabao continued to scream, shaking his head desperately.

...Oh, did this child just not like milk?

Thinking back on it, he always fed the fish babies top-quality fish food and peach blossom pastries. Perhaps that was the problem. The fish babies liked fresh sweets, not bland milk.

But what could he do? At the moment, the babies weren't fully grown and didn't even have teeth. They could only drink milk.

Li Yu said gently, "Dabao, either you drink the milk, or you go hungry."

After being gently threatened by his fish dad, Dabao pouted, then drank the milk in the spoon with tears in his eyes.

Li Yu's first attempt went smoothly, but the next time, Dabao accidentally choked. Now he refused to drink from the spoon no matter what.

Li Yu thought about it, then ordered someone to bring a plate of peach blossom pastries and set them to the side. Dabao stared longingly at the peach blossom pastries with his sparkly black eyes. But it was no use. His unsympathetic fish dad only let him smell the pastry. When Dabao was momentarily distracted, Fish Dad slipped another spoonful of milk into his mouth.

Prince Jing, who had been watching the entire time, realized he'd been mistaken. He'd been expecting a completely different kind of feeding. He walked toward Li Yu. Li Yu was holding Dabao, humming an unknown tune. When Prince Jing approached and saw the gentleness in his eyes, his heart felt soft.

Imitating Li Yu, Prince Jing also picked up a child and fed him milk with another spoon. Occasionally, he'd glance at Li Yu.

Li Yu giggled quietly. Prince Jing had chosen Sibao. The other three all looked like Little Chubs, and only Sibao looked a little bit like Li Yu. Prince Jing really liked to hold Sibao.

Whenever Sibao was being held by his dad, he'd smile happily. As expected of the most confused baby, he hadn't noticed the difference between milk and fish food, and just wanted to be fed by his father. Sibao finished the milk incredibly quickly. When he was done, Prince Jing wanted to pick up Erbao, but Sibao kept his fingers clenched onto his collar, unwilling to leave his father's embrace.

When Dabao was finished eating, he also grabbed onto Li Yu. Then, as he was trying to console him, Erbao and Sanbao started to cry even harder. They hadn't had their turns yet!

Li Yu sighed in resignation. He and Prince Jing had no choice but to hold two children each. He felt like they were much better behaved when they were fish.

When night fell and it was time to sleep, the babies still wouldn't let go. Li Yu discussed the issue with Prince Jing, his face red. "Your

Highness, they're still young. Maybe they're just not used to it. Let's let them sleep together with us..."

Before, when the fish babies were in the tank, they'd stayed in the same room as their dads, and Fish Dad slept beside them all the time. Why did they have to go sleep with a stranger, the wet nurse, now that they were human? None of them were willing to do that. Being a human wasn't better than being a fish at all. They couldn't move or speak, and they could only drink boring old milk. This was way too hard—the fish babies wanted to be held by their fathers, sob sob sob sob sob!

Prince Jing had always doted on Li Yu. Since Li Yu was the one to suggest it, he resisted the urge to kick the four babies out and nodded.

Li Yu first put all the babies on the bed, then lay down himself. These days, he only had four hours to be human. It would be fine if he took a little nap. Prince Jing would take care of everything for him.

But as soon as he lay down, the children immediately craned their necks and stretched out, wanting to stick themselves to him. If they couldn't reach him, they'd start to cry. Li Yu had to make sure each child was touching him.

Dabao claimed one of Li Yu's arms, Erbao and Sanbao claimed the other one, while Sibao grabbed onto Li Yu's leg tightly.

Once Li Yu was completely surrounded, all of the babies were satisfied. But Prince Jing, who felt like his wife was getting further and further away from him, was not.

Li Yu touched his finger, looking at him apologetically. Prince Jing held his hand back, gently pinching his palm.

Babies had very limited energy, and they were now fully fed. They each nodded off to dreamland quickly.

Prince Jing waited until the four of them were fully asleep before handing each of them over to the wet nurse, expression stiff.

Li Yu, surrounded by his babies, was about to nod off, when he suddenly felt cold...

Ah, his husband was here. Li Yu wrapped his arms familiarly around his shoulders. Their married life was very harmonious. Every couple of days, they'd have to absorb essence.

If they ignored the whole pregnancy thing, Li Yu was very happy to absorb essence. But today, Prince Jing was a little different. He absorbed essence incredibly thoroughly.

Li Yu's face was flushed—feeling both numb and tingly—and tears swam in his eyes. Originally, he hadn't thought he was capable either, but now, he felt like something was about to...come out...

Was Prince Jing getting his revenge now for the time Li Yu accidentally bit him on the man tit?

Li Yu couldn't take this kind of stimulation. He felt like his soul was about to be sucked out of his body. He punched Prince Jing a few times, yelping. Prince Jing, who was doing his best to absorb the carp spirit's essence, glanced at the hourglass and then finally let go, holding onto Li Yu's waist instead.

The next day, when they were feeding the babies, Prince Jing was looking down, focusing on feeding Sibao, while Li Yu held Dabao. Li Yu's chest was sore, and his legs were still shaking. Thinking back to the wild night he'd had, Li Yu couldn't resist glaring at the culprit.

Prince Jing felt his fierce gaze. He smiled at him, then licked his lips salaciously.

Seriously? He couldn't even speak and he was still managing to attack Li Yu with brazen flirtation!

...Whatever, it was fine if his husband was like this. It wasn't as if he didn't benefit.

With Li Yu's continuous encouragement, Dabao and the rest of the kids slowly started to get used to being human babies.

That was when the emperor's edict arrived from the capital, appointing Li Yu as Prince Jing's official consort. Prince Jing had done exactly as he'd promised and gotten Li Yu the title. Li Yu almost couldn't believe it himself.

This wasn't just something the villagers on the streets called him casually. He was now Prince Jing's official consort, recognized by the emperor himself. He was going to be recorded into the official family tree. Their marriage was set in stone.

On the day the edict arrived, Prince Jing decided on the date of the wedding. Wang Xi had been preparing for it for a long time and everything was ready, so they could hold the wedding whenever they wanted. Prince Jing was just annoyed that all the auspicious days were too far away and that he had to wait even longer. Li Yu was amused by this rare childishness from his husband. Thinking about how Prince Jing wanted to give him an official wedding even though they already had children, Li Yu's heart felt like it was coated in sugar.

"The emperor has already agreed, it's just a matter of time," Li Yu placated him, chuckling. "Don't be impatient, Your Highness."

Having tasted the sweetness of Li Yu's particular sort of comfort, Prince Jing continued to pout childishly, only calming down when Li Yu continued. At the same time, he asked Wang Xi to double check everything that had to do with the wedding.

It didn't take Wang-gonggong long to check it all. The only thing that was left was the most important aspect of the wedding: the wedding robes.

Prince Jing's robes had been made to order far in advance, and there were several backup sets waiting. Every single stitch had been inspected by Prince Jing, and all the accessories were made by artisans according to Prince Jing's designs, ensuring that each piece was completely unique.

Li Yu hadn't tried on the consort's robes and accessories yet, but with Prince Jing's experience designing clothes for him, there was nothing to be worried about.

Finally, the day of the wedding came. Prince Jing handed Li Yu his robes personally. There weren't that many servants, and Li Yu didn't have any family, so Prince Jing helped him change and do his hair himself.

Soon, Li Yu was dressed in his bright red robes edged in gold, made from Yuehua brocade. Apparently, clothes made from Yuehua brocade gave off a serene radiance like the light of the moon, which was how it got the name "radiant moon brocade." The Yuehua brocade was woven with gold thread and phoenix feather thread, and embroidered with a majestic koi fish leaping amongst the clouds over a gate. A fish pattern was embroidered all along the collar and long train, shimmering with extraordinary brilliance.

The belt was woven from soft gold thread and made to look like aquatic plant leaves. Though it appeared thick, it was actually very light. A few small, cute, golden fish hung from the belt, tinkling as they moved.

To match the outfit, there was a ruby and pearl headpiece, topped with a circle of thirty-six small, golden fish. Each fish was encrusted with rubies, and strings of pearls fell from the fishes' mouths, covering Li Yu's face slightly to keep him partially hidden.

Li Yu had never put on makeup before, but on this joyous day, he put on a bit of blush and lipstick, making him look even more radiant.

After he'd made sure that Li Yu's entire outfit fit him perfectly, Prince Jing gave a small smile and went to change himself. Wang Xi waited on him and couldn't help but speak for his master. "Consort, according to the rules, your robes should be embroidered with a phoenix. His Highness asked the emperor specifically for the changes to your robe..."

Wang Xi had been in charge of planning the wedding, so he knew exactly which things Prince Jing had worried about. Prince Jing didn't need Li Yu's gratitude, but Wang-gonggong was very chatty and immediately revealed everything to the consort.

Li Yu had seen Ye Qinghuan and the princess's wedding robes. He hadn't realized that even just the embroidery would require so much thought. He was suddenly overcome with gratitude.

Soon Prince Jing finished changing into matching wedding robes, except in black. Li Yu took a careful look and saw that Prince Jing's robes were still embroidered with the four clawed dragon, as expected of a prince. But their belts were the same—in the shape of aquatic leaves—and he'd tied the silver bead that Li Yu had once given him onto his belt as well. His sleeves and hem were also embroidered with the same fish pattern as Li Yu's robes.

Wasn't he secretly showing off their love?

Li Yu gave himself a thumbs-up for being so perceptive and noticing all the beauty in the world.

Prince Jing walked over, lowering his head as though he wanted to kiss him. As he did so, a section of red string appeared from beneath his robes. Li Yu smirked and pulled it out. He wanted to know what the prince was wearing on such an important day.

Li Yu was wearing Prince Jing's little jade figure. As he suspected, Prince Jing was wearing his fishy rock.

Put together, they were a match made in heaven.

"Your Highness, Consort, the time has come." Wang Xi was so happy, he kept wiping his eyes.

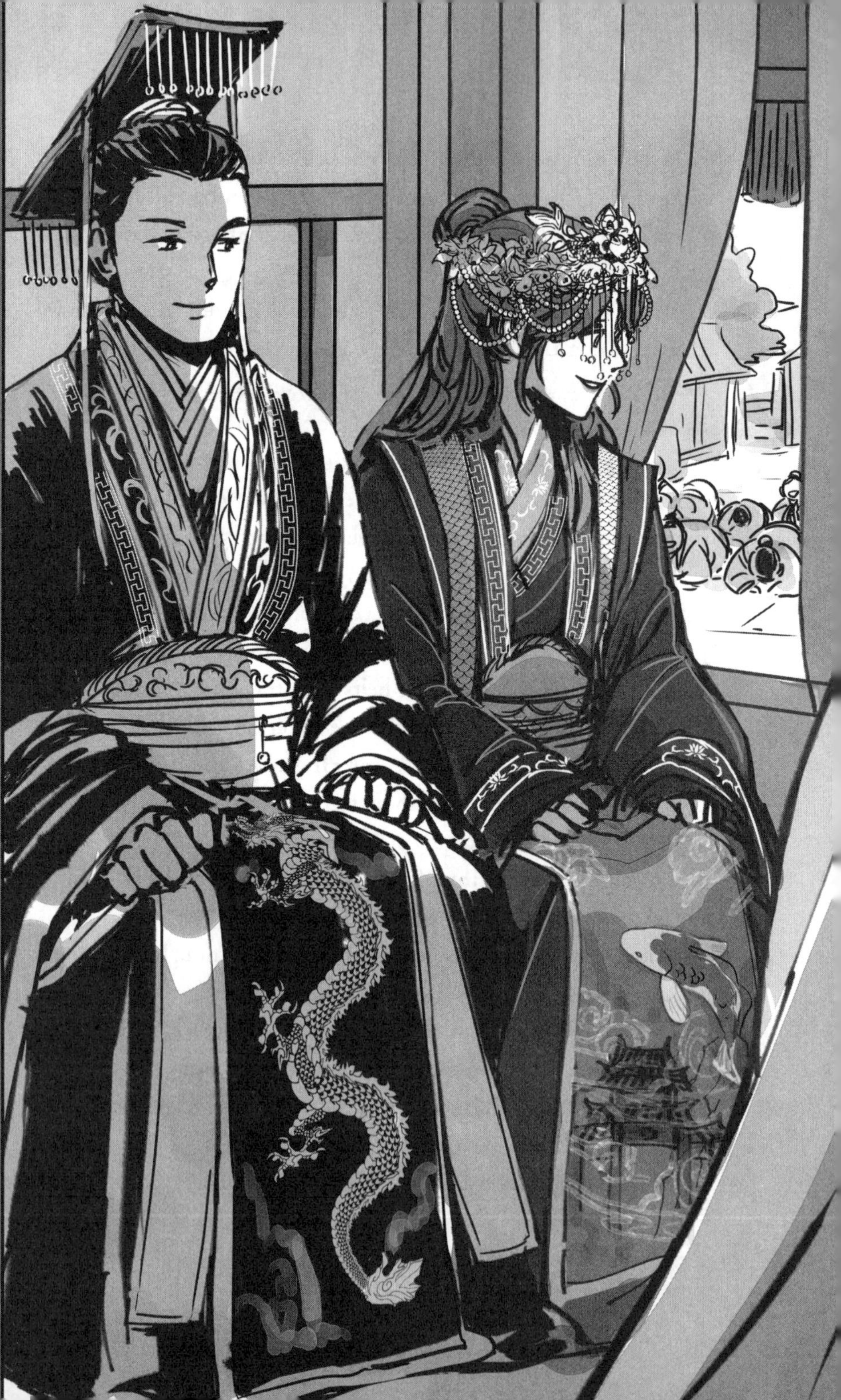

Prince Jing felt for Li Yu's hand beneath their robes, and the two exchanged a glance.

Li Yu didn't have any family; his family was Prince Jing. Prince Jing helped him onto the wedding carriage, then sat inside himself. The red and green wedding carriage made a lap around Luofeng Village, then returned to Prince Jing's residence for the bows.

Plenty of villagers had come to witness the joyous occasion and followed behind the carriage.

Li Yu lifted the curtain, feeling nervous as he looked down at the crowd of people. Prince Jing gave him an encouraging glance, and Li Yu gave a tentative wave to the audience.

The villagers all knelt on the ground and cheered loudly, "Long live the consort!" The noise startled all the surrounding magpies into the air.

Li Yu's heart leapt. In this moment, he really felt like he belonged in this ancient world.

Dabao, Erbao, Sanbao, and Sibao were lying in a row on the bed.

Today, there was only the wet nurse and no dads. They were utterly dejected.

Faint music could be heard from outside.

Sibao remembered that the wet nurse had said his dads were getting married today. He didn't know what getting married meant, but it must have been a good thing.

Sibao attempted to flip himself upright but failed.

He waved his arms around angrily. "Ahhhhhhhh!" *I want to go to our daddies' wedding!*

Sanbao also started to wave his limbs around, following his example. "Ahh!" *I want to go!*

Erbao turned to look at them. "Ahh?" *How?*

Erbao, Sanbao, and Sibao each took turns "ah"ing at each other. After coming to an agreement, with Sibao in the lead, they all did their best to roll down from the bed.

If they wanted to see their dads get married, they first had to get off the bed. Although babies weren't very strong, they could still achieve their goal by rolling.

But they weren't even a month old yet. Once they rolled over, they couldn't roll back. Erbao, Sanbao, and Sibao all lay face down on the bed.

"Ahhhh!!!" *Save us!!!*

Dabao had witnessed everything... He gave a dismissive wave of his hand. "Ahhhhhhh!" *You're all so stupid!*

One Fishy Family

PRINCE JING MENTALLY kept track of Xiaoyu's transformation time. Although they took a lap around the village, the carriage sped up as much as possible when there were not a lot of people.

The carriage driver had received a unique task. On the day of the wedding, he had to drive quickly, but not so quickly it disturbed Prince Jing and his consort. The driver was an old servant of Prince Jing's. In order to celebrate him finally getting married, he really went all out, practicing for this specifically for a month.

Along the way, Prince Jing's guards were in charge of security, stopping any overexcited villagers from getting too close. Once the carriage safely returned to Prince Jing's residence, the next step was the wedding bows.

The emperor was in the faraway capital, unable to attend Prince Jing's wedding, but that didn't stop his need to reward, reward, reward. It took Wang Xi over an hour just to read the gift list. The group bearing gifts from the emperor lined up all the way from the room where the ceremony was taking place to the outside of the entire residence.

There weren't too many guests invited to this wedding. Prince Jing wasn't a fan of commotion, but this was his and Xiaoyu's wedding; he couldn't just have a bunch of empty seats! So, he asked the village head to bring some of the respected elders in the village as important guests. Auntie Xu, who was close with Li Yu, was also invited. Most of the guests weren't nobles or aristocrats, but the couple didn't receive any less congratulations.

At the ceremony, where one's parents would usually sit, sat the emperor's edict, as well as Empress Xiaohui's memorial tablet.

Just as Prince Jing signaled for the host to start the ceremony, a horse suddenly arrived. Ye Qinghuan got off the horse, travel-worn, and rushed to the ceremony excitedly.

After they found out about Prince Jing's wedding, the House of Cheng'en had to send someone no matter what. Ye-shizi had volunteered, at least in part because he missed his cousin who he hadn't seen in nearly a year.

"Tianchi, it's finally my turn to congratulate you on your marriage!" Ye Qinghuan smiled and patted Prince Jing on the shoulder.

For once, Prince Jing didn't brush him off. Instead, he smiled lightly and ordered Wang Xi to bring over a cup of wine. They drank it together.

After drinking the marriage wine, Ye Qinghuan was feeling chatty. Besides, he had a lot to talk about.

When Prince Jing had first left the capital, he'd sent a letter to the House of Cheng'en, asking them to be patient, observant, and flexible. They could not beg for mercy on his behalf, nor should they write any letters to the western border. After Prince Jing left, aside from the old Duke of Cheng'en who seemed to have limitless patience, everyone else was worried for him. In the past year, Prince Jing had suffered bandit attacks and locust infestations, and had even had to give away his job at the Ministry of Works to the sixth prince. Ye Qinghuan nearly went to beg the emperor to let Prince Jing come back.

Fortunately, the old Duke of Cheng'en had managed to convince him in time, asking him to trust Prince Jing. The old Duke of Cheng'en could see what was going on. Prince Jing was currently in a very delicate situation. If the House of Cheng'en stepped up, not only would they be unable to help Prince Jing, they would cause all of Prince Jing's efforts to go to waste. Ye Qinghuan could only wait for something to happen.

The wait lasted until Prince Jing asked the emperor for Li Yu's hand in marriage, and the emperor agreed. Ye Qinghuan had met Li-gongzi before. Not only had they met, the entire House of Cheng'en loved Li-gongzi and they all thought this was a good match. Ye Qinghuan kept following the former duke's orders and never said anything. But Li-gongzi was a man—that was an indisputable fact. What about Prince Jing's future children?

Ye Qian kept his mouth shut too and didn't tell Ye Qinghuan that Li Yu had already given Prince Jing four little gongzi and the matter of heirs had long since been a nonissue. As a result, currently Ye Qinghuan really wanted to comfort Prince Jing.

"Don't worry, there will always be solutions when it comes to your heirs," Ye Qinghuan said quietly, pulling Prince Jing to the side. "I shouldn't say this to ruin your special day, but my parents have both worked out a solution for you. As long as you have children, Li-gongzi won't have to face judgment and blame in the future. If you don't want Li-gongzi to suffer, you can find a kid of royal blood and adopt them. There must be someone suitable."

Prince Jing raised a brow, put down his cup, and shook his head.

Ye Qinghuan thought he knew Prince Jing well enough to guess his thoughts and tried, "You... Do you perhaps look down on other people's blood?"

He didn't just look down on them. Prince Jing nodded.

Ye Qinghuan said, "If no one else, what about me?" He scratched his head, saying, "This is just a thought. The princess is already pregnant. I should be able to convince her to give you our next son... Don't misunderstand, I don't want to do this either. If it doesn't suit you, of course I would be happy to keep him." Ye Qinghuan's tone grew solemn, as though he couldn't bear to part with his flesh and blood.

Prince Jing didn't know how Ye Qinghuan had ended up here. He coughed lightly. When Wang Xi heard, he immediately brought the wet nurse over with a child.

"Your Highness, the young masters are crying so hard. This old servant had no choice but to bring them to the ceremony..."

Wang Xi didn't dare tell him that in the brief moment the wet nurse had left, three out of the four young masters had flipped over and couldn't get back up again. They had nearly drowned in their tears and were inconsolable, no matter what the wet nurse did. Wang Xi thought that since it was lively here, perhaps the young masters would enjoy it, and decided to bring them to the ceremony. But now that they were out and had spotted Prince Jing and his consort, there was no way they would leave. The young masters wanted to see their dads get married.

Prince Jing also missed his sons and gestured Ye Qinghuan over to take a look.

Ye Qinghuan was completely bewildered when he saw the four babies. Each one was wrapped in a different colored swaddling cloth—gold, gold and silver mixed, silver, and black—and held in the arms of Wang Xi and a woman. Who was this? What relationship did she have with Prince Jing? Ye Qinghuan was confused.

Wang Xi chuckled, "The young masters insisted on wearing this. The wet nurse wanted to change them into something more celebratory, but they wouldn't let her—they started crying immediately."

Prince Jing nodded, not assigning any blame. Wang Xi didn't know, but *he* knew the colors of these swaddles were the fish babies' original colors. Prince Jing took Sibao from the wet nurse and expertly patted his back.

Ye Qinghuan's eyeballs nearly popped out of his head. He couldn't help but ask, "Wang Xi, whose babies are...?"

Why did Wang Xi call them "young masters"? And why was Prince Jing...so experienced with picking them up?

Wang Xi slapped himself on the forehead and said, "Ye-shizi, so sorry. This old servant was so busy being happy he forgot to introduce you. These are His Highness's children. Li...ah, the consort gave birth to them."

Li Yu could give birth?

Ye Qinghuan was thoroughly stunned. He slowly turned around to stare at Prince Jing, whose expression was full of pride.

Wang Xi's words were too shocking. Ye Qinghuan needed time to adjust.

Li Yu had given Prince Jing four kids?

Men could get pregnant too?!

Wang Xi had no choice but to give Ye-shizi, who was about to pass out, a brief explanation. Although Wang-gonggong wasn't clear on the details either, Prince Jing had seen the whole process through. Plus, there was the gynecological expert, the other physicians, and the four young masters as proof. He could swear to the heavens it was real.

Ye Qinghuan could also tell that three of the babies looked a lot like Prince Jing when he was younger. The one that Prince Jing was holding looked a lot like Li Yu... If it was fake, how could it all seem so real?

...Wait, Ye Qinghuan suddenly realized. He'd thought Prince Jing was childless, but he actually already had four healthy sons.

Meanwhile, he, whose wife was still pregnant, had lost again.

Prince Jing knew Ye Qinghuan had mentioned adopting because he was being considerate of him, not because he wanted to be offensive, so he wasn't angry. He was just annoyed Ye Qinghuan was still standing there being a bother. They'd only had a brief moment of brotherly companionship before he wanted Ye-shizi to go somewhere else.

There wasn't much time left, so the wedding bows had to happen soon. They had to do it during the pre-calculated, auspicious time. Prince Jing gave the host another look, and they immediately started the ceremony.

Li Yu wasn't used to such finery; all the pearls dangling into his field of vision were a little distracting. Prince Jing quickly walked to his side.

"Your Highness," Li Yu called out with a smile.

Prince Jing really couldn't smile enough today. He reached out, and a warm hand enveloped his. As soon as their hands touched, all the commotion in the room settled down.

Li Yu eyed a brazier to the side. What was going on? Did the consort have to step over it too?[10] He was worried he'd kick the brazier over with how clumsy he was, or burn the expensive wedding robes. Neither seemed particularly lucky. But as he was fretting, Prince Jing wrapped his arms around him and picked him up lightly. Li Yu felt his feet leave the ground, and his mind went blank.

In an instant, he was back on the ground, with the brazier behind him.

Li Yu's face was bright red; not even the pearls on his headdress could hide his embarrassment. Prince Jing had actually carried him over the brazier, in front of everyone. The prince was so smooth,

---

10 Stepping over a fire (跳火盆) is a traditional wedding custom to burn away bad luck.

the guests all laughed amicably. Ye Qinghuan laughed the loudest, and the xiniang[11] behind them also went bright red.

It was finally time to do their bows.

Li Yu stood at Prince Jing's side. The two of them sincerely bowed to the heavens and earth, and Prince Jing's parents.

Finally, there was a deep bow between the couple.

To be honest, they had been married since the day they signed the wedding contract. This was just a declaration to the rest of the world: declaring that from now on, you are mine, and I'm yours.

Prince Jing told Wang Xi to take care of the guests as he and Li Yu went back to their room.

He'd already formed the habit of regularly checking the silver hourglass. Xiaoyu's transformation time was almost up, so he had to keep an eye on him. On such a special day, he couldn't let Xiaoyu experience even a sliver of panic or shock.

Once all the guests had left, Prince Jing used a traditional rod[12] to part the pearls covering Li Yu's face. The two of them stared at each other for a while, then smiled at the same time.

Prince Jing reached into his sleeve as Li Yu stared at him in anticipation. He guessed the prince had some notes prepared, or perhaps a special gift for the occasion.

But Prince Jing didn't produce anything strange. It was just a long, oval box. Inside, was a rolled-up painting.

Li Yu unrolled the painting under Prince Jing's watchful gaze. Prince Jing had painted a school of fish. There was a total of six life-like fish, two large and four small. One of the big ones was silver speckled with gold, exactly like Li Yu's fish form, and the small ones

---

11 A xiniang (喜娘) is a woman who accompanies the bride when she is married into her husband's family. A xiniang is responsible for teaching the bride proper etiquette.

12 A xicheng (喜秤) is a traditional Chinese handheld weighing scale which is used to lift the bride's veil. The scale has a long handle so it can be used for this purpose.

were gold, silver, gold and silver, and black. It was clearly the four fish babies.

But that wasn't right. Li Yu counted again and again. Him and the babies should make five fish. Who was the extra-large black fish in the painting...? Li Yu thought about it for a while. It wasn't until he caught sight of Prince Jing's black robes that he realized Prince Jing had drawn himself as a big black fish. This was clearly a painting of their family.

Li Yu especially liked this large, majestic black fish. He looked at it for a while before he finally, a little reluctantly, put the painting away. "Thank you for the gift, Your Highness."

Having given his wedding gift, Prince Jing once again picked up the pair of jade cups they'd drunk from the day they consummated their marriage, and filled them with green plum wine.

This time, Li Yu drank first and playfully passed the wine to him with his mouth.

Sand slowly trickled down the silver hourglass. Two figures rolled together on the marital bed, unable to part. Just as things were at a burning point, wave after wave of infant wails came from the next room.

The two of them stopped and stared at each other.

Li Yu was still panting. "Y-Your Highness," he pleaded pitifully, "the children..."

This was the annoying part about being a dad. You couldn't just enjoy yourself and forget about the kids.

Prince Jing caught his breath, resigned, and went to the next room to bring the kids over.

Dabao, Erbao, Sanbao, and Sibao's faces were all scrunched up from crying. They'd finally made it to the marriage ceremony, but their fish dad hadn't even noticed them. Soon after, their dads had disappeared, and their wet nurse had brought them back. They hadn't even received a comforting hug. Even Dabao, who considered himself the most mature, was about to explode.

Prince Jing was the first one to appear. The other babies all quieted down immediately, but Sibao, who was crying too hard and couldn't stop, accidentally started to hiccup.

Prince Jing shook his head. With two children in each arm, he moved them all to their room.

The babies finally saw their fish dad on the marital bed, and they all grabbed at him, wanting to sleep with him.

Li Yu was surrounded again...

He thought he had made another mistake. His lovely wedding night was ruined just like that. He was just about to apologize to Prince Jing, when Prince Jing lay down, blinked at him, and then pulled him down into his arms to rest on top of him.

That way, even if they were surrounded by their children, the two of them wouldn't be separated.

"Your Highness, aren't I heavy?" Li Yu rested his head on Prince Jing's shoulder, afraid of crushing the man under him.

Prince Jing shook his head and turned all the children's faces away. Wrapping his arms around Li Yu's waist, while Li Yu was still talking, he planted kisses on his lips, again and again.

Li Yu had no choice but to shut up. The kids were right there—he couldn't make any weird noises. Squeezed tightly together, the two of them continued to kiss, on and off, full of love.

They waited for the kids to fall asleep, for Li Yu's time to run out, and for him to transform into a fish. Then, when it was past midnight again, he could turn back into a human. No matter how long the wait was, they would always find the time that belonged only to the two of them, and devour each other to their hearts' content.

Merman Manmer

NO ORDINARY PERSON would dare disturb Prince Jing's marital night... But Ye Qinghuan was not an ordinary person.

Wang Xi had taken care of all the guests. After everyone had a few cups of celebratory wine, they all bid their goodbyes. Only Ye Qinghuan made his way to the bedroom.

Wang Xi stopped him with a smile. "Ye-shizi, did you want to be thrown out by His Highness again?"

Prince Jing had ordered that no one be allowed near their bedroom. Even if Wang Xi himself wanted to interrupt, he was powerless.

"There's a 'Quanjude' in town, a roast duck restaurant. His Highness had it opened for the consort. Due to the special occasion, all the roast duck is free today. If Ye-shizi is bored, you can take a walk there."

Wang Xi had even planned a place for Ye-shizi to go.

Ye Qinghuan had originally wanted to sneak a listen so he could make fun of Prince Jing a little in the future, but he hadn't expected Wang Xi to stop him like this. He'd even been forced to witness Wang-gonggong showing off his master's generosity, and now he was too embarrassed to stay.

The candles had already been blown out inside, so there wasn't anything fun he could witness anyway.

Just as he was thinking roast duck actually sounded pretty good, the door was suddenly opened from the inside. Prince Jing walked out, half-naked, in a hurry, holding something wrapped up in a piece of clothing in his hand, and ran right into Wang Xi and Ye Qinghuan.

Prince Jing nodded calmly, protecting the thing in his arms without blinking, and walked next door.

Ye Qinghuan and Wang Xi were stunned into silence.

Ye Qinghuan had good eyesight. Within the clothing in Prince Jing's arms, he'd caught a glimpse of a section of a fish's tail: the tail of Prince Jing's favorite fish. The one that was silver speckled with gold. Ye Qinghuan remembered it well—there's no way he could've mistaken it.

What had happened just now?

Ye Qinghuan was shocked. After a while, he asked Wang Xi, stammering, "Wang-gonggong, Prince Jing, he..." How could he run out carrying a fish on the night of his wedding? And in such a state of undress?!

Wang Xi was also very shocked, but clearly had more experience than Ye-shizi. In his eyes, Prince Jing could do no wrong. He quickly recovered and said, as though it were no big deal, "Shizi, His Highness is just like that."

...Like what?

Was Prince Jing into...*that* kind of thing?!

Ye Qinghuan didn't know if he should sympathize with the newlywed consort or the fish in Prince Jing's hands.

Li Yu hid himself in Prince Jing's arms, too afraid to peek out. This wasn't the first time Prince Jing had taken care of him after he transformed, so he wasn't worried at all. But because this was the night of their marriage, they hadn't had much opportunity to think after the fish babies went to sleep. They didn't realize until Li Yu was about to transform that...there was no fish tank in the bedroom.

Wang Xi had good intentions: when he arranged the room, he'd been afraid that the two masters would knock into it if they got too drunk, so he had the fish tank moved next door. Since it was their wedding night, Li Yu and Prince Jing were so focused on each other that they hadn't noticed in time...

Li Yu only realized what was wrong when he'd already transformed. Prince Jing had an idea where the fish tank might have been moved to and rushed out with Li Yu to find it. At least they could say they were the only ones in history to experience a wedding night this chaotic.

Prince Jing moved very quickly, not wanting to alert anyone, but he never expected to run into Ye Qinghuan and Wang Xi.

Li Yu took a deep breath. Good thing those two didn't know anything. Otherwise, as a consort, he would never be able to face anyone ever again!

Prince Jing put Li Yu safely in the tank. While he waited to turn back into a human, Li Yu started to wonder whether or not he should ask the system when he could end this lifestyle of transforming back and forth all the time.

It would be several years before the fish babies had to transform again. It wasn't fair that he, their fish dad, always had to live in fear that his identity would be revealed, right?

Since the "Growing Up" quest, the system had disappeared. No further quests had popped up. Prince Jing took good care of Li Yu, his days passing peacefully. Sometimes, he couldn't help but think that continuing like this would be fine too. But after this heart-pounding experience, he wanted to turn completely into a human.

Before he got to any of that, though, he had the rest of his wedding night left.

The kids were still asleep in the bedroom. They might as well use this as a chance to escape and change the scenery...

In the end, Prince Jing and his consort spent their wedding night next door.

The next morning, Li Yu was draped over his silver rock bed like a fish pancake. Prince Jing prepared his favorite food, wrapped him in the leaf blanket, and then went to see the fish babies, feeling refreshed.

As the man with the most authority in the western border, Prince Jing hadn't just given himself a wedding vacation, all the villagers were given time off to celebrate too. But as soon as he turned the corner, he ran into Ye-shizi, with dark circles under his eyes.

Ye Qinghuan had accidentally discovered Prince Jing's secret, and he couldn't be more anxious. He'd gone to Quanjude and devoured three whole roast ducks, but it hadn't helped. When he got back, he realized Prince Jing still hadn't returned to his bedroom, so his worry only grew.

Li Yu was his friend, and Prince Jing was his cousin, someone the entire House of Cheng'en had to follow. Rationally, Ye Qinghuan knew whose side he should be on. But emotionally, he couldn't just do nothing.

"You've only just gotten married to Li-gongzi! Don't do anything that would hurt him!" Ye Qinghuan threw down those words, then left.

Prince Jing had no idea what that was about. He decided to ignore him.

Some time later, Wang Xi came over, not sure what to say to him. "Your Highness, this old servant will just say o-one thing. You...you have to be good to the consort in the future."

Prince Jing really didn't know what those two were thinking.

Li Yu, the fish pancake, entered the system after catching up on his sleep. He'd felt like he vaguely heard the system last night, but he wasn't sure. The system always tried to give him notifications when he was busy doing things!

Now that he thought about it, he realized he hadn't entered this mental world in a while. The last time was when he'd collected the reward for "Growing Up." The fish babies had all turned into human babies that time, and he was worried about how to explain the fish's absence to Wang-gonggong. The four fish babies "disappeared" together, then he "gave birth" to four children. Was that suspicious?

Fortunately, the reward from the system was four plushies that corresponded with the baby fish. That had saved him a lot of worry.

The fish babies now each had their own fish plushies, and Li Yu had a great idea. With the help of Prince Jing, he'd attached a magnet to each baby fish's mouth and tail, as well as his own plush. That way, the plushies could form a line, the same way he would play with the babies.

Although the fish-scamming system was a huge fraud most of the time, sometimes, it really did pay attention to the details.

After transmigrating as a fish, he'd been forced to complete many quests, all because of the system. But he'd found his other half in this book, and that was because of the system too. Li Yu had once hated the system, but now, he wasn't sure how he felt.

He checked the main quest line as usual and noticed a new quest had lit up.

So there really had been a notification last night. After all, they were officially husbands now—they even had the emperor's approval. Their relationship had gone up another level, so it was time for the main quest to update. The next quest was—

"Postpartum Care for Fish."

Li Yu felt incredibly embarrassed. Before, he'd just thought all the quest names were slightly weird. He'd already given birth to the fish, so what was there to still care for?

Oh right. He was now considered "postpartum," right?

Li Yu looked at the description calmly.

With the system's usual behavior, it once again had to be separated into steps. You thought there was only one quest—actually, it's several quests dressed up as one! This quest line... Wait, Li Yu suddenly realized that two of the steps were already completed!

Postpartum care step one: incubate and hatch the eggs. Complete, reward awaiting collection.

Postpartum care step two: feed the young fish. Complete, reward awaiting collection.

Li Yu thought about it for a moment. Hadn't these two steps happened while he and Prince Jing were just learning how to take care of the fish babies? At the time, the main quest was still under determination, and nothing had happened.

<After getting married, the user and the tyrant can no longer be separated,> the system explained. *<You have now reached the requirements for the next quest line: "Postpartum Care." This questline is different from the others—it will mainly be the tyrant who will be completing these quests. When the first two steps were in progress, although the quest line hadn't begun yet, it still had a great effect on the fish babies. Now, the system has completed its determination.>*

Li Yu understood. "Postpartum Care" was mainly Prince Jing's responsibility. All he had to do was lay there. It wasn't his fault he and the babies were the ones who needed care. As expected of the protagonist, though, Prince Jing had managed to complete two in one go.

<What rewards do these two steps give?> asked Li Yu, curious. <If the person completing the quests is Prince Jing, does he get the rewards?>

But his husband probably didn't need anything—other than him.

<The user will still receive the rewards. Each reward is one of the tyrant's secrets.>

More secrets. Li Yu was in no hurry to claim them. He'd just save them; perhaps they'd be useful in the future. Compared to Prince Jing's secrets, he was more concerned with how to become a proper human, so he asked, <This is already the third main quest line. When can I become a human?>

A notification immediately popped up: <The third quest in the "Postpartum Care" questline is the time-limited quest 'Protect the Pet Fish.' The reward involves returning to human form. Do you want to start the quest?>

Li Yu was delighted. Every other time he asked about this, he'd never gotten an answer. This time, the answer came immediately. He could see the light at the end of the tunnel!

<What kind of quest is it exactly?> he asked. "Protect the Pet Fish" was way too general.

Since this related to whether the user could return to human form permanently, the system explained in detail for once. <The time limit is three days. After accepting the quest, the user will turn into a Merman or Manmer and be unable to move freely. You need the tyrant

to protect you during this time. If you are discovered at any point, you will fail the quest. Please choose carefully, user.>

...So, a quest where he needed to be protected?

He knew what a Merman was, but what was a Manmer?

<Mermen are human on top, and fish on the bottom. Manmers are the opposite: fish on top and human on the bottom.>

In other words, in this quest, he will become half-human, half-fish, but also not a human and not a fish...

It was so over. Now he was going to seem even more like a carp spirit.

It was fine if he just turned into a fish. If he turned into a Merman or Manmer, he'd be lucky to get Prince Jing to stay in the room with him, let alone protect him. In Legend of the White Snake, the half-human half-snake yao had scared the scholar to death. Did anyone wanna read more about that?

Li Yu forced himself to calm down. If he accidentally pressed accept because he was shaking, he might immediately turn into a creature that was neither human nor fish. He only had one chance to complete this quest, so it was probably best to warn Prince Jing first. He wanted to succeed, of course—once he did, his happy future was waiting for him.

Li Yu exited the system. Once he found a good opportunity to turn human, he asked in a quiet voice, "Your Highness, I have a... tribulation I need to get through. Can you help me?"

Fishy Tribulation

BECAUSE LI YU kept the system a secret and pretended he was a carp spirit, when he explained what was going on to Prince Jing, he framed it as a tribulation.

Essentially, he had to pick a time to go through this "tribulation," lasting around three days. He'd be in a half-human, half-fish state and needed Prince Jing's protection and care.

Prince Jing listened quietly, holding his hand tightly as Li Yu recounted the task quickly. Occasionally, Prince Jing's brow would furrow in thought. But he never let go of his hand.

"I don't have to go through it immediately," he said, not wanting to put too much pressure on Prince Jing. "We can take it slow and choose somewhere no one will disturb me... But when the time comes, I'll look really weird, and I won't be able to move. Please prepare lots of fresh water and food for me, and don't let anyone see me. That's all."

Although the task was "Protect the Pet Fish," he'd be turning into something that wasn't quite human or fish. He definitely would be staying inside so he wouldn't put himself in danger. That way, the quest would be a little easier too.

Prince Jing, however, gave it a lot more consideration than him. Picking up a brush and paper, he wrote, *Wait for me for a few days. I'll ensure your safety.*

Li Yu read the words over and over again, his chest feeling warm. "Your Highness, don't you want to ask what I will turn into?"

Prince Jing held his hand and smiled. He wrote, *No matter what you look like, you are you.*

"All right... Then please don't laugh at me when the time comes, Your Highness," Li Yu said, trying to sound casual.

When people were in love, they often hoped to look their best in front of the person they loved. Li Yu secretly felt like that as well. He'd only just gotten married, and although he wasn't beautiful enough to cause the downfall of a country, he was at least a pretty little cutie. Subconsciously, he didn't want Prince Jing to see him as a weird fish-human monstrosity.

Being a Merman was fine, but if he was fish on top and human on the bottom, he'd be basically a monster. It was already difficult enough to turn into a fish in front of Prince Jing, and now the system wanted him to be something in between? Time after time, the fish system only got more scammy instead of less.

If he wanted to complete this mission and become human for good, he had no other choice, no matter how reluctant he felt. Prince Jing had to be the one to complete this mission. He couldn't just get around it with a lie. Even if Prince Jing had always treated him well, Li Yu was still uneasy. But just a few words from Prince Jing were enough to chase away all his worries. For a moment, he couldn't control his own emotions; he had to turn around.

Don't misunderstand, he only cried when he was sad. Right now, he was just so moved that his throat felt a little uncomfortable.

Thinking of all the ways Prince Jing took care of him, Li Yu thought he should trust him. Perhaps a Merman and a Manmer would be very scary, perhaps Prince Jing would be shocked—but he would never let him down.

Prince Jing misinterpreted Li Yu's emotional turmoil, thinking he was worried that his tribulation wouldn't go well. He wrote more: *Don't worry, I won't make you wait long.*

Li Yu's lips curved up, and he nodded forcefully. Ever since he got together with Prince Jing and they got married, he'd always felt very safe.

Now that they'd talked about it, Prince Jing knew Li Yu had to go through a "tribulation," so he made a lot of preparations. The emperor often mentioned the babies in his letters these days—although it was just a sentence here or there, Prince Jing suspected his family of six wouldn't be stuck at the western border for much longer. But the babies were still young. Even if the emperor wanted to see them, Prince Jing didn't want them to suffer through traveling. He would at least try to delay until they stopped breastfeeding...

Although Xiaoyu said he wasn't in a rush to go through his tribulation and that they could take their time, he thought it was best if they did it sooner rather than later. It would be better to do it while they were still on the western border, because here, he was in charge. He could even make up excuses for Li Yu getting pregnant and giving birth. If they returned to the capital, there would be many restrictions, and he was worried Xiaoyu's identity would be revealed.

As he saw it, these few days right after the wedding were the best time. He'd taken care of most of his work in advance, and no one would disturb him while he was on this break.

But if he and Xiaoyu went to deal with this tribulation, they would have to leave the kids to Wang Xi. Luckily, Ye Qinghuan hadn't left yet, so they could at least conscript him to help.

At Luofeng Village, apart from the residence the village head had prepared for Prince Jing, Wang Xi had also secretly purchased a few different properties, just in case. Prince Jing picked one that was not far from his regular residence. It was connected via a secret tunnel, making it perfect for this situation. If anything were to happen, he could return quickly.

With the location chosen, Prince Jing told Li Yu his plans. Li Yu was shocked at how fastidious Prince Jing was. He was rather embarrassed—he'd only thought of preparing food and water, but Prince Jing had thought about where to stay and what to do about the kids. He really didn't have anything to add. Li Yu didn't need to worry about anything.

Prince Jing secretly ordered the house to be cleaned out and prepared as soon as possible, then ordered Auntie Xu to prepare lots of Li Yu's favorite foods. Altogether, the human and fish food took up an entire cart. Never mind three days, they were prepared for thirty.

Prince Jing was the person who commanded the most authority and respect in the western border. He didn't need to let anyone know where he was taking his consort. But he still had to give everyone other than Wang Xi and Ye Qinghuan an explanation. His first thought was to pretend to go hunting, but he rarely hunted even when he was at the capital, so this excuse was a little bit flimsy. Li Yu wanted to help. He suddenly had an idea: the honeymoon excuse.

"Your Highness, where I'm from, after they get married, people usually have a honeymoon, which is when the newlyweds go on a trip to have fun and relax."

Li Yu thought he'd lost a great opportunity. Why did he have to be so honest and tell Prince Jing the quest would take three days? He should've said it would take longer so they could have more time together in their own little world.

Prince Jing fully believed him about the honeymoon, though, and relayed the information to Ye Qinghuan and Wang Xi.

When Wang-gonggong found out His Highness and the consort were going somewhere alone, he couldn't be happier. There were already four young masters—perhaps this time they could return with a few new young ladies?

Wang-gonggong agreed happily and immediately used what he'd just learned to wish His Highness and the consort a happy honeymoon.

Ye Qinghuan was not so happy. Ye-shizi, who had been recruited to work, said with a fierce expression, "Why do I have to take care of your children for you while you go on your honey...honeymoon?"

Prince Jing glanced at Wang Xi, and Wang Xi laughed. "Shizi, His Highness says letting you take care of them is a way of showing you respect."

"Bullshit!" Ye Qinghuan said. "I came to drink your marriage wine, I'm a guest. How can you make a guest work for you? Either way, you have to let me come along during the honeymoon."

Prince Jing glared at him judgmentally. Xiaoyu had said honeymoons were for couples. Those who wanted to interrupt a couple's honeymoon were what Xiaoyu had called "wheels."

It didn't matter whether or not Ye Qinghuan agreed. When the time came, Prince Jing left with Li Yu, and the four kids were handed to Ye Qinghuan.

The fish babies couldn't speak or move right now, but they could listen. Through various conversations, they'd figured out their dads were leaving, and were handing them over to Wang-gonggong and Ye-shushu.

The fish babies were very familiar with Wang-gonggong. When Wang-gonggong was looking after them, all of them were very well behaved. But this was the first time they were meeting Ye-shushu. The babies were never very polite when it came to strangers.

Ye Qinghuan was about to become a dad himself. Just because Prince Jing was rude didn't mean Ye-shizi couldn't take good care of the kids. But he'd only just met these three chubby babies who all looked a lot like a younger Prince Jing, so it took a long time before he finally managed to differentiate Dabao, Erbao, and Sanbao. Out of the three, Erbao and Sanbao started crying as soon as they saw him, giving him a headache. Dabao's expression remained serious.

Ye Qinghuan had been beaten up by Little Chubs when he was young. For a moment, he thought he was looking at the real deal and felt a little fear in his heart. He touched his nose, feeling like he was thinking too much, but then his eyes met the judgmental gaze of this child.

...What's going on?! I want to beat him up!

But Ye-shizi was an adult. He couldn't harm a defenseless baby who didn't know anything, so nothing ended up happening.

Ye Qinghuan picked up Erbao and Sanbao, then stuffed Dabao into his arms as well, his movements clumsy. He took this opportunity to practice—soon, his own child would be born, after all.

Ye Qinghuan touched the three children's heads and couldn't help but smile.

Oh, there was also Sibao. He looked a lot like Li Yu and didn't seem as mischievous as the other three. He was always smiling brightly.

"Sibao, call me shushu!" Ye Qinghuan got excited, pinching Sibao on one tender cheek. What a classic example of bullying the weak.

Sibao remained smiling...then suddenly bit Ye-shizi's hand. Although he had no teeth, his gums left two red marks behind.

Ye-shizi howled like a banshee.

Li Yu and Prince Jing soon arrived at the secret residence. Prince Jing wasted no time sending everyone off, leaving only the two of them.

They had brought plenty of food, and Prince Jing had ordered someone to dig a pond in the garden. It was filled with clear water, and they had brought the fish tank along as well.

"Your Highness," Li Yu announced, "I...am going to start."

Prince Jing grabbed him and pulled out a silk pouch, handing it to Li Yu.

"What's this?" Li Yu asked. Prince Jing was always finding new gifts to give him. Prince Jing gestured for him to open it, so Li Yu did. Inside lay an old protective charm and a note.

The note described where the protective charm came from. This was the protective charm Empress Xiaohui had gotten for Prince Jing before he was born. This was technically something she passed down to him, so Prince Jing had kept it safe ever since and had never worn it.

The night before he came to the western border, he'd made sure to ask someone to bring the charm to Liao Ran for him to bless. It had all been for this moment. Tribulations for yao were usually very dangerous. Prince Jing firmly believed this protective charm would keep Li Yu safe.

"Your Highness, thank you..." Li Yu sniffled and hung the charm around his neck. His emotions were complicated. He knew very well that he wasn't going through any tribulation, and this charm was just a piece of paper. Even if anything did happen, the charm would be completely useless. But now all of Prince Jing's trust and sincerity would be concentrated in this charm, all because of a white lie he had told.

He knew he'd had no other choice, but he still felt regretful at this moment.

It was time to start. Prince Jing nodded at him slightly.

Li Yu made his last request. "Your Highness, can you turn around?" He didn't know what he was going to look like. He had to give both Prince Jing and himself a bit of a buffer.

Prince Jing was always very understanding when it came to him, and he immediately turned around as asked. Li Yu gritted his teeth and quickly entered the system. When the system asked him if he'd like to start the quest, he chose yes without hesitating.

Something abruptly occurred to him. The system said he would appear as a Merman and Manmer one after another. Which would be first?

...

When Li Yu came to again, he felt surrounded by coldness. His face felt a little itchy, and when he looked down, his feet and legs were all accounted for.

Li Yu thought he hadn't changed yet, but when he opened his mouth, he found he couldn't speak. When he took another look, he realized his hands had turned into fins... That was when he realized the quest had already started.

It was different from his fish form. His fish form was a whole fish, and much smaller than a human. But right now, his legs and feet were still human, meaning he hadn't changed in size, but his hands...

Ahhhhh, he was a Manmer!

The bottom half was human, and the top half was...!!!

Li Yu immediately tried to cover his face, but his fins were too short. Soon, he could no longer breathe. Even though he was half-human and half-fish, the fish half still needed water.

Li Yu didn't even dare look at himself, let alone tell Prince Jing to turn around. He quickly used his foot to hook over a piece of cloth he'd prepared beforehand and tried to cover up his top half.

With the cloth draped over his fish head, Li Yu ran into the garden and threw himself into the water. Even if he had faith in Prince Jing, he still didn't want... Sob sob sob, he didn't dare look at himself, so he wanted Prince Jing to see him even less!

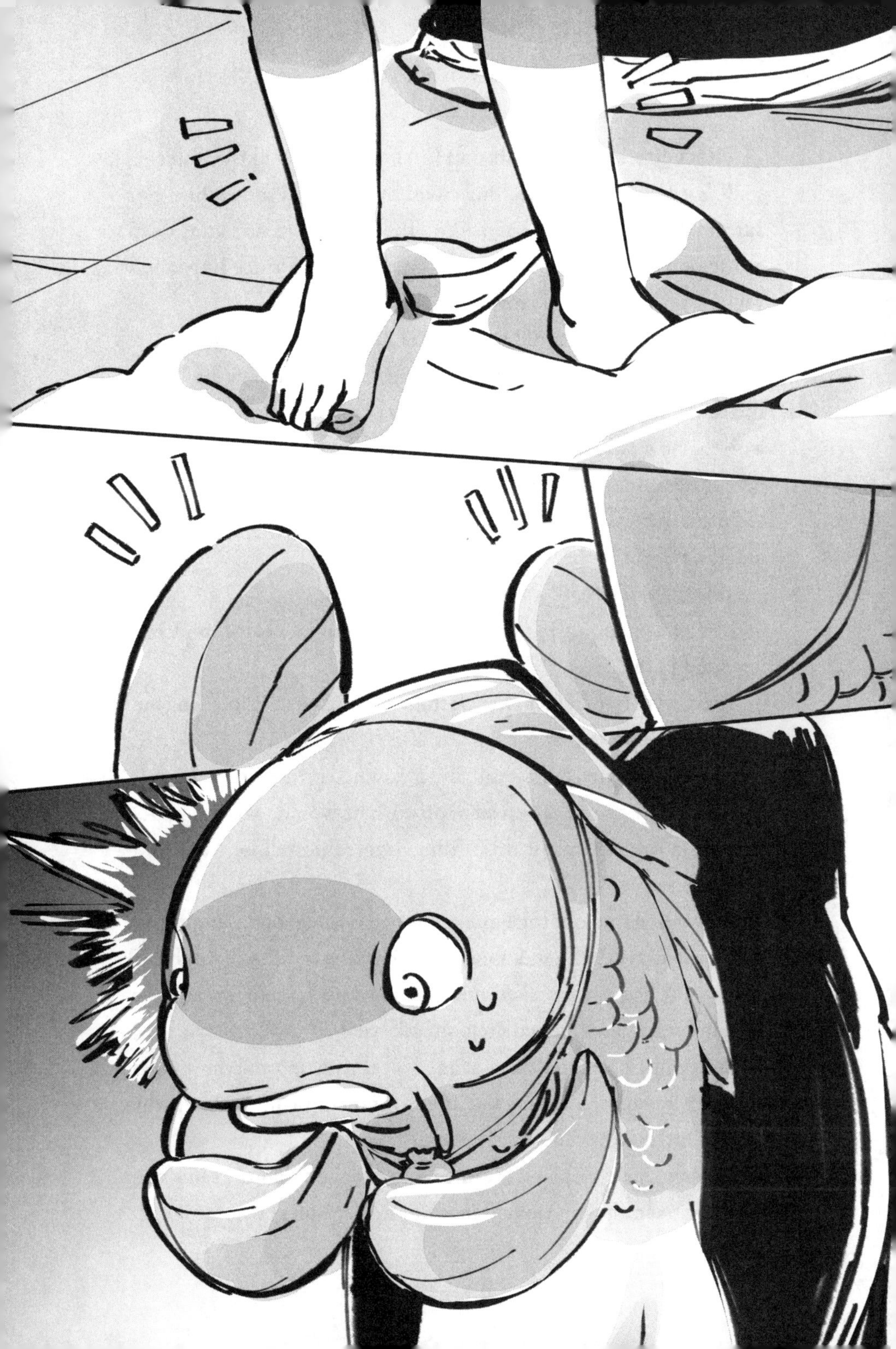

Prince Jing heard a splash, and Li Yu was already in the water.

What happened? Prince Jing stood by the pond for a while, not sure what had happened to Li Yu. The pond here wasn't as deep as the one in Prince Jing's manor. On the shore, Prince Jing could vaguely make out Li Yu's form.

He realized Xiaoyu didn't seem to have fully transformed.

Considering Li Yu had suffered a cold the last time he hid at the bottom of the pool and refused to come out, Prince Jing was worried he would catch one this time as well. Soon, he decided to get in the water too.

Just as he was about to take off his outer robe, the water rippled, and the person in the water came to the surface.

Xiaoyu? Prince Jing was very worried.

Li Yu was standing in the water silently, his upper half completely wrapped in the cloth.

There were two holes in the cloth. Li Yu looked at Prince Jing out of them. *Sob sob sob, Your Highness, don't come closer!*

Neither of them could speak. Li Yu watched Prince Jing nervously. As soon as the prince took a step forward, he would take one back.

After a few repeats of this, Prince Jing could tell he was avoiding him.

Prince Jing thought for a moment, then reached out to pull Li Yu out of the water. Li Yu was about to reach back for him out of habit, but his fin had only peeked out a little when he remembered he couldn't reach, and immediately shrank back.

Prince Jing had good eyesight and had already spotted the hidden fin. He was stunned at first, but after a moment he figured out why Xiaoyu had to cover his face and upper body.

...It was a little surprising. Prince Jing coughed slightly. How was he going to comfort Xiaoyu if he wouldn't let him get close?

Looking around, Prince Jing spotted a bamboo stick.

Li Yu noticed it as well. He and Prince Jing had to communicate somehow. Perhaps they could use this bamboo stick to pass along messages?

Li Yu waited for him eagerly, but then, as he watched, Prince Jing cut off half of his sleeve, tied it to the bamboo stick, and slowly brought the stick closer to him.

The sleeve on the bamboo stick lightly caressed the top of his head. This movement... Li Yu froze.

It was like Prince Jing was gently touching his head, the same way he'd done countless times before.

Merman Play

YOU BASTARD! *Do you think you're fishing?*

Li Yu giggled at the method Prince Jing had chosen to pat him. He paused, then used his fin to grab the corner of the sleeve on the bamboo pole.

Prince Jing tried to pull the bamboo pole back, and Li Yu moved with it to stop in front of him.

Prince Jing wasn't fishing, but Li Yu was hooked.

Prince Jing let go of the bamboo pole and reached his hand out. This time, Li Yu gave up his shiny, fat, short fins, and Prince Jing held them without any hesitation.

Prince Jing patted his fins. *Don't be afraid.*

This was something Prince Jing did often, so there was no way Li Yu could misunderstand him.

Dummy... Li Yu thought to himself. *Isn't it obvious? I'm afraid that you'll be afraid.*

He stopped hiding and leaped into Prince Jing's arms, the cloth still over his head. In Manmer form, it was easy for his upper body to get dehydrated, but his legs and feet were still very agile.

Prince Jing was afraid that he wouldn't be able to breathe, so he stayed with Li Yu in the water.

Li Yu swam around occasionally—a Manmer usually relied on their fins and feet to tread water—but since the water wasn't deep,

Li Yu was lazy and just walked in the water with his feet. He was really taking "neither fish nor fowl" to the extreme.

Li Yu walked around in the water playfully and even childishly splashed water onto Prince Jing, before stomping on Prince Jing's feet and then trying to make his escape.

But Prince Jing expressionlessly grabbed his ankles and dragged him back.

This position made Li Yu recognize the danger he was in. Though his upper body was that of a fish, his lower body was still a human's. He still had all the right parts—oh no, would he incite Prince Jing into an animalistic fervor toward his pitiful, weak, and helpless self if he struggled?

No thanks! A Manmer was way too much of a turn off, and Li Yu was afraid he might throw up even thinking about it. He didn't dare to move or think carelessly, so he just leaned against Prince Jing with the cloth still covering his head.

Hugging was okay, but his cloth couldn't come off!

Li Yu's mind was racing with thoughts, but Prince Jing seemed determined to stay with him through his trial. As if he knew that Li Yu didn't want his fish face to be seen, as long as Li Yu didn't try taking off the cloth, Prince Jing didn't try to force anything and treated him normally.

Li Yu thus barely managed to maintain his image.

The first day passed uneventfully, and Li Yu fell asleep in Prince Jing's arms.

When he woke up, he realized he was still covered with the cloth and that it was the next day. The first thing he did was look down at his hands.

The mission was supposed to last for three days, and he would switch forms during that time. The appearance of his hands was all-important: he was more experienced now, and he knew that if his hand was a fin, then he must still be in Manmer form.

He hoped he was a Merman this time, but even if he was a Manmer again, Prince Jing would protect him, so he didn't need to worry about anything.

It was easy to be disappointed if one's hopes were too high. Li Yu didn't want to be disappointed, so he only allowed himself a tiny bit of hope and took a quick glance.

Now that it was the next day, he saw that his short fins...were gone! Before him were a pair of hands with proper fingers.

Li Yu suppressed his excitement and tried to clench his hands. After he made sure he wasn't dreaming, he used those hands to rub his face aggressively.

His face hurt, and there were no scales!

Li Yu happily tossed the cloth to the side and took in lungfuls of air.

Since his face and hands were both human, then he was definitely a Merman this time!

Li Yu looked down at his legs. As expected, he saw a silver fish tail with gold sprinkled throughout.

When he was a fish, he saw his tail all the time and never thought much about it. Now that his fish tail was bigger, though, it seemed a lot more impressive. It was almost as long as his legs, and the silver scales started about three inches below his navel. The fish tail replaced the legs of his human body, making for a very fetching appearance.

The Merman form he was in now was more like the Merman he imagined at first, and thankfully not a dugong. He'd transformed from a food carp into a koi carp, and then into a Merman. This really was quite...

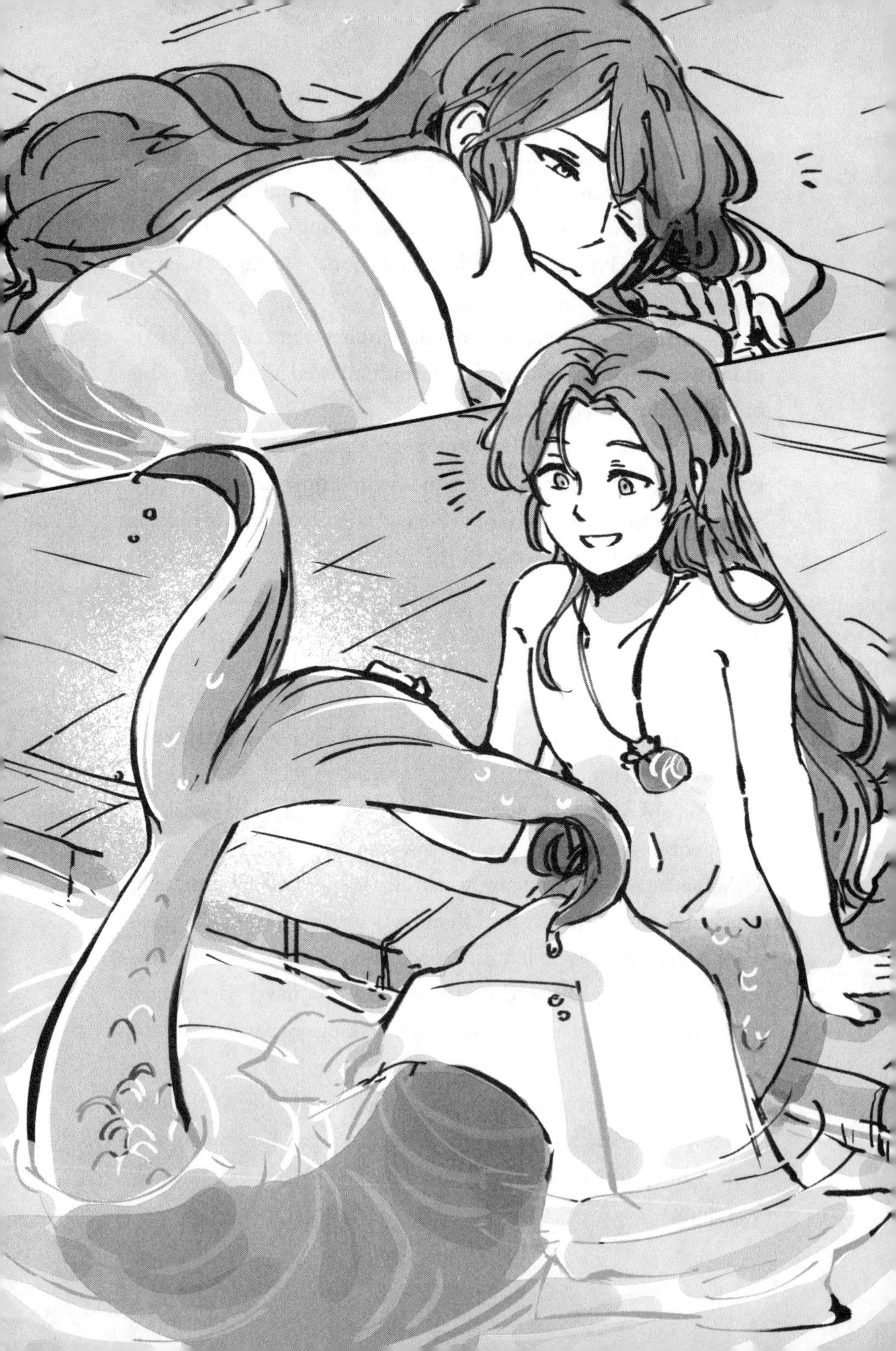

He'd wanted to cry when he was a Manmer, but now, as a Merman, he wanted to laugh loudly. Humans were truly irrational creatures!

Li Yu admired his Merman reflection in the water and started getting used to his new form. First, he rubbed his own tail. That's right, he'd never petted himself before. A Merman could do something a fish couldn't do! So, this was how weird petting a fish felt!

When he was done stroking it, he tried flapping his tail. His silver tail drew a pretty arc in the water, and even Li Yu himself was amazed.

He wanted to try something out with his Merman tail, so he wriggled up onto the shore. He could use his tail as a skateboard when he was a fish, but he wasn't sure yet if a Merman could do that.

Since his upper half was human, breathing out of the water wasn't a problem. Li Yu did his best to stand on his tail...but perhaps because his size had changed too much, it was hard to balance. His tail couldn't support his body to walk on the ground.

Next, Li Yu tried to jump. His tail strength was still the same, so he was able to get off the ground, but he was a bit unstable when he landed. Li Yu took some time to recover and then jumped up again—even though he couldn't walk, he could move a bit by jumping around.

The only inconvenience was that when he was on land for too long, his tail would become dry and sore, similar to chapped skin. However, it was much better than being unable to breathe in his Manmer form, and he only had to put his tail in the water to alleviate most of the pain.

Overall, the Merman form was prettier, and a much better deal than the Manmer form!

Li Yu happily jumped back and forth from land to water, loud enough that he woke up Prince Jing.

Li Yu saw his feather-like eyelashes tremble slightly and knew that he was close to waking up, so he leaped into the water and hid his tail.

As soon as he awoke, Prince Jing saw Li Yu, with his human upper body, resting on his arms and looking at him.

Xiaoyu? Prince Jing smiled and patted Li Yu's head.

Li Yu smiled mischievously and cocked his head at Prince Jing, and Prince Jing saw a silver and gold tail rush to the surface and rise slowly from the water behind Li Yu.

Surprise flashed across Prince Jing's face for a moment when he realized who the tail belonged to. Xiaoyu had fins and a human lower body before, but now...it was flipped? In front of him was a young man, beautiful as always, but his lower body was now a dazzling, splendid tail. Prince Jing had never seen such a scene in his life—so innocent yet seductive, so mysterious and beautiful.

This was the most beautiful yao he'd ever seen.

Li Yu had been waiting this entire time for Prince Jing to find out how beautiful Mermen were. He thought so himself, and not only did he not want to hide it, he even looked forward to Prince Jing seeing him.

He purposely swam slowly around Prince Jing. His tail was soft, and he would occasionally brush past Prince Jing's hands and feet.

Once he was sure that Prince Jing had no plans to run away, Li "Devious" Yu decided to go all out and wrapped his entire tail around Prince Jing.

He used to wrap his tail tightly around Prince Jing's fingers, but now he wanted to wrap his tail tightly around his body.

Li Yu had wanted to do this ever since he found out Prince Jing didn't look upon his Manmer form with disdain and was still willing to protect him. Opening his arms, Li Yu threw them around his husband's neck.

"Your Highness, do you like it?" Li Yu asked softly, leaning in to kiss Prince Jing.

Li Yu's scent was everywhere: in Prince Jing's arms and on his upper lip. He couldn't stand the teasing and could barely control himself. But he remembered that Xiaoyu was in the middle of a tribulation, so he couldn't respond hastily. Instead, with great restraint, he hugged the Merman tightly, his ears turning slightly red.

He had petted the tail that was encircling him countless times before. To distract himself, Prince Jing tried to pet the tail again.

The tip of the tail shivered violently, and, to his own surprise, Li Yu let out an "Ah~"

The tail was actually very sensitive. When he was a fish, petting it just felt comfortable, but when he was a Merman, the feeling was amplified several times over. Li Yu could hear the indecency in his own voice. It wasn't a noise of surprise—it was practically a moan.

Prince Jing's whole body stiffened. Because of that light moan, he didn't dare move. His ears turned even redder.

Li Yu was still in his arms, and could clearly feel the ways he was reacting... His tail began to move, rubbing with persistence. He kissed Prince Jing wetly on his earlobe and whispered in his ear, "Your Highness, do you want it?"

This was probably the only time he'd get to be a Merman; it would be a waste if they just stared at each other.

Sure, he was probably the first fish to want it while completing a mission, but since the system didn't do anything to stop him, it was probably fine.

Prince Jing's throat bobbed. Staring into the dark, wet eyes of the person in his arms... Who could resist such a sight? But he was still undergoing a tribulation...

Li Yu was afraid that Prince Jing wouldn't be able to come to terms with it and they'd waste this excellent opportunity, so he wheedled, "Your Highness, it's all right. This is also part of my tribulation."

Prince Jing paused. *This was part of it?*

"Yes." Li Yu smiled naughtily. "It's a love tribulation, so a carp spirit has to absorb essence."

Prince Jing came back to his senses and held the restless fish. He picked an open spot next to the pond, took off his robes, and laid them out onto the ground. Li Yu lay down with his tail just close enough to trail into the water, so he'd be comfortable no matter how he moved.

"Your Highness, let me tell you..." Li Yu lay next to Prince Jing's ear, smiling and talking.

A fish's structure was different from a human's, but Li Yu hadn't looked into it much beyond the obvious. Fortunately, Prince Jing was on board to help research the matter, and a whole new world awaited them. Li Yu's tail was so excited that it started slapping the water loudly. They finally found the right location and did everything they wanted.

After the fun, Li Yu fell asleep.

Prince Jing put on a random undershirt, carried him back inside, and wiped off all the gravel on his tail. Li Yu hummed quietly as he was wrapped in a quilt, his eyebrows slightly knitting together.

Prince Jing examined his scales closely and found that they were a little dry. He remembered that Li Yu's tail was very lively earlier when it was in the water, so perhaps his scales were somewhat dehydrated now. Thus, Prince Jing used a wet cloth to continuously wipe his tail. Li Yu's brows relaxed, and he finally slept soundly.

But before the day was over, as night approached, the sudden noise of drums and a crowd could be heard outside.

Li Yu jolted awake on Prince Jing's lap. He was afraid something huge had happened, and he wanted Prince Jing to check it out. But Prince Jing didn't want to. He'd already prepared everything beforehand and had no intention of leaving Xiaoyu's side.

Before long, a servant reported that bandits had taken advantage of the commotion surrounding Prince Jing's wedding to attack Luofeng Village.

The leader of the bandits, who'd suffered several defeats, assumed that Prince Jing would let down his guard during his wedding. Most of the officials and soldiers in Luofeng Village were on vacation too. What a heaven-sent chance.

A heaven-sent chance indeed.

Prince Jing smiled coldly. Li Yu, who was about to push him to accept the battle, had the sense of "The weather is getting colder, so the bandits should die."

Tricked Fishy

PRINCE JING HANDED Li Yu a secret report. Li Yu glanced over it and found that the ambush on the village was part of Prince Jing's Wedding Leave Plan.

The bandits wanted to attack during Prince Jing's wedding when his guard was down, but Prince Jing had already anticipated this.

Luofeng Village's advantage lay in its secret passages. Prince Jing had been there for nearly a year and had been training the local guards to be proficient at using those passages during battle. Prince Jing had given everyone in the village a vacation because of his wedding, making it seem as if everyone's guard was down. In reality, the security in Luofeng Village was relaxed on the outside but alert on the inside. Word had spread that the citizens were gone to visit friends and family, so if the bandits were really thinking about making a move right now, they'd make themselves an easy target.

Prince Jing knew that he wouldn't be able to stay on the western border for long, so he wanted to get rid of the bandits as soon as possible so that danger could be fully eliminated.

Li Yu was mostly relieved when he saw all the details on the secret report. As long as Prince Jing was prepared, then a dilettante like himself had nothing to worry about. Come to think of it, Prince Jing had made so many preparations to aid him in his "tribulation" that there was no way he would've been so negligent as to ignore something as important as defense.

Prince Jing comforted him and handed him a note, telling him to be patient and wait for results within four hours. Li Yu nodded. It was almost the last day of his mission too, so he hoped that the bandits could be caught as soon as possible and nothing unexpected would happen.

Outside, a fight was about to start, so he couldn't fall asleep even if he wanted to. Prince Jing hugged him, and Li Yu leaned against Prince Jing's shoulder. The two of them listened to what was happening outside.

After some time had passed, the sound of children crying could be heard, as if several children were crying at once. Li Yu's hands shook, and his heart skipped a beat.

He thought the crying sounded like Dabao. He and Prince Jing were in a secret residence to complete the mission, but the children had been left in the manor and weren't with them. Earlier, he'd only been thinking of the village's defenses, not his own children, but if a fight were to really break out...would they be in danger?

Wang-gonggong and Ye Qinghuan were keeping guard at the residence, but would they be as wary of bandits as Prince Jing was?

What if bandits broke through the defenses and rushed into the manor during the battle?

Li Yu didn't dare keep going down this line of thought.

Prince Jing only needed a glance to know that Li Yu was seriously worried, so he held his hand tightly and gave him a determined look. *We're baiting the enemy. Don't fall for it.*

Wang Xi had been with Prince Jing for many years, and Ye Qinghuan was Prince Jing's cousin. They were both trustworthy. In the very unlikely event that the bandits actually broke into the residence, there were numerous loyal guards who were willing to risk their lives to protect the four children. Even without them, Ye Qinghuan was skilled in martial arts and Wang Xi was meticulous and careful. They were more than enough to protect the children.

Prince Jing tried his best to let Li Yu know that the children weren't in any danger, but the children outside kept wailing, sounding more devastated by the second. Li Yu's heart twisted into a knot. He was already a father—Dabao, Erbao, Sanbao, and Sibao were his own flesh—and normally, just a single tear from one of his children was absolutely heart-wrenching. Even if the children outside weren't his own, he thought of his children when he heard these cries.

Li Yu held Prince Jing's hand and begged softly. "Your Highness..."

Prince Jing knew what he wanted. It wasn't unusual for Xiaoyu to lose his composure out of concern for the children, so the easiest way for him to calm down would be to send someone outside to see what was going on and tell them what happened.

Prince Jing had actually already sent people to inquire, but they still hadn't come back for some reason. It would be quickest for him to go himself.

There wasn't anything wrong with that; Prince Jing was confident in his own skills, even if he encountered bandits. But he was worried that Xiaoyu's tribulation would be affected. There was still one day to go. He'd heard that the biggest obstacles usually came during the final day.

"Your Highness, I promise I'll stay right here and wait for you to come back," Li Yu pleaded. "Take a look for me, please?" If it weren't for the fact that he was half-human and half-fish, he probably would have gone already himself.

Prince Jing couldn't resist him, and didn't want him to be disappointed. Surely it should be safe as long as the fish stayed in the residence... On the other hand, he was afraid that Li Yu wouldn't be able to concentrate and overcome his tribulation if he was afraid and on edge.

I'll be back soon. Prince Jing agreed, and after touching the charm on Li Yu's neck and giving him a token that represented the prince's authority just in case, he strode out. The guards immediately greeted him, and Prince Jing signaled for them to protect the consort, but not to enter and disturb him.

Li Yu watched him leave. After Prince Jing left, it calmed down a bit outside. Li Yu thought that Prince Jing would be back soon, but he waited a long time, and not only did Prince Jing not return, but the sound of children crying started up again.

What was going on? Had something happened that even Prince Jing couldn't handle?

Li Yu was extremely anxious. Having absolutely no clue what was happening outside only made him more worried. He was also worried for Prince Jing; he should've insisted on going outside with him.

But he was still in Merman form—even if he didn't mind it, he couldn't walk outside.

Just as that thought crossed his mind, Li Yu realized that his tail was gone and had been replaced by human legs and feet.

Somehow, the third day had arrived, and he transformed from a Merman back into a Manmer.

Turning into a Manmer right now wasn't the worst thing that could have happened. He didn't look as nice as a he did as a Merman, but he had legs and feet and could move around as he pleased. But a Manmer couldn't breathe air, so he couldn't leave the water for too long...and he might scare others with his appearance if he went out like this. There were a lot of factors to consider.

But Prince Jing hadn't returned, so he had no choice but to look for information on his own. He had promised Prince Jing that he wouldn't leave the secret residence, but the situation outside and his husband's safety were more important to him. He wanted to find Prince Jing as soon as possible.

Li Yu's gaze fell on the cloth that he'd thrown to the side. It was a rather large piece of cloth, big enough to cover his upper body and fins. Plus...if he needed water, he still had his inventory and could bring some with him!

Li Yu rummaged through the room and found a fish tank, put it in his inventory, and filled both the fish tank and his inventory with clear water. In case of an emergency, he could take it out and put his head in the fish tank.

Li Yu finished preparing everything and got ready to leave. The guards outside stopped him, but Li Yu immediately showed them Prince Jing's token. Prince Jing had given it to him so he could protect himself. Since he had the token, the guards had no choice but to let him go. Prince Jing had only thought to ask them to protect the consort—he didn't think that the consort would ask to leave himself.

The guards obeyed the order and followed Li Yu closely. Li Yu didn't scold them. He was the one who insisted on leaving and broke his promise, but he should be safe with the guards watching over him.

He saw a good number of people on this outing. Li Yu followed the sound of crying. He didn't need to go far before he ran into some people dressed as bandits, with their heads covered. They were holding something and trying to leave in a panic.

Li Yu's sharp eyes recognized that they were holding a swaddled baby, wrapped in a cloth with a golden hem. Li Yu's heart skipped a beat, and he ordered the guards to chase after them.

There weren't many bandits, and the guards were extremely skilled, so it didn't take long for them to capture the bandits. Li Yu felt like he was going to stop breathing, but he still took the swaddled baby from the bandit and looked at it.

This child…wasn't Dabao!

Li Yu was surprised and gave the child to a guard to look after. He ran into a corner just out of view, brought out the water in his inventory, and took some time to recover.

Just as he put away the fish tank and was about to turn around, a smoke bomb landed at his feet, spewing white smoke.

Oh no! I was tricked! Li Yu realized as he fainted.

When he woke up again, he was floating in some water with the cloth still wrapped around his head. Before he left, Li Yu was afraid that the cloth would fall off and he would scare others with his fish face, so he'd purposely tied a strip of sturdy leather several times around his body and found some cloth strips to hide his fins. The large cloth and cloth strips were still there.

Li Yu remembered that he'd fainted from the white smoke. It was dangerous for him to lose consciousness as a Manmer; why had he woken up in the water?

Had Prince Jing come back to save him?

There were voices by his ear. Li Yu quickly realized that it wasn't Prince Jing but several other people. From their clothing, they appeared to be a group of bandits.

This group was noisy—Li Yu listened for a while before he figured out what was happening. The bandits had just broken into Luofeng Village when they'd been beaten up badly by Prince Jing's ambush. They were going to retreat to their base, but the bandit leader decided to listen to his tactician, who wanted to grab some important hostages from Luofeng Village to knock down Prince Jing's confidence.

This tactician had come to the western border recently and just joined this group of bandits. Somehow, he'd managed to get the head of the bandits to obey him, and at a crucial moment, on his instruction, the bandit leader didn't just try to escape but came back to kidnap people instead.

The tactician found babies about a month old and placed them in golden-hemmed swaddling clothes. Then, he had the bandits make the babies cry, and made them run around the village to lure people out with their wailing. The bandits didn't really understand why. Why couldn't they just use the children as hostages? Why did they need to lure other people out?

The tactician wouldn't explain, just insisted they should do as they were told. The first time they ran into Prince Jing, he beat the bandits up, and only a couple of them were left. In the end, the bandit leader decided to sacrifice himself and lure Prince Jing away, while the tactician had the rest of the bandits keep trying to lure other people out.

But the remaining bandits were confused—when another person came out, they ended up being beaten to a pulp again.

The exhausted bandits took the unconscious Li Yu to a run-down temple. Near the temple, there was a shallow river. Li Yu's leather strip was thick and hard to break, so the bandits hadn't been able to take off the cloth. Since they couldn't see him or identify him, they could only toss him into the river and hope that he would wake up soon so they could interrogate him.

Li Yu had worked it out now and thought to himself that Prince Jing was right. This was a trap all along, and he'd fallen right into it. The bandits' strategists held ill intentions, and they used swaddled babies—a very particular choice. They must have been targeting him and his children, so he and Prince Jing had to be careful.

They were separated; though that initially seemed pretty bad, the guards responsible for guarding him should have realized that he was kidnapped by now. The bandits were dressed conspicuously, and Prince Jing would definitely find him soon.

He'd messed up again.

He hadn't trusted Prince Jing and had made his own rash decisions. But he had heard a baby's cry... If he were to do it all over again, he would probably make the same choices.

Li Yu couldn't imagine himself being so reckless in the past, but there was nothing he could do about it. He was worried about his children and couldn't just stand by—a father's instinct.

Fishy Punishment

L I YU WAS SAFE for now as long as he stayed in the river, but he couldn't just wait for Prince Jing to rescue him. If the bandits suddenly decided to deal with him, then it would be too late.

At least now he knew Dabao and the others weren't in the bandits' hands—plus, the bandits that caught him didn't know who he was, so they couldn't use him to threaten Prince Jing. Li Yu comforted himself with this silver lining, forcing himself to calm down a bit and consider the situation carefully.

He naturally wanted to escape. Manmers had nimble legs and feet; what if he made a break for it while the bandits were distracted?

As he was thinking, a bandit came over and Li Yu did his best to hide in the water.

When the bandit saw him, he swore a bit and reached for Li Yu. Li Yu didn't want to be caught, so he kicked out forcefully and managed to connect with the bandit's arm.

The bandit, hit unexpectedly, became furious and drew out the sharp knife he was carrying.

Li Yu started to regret not bringing a weapon with him when he left. He'd been too worried about the chaos outside and didn't think he'd be caught by the bandits—and as a Manmer, he couldn't hold anything anyway.

It would be nice if he had his tail...

He'd never wished for a tail so much. His legs were still a bit weaker than a tail, and though the scales on his upper body provided some protection, he wasn't sure if they'd be able to withstand a knife. And his short fins couldn't even reach far enough to slap people.

As soon as he'd thought that, at this critical moment, his body changed again. He'd been a Manmer just now, but his lower body suddenly felt light, as if he had his flowing tail. Li Yu gently flicked it to confirm the feeling. His tail really was there. Before, he'd stayed one or the other for a whole day, but he didn't think that on the third day the mission would...

...change up the rhythm like this!

Great timing! Let's handle the bandits first!

The bandit slashed at Li Yu, but Li Yu deftly hid in the water. When he couldn't catch him, the bandit rushed into the river angrily, and Li Yu hid his tail in a dark spot to trip him, making the bandit fall into the water.

Before he could get up, Li Yu lifted his tail up high and slapped it down on the bandit's forehead. The bandit didn't even have time to make a noise before he was knocked unconscious.

Li Yu quickly dragged the unconscious bandit behind a rock.

If another bandit came to check on him alone, he could deal with him. But if several came at once, he was just a single fish with a single tail and probably wouldn't be able to handle all of them. What's more, his tail could knock a bandit unconscious, but he couldn't escape with it. His goal was still to escape.

Wait. Li Yu had just thought about the advantages of legs when he realized his body had changed again. His tail had once more turned into legs.

...It was going to change that frequently?

When Li Yu was calm, he was quite clever.

He started to analyze all the times he'd transformed today.

The first time, he'd turned into a Manmer when he was impatient to run outside to see if it was Dabao crying.

The second time, he'd turned into a Merman when the urge to beat up the bandits was strong.

Just now, he thought about running away with his legs, and turned into a Manmer.

So, could he transform at will on the last day?

Then—he really wanted to transform into a human!

Li Yu waited for a long time, but nothing changed. His fins were still short and stubby, unable to hold or grasp.

It looked like he'd been wrong, then. When he first started the mission, he'd tried turning into a human, but it didn't work. Since the fish-scamming system had essentially banned the skill, it wouldn't just let him turn into a human so easily, right?

...If he couldn't turn completely into a human, then what about a fish?

This time, it was just a casual thought, but his line of sight suddenly dropped, and his height shrank.

Whoa! It seemed like he couldn't just absently think about turning into a fish, because he really would turn back into a fish!

This fish form was still the original size too! Li Yu couldn't believe his luck. The cloth and strips used to cover his body scattered and fell, and he escaped from them easily.

Turning into a fish was the best-case scenario right now. Li Yu hid in the aquatic plants and coldly observed the bandits. There was no way the bandits would guess that their hostage had turned into a fish and hidden in the water. They'd only think that their hostage had somehow escaped.

The bandits talked loudly among themselves for a bit, but they finally noticed that their comrade who'd gone to check on the hostage hadn't returned for some time.

They made their way over, loud and cursing...only to see him lying in the river. The cloth and strips that had been wrapped around the hostage were all still there, but the hostage himself was gone.

"What happened? Where'd the hostage go?!"

An ill-tempered bandit pulled up the unconscious man and slapped him a few times.

The bandit woke up, his eyes unfocused. He obviously hadn't seen a thing when he was knocked unconscious by Li Yu's tail.

"What are you just standing around for? Chase after him!" someone shouted, and the bandits all rushed out to find the hostage.

Li Yu held his breath and waited for a bit.

One bandit, with his face covered, didn't leave with the rest. Instead, he walked to the riverbank and searched around, but didn't find anything.

He didn't give up, though. He squatted and stuck his hand in the river. Li Yu tried to avoid his wandering hand and inadvertently got a look at it. There was a scar on the man's hand that looked a lot like an animal bite.

The man didn't find anything in the river. Just as he was about to stand up, a racket started coming from the run-down temple.

The bandits who had run out before came running back, shouting in panic, "Tactician, it's not looking good! Prince Jing is on his way over!"

So, this was the tactician. Li Yu swung his tail excitedly; His Highness had come so quickly to save him!

As soon as the bandits finished speaking, Prince Jing broke into the temple, covered in blood. A bandit gritted his teeth and rushed forward with a knife, but was immediately cut down by Prince Jing's sword.

Prince Jing had a murderous aura about him, and his eyes were terrifying. He cut down anyone in his way, and very soon, the bandits had all fallen.

Only the tactician was left standing.

He slowly raised his hand. Li Yu thought he was going to surrender, but without warning and quick as a flash, he threw a smoke bomb!

Your Highness, watch out! Li Yu was fearful; the smoke could render one unconscious. He'd suffered from it once before and was afraid that Prince Jing would too.

Luckily, Prince Jing reacted quickly and knocked the smoke bomb away with his sword.

The tactician drew his sword and stepped forward to battle with Prince Jing. Prince Jing fought for a while, but he couldn't gain the upper hand, which made Li Yu anxious. Why had Prince Jing come to save him without any of his guards?

The tactician parried Prince Jing's sword with his own, and when he got closer, threw a handful of white powder at him.

This bastard! How shameless!

Li Yu was so anxious that he wanted to turn into a Manmer and run into this disgraceful man to kill him.

Prince Jing swayed a bit and lifted his hand to cover his eyes. He seemed to have fallen for the trick.

The tactician coldly chuckled, knocked Prince Jing's sword aside, and then made a strange move to stab Prince Jing's calf. But although Prince Jing shouldn't have been able to see anything, in one fluid motion he dodged cleanly, swerved behind the tactician, pulled out a dagger from his sleeve, and stabbed it into the man's back.

Every move was accurate and merciless. The tactician's plot, the attempt to stab Prince Jing in the leg, and Prince Jing's dodge and counterattack all happened in a split second.

"Y-you didn't..." The tactician met Prince Jing's dark eyes and suddenly came to his senses. But before he could finish his sentence, Prince Jing twisted the dagger and sent him to meet his maker.

Li Yu had transformed into a Manmer again. He stood up from the river and rushed over like a cannonball to save his husband—only to find that Prince Jing was fine, and had even killed the tactician already...

Prince Jing had noticed him, though. With his lips pursed, he strode over to him, getting faster with each step.

Your Highness... Li Yu closed his eyes instinctively.

He wasn't afraid of Prince Jing because he'd killed the bandits. He was afraid that Prince Jing was mad at him. Li Yu had impulsively left the secret residence. Prince Jing must have gone through a lot to find him.

When he saw Prince Jing earlier, he noticed that Prince Jing's face was pale, the corners of his eyes were red, and he looked furious. Prince Jing had never hit him before, but Li Yu knew that he'd crossed the line this time.

Li Yu knew he was in the wrong. He turned into a Merman again to apologize. "Your Highness, I'm sorry..." But he wasn't used to standing on his tail, and almost collapsed to the ground.

None of his forms were what he wanted, and he felt a bit frustrated.

Prince Jing reached a hand out to help him up, then hugged him, despite everything.

Li Yu leaned on his shoulder, sniffled, and said apologetically, "I'm sorry, I shouldn't have left..."

But he really hadn't been able to ignore the children's cries—he was a father now, and it was a father's instinct. Even if he knew logically that he should trust Prince Jing and that it was most likely a scheme by the bandits, he couldn't just let it go. Sometimes, logic couldn't control emotions.

Prince Jing and his four children were his weak spot, the kind he would go crazy for, the kind where he only realized how ridiculous he was being after his impulsiveness passed. But if he had to do it again, he would make the same decision.

"Your Highness, it was my fault. You can punish me." Domestic violence was no good, but Li Yu thought he deserved it.

Prince Jing shook his head, hugged him with reddened eyes, and shoved something into his hand.

Li Yu looked at it. It was the charm Prince Jing had given him before.

When the bandits kidnapped him, the charm had fallen to the ground, and Prince Jing found it.

Li Yu gazed into Prince Jing's reddened eyes and lowered his own, embarrassed.

Prince Jing looked at him, suddenly took his hand, and wrote on his palm. *It's not your fault, it's mine. I was late.*

"No..." Li Yu hurriedly waved his hands. "Your Highness came in time to save me. It was my fault."

It was my fault that I didn't come back sooner and made you worry. It was my fault, Prince Jing wrote.

"Your Highness, let's not fight, okay?" Li Yu sniffled emotionally. "Why didn't you come back?"

Same reason as you. Prince Jing's lips turned up in a small curve.

Li Yu blinked and stared at him. After a moment, he understood—was Prince Jing late because he also thought the bandits had captured Dabao, and he had to go and deal with them?

"Your Highness, do you also lose control of your emotions and get carried away?" Li Yu asked.

Prince Jing nodded.

Li Yu thought to himself: *Then we really did make the same mistake.* With Prince Jing's explanation, Li Yu felt a lot better.

In the future, trust me. I'll take care of it, Prince Jing wrote.

Li Yu smiled and nodded. *Okay!*

Prince Jing didn't mention that he'd run into the head of the bandits and had a fight to the death. The golden swaddle in the bandit's arms hadn't tricked him, but when he returned to the residence, he'd discovered that Xiaoyu was gone. When he found the charm later, he realized that Xiaoyu had been knocked unconscious and kidnapped by the bandits. In that moment, he felt like he'd fallen into hell.

Though he seemed calm, he started killing immediately. All the bandits who tormented Xiaoyu needed to die!

He didn't know how much longer he would have gone on killing if he hadn't found Xiaoyu. Only when he saw Xiaoyu with his own eyes did the anger in his heart start to dissipate.

He really could understand the feeling of losing control that Xiaoyu described.

When they finished talking, Prince Jing took off his outer robe, wrapped it around Li Yu, covering his fish tail, and picked him up.

Everything was ready. The guards waiting outside of the rundown temple were now allowed inside to deal with the rest of the bandits. Prince Jing had entered the temple alone, with the guards outside tasked with killing any bandits that escaped.

While the guards were busy with their task, Li Yu and Prince Jing secretly returned to their original residence.

Li Yu and Prince Jing had just begun to watch the manor from a distance when Wang Xi spotted Prince Jing and intended to run over. But Prince Jing held out his hand to stop him while protecting Li Yu with his other hand. Wang Xi guessed that they were in the middle of something, so he knew better than to disturb them.

In their room, Ye-shushu, who was so bored he almost started growing grass on his head, was playing with the children.

Ye Qinghuan let Sibao sit in his lap and Erbao and Sanbao lay on his back while they all made faces at Dabao. Ye-shizi had sworn to make the serious, chubby little child laugh out loud. But the other three children started laughing first.

Dabao thought human life was very difficult and that he would rather be a fish...

Don't worry. Prince Jing held Li Yu's hand.

Li Yu understood what he meant. Prince Jing wanted him to see that the children were fine. He nodded, signaling that he understood.

After they watched the children for a bit, Prince Jing looked at Li Yu and raised his right hand.

Was he finally going to be punished? Li Yu bit his lip and didn't dodge.

Prince Jing's hand came down and patted his head softly.

Your Highness? Li Yu looked at him, confused.

With the punishment over, Prince Jing curled his lips into a smile.

Now, they still had to overcome the tribulation.

Protecting the Pet Fish

L I YU WASN'T actually sure how the mission was going.

On one hand, the bandits came suddenly and he rushed out in the middle, not caring about anything else. He'd only barely covered himself up, so what would he have done if someone saw him? But at the time, he couldn't care less.

On the other hand, there had been no notifications from the system. From his past experience, this meant the mission was still in progress and that he probably hadn't failed yet. The system had told him before that if he failed a main mission, he would turn into fish bones and fish ash. Since he could still transform into a Manmer and Merman whenever he wanted and was fine... Well, no news was good news.

Prince Jing put the charm around Li Yu's neck again and guarded him for the next couple of hours. During this time, Li Yu clung to him like an octopus, determined that even if the Heavenly Emperor came knocking, he wouldn't be tricked again. Prince Jing had only punished him by patting his head, which made him even more embarrassed.

If it hadn't been for him, Prince Jing would have been able to kill all the bandits in a jiffy. He wanted to make up for all the worry and burden he'd put on Prince Jing's shoulders.

"Oh, right, Your Highness. Don't forget to look into that tactician."

Li Yu had heard a lot about the tactician from the bandits. Other than the fact that his face was always covered and his name was a mystery, the tactician also strategically used children and golden swaddles as bait, which was different from the bandits' usual recklessness. He felt that the tactician was probably targeting him and Prince Jing.

It was well-known at the western border that Prince Jing had just gotten four little gongzi and that the golden swaddle was only for Dabao. Ordinary people wouldn't use such a color, and it was easy to find out this information if one was interested. The tactician must have asked around beforehand.

Li Yu's suspicion was logical. Prince Jing had thought the same thing.

The bandits had been almost completely wiped out in this fight, and the few that were left were the ones who hadn't ventured out. Prince Jing ordered his guards to torture and interrogate them to find out who the tactician was.

The tactician felt eerily familiar.

Throwing white powder at him and then attacking his leg when he thought he was blinded seemed unnecessary, but in the past, Prince Jing had always kept a dagger hidden in his boot in case of emergencies. He'd brought a dagger this time as well, but he'd placed it in his sleeve during his killing rampage. It was this dagger that he ended up counterattacking with.

The tactician had attacked the spot where he usually kept daggers. Was he trying to stop him from pulling it out?

In any case, the tactician must have been somewhat familiar with him, otherwise he wouldn't have used a baby as bait. But how did he know where the dagger should have been hidden? Apart from this time, he'd only used a dagger in public once before—during an assassination attempt where his eyes were affected, after which he was saved by Xiaoyu!

It was precisely because of that experience that Prince Jing had become more careful when fighting in close quarters. He'd been able to avoid the smoke bomb in time and even pretended his eyes were injured.

The tactician had used powder too, just like before. Since he also knew that Prince Jing had a habit of hiding daggers, Prince Jing had reason to believe that the tactician was the one who'd attacked him that night!

"Your Highness, I saw by accident that the tactician had a scar that looked like an animal bite on his hand..." Li Yu had a piece of evidence. He didn't know if it would be useful, but he might as well say it since he remembered it.

As soon as Li Yu mentioned it, Prince Jing immediately remembered that his attacker in the palace had kept covering his hand, as if he was injured.

Prince Jing wrote down the events of that day. Li Yu hadn't realized there were so many details behind Prince Jing's eye injury.

"Your Highness, are you thinking that the tactician is the same one who attacked you that day?" Li Yu asked, mulling over it.

Prince Jing nodded.

On the western border, his only enemies were the bandits. The tactician had only come to the western border a short while ago and wasn't previously a bandit—that meant he must be from the capital.

Li Yu thought about the scars on the man's hands and the other events of the day Prince Jing's eyes were injured. It couldn't be just a coincidence, right?

"Your Highness, remember the day Xiongfeng and I encountered a masked man? The one that tried to poison the fish food? Xiongfeng bit him...on the hand!"

When Li Yu mentioned Xiongfeng, Prince Jing visibly paused before he realized that Li Yu was talking about his experience as a fish, and that Xiongfeng was Ye Qinghuan's dog. Hearing Xiaoyu suddenly call out another name so familiarly had made Prince Jing a little uncomfortable, but he soon managed to turn his attention back to business.

The person that poisoned the food had been bitten by Ye Qinghuan's dog, and the tactician had a scar from an animal bite on his hand—it matched.

The tactician was from the capital and had run into both of them long ago, as the same person who poisoned the fish food and then turned around to attack him.

"Is it...the second prince?" Li Yu asked cautiously.

When the masked man poisoned the fish food, the second prince had been plotting against the House of Cheng'en and had asked someone to buy arsenic. Prince Jing and Wang-gonggong had thus concluded that the poisoner was sent by the second prince, who wanted to vent his anger.

Back then, the second prince had been under the most suspicion, but the situation was different now. After Prince Jing had dealt with him, the second prince was left confused and mentally broken; how could a person who was out of the running for such a long time still have an accomplice? And for it to be the same masked poisoner...?

It didn't make sense. Prince Jing had someone in the second prince's residence keeping an eye on him, and he knew exactly what state Mu Tianzhao was in, so it couldn't be him. That only left one possibility that they hadn't thought of before—that the poisoner had never been sent by the second prince in the first place, and the second prince had only taken the blame for the event.

If it wasn't the second prince, it could only be the third or sixth prince.

In the past, Prince Jing might have suspected the third prince, but right now it was hard for the third prince to even protect himself. The emperor had found out about someone passing messages between the western border and the capital under the third prince's name, and the third prince had suffered for it…

Wasn't that quite similar to the way the second prince had been framed?

Prince Jing thought for a while and then wrote a "six" that bled through the paper.

Xiaoyu had been right. Mu Tianxiao was his biggest enemy. And he'd been secretly plotting against him for so long.

"So, it was him…" Li Yu sighed lightly. Everything could be explained if the devious sixth prince was behind it.

The tactician was loyal to the sixth prince; the sixth prince was the only person with time to come out to the west to do something like this.

Before, the sixth prince had hidden behind the third prince, and before that it had been the second prince. If he made a move, nobody would think of this unwanted, invisible person. Now that the sixth prince got rid of the third prince and became "the emperor's only adult prince in the capital," he was in the limelight at court…but he was also no longer hidden.

He had no shield anymore.

Now that he knew it was the sixth prince's doing, Prince Jing wasn't going to hold back. A month later, the people at Prince Jing's manor in the capital received a secret letter from Wang-gonggong.

There was only one line on the letter: *Teach him a little lesson.*

They would have to find out who "him" was through other means. That was how secrets were kept in Prince Jing's manor.

These people would follow Prince Jing through hell and high water, but they'd been bored guarding the huge manor. Now that they finally had an order from their master, they immediately flew into action.

Soon afterward, Zheng Jing from the Ministry of Works reported to the emperor that the sixth prince had taken bribes while he was in charge of repairs for Zhongcui Palace and switched out quality materials for inferior ones.

Mu Tianxiao's expression twisted as he denied it, saying he was just following regulations.

Zheng Jing, filled with righteous indignation, countered him and took out the original blueprints of Zhongcui Palace. The Zhongcui Palace that the sixth prince had renovated looked the same, but it was clear that the wood used didn't match the plans. Instead, second-grade wood had been used, even for the beams.

The emperor was extremely shocked. He immediately ordered the removal of the beams from Zhongcui Palace for examination and called upon more than a dozen carpenters to inspect it—he was worried that someone might even be framing the sixth prince, so he chose the carpenters himself. But the carpenters confirmed that the wood didn't match the original plans.

In actuality, it wasn't the first time the repairs had differed from the blueprints. It could be explained logically if need be, but unfortunately, the numbers the sixth prince had reported to the emperor and the Ministry of Revenue were based on top-quality wood. The accounts had one price and reality had another—so where had the difference disappeared to?

As the supervisor of the project, the sixth prince had to have seen what wood was being used. That was part of his responsibility. He simply had no leg to stand on.

He'd just gotten married a month ago. Normally, a prince's wedding was held by the Ministry of Rites. The only exception was Prince Jing, who was in the western border and had the emperor's permission to hold his own wedding. All the other princes' weddings were carried out by the Ministry of Rites, and they were all quite similar. But it was said that the sixth prince had given his fiancée, Marquis Dingbei's di daughter, quite a few more gifts than usual, which were all added to her dowry and carried to the sixth prince's manor.

Marquis Dingbei loved to show off and had already made a ruckus about the gifts from his future son-in-law, the prince. Anyone with eyes could see which gifts were the sixth prince's; gold and silver jewelry were considered inconspicuous among the pearls, agate, coral, jade, and ivory, which all came in boxes of two or more. There were countless ancient books and paintings as well, even though the sixth prince had claimed that he couldn't even prepare a decent gift for the emperor's birthday.

And that was the problem. How could the sixth prince get his hands on so much money within a single year? With the prince's status and salary, he definitely wouldn't be able to afford all this. The sixth prince's mother was a palace maid, and her family was poor—that was why he'd always been so poor in the past.

Either he'd lied to the emperor during his birthday, or the money came from dishonest means.

Some court officials had suspected him before, but the sixth prince was the only adult prince by the emperor's side now and his status had risen rapidly, so these officials weren't inclined to offend the possible future emperor. Even Zheng Jing had to think twice before exposing him after he received evidence that the sixth prince had accepted bribes.

Zheng Jing was extremely familiar with the sixth prince's job in the Ministry of Works. When he learned that the wood used for renovating Zhongcui Palace was different from the wood in the plans and that the sixth prince had never mentioned such a thing, he knew something was fishy. It didn't take much thought to work out who benefitted from this.

Zheng Jing ordered people to follow the servants of the sixth prince, and then remembered that when Zhongcui Palace was being renovated, the sixth prince had sent servants to pawn off some rosewood boxes. Zheng Jing put in a lot of effort to retrieve them, only to find that they were heirlooms from the imperial merchant who was in charge of wood. That showed where the sixth prince's money was coming from.

Zheng Jing presented the pawn tickets and the pawned heirlooms as evidence. The emperor interrogated the sixth prince, and the sixth prince insisted that his confidant had done it behind his back. He said his confidant had taken the money for himself, deceived him while he was in charge of the project, and substituted the good wood with the bad. The sixth prince didn't suspect him because he trusted him—all in all, he managed to push the blame onto someone else completely.

The emperor's expression remained icy cold as he stared at the sixth prince. The sixth prince felt like he had nowhere to hide under the emperor's piercing gaze, but he could only grit his teeth and continue his innocent act.

The emperor finally accepted the sixth prince's explanation. But because of this, everyone around the sixth prince was replaced.

That was another story, though.

Li Yu was finally at the last stage of "Protecting the Pet Fish."

The long-awaited system notification sounded, but instead of notifying him whether the mission was completed or not, it asked him to enter the system and check himself. It was a little different from how the fish-scamming system usually worked, so Li Yu felt a bit anxious.

He was sort of scared that he'd failed the mission.

After making a brief explanation to Prince Jing, Li Yu entered the system at once.

The main mission "Postpartum Care" was still lit up, and the "Protecting the Pet Fish" step was followed by color-changing small squares that would determine the final outcome.

So, this step also required assessment?

<*This mission was for the tyrant to protect his pet fish,*> the system explained. <*If the transforming pet fish was found by others, then it would be a fail...*>

<*I covered myself, so they didn't see my real appearance,*> Li Yu replied. <*It shouldn't count as being discovered, right?*>

<*It doesn't count. But there were two bandits who were killed by the tyrant after they saw the user's Merman form. The mission can't be classified as a success or a failure. It can only be reassessed based on the tyrant's actions.*>

So dangerous. Li Yu breathed a sigh of relief. Thankfully, it didn't count as a failure; he'd been assessed several times before, and Prince Jing always did great. There shouldn't be a problem this time either.

Li Yu stared intently at the small square that would indicate the results. Green meant success, red meant failure. He remembered that the square had turned rainbow-colored once—what would it be this time?

The little square changed colors faster and faster until it suddenly stopped.

It was yellow.

...This was such an unexpected color!

Thinking about what he and Prince Jing had done during the mission, Li Yu couldn't help but complain. Did the system think he and Prince Jing were too horny?[13]

---

13   In Chinese, "yellow" is a euphemism for pornographic material; an erotic book might be referred to as a "yellow book."

Fish Calling His Name

THE SYSTEM COULD hear Li Yu's thoughts and was rendered speechless for a moment because of the user's derailment.

‹Yellow means a partial pass,› the system corrected him.

Otherwise, the user might imagine some strange things on his own.

Huh?

‹The tyrant used excessive violence, but it was to save the pet fish. Since the system cannot deny the tyrant's protection of the pet fish, that is the result of the assessment.›

It was as if this was a test—Prince Jing had answered well at first but accidentally spilled ink on the paper. Li Yu had expected that the system would balance the pros and cons, but instead, to his surprise, the system simply disregarded the part of the paper with ink on it and just graded what was left.

...Prince Jing was actually the one who made the system, wasn't he? Why was the system always giving him a pass?

But thankfully, a partial pass was still a pass.

‹Yes, that's true,› the system agreed. *‹However, the reward will also be affected, and you can only receive part of it. User, please accept the reward.›*

"Protecting the Pet Fish" was the last step of "Postpartum Care." The system tried to keep him guessing by having the reward appear as a large mystery box.

Li Yu had been assuming he would be able to turn into a human now, but the reward seemed different from what he had imagined. What would a partial reward be?

Could it be that he would turn back into a half-human, half-fish? Then he might as well continue being a fish!

The system comforted him, saying, *<Please relax, user.>*

Li Yu accepted the reward cautiously, expecting to be scammed.

A dazzling white light enveloped him. When it dissipated, two new scales appeared next to the jade scale that allowed him to transform into a human.

Li Yu glanced at the description. The two new skills were: "Turn into a Manmer" and "Turn into a Merman."

He paid special attention to the duration of all his skills. The duration had also changed—it was now twenty-four hours, a whole day. It could be used once a day and could also be canceled.

The addition of the two new skills meant that the system had given him the ability to transform into different forms. He could transform as he needed, and even though he hadn't turned fully back into a human, transforming once a day for an entire day was basically the same as being fully human again, as long as there weren't any accidents.

As for the other forms—he could turn into a fish to avoid danger, and since the Manmer and Merman forms wouldn't be used daily, he could have fun with them in the privacy of his room. A Merman was a different type of flavor, after all, and he wanted to try it out again.

Li Yu felt that these new skills were somewhat similar to the way he'd continuously changed forms on the third day of the "Protecting the Pet Fish" mission. During the mission, though, he changed forms too easily, and he'd almost lost control of it. The new skills required him to choose to press the jade scales to use them, which was much more reliable than changing at will.

Plus, the jade scales could only be used if Li Yu was the one to press them. Even though Prince Jing could see them, the skill wouldn't be triggered if he did it—to anyone else, it was basically a tattoo.

Two new skills and a change to the duration of the transformation were the first part of the mystery box of rewards.

The mystery box had a second set of rewards, represented by a cute fish-shaped symbol. After he collected the first batch of rewards, Li Yu found that other than the "main quest" and "side quest" categories, there was another "fish children status" that had appeared.

<What's this for? Does it have to do with Dabao and the others?> Li Yu asked curiously.

Though the children were considered part of Li Yu's team after they hatched, Li Yu hadn't experienced any benefits of being on a team. The children were just a few simple fish-shaped symbols, and Li Yu suspected that these were just decorations.

Since there was now a "fish children status," the system asked him to check it out. When it expanded, there were four fish children symbols. Li Yu thought about it for a moment, then pressed the golden symbol that represented Dabao. A transparent box popped up, showing Dabao sleeping as Wang-gonggong placed a small blanket on him.

...Was this...?!

Li Yu's little heart was pounding, and he happily clicked on Sibao.

The fish babies were usually doing the same thing at the same time—since Dabao was sleeping, so was Sibao. But Sibao was sleeping on Ye Qinghuan's stomach, with Erbao and Sanbao next to him. The three children and Ye Qinghuan were fast asleep.

Sibao was soundly sleeping, his mouth opening and closing repeatedly. He probably still thought he was a fish and was imagining blowing a bubble.

Li Yu checked on the fish children one by one. He couldn't look away.

The system took some time to explain: *‹The user can check the current status of the young fish here. It only works with the ones on your team and can be used up to three times a day for each young fish.›*

Li Yu's eyes lit up with excitement. Wasn't this the fish-scamming system's version of a baby monitor? One where you could see the fish babies!

He'd fallen into the bandits' trap because he couldn't ascertain the children's safety and acted impulsively. In the end, it was because communication in ancient times was inconvenient—really, the best you could do was shout. If it could be like the modern world he came from, with well-developed communication tools like a phone, where one could make a quick phone call to see if the children were safe, how could those criminals have taken advantage of him?

Though the system hadn't rewarded him with a phone, it gave him the opportunity to see his children whenever he wanted to. Even if there were only three chances a day for each child, it was the best reward for a fish father who often worried about his children.

...Many thanks, System.

From the bottom of his heart, Li Yu was grateful.

However, the system had more to say. *‹User, "Postpartum Care" is only partially completed. This was supposed to be the last of the main missions, but since it was only partially completed, the requirements for closing out the main line have not been met. After the system's assessment, a new main line of missions will be added to make up for it.*

The rewards that the user was not able to obtain can also be obtained after completing the new main missions.>

...He really wanted to take back his thanks.

He'd thought he would be able to become human after completing these missions and could finally escape the system, but he still had to complete Moe Pet System missions?!

<No matter what form you're in, the user is the user. This will definitely be the last main quest line; after completing these missions, there will be no more. The user can choose a side mission to complete as required, and failing the side mission will have no negative consequences.>

Okay, that sounded pretty good, actually.

Li Yu wanted to be rid of the system because he didn't want to complete missions all the time and worry about failing them. If he could just do missions at his leisure in the future, then it didn't really matter if the system was there or not.

Besides, he'd gotten used to the system talking to him and giving him weird power ups...

<Since there are still main missions, you should hurry up and assess,> said Li Yu mischievously. *<Don't get in the way of me completing missions and receiving rewards.>*

The system seemed bemused.

<Oh, and one more thing...> Li Yu asked, stammering a little, *<Can the system see Prince Jing and I when we...>*

When Li Yu was thinking clearly, he was actually pretty smart, even if his reaction time was a little slow, but he was only just considering this issue. There was no privacy with the system.

The system was just a system. Li Yu wasn't worried about it being awkward, but he was worried about Prince Jing's secrets being stored in the system. Would they end up turning into viral videos?

So, was he watching, "watching," or *watching*?

The system had nothing to say. The extremely ridiculous user was kicked out.

Li Yu "woke up" in a great mood.

He lost consciousness every time he entered the system, and this time, he'd entered as a Merman. When he came to, he was sitting in Prince Jing's arms, carefully protected.

The Merman form's tail was easily dehydrated, so Li Yu impatiently turned back into a human. But his timing was a bit off. Originally, his tail had been cutely wrapped around Prince Jing, but when it turned into legs, it was in a weird position that made his imagination run wild.

Li Yu blushed and lowered his legs from around Prince Jing's waist. Then he looked up to meet Prince Jing's eyes.

Prince Jing smiled and touched Li Yu's face. *What's wrong?*

Li Yu hugged him and nuzzled up to him, unable to control his happiness. "Your Highness, I have good news for you. The duration for my human form has been extended, and after one more tribulation, I can return..."

Ah! It suddenly occurred to him that this explanation wasn't quite right. No matter what progress he'd made with the missions, he was still just a carp spirit to Prince Jing. A carp spirit would want to turn into a human completely, not *return* to human form. He couldn't get that wrong!

Li Yu paused and tried again. "Next time. If I pass through the next tribulation, I'll be a human forever."

Prince Jing smiled slightly and nodded. *All right. I'll protect you during the next tribulation too.*

Li Yu couldn't help but smile. "I'm so lucky you're here, Your Highness," he said, and let out a heartfelt sigh.

It was all right even if he had to do one more round of missions.

His missions would be completed one day, but he didn't know where he'd be now if not for Prince Jing.

Li Yu scooted closer and pulled Prince Jing in. The atmosphere was just right, and the fish was about to kiss him. He exaggeratedly pouted his lips out and kissed Prince Jing's cheek. It was a kiss as light as a feather, making one's heart ripple like water.

Prince Jing raised his eyebrows, his lips moving.

"Do you want to say something, Your Highness?" Li Yu asked. He noticed that Prince Jing's expression was a little different.

Prince Jing glanced at him quickly and hesitantly took out a note.

...He made a random guess, but there really was something?

Li Yu took the note. He was curious about what Prince Jing wrote, but he only saw Prince Jing's name, *Tianchi*, on it.

"...I know your name, Your Highness—"

Why did His Highness want him to see this?

Seeing that he still didn't understand, Prince Jing took Li Yu's reddened lips into his and bit down softly when he said "Your Highness."

Li Yu, confused as he was teased, said again, "Your Highness..."

Prince Jing sidled up to him before he finished speaking, and Li Yu got bitten again.

"Your..."

Prince Jing hugged him and bit once more.

Li Yu didn't dare speak anymore and blinked. Was he not allowed to say "Your Highness"? He was going to be kissed every time he did?

Prince Jing, seeing that he was starting to understand, handed him the note with his name on it again. Li Yu suddenly got it.

"Y-Your...no, are you asking me to call you by your name?"

Prince Jing nodded seriously.

He finally got it right!

Tears sprang to Li Yu's eyes. Prince Jing wanted him to call him by his name—this was perfectly normal, since they were married now. It seemed a bit distant to be calling him "Your Highness" all the time.

Prince Jing didn't want him to be distant.

"Then...Tianchi." Li Yu smiled shyly. Prince Jing's name was quite tasteful, so he couldn't help saying it again after the first time. "Tianchi!"

Prince Jing responded. A smile spread across his face, and he held Li Yu's hand.

It was such a small thing; why not write it out?

Because he wanted Xiaoyu to realize it himself. He didn't want to ask for it.

If he could say Xiongfeng's name so easily, then why not his too?

Fish Babies Write
a Letter

THE LAST LINE of main missions still hadn't been revealed yet, so Li Yu didn't have any tasks he had to run around completing. Prince Jing's manor was managed well by Wang Xi, and he didn't have much to do as the consort. He just had to educate the children every day and give Prince Jing some ideas from time to time. From this angle, life was still the way he liked it and hadn't changed just because he became a consort.

This was the kind of life he always wanted, and it was also a result of Prince Jing's doting.

Prince Jing did whatever he asked. Quanjude Roast Duck Restaurant was opened for him simply because he said he wanted to eat it; now, it had become a famous delicacy known far and wide, and even the Duke of Cheng'en's son from the capital praised it wholeheartedly.

The days passed quickly. With Prince Jing's hard work, the locusts, which was a major threat on the western border, had been eradicated, and another major threat, the bandits, were too dead or injured to cause any more trouble.

The western border was now stable, and there was much less chaos near the border.

In the blink of an eye, the little fish babies turned one hundred days old.

Prince Jing held a grand celebration for them, just like a wedding. There was a huge banquet, and numerous guests were invited— a lively scene.

After one hundred days, Ye Qinghuan came to say goodbye.

Ye-shizi had come to visit partially because the House of Cheng'en wanted him to, and he'd asked the emperor especially for the time off. He'd helped Prince Jing a lot during the hundred days he'd been here, but since his wife was pregnant and the bandits Prince Jing was dealing with were pretty much gone, it was time to leave.

Before he left, Prince Jing had a deep talk with Ye-shizi and told him that he wanted to write a letter of gratitude for him to bring back. Ye Qinghuan had a good relationship with Prince Jing. He agreed readily.

When Prince Jing was writing the letter, Li Yu and Wang Xi came to visit with two children each in their arms. The human-shaped fish children had accepted reality and were living happily—except for Dabao, who still had his reservations. They ate and slept, slept and pooped every day. Dabao, who just wanted to grow up, felt himself going numb.

No matter how unhappy he was, all he could do was cry. But if he cried too much, his fish dad would start to feed him milk again, and Dabao hated drinking milk from the bottom of his heart. He missed the fragrant, sweet peach blossom pastry dearly.

Unfortunately, he'd heard the wet nurse say that babies needed to drink milk for six months before they could eat other things. Dabao used all his fingers and toes and still didn't manage to count six months, and he felt like the peach blossom pastry was getting farther and farther away.

He didn't really get it, and he couldn't understand why his younger brothers accepted it so readily, especially Sibao. That fish was never worried.

Dabao was right next to Sibao at the moment, and Sibao, who was being held by their fish dad as well, was currently munching on his hands. Dabao admired him for that, and his baby instincts made him want to lift his own chubby fingers and shove them in his mouth.

No, no, Dabao told himself repeatedly. *I'm a responsible older fish brother and can't eat my hands like my younger brother is doing.*

But...my mouth is itchy and I want to chew...

Dabao, the most proper baby in the world, was holding himself back so much that he almost shed a tear.

Sibao was enjoying munching away when he found Dabao looking at him. The naive Sibao smiled lazily and warmly at his older brother, smeared his drool all over Dabao's face, and went back to chewing on his fingies.

Dabao wanted to cry. Sibao's saliva was so gross, but why did he also want to do the same thing?

Li Yu had been watching them secretly for a long time as he held them in his arms, and he couldn't hold back his laughter. When he saw Prince Jing writing the letter, he had an idea. "Dabao, Erbao, Sanbao, Sibao, why don't we write a letter to Grandpa too?"

The fish babies didn't know what an emperor was yet. Li Yu always called the emperor "Grandpa" in front of them, because that's exactly who he was to them.

Dabao nodded quickly, excited. It'd been such a long time since his fish dad called out to him for something other than nursing! Sibao was a bit confused and didn't know what writing a letter meant, but he liked his fish dad, so he'd do whatever he wanted him to. He nodded along with Dabao.

"Tianchi, is that all right?" Li Yu asked, tugging on Prince Jing's sleeve.

Prince Jing loved hearing Xiaoyu call him by his name. He smiled and got out of his seat; Li Yu put the two babies on the table as the other babies in Wang Xi's arms cried and fussed, wanting to reunite with the other two.

The children's small bodies wrinkled the high-quality rice paper placed on the table, but Prince Jing, the paper's owner, wasn't distressed by this at all. The children couldn't touch the ink next to the paper, but Prince Jing was astute; he'd had the kitchen mix together some dark, harmless juice for them to use.

Li Yu, who had checked with the wet nurse beforehand, applied the juice on the babies' hands. He'd heard that the emperor would often ask after the children, so Li Yu thought that he might appreciate something the children made themselves. The emperor had also conferred titles onto all four of the children, so they already had salaries. They should give thanks to the emperor for the fact that they'd never have to worry about money.

Instead of pondering over what gift to send in the children's name, why not let them write a letter with their father? It was a nice idea.

The children were placed together on the table and greeted each other with cries of "Aaahhh!"

Their hands were smeared with the "ink," and they were all seated on the paper. There was no need to tell them what to do, they all got started immediately.

When Dabao was still a tiny, tiny fish, he'd seen a lot of words when he followed his father. Dabao thought about it and determined he could probably write the word "Da" out. He started to concentrate on writing.

Erbao and Sanbao didn't know what they should do, but when they saw Dabao begin, they followed his example and started to "write" the same word.

Dabao stopped immediately. "Aaaahhh!" *No!* This was something that only belonged to Dabao! The younger brothers couldn't write it!

Dabao used his hands and feet to write "Er" and "San" hurriedly, then pushed it to his younger brothers.

After a moment of contemplation, Erbao and Sanbao decided they didn't like it. They still thought their elder brother's "Da" looked nicer. "Aaaahhhh!" *We want older brothers!* Erbao widened his eyes, like little glass beads, and Sanbao reached out his chubby fingers. Their wails mingled together.

Li Yu almost couldn't breathe from laughter. He turned Dabao, Erbao, and Sanbao away from each other so they could each do their own thing. What kind of proper letter could such tiny babies write? The most they could do was probably a handprint.

Meanwhile, Sibao felt sleepy as soon as he saw the rice paper, and was now sleeping face down on the paper with his butt in the air.

...Which one of them did this child resemble?!

In the end, Dabao finally "wrote" the "Da" he remembered, and Erbao and Sanbao both left a handprint. Sibao was still sleepy, and accidentally left half of his face for his grandpa because he got "ink" on his cheek.

Li Yu carefully blew the children's letters dry, folded them, and handed it all to Prince Jing. "The emperor won't be angry, right?" he asked, worried.

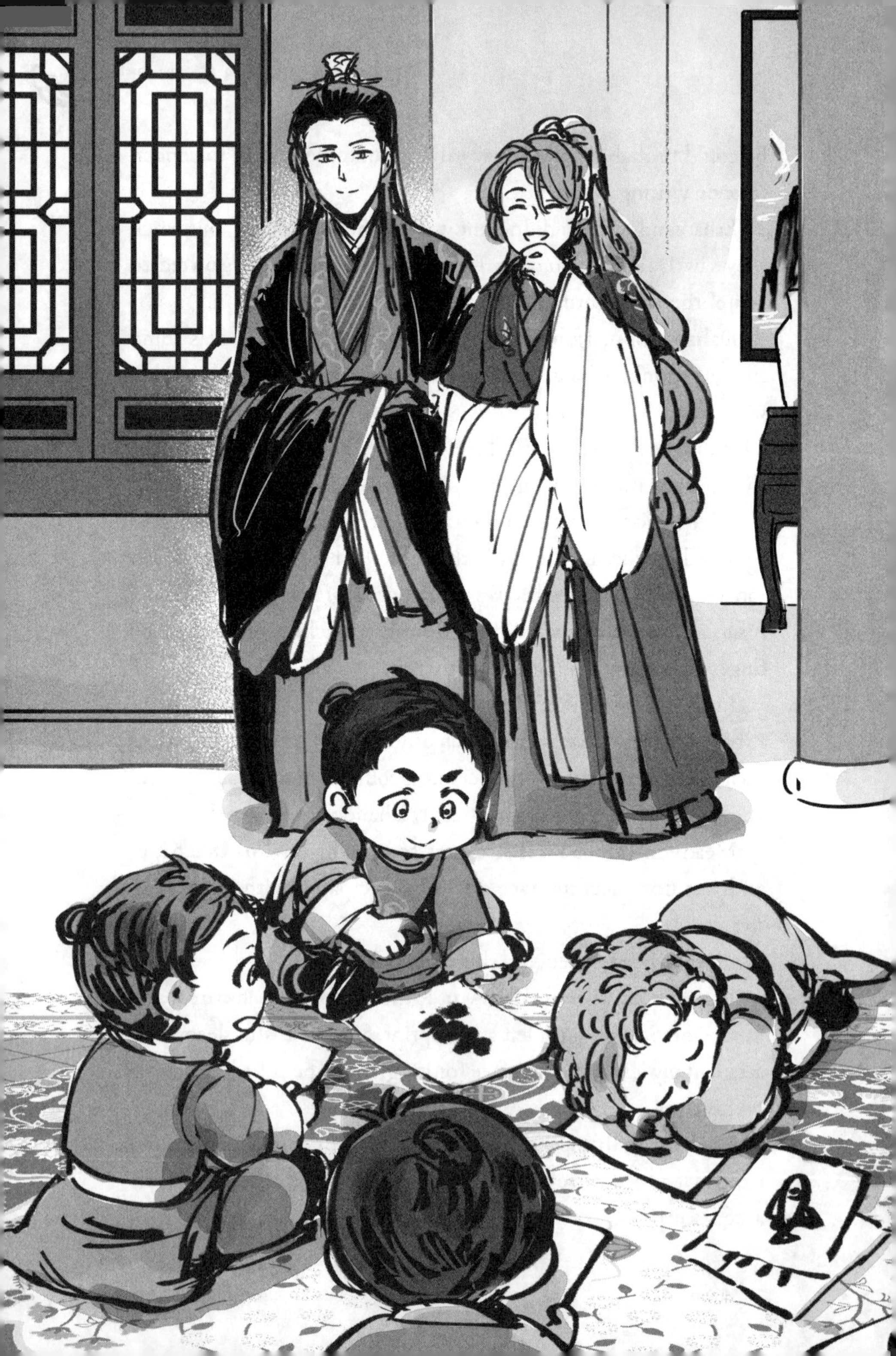

Prince Jing smiled and shook his head. This fish. He was the one who came up with the idea, but he was also the one worrying about it afterward.

Prince Jing put the children's "letters" with his letter of thanks in a large envelope and entrusted this huge responsibility to Ye Qinghuan.

This envelope reset Ye Qinghuan's understanding of "a letter." Prince Jing said it was a letter of gratitude—why was it so thick? He'd always thought Prince Jing was cold and didn't care to please the emperor. Who knew he'd write so much? He was obviously as talkative as Wang-gonggong!

Li Yu prepared a gift for the princess of Jinjue too and asked Ye Qinghuan to give it to her. The princess was pregnant, but he and Prince Jing were far away in the west. Li Yu probably wouldn't be able to congratulate her in person when the child was born, so he wanted to send gifts to her and the child in advance.

He had a craftsman melt the small golden bracelets Dabao and the others wore into a pretty lock charm.[14]

There was probably no lack of children's accessories at the House of Cheng'en, but Li Yu had heard from Auntie Xu that things that children had worn were touched with good fortune. Since his four children were safe and healthy, combining the four bracelets together would give four times the fortune. To a pregnant woman, there was nothing more important than the safety of the mother and child.

Ye Qinghuan accepted the gift on the princess's behalf, his eyes a little red. "Thank you, cousin-in-law." He bowed with full respect.

---

14 Lock charms (长命锁) are common gifts for children, meant to "lock" their safety and good luck to them.

Ye Qinghuan and the princess both knew Li Yu, so they usually called him Li-gongzi or Consort. The sudden "cousin-in-law" surprised him, and he realized that it meant Ye Qinghuan recognized him as part of the family. Li Yu responded happily.

Prince Jing glanced at Ye Qinghuan. This younger cousin of his that he always looked at with slight disdain was finally a bit more pleasing to the eyes.

Ye Qinghuan hurried back to the capital. When the emperor received news from Prince Jing—or more precisely, when he received the letter that came with several more pages of rice paper that the children "wrote," he was so excited that his hands started trembling.

Prince Jing's children were only one hundred days old. Were they able to write letters already? Curiosity piqued, the emperor unfolded the "letters."

The first piece of paper had a crooked word that looked like "Oa."

The second and third pieces of paper had little handprints.

And the fourth one...

The emperor couldn't control the smile that rose to his lips. Wasn't this just a little baby's face? With a few drops of saliva too.

He'd never met Prince Jing's children, but he could sense their vivid personalities through these papers.

"Luo Ruisheng, what do you think this means?" The emperor pulled out the first piece of paper again and showed it to Luo Ruisheng.

Luo Ruisheng looked at it for a bit and shook his head.

The emperor read Prince Jing's letter again. At the end he mentioned that these four papers were written by the children. The emperor realized that the first piece of paper must have come from Prince Jing's eldest son, who he'd already named as heir.

Luo Ruisheng immediately said, "Your Majesty, I do not know what the little shizi meant when he wrote this word, but in all my life so far, I have never seen a child start writing so young. The little shizi will definitely be well educated in the future!"

Luo Ruisheng knew the emperor well, so he started praising Prince Jing's heir as soon as he opened his mouth. Of course, he wasn't permitted to casually speak about the royal grandson's future, lest he imply anything about anyone taking the throne from the emperor, but there was nothing wrong with saying he'd be well educated!

This resounding flattery hit the emperor in the right spot, and he felt at peace as he admired the "Oa." He stared at it for a long time; he even wanted to ask Luo Ruisheng to frame it and hang it in Qianqing Palace.

Prince Jing's shizi was so promising that it made the emperor think of the seventh and eighth princes in the palace.

The two princes were still studying in the imperial study room. The emperor paid a visit himself to encourage them gently and give them a lot of homework, which included writing. An emperor's son couldn't do worse than an emperor's grandson who wasn't even a year old yet, right?

The little princes were suddenly burdened by homework and had no idea why.

Not only was the emperor pleasant and cheerful to the seventh and eighth princes, but he also decided to choose the two most excellent students from the Hanlin Academy as future teachers for Prince Jing's children. Prince Jing had originally chosen a couple of teachers from the capital, but they weren't going to be needed anymore.

News of the emperor's preparations made its way to the west. Li Yu was a bit speechless when he heard; wasn't the emperor doting on these little babies too much?

"Tianchi, what does the 'Oa' that Dabao wrote mean?" Li Yu couldn't help but quietly ask Prince Jing. "Why does the emperor like it so much?"

Prince Jing shook his head. He didn't know either.

When he heard his fathers talking, Dabao looked at his tender little hands and felt sorry for himself. Oa? He'd clearly written "Da," for Dabao.

Fish Children Kissy

THE WORD DABAO had "written" so carefully turned out to be wrong. Dabao was unhappy.

Even the peach blossom pastries his fish dad put to the side while he was nursing didn't seem so fragrant anymore.

Li Yu cared for the children very much, so he quickly realized Dabao was feeling off. He didn't know why, but usually spending time with his brothers helped him feel better when he was in a bad mood. Thus, Li Yu gathered the fish children in hopes that Erbao, Sanbao, and Sibao could make Dabao feel better.

Erbao, Sanbao, and Sibao surrounded Dabao, who turned his chubby face away with tears in his eyes. His three brothers all had the same thought: *Why is he unhappy?*

Even though they looked like babies, they were fish brothers who had been together for a long time and were very close to each other.

Sibao remembered that when he felt sad, his fish dad would use his mouth to rub him, which made him very happy. Fish Daddy said this was a kissy and that he should kiss the people he liked. Sibao liked his fathers and his brothers, so he could give his brother a kissy to make him happy!

I got it! "Aaahhh," Sibao yelled, making Erbao and Sanbao look over.

Sibao gave them a demonstration, puckering his lips and smacking a kiss on Dabao's cheek.

Dabao wasn't sure what had just happened. But Erbao and Sanbao understood. They puckered their lips as well and moved closer.

Dabao was so terrified that his voice broke. "Aaahhhhh!" *What are you guys doing?!*

Smooch, smooch!

"Aaahhh!" *Save me!*

Dabao was continuously baptized by the love of his fish brothers, and he couldn't hold it together anymore.

Erbao and Sanbao were all right with just kissing him, but Sibao was a weird one. Not only did he kiss his older brother, he wanted his older brother to kiss him back—he'd keep kissing Dabao until he did!

Dabao, who was kissed so much by Sibao that his face was covered with drool, couldn't bear it anymore and gave in. *Isn't it just a kissy? I-I can do it too!*

Dabao's eyes were filled with tears that threatened to spill over. He hugged Sibao with his little arms and little legs, then gave him a little kiss.

Li Yu was watching the entire time. "Ha ha ha, as expected of Sibao!"

Sibao was able to accomplish what Ye Qinghuan couldn't!

After this incident, Li Yu found that Dabao had become much livelier than before. In the past, he usually stayed alone; he was just a baby, but he was always straight-faced and didn't mingle with the others. Now, whenever he saw the other children, his arms and legs would start dancing.

Gege, we're coming to kissy! said Erbao, Sanbao, and the happy Sibao.

Dabao disdainfully shouted, "Aaaah!" *Get away!*

The boys were in chaos. "Look, Tianchi," Li Yu said to Prince Jing, feeling accomplished. "Children have to be together to be happy."

The corner of Prince Jing's mouth twitched. From what he could see, Dabao wasn't happy. But he wasn't going to reveal that. The most important thing was to make Xiaoyu happy.

Mu Tianxiao was impeached for accepting bribes. He never committed any of the crimes himself, though, and just like every other time, someone under him took the blame instead. The emperor couldn't punish him directly but had switched out all the people around him. That left a bad taste in his mouth.

Mu Tianxiao had acquired his current position by betraying the third prince, so he never trusted his subordinates too much. He had very, very few trustworthy confidants. On the positive side, it was hard for secrets to be leaked, but on the other hand, with this single decree from the emperor, he no longer had anyone he could actually utilize.

And it was all just because he desperately wanted to win over the Marquis of Dingbei of the Yue family. The Marquis of Dingbei's family and the House of Cheng'en were both centuries-old families. The Marquis was extremely hard to please, and he rarely helped his relatives out or did favors for them. The only person he doted on was his daughter, so Mu Tianxiao wanted to lock down the marriage. The Marquis of Dingbei and his daughter were true nobility and had a lot of experience, so Mu Tianxiao couldn't win him over with a few petty tricks. He had to take some risks to convince Marquis Dingbei to help him.

His siphoning money from repairing Zhongcui Palace shouldn't have been discovered so easily. Once everything was built and painted over, nobody would take it apart to look at it. So, when the wood merchant contacted him through his connections and wanted to do business with him, Mu Tianxiao knew that his opportunity to make a fortune had arrived.

Additionally, he had subordinates who wanted to kiss up to him. This marriage hadn't been easy for Mu Tianxiao to achieve—who could have predicted that Zheng Jing would find out, even though everything was so secretive? Zheng Jing even reported him to the emperor to get him impeached—wasn't he afraid of offending him?!

Mu Tianxiao remembered that when he was ordered to renovate Zhongcui Palace, Zheng Jing had taken him under his wing like he had for Prince Jing. He was kind and caring toward him, so Mu Tianxiao had assumed that he was someone who had a discerning eye—but he was actually quite ruthless, and stabbed him in the back. Mu Tianxiao wanted to get back at Zheng Jing, but firstly, he didn't have anyone to use, and secondly, Zheng Jing was an upright person. He was like a sheet of metal—he didn't have any weak spots for Mu Tianxiao to sink his teeth into.

But no matter how ruthless Zheng Jing was, the emperor was more so. The decree the emperor issued seemed to preserve a lot of the sixth prince's dignity, since he wasn't given most of the blame and wasn't beaten, but the subordinates he had worked so hard to get were all gone.

Mu Tianxiao hated the emperor, and he hated Zheng Jing even more. But this type of hate was the same as his background: feeble and powerless. He would rather have the emperor beat him a couple dozen times more.

"Tianxiao, it's just fewer people serving you." Mu Tianxiao's mother, Consort Zhang, comforted him gently. "Don't feel so bad. Why don't I give you some more maids?"

Since Mu Tianxiao's status had improved, there were people who had started trying to cling to Consort Zhang, so she had much more confidence when speaking to her son now.

But her words almost made Mu Tianxiao laugh.

He couldn't help but tremble slightly. How funny. His mother could wear silver and gold because of him, but she didn't know what he needed the most. Meanwhile, Empress Xiaohui had been dead for twenty years, but she was still able to protect Prince Jing. The House of Cheng'en, Empress Xiaohui's family, all supported Prince Jing so much—this was the difference between an empress and a palace servant!

Mu Tianxiao never blamed his mother outright, but he told Consort Zhang to be careful what she did. He couldn't let the emperor find any further fault with him.

Consort Zhang agreed. With the second and third prince as examples, at most she was just a bit more imposing behind closed doors. In front of the emperor, she was still a well-behaved quail. However, even though Consort Zhang agreed to what Mu Tianxiao mentioned, she didn't think his caution was all that necessary. Right now, who else other than her son could the emperor choose?

Mu Tianxiao had no manpower and couldn't act recklessly. He'd always suspected that there was something going on with Prince Jing's children too, and he doubted Prince Jing's consort. Mu Tianxiao had sent a confidant to the west to investigate, who'd told him that he had a plan to capture the consort, but there'd been no further news.

Mu Tianxiao was afraid that this confidant had disappeared, but he still hoped that he would actually find something to hold over Prince Jing, so he waited every day.

But, with a start, he realized that he had no time to relax when the emperor was visiting the imperial study and treating the seventh and eighth princes differently.

Apart from Prince Jing, the emperor still had two younger sons who could ascend to the throne.

Mu Tianxiao wanted the two younger princes to lose the emperor's favor somehow, but all of his confidants were gone, and he couldn't find anyone else to help him. Even though the two princes were still young and wouldn't be hard to deal with, he had no way to touch them himself.

Just as he was mulling the issue over, someone came to him.

"Your Highness, I can help you and solve your problems." Chu Yanyu's misty eyes peeked out from behind the dangling veil of his bamboo hat, unblinking.

Mu Tianxiao was quite shocked when he saw him.

After Prince Jing had left the capital for the western border, the people residing in Qingxi Garden in his manor were each asked individually what they wanted to do. The ones who wanted to leave were allowed to leave.

That was when Chu Yanyu left Prince Jing's manor.

He'd been with Mu Tianxiao since he was a child and had nowhere else to go. He went to the sixth prince's manor to find him.

Mu Tianxiao had let him stay, but at that time, he'd learned that he was about to get married, so even though Chu Yanyu was right in front of him, he didn't get too close to him. And Chu Yanyu acted like he didn't exist. The only thing he did was run right up to Mu Tianxiao before he was leaving to meet his in-laws, to ask if Mu Tianxiao was really getting married.

Mu Tianxiao had nothing to hide. When he'd shoved Chu Yanyu into Prince Jing's manor, Chu Yanyu should have known then that they would never be able to openly be together before the sixth prince reached his goals.

The sixth prince had promised him that he would have a place for Chu Yanyu by his side, but it wouldn't be as his lawfully wedded partner. Even if the wife's position was vacant, it still wouldn't be Chu Yanyu. Mu Tianxiao desperately needed an heir.

Mu Tianxiao was worried that Chu Yanyu would do something outlandish, but Chu Yanyu had just stood there in a daze and then walked away crestfallen.

Even now that the sixth prince's consort had officially married into the family, she didn't know there was a Chu-gongzi in this manor.

"You... Yu-er, what are you saying? How are you going to help me?" Mu Tianxiao asked carefully, slightly expectant. Chu Yanyu was smart, and Mu Tianxiao knew he'd always had a place in Chu Yanyu's heart, ever since they were children. He trusted Chu Yanyu. The previous lack of progress at Prince Jing's manor was because Prince Jing had a strange personality—it couldn't be blamed on Chu Yanyu.

Chu Yanyu paused. "You need someone," he said. "I can be your eyes and support in the harem."

For real?!

Mu Tianxiao was ecstatic. His mother was slow witted and wasn't favored, so if he had another form of support in the harem, that would be better than having a lot of subordinates.

"But you just came back from Prince Jing's. Is that...possible?" Mu Tianxiao asked tentatively.

"Your Highness, you know that I have no relationship with Prince Jing." Chu Yanyu's voice was soft, tinged with the aggrievement that only existed between lovers.

He had grown sallow and skinny at Prince Jing's manor; not pretty at all. But now that he was at the sixth prince's manor, he had returned to his previously alluring self...

Mu Tianxiao's heart thudded as he held one of Chu Yanyu's hands. "I mean, you were at Prince Jing's manor before and now you want to become an imperial concubine. Isn't that asking too much of you? Yu-er, if you don't want to, you must tell me. You know I'm reluctant to part with you."

Chu Yanyu shook his head gently. "I only have one wish now, and that is to help you fulfill your goals. Please allow me."

Chu Yanyu started to kneel as he said this, but Mu Tianxiao stopped him.

He didn't doubt Chu Yanyu's feelings for him—otherwise, why would he have agreed to enter Prince Jing's manor in the past?

If Chu Yanyu could enter the palace...

Mu Tianxiao's thoughts raced. Gorgeous women couldn't compare to Chu Yanyu's looks; and he would be the most beautiful in the emperor's harem as it was right now. As long as Chu Yanyu was willing to do it, Mu Tianxiao felt quite confident in him.

Mu Tianxiao made up his mind. He helped Chu Yanyu up, warmly saying, "Come, get up. I'll leave it to you from now on, then."

Chu Yanyu nodded. Through the veil, Mu Tianxiao couldn't see the slightly cryptic smile spreading across his face. "It's my duty to help you, Your Highness." Chu Yanyu had been waiting for this moment for a long time.

Mu Tianxiao was clever in placing Chu Yanyu. He took him to the palace as a bodyguard first, and Consort Zhang, as a maid who'd climbed into the emperor's bed while he was drunk, had some unique tricks.

Shortly after, during the Double Ninth Festival, the emperor drank a little too much and stayed nearby in Consort Zhang's Yongfu Palace. The next day, there was a new person with charming looks that appeared in the palace: Noble Lord Chu.

"Ch-Chu Yanyu is—a male imperial concubine now?!"

When Wang Xi brought up the subject lightheartedly, Li Yu was shell-shocked. Could there be anything more bizarre than that? In the original book, there was one top and one bottom. Li Yu had married the top and had a bunch of fish children, but the bottom went to be together with the top's father? To become...the top's stepfather?

No, a male concubine was still a concubine, so he couldn't be his stepfather. Ah, Li Yu didn't know what to call him anymore.

"Wasn't he in the manor? How did he get into the palace?" Li Yu was stunned for a while before it occurred to him to ask this question.

Li Yu had originally thought that when they returned, Chu Yanyu would have been living in the manor for a whole year, so Prince Jing's anger would've subsided. Then, he could ask Prince Jing to let Chu Yanyu go. But he never expected that Chu Yanyu would become an imperial concubine—how did he do that?

Wang Xi glanced at Prince Jing's expression and said, "When His Highness and the consort left the capital, a lot of people in the manor were let go."

So that was what happened. Prince Jing had allowed him to leave. Chu Yanyu hadn't escaped.

Li Yu understood that Chu Yanyu didn't have any future in Prince Jing's manor, so after he was released, he would definitely go to the lover of his dreams, the sixth prince. So how had he ended up in the palace?

"His Majesty got drunk at the banquet, and the sixth prince happened to go to Consort Zhang's palace with his guards," Wang Xi said vaguely. "I heard that Noble Lord Chu was bestowed the title in Yongfu Palace."

Wang Xi's words were veiled, but Li had gleaned his meaning. Wasn't that just...the sixth prince giving Chu Yanyu to the emperor?

Mu Tianxiao was still the same scumbag after a whole year. Was Chu Yanyu happy about that?!

...Oh, he probably was. After all, Chu Yanyu's logic was different from other people's; he'd entered Prince Jing's manor for the sixth prince too.

Perhaps to Chu Yanyu, there wasn't much difference between belonging to Prince Jing or belonging to the emperor?

Li Yu's thoughts ran wild, until he noticed that the children were listening—especially Sibao, whose eyes were flickering. Li Yu knew that they could understand and quickly covered their ears.

Getting drunk and bestowing favor on someone... Grandpa was a bit irresponsible. The children shouldn't be led astray by this.

At the same time, Li Yu was also worried about Prince Jing.

He wasn't afraid that Prince Jing had feelings for Chu Yanyu— that was impossible—but he was worried that this would affect Prince Jing's opinion of the emperor. As far as Prince Jing was concerned, and in the eyes of many others, the emperor held deep feelings for Empress Xiaohui. Would Prince Jing think that the emperor had failed his mother?

With these thoughts in mind, Li Yu forgot about covering the children's ears. He held Prince Jing's hand and said, "Tianchi, don't feel bad."

...The emperor had an entire harem; why would Prince Jing care? He didn't want to comment on the emperor's decision. Purely to cooperate with Li Yu comforting him, the corners of Prince Jing's mouth pulled downward, but his eyes were full of deep affection.

Li Yu held his arm and casually said, "Don't read too much into it. Why don't we try out the Merman tonight?" He wanted to change things up so that the prince wouldn't be sad.

Prince Jing's lips curved, and he nodded obediently. *Okay.*

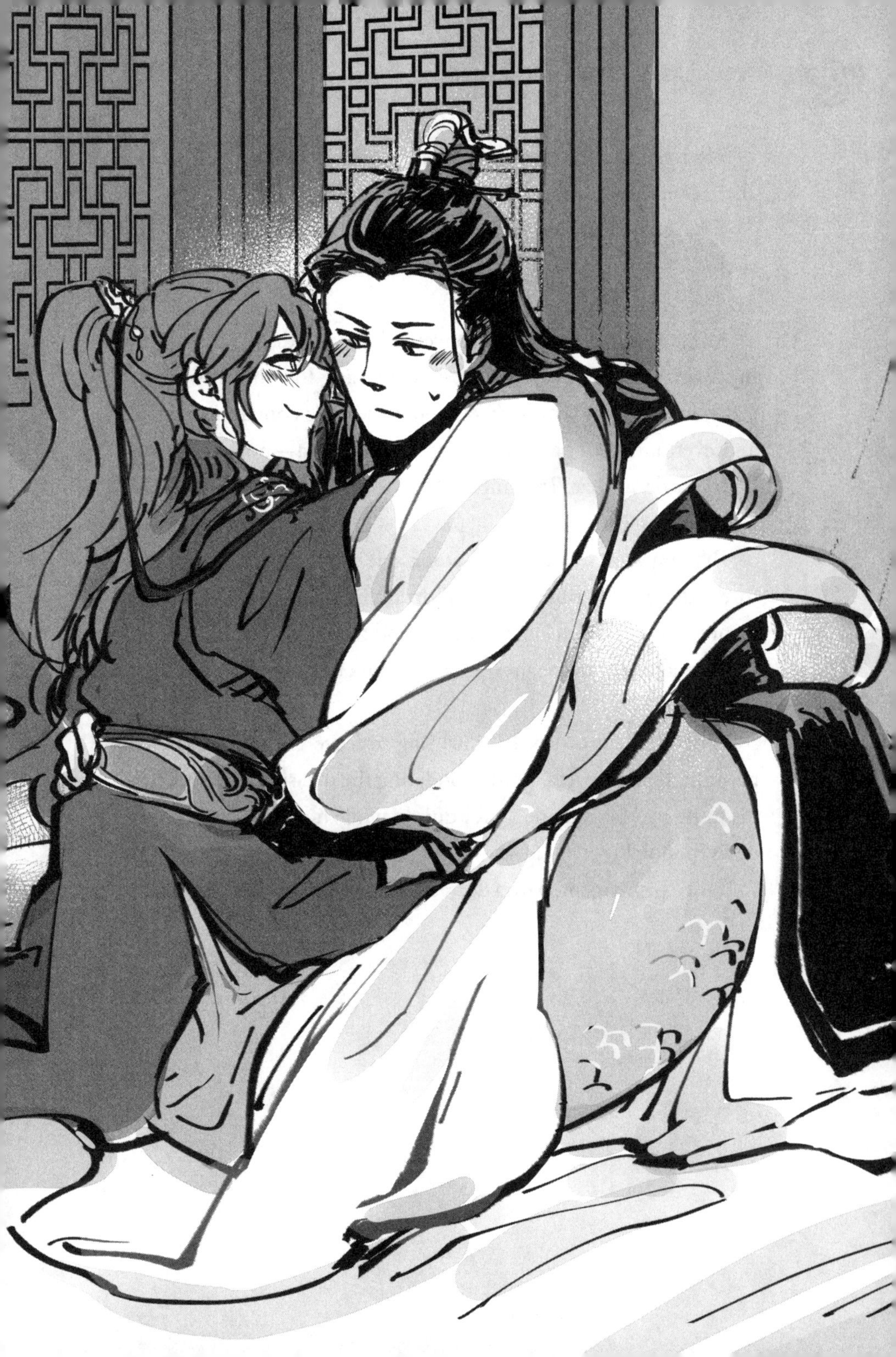

After the Double Ninth Festival, the west had become colder. They could heat up the rooms and prepare a large tub...

If he wasn't mistaken, their family would probably be setting off soon.

As far as the emperor was concerned, getting drunk and bestowing favor on someone was very embarrassing for him. It was especially embarrassing that it had happened in his concubine's palace, and even more embarrassing that it was a man—one of his son's bodyguards, at that. The emperor had to assume responsibility and take the man in.

The emperor was quite ashamed. He'd felt this annoyance before—there was a time he'd been drunk in Changchun Palace and favored a maid called Zhang there—and here it was again.

To make the annoyance go away, the emperor thought about Prince Jing.

When he had ordered Prince Jing to leave the capital, the emperor had spent several hours pondering the decision. But this time his mind had been made up for quite a while now, and he made the decision quickly.

"Luo Ruisheng, prepare a decree and have Prince Jing come back."

Fishy Back in the City

WHEN THE EMPEROR'S EDICT summoning Prince Jing back to the capital arrived, the children were already six months old. They could now eat some mushed rice in addition to drinking milk, and the peach blossom pastries they'd longed for all this time could be made into a paste and eaten too.

In ancient times, though, the imperial family was usually in no hurry to wean the children off of milk and would let them drink it for as long as they wanted. The wet nurse thought it would be the same at Prince Jing's home. Li Yu knew that in modern times, babies could be weaned at six months, but local customs said that milk was nutritious and it was fine to drink it for longer. Unexpectedly, though, Dabao refused to drink milk as soon as he hit six months and would only eat paste, so he weaned himself quickly off milk.

Following Dabao's leadership, Erbao, Sanbao, and Sibao soon also refused to drink milk. They stuck out their necks and clamored for rice mush, completely ignoring the wet nurse. If the wet nurse picked them up and tried to force feed them, even the fourth young master with his lovely temper and ready laughter would get upset, turning his body around and showing the wet nurse his butt.

For the first time, the wet nurse felt alone. She was also having doubts about herself—did the young masters not like her milk?

Li Yu knew what was going on. The fish children weren't normal babies and had their own ideas, but Li Yu couldn't explain that to the wet nurse. He tried to comfort her anyway. When a family like Prince Jing's hired a wet nurse, they would have to take care of her for the rest of her life, so she didn't have to worry about the future. As there was no more need to breastfeed, Li Yu asked her to just look after the children, and she readily agreed. The young masters seemed very smart; perhaps they were just different from the children of a normal family?

At first, Prince Jing was a little worried about the children's health. But Li Yu assured him over and over again that weaning at six months wasn't a problem, and Prince Jing of course believed Xiaoyu. So, the issue of the children's weaning quickly passed, just like that.

As soon as the emperor's edict arrived, Prince Jing ordered their things to be packed. Since he'd been expecting this for a while, the official affairs of the western border were pretty much handled already, so Prince Jing handed over official duties to the village head.

The bandits had been dealt with and the western border was now peaceful. As for the imperial guards that the emperor sent to protect Prince Jing—Prince Jing asked them to stay in the western border for a bit to help the village head. He'd also trained a group of young soldiers, and he handed them over to the village head as well.

Official affairs were progressing smoothly with almost no issues. All that was left was to pack. Prince Jing was still unmarried before he came to the western border and brought his boyfriend, Li-gongzi, along, but now he was returning with his wife and four young

masters. It wasn't just the number of people that had changed—
there was multiple times more luggage than before. The children's
clothes, toys, and diapers took up several carriages alone, and they
had to bring along the wet nurse and other caretakers as well. There
were also several physicians that had come with them to the western
border, and the children's teachers that Prince Jing had hired back in
the capital who he was responsible for bringing back.

Li Yu had married Prince Jing in Luofeng Village and had his
fish children here. The residence in Luofeng Village held immense
significance to him—like another home. He was reluctant to part
with it, and, after making his rounds, he wanted to bring everything
he saw.

The fish tank, crystal bottle, and all the fish plushies had to be
brought along. He also wanted to bring the two ducks they were
raising in the yard; these two ducks were the fluffy ducklings he'd
brought back from the duck farm, which had since grown into fat
ducks. Li Yu had said that the ducks would get ugly once they were
grown up, but he secretly liked them a lot. Sibao, who'd watched the
ducks grow up and get ugly, also liked them. Li Yu liked to eat roast
duck, but he had never thought about roasting these ducks.

Wang Xi followed Li Yu around and wrote down everything he
wanted to bring. When he saw Li Yu hesitate, he smiled and said,
"Consort, please rethink this. The ducks would be difficult to bring
along."

"I really can't?" Li Yu was a little reluctant. "But if they're left
behind, nobody will take care of them."

"The servants in this manor have been hired by the village head,
so there won't be anyone else living here," Wang Xi said. "There will
be some servants left behind who can feed them on time and take
care of them."

"But..." Li Yu knew what Wang Xi meant and knew that this was normal, but if the ducks were left behind, he wouldn't get to see them again.

Prince Jing was destined to become the emperor, and he knew this year they'd spent at the western border was just part of Prince Jing's journey to the throne. When they returned to the capital this time, Prince Jing would definitely show his brilliance, so he and Prince Jing would never be able to set foot on the western border again.

"Wang-gonggong, we really can't take them back? Aren't we bringing the fish too? Ducks don't take up too much space and they can walk on their own, so it should be fine as long as we bring enough food, right?"

Li Yu kept thinking they should be able to find *somewhere* in the carriages to squeeze the ducks in.

Wang-gonggong thought, *How could bringing fish and bringing ducks be the same? Isn't it too crazy to drive two ducks from the western border to the capital?*

Wang Xi's lips twitched. "They may not survive the difficult journey."

Li Yu kept fighting for the ducks. Prince Jing, who could see him feeling troubled from a distance away, came over and held Li Yu's hand while glaring at Wang Xi reproachfully.

A chill went down Wang Xi's spine and he immediately changed his tune. "Yes, we can probably bring them. I'll go make arrangements...to bring these two ducks along."

Prince Jing nodded, satisfied. He didn't necessarily want to blame Wang Xi; Wang Xi's logic was sound, but he knew that this home meant something different for Li Yu.

When they left the capital, Xiaoyu didn't have many objections because he didn't have a proper title yet. Prince Jing's manor in the capital was more like a simple residence to Xiaoyu. But they'd gotten married and had children here, so Xiaoyu was the other master of this residence. He could obviously decide what to bring and what to leave behind.

Just do what the consort wants, Prince Jing signaled with his eyes.

Wang Xi nodded quickly, thinking that he'd probably just been confused earlier. How could he try and persuade Li-gongzi to change his mind? Li-gongzi was the consort and his master. He should fully support what his master wanted to do.

"Please give me a chance, Consort," he said respectfully. "I'll definitely complete the job."

Li Yu didn't know what Prince Jing had hinted to Wang Xi, but since Wang Xi had agreed to take the ducks with them, he was happy beyond belief. "Then I'll leave it to you, Wang-gonggong," he said.

Wang Xi hurriedly replied, "You're welcome," then rushed out to get things ready. He found a properly sized duck cage and asked the servants accompanying them if any of them knew how to take care of ducks. Since ducks couldn't stay in the carriage for too long, he had to prepare another cart and put the duck cage there...

It seemed like it wasn't impossible to bring the ducks after all, they just needed to be transported correctly. After that, no matter what Li Yu wanted to bring, Wang Xi simply nodded and took care of it.

On the day of departure, Li Yu held his children and felt a little embarrassed as he stared at the line of carriages behind him. It seemed like he'd emptied out the entire manor.

Prince Jing smiled and squeezed his hand to tell him, *It's all right,* then gave him a note.

Another note? All right. Consort Yu was used to it by now. He took it to see what Prince Jing wanted to say.

This time, what Prince Jing wanted to say was—

Xiaoyu's dowry.

Li Yu's face instantly turned red. *Dowry, my ass.*

The carriage Li Yu rode on the way here had been very spacious, but Prince Jing made the carriage even bigger this time. Originally, Wang Xi, the wet nurse, and the four children were supposed to be in a different carriage, but Li Yu insisted on keeping the children with him, unbothered by their crying. The fish children also wanted to stay near their fish father, so Prince Jing smiled and agreed. However, he didn't want Li Yu and the wet nurse to stay together for a long period of time in the same carriage, so he gave up his horse and got into the carriage with Li Yu to help look after the children with him.

The wet nurse was left hung out to dry again, and she thought it was somewhat hard to believe. She quietly told Wang Xi about this, and he chuckled and said, "There's nothing strange about that. That's how Prince Jing spoils the consort and the four young masters. You're new, so you don't know yet, but there'll be many more incidents like this."

The wet nurse fully believed Wang-gonggong's words.

They set off with no issues, but after about half a mile, Wang Xi suddenly called for the carriage to stop and asked Li Yu and Prince Jing to look outside.

Prince Jing opened the curtain of the carriage to see the citizens of the western border kneeling.

The village head explained to Prince Jing that when the citizens heard he was returning to the capital, they wanted to come to send him off.

Prince Jing got rid of the bandits, exterminated the locusts, and helped the people flourish. The way they showed their thanks was very simple—they put all the good things they had, food or objects, in bamboo baskets to offer to Prince Jing and his consort.

The old woman that Prince Jing saved was there in the crowd holding her grandson, kowtowing nonstop. And the baby Li Yu had ordered the guards to retrieve from the bandits was also there. The baby's parents had later been found by the guards, and now they'd brought the baby over to see them.

Li Yu's eyes were a little teary. He didn't know what he should say. Without saying a word, he waved to them just like he had on his wedding day.

The people all loudly shouted, "We wish the prince and his consort peace and safety."

The citizens were overly enthusiastic and gave them gifts like chickens, ducks, pigs, and sheep. They couldn't take all of it with them, so Prince Jing asked Li Yu to take care of it. After giving it some thought, Li Yu ordered Wang Xi to keep two red eggs and a roast duck as a souvenir; he knew the citizens didn't have it easy, so he persuaded them to take everything else back.

The citizens sent them off again, and it was two hours before Prince Jing and Li Yu actually managed to leave Luofeng Village.

As Li Yu watched the people turn into small black dots in the distance, he thought to himself that if he had the opportunity in the future, he was going to do more for these lovely people.

Prince Jing and the group had been in no hurry when they left the capital, and they were the same going back. They slowed down even more since the children were with them now, and Li Yu even developed a mood for seeing the sights.

Just like on the way there, every time they passed a town, Prince Jing would change up their diet and take Li Yu to try local foods. When they were wandering around an unfamiliar town, he would grab Li Yu's hand tightly, as if he was afraid Li Yu would suddenly fly away.

Li Yu felt both moved and amused when he thought about the man who would take care of the children with him and always protected him, despite believing Li Yu was a carp spirit. Who said men never continued to cherish their partner after marriage?

Prince Jing, at least, treated him better and better.

The moment they arrived at the capital, the fish-scamming system finally showed its presence with a new mission. It had been so long that Li Yu had almost forgotten it existed.

<Please note: the main quest line "Share the Country with the Tyrant" has begun. User, please view it promptly to obtain the mission information.>

Li Yu was excited when the mission finally appeared, but he calmed down quickly. "Share the country"? Did that mean what he thought it did?

The fish-scamming system's previous missions were mainly about nurturing their relationship, but this last one was a bit too difficult.

Prince Jing could only think of the country after he ascended to the throne, which also meant that completing this mission would have to wait until the fight for the throne was decided in Prince Jing's favor.

He'd been able to complete all the weird quests he'd gotten before, though, so it would be the same this time, right?

Share the country with the tyrant... That was different from simple lovey-dovey behavior—no typical emperor or empress would say such a thing. Li Yu glanced at the man holding his hand, and he wondered if this man really loved him enough to share the country with him.

A country was different from everything else. It was something that many would give up family or love for.

But Li Yu had promised to trust Prince Jing. He'd try to trust that they could finish this last mission with no issue.

When they arrived in the capital, they had to enter the palace immediately to greet the emperor, even though they were all extremely tired.

Prince Jing took Li Yu with him, and they each held two children. Wang Xi quickly ran to Qianqing Palace to deliver the message, and, after receiving the emperor's orders, Luo Ruisheng waited for them outside the palace. As soon as he saw Prince Jing's family from a distance, he immediately rushed forward to greet them.

Luo Ruisheng had never seen Li Yu before, so he bowed to him politely. When he saw Erbao and Sanbao in Li Yu's arms, as well as Dabao and Sibao in Prince Jing's arms, he couldn't help but smile. They really looked alike, especially the little heir. He looked like he was made from the same mold as Prince Jing when he was a baby.

Head Eunuch Luo wanted to say a few more things, but the emperor couldn't wait anymore and walked out himself, calling out loudly, "Where's Prince Jing?"

But before he'd even finished speaking, the emperor stopped in his tracks.

Prince Jing was standing a few feet away, with a delicate and pretty young man cuddling up next to him, and they were both holding two children in their arms.

When Prince Jing saw the emperor, he pulled Li Yu down to kneel in greeting. The emperor ordered Head Eunuch Luo to help them up and stared at Prince Jing for a while, before saying emotionally, "You've gotten more tanned, and you've bulked up."

The emperor then turned to look at Li Yu next to Prince Jing. This young man's luminous eyes and rosy lips were very pleasing to the eye, he thought. He'd already guessed who the young man was, so he smiled and asked, "You're Li Yu?"

Prince Jing gently squeezed Li Yu's hand under their sleeves. Li Yu understood. He and the emperor weren't truly strangers, so he boldly called out, "Royal Father."

The emperor was delighted, as if he'd gained another son. When he looked at the two in front of him, he felt they matched each other well in both appearance and temperament, making them a very suitable couple. He nodded kindly.

Prince Jing was holding Dabao and Sibao. Li Yu had already told the babies on the way there, so Dabao knew that the man wearing strange, bright yellow clothes was his grandpa. But Dabao still didn't know how to talk, and he usually just drooled when he opened his mouth. Dabao was afraid of embarrassing himself, so he didn't open his mouth and instead copied the adults by putting his fists together and stretching them out to his grandpa.

The emperor's gaze landed on Dabao immediately, and he paused. After a while, he smiled and said, "Tianchi, this child looks just like you when you were a child. A little chubs."

Prince Jing, who had been looking for "Little Chubs" for a long time, was stunned to hear this.

Neither Wang Xi, Ye Qinghuan, nor anyone else would ever dare call Prince Jing "Little Chubs." Only the emperor was so fearless.

Prince Jing suddenly realized—was the "Little Chubs" Li Yu was talking about that one time...actually himself?

Fish Children Meeting the Emperor

THE EMPEROR was right in front of them, so Prince Jing couldn't ask Li Yu straight away. He decided to put it aside for now.

The emperor was overjoyed when he saw Dabao, just as Li Yu expected. He glanced at Prince Jing, and then stepped forward with Erbao and Sanbao as well. When the emperor saw the other two chubby children, he was ecstatic.

Erbao and Sanbao weren't as concerned with their image as Dabao was, so when they saw their grandpa, they opened their mouths to shout but ended up just drooling a lot. Erbao pointed to the dragon on the emperor's clothes, then smiled and clapped his hands. He'd seen this before! "Ah!" *Snake!* The sound was clear and crisp, very healthy.

The emperor patted the chubby little boy's head in surprise.

Sanbao, not about to be outdone, yelled back even louder: "Aahhh!" *A centipede!*

The emperor patted the other chubby little boy's head too, amused.

Dabao was sulking on his own. Erbao and Sanbao were dummies—that was a dragon! Fish father had told him before that the long thing on Grandpa's clothes was a dragon.

Stop talking! Listen to me! But as soon as Dabao opened his mouth, drool flowed out...

Dabao decided being embarrassed was fine, so he strained until his face was red to force out a "Pa?"

Dabao wanted to cover his face after he heard his own voice. What was going on? H-he was the first one to say "Daddy" clearly, so why was he saying "Grandpa" all weird? *Being human is too hard. I want to be a fish again!*

The emperor had heard him, and he teased Dabao by asking, "Dabao, what are you trying to say?"

Dabao did his best and clenched his little fists. "Gwam...pa?"

The emperor thought he must have heard incorrectly. Li Yu smiled and confirmed, "Royal Father, he's calling for you. Please forgive me. At home...no, on the western border, we always call you 'Grandpa' in front of him."

The emperor had never had a grandson who'd called him Grandpa before—they all called him the proper "Royal Grandfather." But when Prince Jing's little heir suddenly called him "Grandpa," even though he stuttered and didn't pronounce it quite right, the emperor was so happy that his beard almost stood on end.

This baby could call him Grandpa even though he was only ten months old. He would definitely be a smart child in the future.

Anyway, he was his grandson; it was normal for him to call him Grandpa. Wasn't that what ordinary families did? The position of emperor was a very high one to be in, but he also wanted to experience the simple joys of a family.

The imperial family had a saying: "embrace your grandson but not your son." The emperor had been talking about Prince Jing for months now and Prince Jing was finally back, but the emperor could only say a few things to him; he couldn't be overly affectionate. But the little grandson was different. Since he was from a later generation, the emperor could embrace him however he wanted. The emperor, who forgot his son now that his grandson was here, lifted Dabao up.

Luo Ruisheng and Prince Jing quickly helped the emperor. Dabao was well taken care of, and he was a little heavy. The emperor used quite a bit of strength and held Dabao firmly; after catching his breath, he turned around and smiled at Prince Jing, saying, "Little Chubs is quite heavy."

Prince Jing felt a bit bewildered.

The emperor held Dabao in his embrace, and Dabao was obedient and didn't cry. His little chubby arms went around the emperor's neck, and the grandpa-grandson pair seemed very close.

Li Yu was afraid the emperor would get tired, so he wanted to take Dabao back, but the emperor waved him away. Dabao was a little heavy, but the emperor enjoyed the fact that Dabao wasn't afraid of him. After all, when his other grandsons saw him, they were like mice that had seen a cat. They weren't as close to him as the grandsons from Prince Jing's family.

Not only did the emperor not allow anyone to take Dabao away, but he also waved Li Yu over. Li Yu understood. He walked over with Erbao and Sanbao. The emperor made Luo Ruisheng bring each child over to sit on his lap.

"Royal Father, this is too heavy," Li Yu protested, a bit embarrassed.

The emperor's childishness started showing, and he shushed Li Yu. "Let them sit here for a bit. Since I'm holding Dabao, the others will be upset if I don't hold them too."

Li Yu was speechless. He didn't notice the other children getting unhappy—was the emperor trying to start something?

The emperor counted the little butts in his lap and found he was missing one. "What about Sibao?"

Sibao was sleeping soundly in Prince Jing's arms. He was tired from all the traveling, and the fish children had a very good habit of not waking up once they were asleep. This meeting with the emperor didn't even bother him.

Prince Jing put Sibao in the emperor's arms too, after the emperor kept urging him to. Sibao, who was sleeping very well, was welcomed by his brothers. Erbao and Sanbao started waving their little arms and legs in a dance, patting Sibao awake.

Sibao sat up, rubbed his eyes, and saw the emperor holding him.

Who is this? Sibao ate his hands and tried to recall. His fish dad told him that they were going to see Grandpa, but Sibao got sleepy and took a little nap.

...So this was Grandpa?

"Aahh!" *Grandpa!* In his excitement, Sibao accidentally spit out his drool and nearly choked on his saliva. The emperor almost gave himself an internal injury holding back his laughter.

As soon as Sibao opened his eyes, the emperor could tell that he looked a lot like Li Yu. If he had any doubts that Li Yu had really given birth to the children before, it was gone the moment he saw them. Children resembled their parents. This was an unchanging truth.

The emperor had a bunch of stuff he wanted to tell Prince Jing, but he forgot it all as soon as the children landed in his lap. He became completely engrossed in playing with them. Luo Ruisheng had to remind him quietly several times before he remembered that Prince Jing's family had come to see him first thing when they arrived in the capital. Upon closer inspection, Prince Jing and Li Yu did both look exhausted...

The emperor comforted them a bit, then told them to go get some rest and leave the children with him. But then he looked around and realized that there was no place suitable in the palace for children that small. The children had been forced to travel with the adults, so they must be even more tired. The emperor knew that he couldn't keep them for any longer. He smiled and said, "Rest for three days. Come to the palace afterward and burn some incense for your royal mother so she can see the children. I think she would be very happy."

As the emperor spoke, he looked up at Prince Jing's family and felt a little choked up. If Empress Xiaohui were still here and the eldest and fourth prince were still alive, with Prince Jing...the eldest and fourth prince would have had children by now too. How lovely that would have been...

The emperor's smile faded a little. "Go on, then."

Prince Jing nodded and led Li Yu and the children away.

When they left the palace, Prince Jing patted Li Yu's hand. The emperor's expression hadn't looked so great at the end, so he was afraid Li Yu would misunderstand.

"I know," Li Yu said softly. "I won't take it the wrong way." The emperor had clearly made himself sad by mentioning Empress Xiaohui.

A warm, dry hand held Prince Jing's hand in return. "Tianchi, don't be sad."

Prince Jing stared at Li Yu, and his heart felt like a warm current was flowing through it.

Xiaoyu often told him to not be sad. Truth be told, Prince Jing was used to it by now, so he wasn't sad, but every time Li Yu tried to comfort him and cared for him, Prince Jing felt immensely happy.

Looking down, he saw that all the children were asleep. Sibao rolled over, drooling on Prince Jing.

It was late when they got back to the manor. Wang Xi had already ordered the servants to clean up the rooms and make the beds.

The room was just as it had been when they left, except for the addition of Prince Jing's new painting of a school of carp. It signified that the master had returned.

Prince Jing had just settled the children and the ducks when he turned around and saw Li Yu fall asleep on the bed.

He had buried his head in the green quilt with golden edges and started breathing steadily. He was so exhausted that he hadn't even taken off the shoes on his feet. Prince Jing felt for him, so after a moment of thought, he exited the room quietly and brought back a warm basin of water into the room.

He gently removed Li Yu's shoes and socks, then soaked Li Yu's feet in the water.

During the trip from the western border, there hadn't been much time to relax other than the occasional stay at an inn. Xiaoyu must be tired. It must've been difficult for a carp spirit to follow him around all this way.

Prince Jing wiped down the tops of Li Yu's feet and gently rubbed the soles. Li Yu hummed in comfort, but he didn't wake up. Prince Jing wiped his feet clean, took off his robes, and placed him under the brocade quilt. Then he took off his own clothes and snuggled in as well.

Li Yu hadn't slept on a solid bed for a long time, and he didn't know how long he ended up sleeping for.

He could now transform into a human for a whole day. For convenience, he usually transformed in the middle of the night. He could maintain human form until the midnight of the next day, then transform into a fish for a second before turning human again.

It was a bit troublesome, but he was usually with Prince Jing in the middle of the night. With Prince Jing shielding him, there was nothing that could go wrong, and no need to worry about his secret being revealed during the daytime.

When Li Yu woke up, he automatically felt his body to check. He had arms and legs, so he hadn't turned into a fish. A full day hadn't passed yet.

Prince Jing was lying next to him, eyes closed and unmoving, as if asleep.

Li Yu turned around and kicked off the quilt. His feet had been in unbearable pain when he fell asleep, but they didn't hurt anymore. Not only was the pain gone, but he felt like he could go to the palace and back several times over. Was sleep a cure for foot pain?

Li Yu looked at his feet and noticed that his shoes and socks had been removed. Then, when he glanced at the copper basin on the ground, he realized that the reason why his feet weren't in pain anymore wasn't because of sleeping but because someone had massaged and soaked them.

Who else would do something so extreme besides Prince Jing?

Li Yu laid back down, his face against the other person's sturdy back, smelling his familiar scent. He asked hesitantly, "Tianchi?"

He had only called out once when Prince Jing turned around and stared at him with eyes as deep as a dark pool.

Li Yu clutched his chest. "That scared me. You haven't slept yet?"

Prince Jing nodded.

Why wasn't he asleep? Because of his fish, of course.

It had to do with Little Chubs.

Prince Jing had heard Zen Master Liao Kong mention that Li Yu had saved him from drowning when he was a child. Prince Jing couldn't actually remember much because of the high fever he developed afterward, but he believed it.

Xiaoyu had come because of him. Though Xiaoyu had never mentioned or admitted it, he more or less had enough evidence now.

After Li Yu let "Little Chubs" slip out when he was dreaming, Prince Jing had hunted for that person for a long time—but he never found the culprit. He even got jealous of this mysterious fat man. But now that he'd learned from the emperor that he was called "Little Chubs" when he was younger, he came to a realization.

No wonder he could never find "Little Chubs." *He* was "Little Chubs."

The emperor, Wang Xi, and Ye Qinghuan knowing the nickname was only to be expected. But how could Xiaoyu be aware of it?

It must be because he'd seen him when he was younger. Xiaoyu had saved him.

Prince Jing was extremely happy to learn that his love rival was actually himself. If he'd had a tail, His Highness would probably have started waving it. But Xiaoyu didn't know that he had been looking for Little Chubs this entire time, so Prince Jing couldn't properly express the happiness in his heart.

Xiaoyu had made him promise in the past to not ask where he came from. Prince Jing was sure he had some sort of reason to refuse to admit that he saved him in the past.

All right, he decided. He wouldn't let Xiaoyu know that Little Chubs knew everything.

"Tianchi," Li Yu called out in a soft voice, his eyes bright and gleaming.

Prince Jing turned around and kissed him, interlocking their fingers.

Li Yu was walking a bit stiffly the next day. It was different from the foot pain he'd had—it was his legs that were sore this time.

Fishy Bath

THE DAY AFTER Prince Jing and Li Yu returned home, Ye Qinghuan heard they were back and came to personally announce good news to them.

The princess of Jinjue had given birth to a daughter two months ago, and Ye Qinghuan was beside himself with joy. While Prince Jing and the group were on the road they hadn't really been able to receive any news, so this was the first they'd heard of it.

Ye Qinghuan now had a daughter, and he was like a little honeybee, buzzing about her nonstop. "She's so tiny and her face isn't even as large as my palm, but she's so cute. I-I've never seen such a cute little girl..."

Prince Jing thought he was noisy, but it was Ye Qinghuan's first time being a father, and to a precious daughter at that. He had to yell about it, even if he got kicked out!

Prince Jing wasn't much better in that aspect, though. He had incubated the fish eggs himself, and the day the fish children hatched, he'd been smiling all day. He wasn't any calmer than Ye-shizi. Li Yu, who knew the truth, laughed out loud. A contest between Prince Jing and Ye-shizi over who was the more doting father would be an uncontested draw.

But a daughter...

Li Yu had only interacted with his fish sons, and when he thought about a cute, well-behaved little girl, like a little flower...he quite wanted one himself.

He couldn't help but touch his flat tummy. It'd been a year since he gave birth to the fish children. Since he'd been a fish when it happened, it practically had no effect on his body. After that, he and Prince Jing had done it many times. Though the "One-and-Done" buff was gone, the system said that he could conceive normally, which meant that he could still have children. But he'd been on the receiving end for a year now and still hadn't received anything, so weren't the chances a bit too low?

After seeing how cute the fish children were, Li Yu was willing to try a second time even if it was a little difficult.

Prince Jing had worked really hard last night. They'd been on the road for so long with almost no sex life to speak of, so he'd saved up a lot of energy. Would Li Yu get pregnant from that?

But he was a fish with a system. If he was pregnant, the system would definitely give him a notification, like the last time when he'd had to choose between human form or fish form. It should happen every time he got pregnant, but he didn't hear a notification last night.

...It looked like the revolution was not yet achieved, and Comrade Tianchi needed to work harder.

Li Yu looked at his husband's waist with a smoldering gaze.

Ye Qinghuan was still yapping, but Prince Jing couldn't take it anymore. He ordered Wang Xi to carry him out with two thick red envelopes.

Ye Qinghuan held the red envelope and suddenly realized—

"Tianchi, are you perhaps jealous that I have such a cute daughter?"

Prince Jing stared at him. *I'm not jealous! Get out!*

When Ye Qinghuan and the princess's daughter turned one month old, the emperor gave her the title of Qinghe-junzhu. The emperor was quite generous with the younger generation. The little princess was still too young to visit him, so Li Yu went over to visit Ye Qinghuan and chatted with him for a bit, before agreeing to bring the fish children to the little Qinghe-junzhu's one-hundred-days-old celebration.

"Don't forget to bring Xiaoyu and his little fish too," Ye Qinghuan reminded him. "The princess is always talking about your family's fish."

...I guess I'll have to clone myself somehow, Li Yu thought.

Li Yu quickly looked at Prince Jing, trying to ask for help. He would need to bring his fish children and a bunch of fish plushies, *and* turn into a real fish that day—it was definitely too much for him, so it would be best if Prince Jing could give him a bit of a hand.

Prince Jing lightly coughed and turned his face away, as if he didn't see. Who asked this carp to be so eager to see the little princess?

What??? Li Yu looked sad. Everything had been fine just now, so why did Prince Jing suddenly get all upset?

Ye Qinghuan had just left when Luo-gonggong arrived with a plethora of rewards in tow.

The emperor couldn't give Prince Jing a sizable reward, but he liked the four children a lot, so he gave the rewards to the children instead. The list of rewards was so long that Luo-gonggong's throat nearly started smoking. Wang Xi thoughtfully gave him a cup of tea, and Luo-gonggong took a sip before happily continuing to read.

Li Yu stood next to Prince Jing, respectfully listening and silently speechless.

Jewelry, fabric, antiques, calligraphy—those weren't special. But there were also bows, arrows, horses, and the Four Books and

Five Classics. The emperor had a clear plan for the next decade of the children's lives...

Most of the rewards were given in fours, but the last one was different. The emperor gave Dabao a set of Four Treasures of the Study[15] and a jade ruyi, but the other children each received two bags of golden ingots with the words "peace and auspiciousness" etched onto them. The emperor was clearly giving Dabao special treatment.

Prince Jing smiled and looked at Wang Xi, who immediately explained to Li Yu, "Consort, the eldest young master is the heir, so his reward is a little bigger."

Li Yu nodded. He knew that the eldest son in ancient times held a special position, but the children wouldn't start fighting because of this, right?

He recalled that back when the boys had been fish, when he'd put Sibao on his head the other children would get jealous. Li Yu normally tried to pay attention to this; for example, Dabao was smarter than most babies and attracted more attention, but Prince Jing liked to hold Sibao a little more. When Li Yu realized that, he made sure to hold Erbao and Sanbao more often so they wouldn't feel left out.

But if the gifts were different, how was he going to make the children understand why Dabao was different?

If Prince Jing stayed a prince, then Dabao would inherit the title of prince. If Prince Jing ascended the throne in the future, then Dabao would most likely become the crown prince.

One little difference could change everything.

This was probably the most difficult thing for normal princes to accept.

---

15 *The Four Treasures of the Study: Brush, Ink, Paper, Inkstone* (文房四寶：筆、墨、紙、硯).

Since Li Yu had given birth to the fish children, di or shu wasn't a consideration—only their age. But truthfully, age was a bit confusing too, because Li Yu had laid the eggs in his sleep and didn't know which baby's egg came out first. Prince Jing had determined their ages when they hatched, but if they went by the order their eggs were laid in, Dabao might not be the actual eldest son.

Would the other children be unhappy because of that?

Li Yu carefully observed them for two days. The fish children ate and slept as normal; there was no unhappiness to speak of. Except on the day the gifts were given, Dabao was almost covered in drool from the kisses the other children gave him.

Li Yu concluded that the fish children were still too young to worry about it. Even if they were different from normal children and had spent some time as young fish, they still couldn't understand complex things like rights and status. It was better to leave such things for later and let them live a happy childhood. Their father, Prince Jing, hadn't ascended the throne yet, so there wasn't any need to worry about all that for now.

Just as he was deciding to let this go, something else unexpected happened. All at once, the fish children started throwing tantrums.

Li Yu remembered the last time they were this upset was because they were getting weaned from milk, so he was confused. The conditions in the capital were better, so shouldn't the fish children be happier? Li Yu himself was definitely happier. When they got back, he "overheard" Wang-gonggong saying that Prince Jing had brought a Quanjude roast duck master from the western border to open another location in the capital. Wasn't that just to make him happy?

Li Yu was very self-aware. He was waiting for Prince Jing to take him to eat roast duck.

...Aaahhh, why did he suddenly start thinking about food? Li Yu quickly wiped away the drool on his face. He was trying to care for his fish children.

The fish children had just moved back into the manor and were doing fine. They started throwing tantrums...the day after Prince Jing and Li Yu held them in their arms and showed them around the manor.

The manor was their home—was there something wrong with walking through your own home?

After Li Yu gave it a lot of thought, he realized that Sibao was facing the window yelling "Aahhh!" as if he wanted to see something.

Li Yu carried Sibao over. Outside the window was a corner of the huge fishpond that Prince Jing had built for him, the clear water rippling.

"Aaahhh!" *I want to swim!* Sibao raised his chubby hand, pointed at the pond, and looked back at his fish father with tears in his eyes. Now that Sibao had expressed his desires, the other fish children started pointing to the pond as well, calling out to their fish father. Dabao, who was the most mature, yelled the loudest.

So that's what it was!

Li Yu finally understood why the fish children weren't happy. The children could only look at the huge pond in the manor, they couldn't swim in it—no wonder they were upset.

Prince Jing wasn't in the manor because he had some business to attend to, but Li Yu had an idea. He had Wang Xi bring a large bathtub filled with warm water. He undressed the children, put a little towel around each of them, hung a small piece of wood around their bodies, and let them swim in the water while they held the wood.

When the four children got in the water and found they couldn't swim like they used to, they realized they had no tail on their butt to swing around anymore. They were incredibly sad and all started crying and wailing at once.

Li Yu hadn't expected them to cry when they were in the water too, so he got in the water and stayed with them.

Crowding around Li Yu like when they were young fish, the fish children felt a little better.

Li Yu stayed in the bathtub for a while. Something suddenly occurred to him: How could he forget the bubbles?

He took a dry piece of cloth to hastily cover himself up. He had cleared out all the servants in the room, so it was only him and his fish children. Kind-of-streaking-but-not-really shouldn't be a problem, right?

With his modesty thus preserved, Li Yu ran out of the bathtub and grabbed a bunch of bath beans, which were the ancient version of soap. He ground up a bath bean and dissolved it in a bamboo container, then twisted some wire to make a good-sized loop.

Now that he was ready, Li Yu ran back to the babies, dipped the wire into the soapy water of the bamboo tube, puffed up his cheeks, and blew in the direction of the tub.

His efforts were rewarded: he actually blew an iridescent bubble.

Wow!!! Fish Dad was blowing bubbles! The fish children in the bathtub immediately forgot about the no-tail problem and swarmed around chasing the bubbles.

Prince Jing had gone out to do business, but when he came back, he found that the door to Xiaoyu's room was closed and the servants had gone elsewhere. Prince Jing opened the door to take a peek, curious, and saw the carp spirit wrapped in a cloth, running back and forth, his long slender legs dazzling.

So, Li Yu was taking a bath with the fish children. Prince Jing remembered the time he'd played with Xiaoyu in the bathtub before—

how could he miss out now? He immediately got into the bathtub with a smile.

After three days of carefree respite in the manor, the day they'd been ordered to return to the palace came. Head Eunuch Luo sent someone to Prince Jing's manor early in the morning to remind him.

Li Yu put the fish children in little bright red robes and tied bibs around their necks. Each bib's color was the original color of the corresponding fish child, and there was a circle of swimming fish around the edges.

He and Prince Jing changed into clothes appropriate for a prince and his consort. When they met the emperor the first time, they had just gotten back, so they didn't place too much importance on their attire. This meeting, however, was much more formal. The dragon on Prince Jing's clothing and the phoenix on Li Yu's were indispensable, but there were also fish embroidered onto inconspicuous places like his cuffs and collar—and the patterns were complementary.

Now, after the wedding, Li Yu felt that Prince Jing's expressions of affection both openly and secretly had improved.

Though the main goal of the trip this time was to greet Empress Xiaohui in Changchun Palace, they still had to meet the emperor first. However, before they set foot into Qianqing Palace, Head Eunuch Luo came out to tell them that the emperor was currently meeting someone else inside.

Head Eunuch Luo stuck out his thumb and pinky, making a "six" gesture, and sighed. "The emperor didn't expect this either. He usually enters the palace around noon, but he came early in the morning this time and even brought his consort. It seems like he's waiting for Your Highness."

Li Yu gently clasped his hands together in gratitude to Head Eunuch Luo for warning Prince Jing. Luo Ruisheng often spoke in favor of Prince Jing, but it was inconvenient for a prince to express his thanks, so Li Yu thanked him in his place.

As the famous saying went—a husband and husband are one!

Luo Ruisheng hurriedly said there was no need, and Li Yu quickly finished his bow. Prince Jing smiled and rubbed the top of his head.

Who cared about the sixth prince anyway? Li Yu and Prince Jing still carried their children into the palace. Mu Tianxiao was talking to the emperor, his voice full of joy.

"...When I heard such great news, I came to tell you immediately, Royal Father," Mu Tianxiao said with a smile.

Li Yu had only heard the tail end of it, so he had no idea what the great news was. But even though the emperor had heard all of it, his reaction was much less enthusiastic than the sixth prince had expected. He just furrowed his brows and stared inquiringly at the sixth prince's consort beside him.

The consort nodded, embarrassed, and the emperor quickly ordered Head Eunuch Luo to bring a chair over for her to sit down and rest—but there was no chair for the sixth prince. Mu Tianxiao was the only one left standing, and he looked a bit awkward.

"Royal Father!" Li Yu called from behind.

Dabao knew his grandpa now, and even though they were still far away, he opened his arms and laughed, drool falling from his mouth. "Gwampa!"

The emperor acknowledged his response and said happily, "I haven't seen him in three days, but it feels like Dabao is already getting better at speaking."

Li Yu couldn't believe it. *He's not! Dabao isn't! Emperor, please don't get too excited!*

The emperor held Dabao on his lap, and Mu Tianxiao's eyes widened in disbelief. Since when was the emperor so affectionate with his grandchildren?

Dabao took out a calligraphy brush from his little robes; he'd insisted on taking it with him before they left. It was one of the gifts the emperor had sent a few days ago.

"Dabao, you're so smart. Do you want to learn how to write? Grandpa will teach you how to hold it," the emperor said, smiling and holding Dabao's chubby little hand.

Li Yu thought it was too tragic to look at. Dabao had to hold the brush with both hands, and it was almost as large as he was. How was he going to write? But if the emperor thought he could, then so be it. He gave Dabao some pointers with great enthusiasm.

Dabao put on his serious face and listened carefully.

When Dabao scribbled "Oa" again, the emperor's smile practically split his face in half. Li Yu was convinced that the emperor had fallen under Dabao's spell!

It was inconvenient for the emperor to hold the other children at the same time, but he held Erbao and Sanbao's tender little hands and got covered with Sibao's happy drool, laughing heartily.

The sixth prince stared at Dabao in the emperor's arms with a sinister gaze, and he couldn't help but say, "Royal Father, Suyun is also..."

"If she's pregnant, then take good care of her," the emperor said mildly, without looking up. He was still playing with Dabao. "You don't have to come tell me yourself. I will send an imperial physician to check her pulse every day."

The emperor didn't bother hiding his dissatisfaction with the sixth prince. The sixth prince's consort being pregnant was a good thing, and he was very happy when he heard the news. But the sixth prince was announcing it too deliberately, and he'd even dragged his consort with him when he came. How could he make his newly pregnant wife kneel to greet the emperor and force her to run around everywhere to report the news?

The sixth prince's actions could, at best, be interpreted as the ignorance of a new father, but at worst, he was using his child to gain favor and didn't actually care for the little life that was in his princess consort's belly.

Coupled with the timing of when the sixth prince had entered the palace—how could the emperor not notice what his intention was?

Dabao was the smartest. What was the problem with spoiling him a little more?

The emperor coldly thought, *Why are you competing for my favor when your child isn't even born yet?*

Fish Children's Friendliness

MU TIANXIAO SENSED the emperor's coldness and retreated angrily, pulling his consort out of the palace.

His consort, Liang Suyun, wanted to watch Prince Jing's children a bit longer. The elders said that one was more likely to birth a son if one looked at boys while one was pregnant. She knew that her husband was a prince, so he'd be eager for his first child to be a son.

She didn't really want to go, but Mu Tianxiao pulled her away with a lot of strength, and she was practically dragged away. She couldn't damage the sixth prince's reputation while in Qianqing Palace, so she waited until they'd left the palace before she rubbed her wrists vigorously, complaining a bit. Before she had been married, she was dearly loved by her parents and had never suffered. After she married the sixth prince, Mu Tianxiao had been attentive to her every want and never so much as lost his temper around her. Why was he so rough with her now that she was pregnant?

Mu Tianxiao's face was dark and unreadable. After his consort complained a bit, he came back to his senses and returned to his usual gentle, considerate self. He said apologetically, "I'm sorry, I got too excited; I forgot that you need to be treated with special care now."

Mu Tianxiao was very good at concealing his emotions and lying. For a moment, Liang Suyun thought she had made a mistake.

She wanted to have a good life with him, so she smiled and said, "I'm fine, there's no need to be so nervous. I was just thinking that it would be nice to have a child like Prince Jing's heir."

When Mu Tianxiao thought of the boy in the emperor's arms, the corners of his lips twitched and he smiled strangely. "Yes, it would be nice."

Mu Tianxiao had originally been very happy when he found out about Lady Liang's pregnancy. This child was like rain in the midst of a drought: he would soon have what Prince Jing had. Originally, he'd been trying to figure out how to subtly steal the emperor's attention from Prince Jing. When he heard that the emperor had rewarded Prince Jing's children with many things upon their arrival at the capital, Mu Tianxiao thought the emperor must be getting on in age, making him more inclined to dote on his grandsons. If he informed the emperor that Lady Liang was pregnant, the emperor would have to pay attention to more than just Prince Jing's children.

He'd been so hopeful, but the emperor was still so cold toward him and his future child. Even worse, the emperor treated Prince Jing's eldest son much too warmly. He was just a tiny child, yet the emperor sat him on his knee! Mu Tianxiao was resentful. He had always known that the emperor didn't like him because his mother, Consort Zhang, used to be Empress Xiaohui's servant. Ever since he could remember, the emperor never asked to see his mother, and she'd held the lowest rank of Second Class Attendant throughout his childhood. His mother hadn't reached consort status until he was an adult. By then, the emperor would only occasionally visit Yongfu Palace, on account of the prince.

Before, he thought that even if the emperor didn't like him, he would at least like his children. During festivals and holidays, the emperor would summon even the Marquis of Ping and Marquis of

An's children, and he sat Prince Jing's eldest son on his knee as soon as he arrived. Why was he so cold to just the sixth prince's child?

It was clear that in the emperor's heart, he was still inferior to Prince Jing—and even inferior to the second prince and third prince!

Even though he brought his consort with him to announce the good news in person, it was useless; the emperor still never mentioned giving him another job. Was he really just going to spend his consort's entire pregnancy keeping her company?

Mu Tianxiao started to hate the emperor again.

Having said that, though...although this trip hadn't turned out the way he expected, it wasn't fruitless.

He'd been in a rush to bring his princess consort into the palace because he'd heard that Prince Jing's family was also entering the palace today. He wanted to use the opportunity to see Prince Jing's children himself.

The confidant he'd sent to the western border never responded, so Mu Tianxiao had given up waiting and decided that his confidant was gone—he'd most likely found something out and been silenced by Prince Jing. But Mu Tianxiao didn't know the specific reason. He didn't have anyone to help him anymore, so he had to use any opportunity he got to see things for himself.

And it was lucky he'd entered the palace. Though his child wasn't favored, he'd discovered one of Prince Jing's secrets.

Prince Jing's sons didn't look like him.

The emperor and Luo Ruisheng said that they looked a lot like Prince Jing, but unless Mu Tianxiao had gone blind, those were just polite comments!

Since he was a couple years younger than Prince Jing, Mu Tianxiao didn't know what Prince Jing had looked like as a child. The more he thought, the more he drove himself into a corner, the more he convinced himself he must be right.

Regardless of whether the male consort really did give birth to the children or not, the imperial physicians had said before that Prince Jing's children would most likely suffer from the same mute condition as Prince Jing did. But the reality Mu Tianxiao saw was that none of the children were mute, and none of them looked like Prince Jing. That was suspicious.

The imperial physician that the emperor sent had definitely tested their legitimacy, but the western border was Prince Jing's territory. Wouldn't he get whatever results he wanted?

Yes, that must be what had happened. Prince Jing knew that his muteness was a disadvantage, but if he had healthy children, it wouldn't be such a big deal.

Prince Jing was determined to fight for the throne, so it was very likely that he took the risk to disguise the children as his own. As for the male consort giving birth...

Mu Tianxiao thought it was quite an attention-seeking strategy, or perhaps... He had a bolder theory: there was one child within the four that did look a lot like the male consort. Could it be that these healthy babies were the children of the male consort and another woman, and Prince Jing had simply recorded them under his name?

If that was the case, Prince Jing truly was fearless!

Mu Tianxiao was certain that he'd gotten some dirt on Prince Jing. He'd use this to make a plan and hit him where it hurt.

The emperor was too biased. But what would happen if he found out that the grandson he doted on wasn't Prince Jing's real offspring? He couldn't wait to see the emperor's reaction. Even Empress Xiaohui's son wouldn't be able to recover from muddying the imperial bloodline.

But what if he was wrong? Would he suffer because of his own meddling?

...No, not as long as he made sure they were "illegitimate."

When Mu Tianxiao thought of this, the humiliation he'd suffered earlier meant nothing. His mood improved and he smiled, saying, "I think the little heir is quite interesting. It would be nice if we could meet him again."

Liang Suyun didn't know the truth. She thought the sixth prince just liked children.

As for Li Yu—after seeing the emperor and waiting until the emperor had held Dabao for a sufficiently long amount of time, he took the children to Changchun Palace.

He'd been to Changchun Palace when he was a fish, but it was his first time as a human and as Prince Jing's consort. He had his guard up carefully, afraid that he would arouse suspicion by showing his familiarity with the area. After all, they were at the palace.

Don't worry. Prince Jing warmly patted the back of his hand, telling him to not be so nervous. Ever since they'd entered the palace, he'd been with him and had never left his side.

Li Yu followed Prince Jing, comforted.

The servants at Changchun Palace had been informed in advance that they were coming. The cloth and silk to pay homage to the late empress was laid out, and the main hall had been tidied up, candles flickering.

Prince Jing lit three sticks of incense as usual, and the family of six bowed to Empress Xiaohui's tablet over and over again.

This scene reminded Li Yu of the secret from Prince Jing's infancy that took place in Changchun Palace, that he had seen in the system. He had never understood this secret, and he hadn't had time to ponder it after he had his fish children; he was too busy raising them.

Maybe he should take this opportunity to find time and wander around Changchun Palace? He might be able to locate the room and find some clues. He thought this was a pretty good idea.

Wang Xi found two chairs for Prince Jing and Li Yu, and they both sat down. Sibao suddenly opened his little eyes and pointed somewhere, shouting, "Aaahhh!"

Li Yu looked at where the chubby hand was pointing and saw a box placed on the shelf. There was something on the box that looked like a golden pouch.

That was a little strange, he thought. Why hadn't he seen this when he came last time? But Changchun Palace had been cleaned since then, so perhaps it was originally somewhere else and the staff had just moved it here recently.

Prince Jing's gaze ordered Wang Xi to go over and take a look. Soon after, he brought back an old cloth tiger.

"Aahh!" *Tiger!*

This cloth tiger attracted all the children's attention, and they all started wailing. They had a lot of toys, so of course they couldn't miss out on a cloth tiger.

The children all wanted the cloth tiger. Wang Xi didn't dare give it to them directly, so after he'd tested it with a silver needle, he cleaned off the dust on it and wiped it with a cloth a few times before handing it to Prince Jing. It could only be given to the children after Prince Jing approved.

Prince Jing took the cloth tiger and glanced at it with a look of nostalgia.

Li Yu had seen an older woman sewing a cloth tiger in the memory, and he'd seen another cloth tiger in Empress Xiaohui's room in the Cheng'en Manor. Now there was another one—where had it come from?

"Tianchi, do you have memories of this?" Li Yu asked.

Prince Jing nodded and showed Li Yu a stitch on the cloth tiger's tail that had been sewn back together after it broke.

"This..." Li Yu laughed. "Did you play with it when you were younger?" Empress Xiaohui liked to make cloth tigers for her son, so Prince Jing must have had one.

His guess was right. Prince Jing nodded again.

Li Yu recalled the secret and asked, probing, "Then...do you remember a wet nurse you had who was in her thirties when you were a child?"

Prince Jing slowly shook his head.

This wasn't the first time Li Yu had asked this. He didn't have much hope to begin with; the Prince Jing in the memory had still been an infant. He'd looked even younger than Dabao and the others, so how could the adult Prince Jing remember?

Wang Xi didn't know either. Li Yu had asked before and found out that Wang Xi had only begun accompanying Prince Jing after Empress Xiaohui passed away. Wang-gonggong did know a wet nurse who had served Prince Jing before, but that wet nurse was tall and strong, which didn't match the wet nurse in the memory. However, Li Yu assumed a prince would have several wet nurses, and concluded that the one he saw in the memory was only one of them. Unfortunately, neither Wang Xi nor the other wet nurse knew anything about her.

He wouldn't have to ask Head Eunuch Luo, right?

After much thought, Li Yu decided that this was the only other person he could ask. But would Head Eunuch Luo help him?

Prince Jing looked over the cloth tiger, squeezed it, and after determining that nothing was wrong with it, put it in Sibao's hand. Sibao held the cloth tiger that Daddy Prince Jing gave him and yelled in happiness. But soon, the other three children targeted him.

Dabao, Erbao, and Sanbao all yelled, "Aaahhh!" *Everyone who saw it gets a share!*

Sibao wasn't having it! Daddy Prince Jing gave him this toy! It was only Sibao's! Sibao put the cloth tiger under his arm. He could roll and sit, but he couldn't walk yet, so he rolled on the spot with the cloth tiger in his arms, planning to escape.

Dabao, Erbao, and Sanbao quickly blocked Sibao with their round little bodies. When Sibao stopped rolling, Erbao grabbed the cloth tiger's tail, Dabao and Sanbao each grabbed a tiger's leg, and Sibao held the tiger's head. Nobody was willing to let go.

After a short stalemate, a ripping sound was heard. The cloth tiger was quite old and had been ripped once before, so it was easy for it to get torn in the children's scuffle. Dabao, Erbao, and Sanbao were dazed and quickly let go of the toy. Sibao grabbed the broken tiger, his lip trembling, wanting to cry.

Li Yu almost cried himself, from laughter. He rushed forward to hold Sibao, who buried his head in his fish father's arms and sobbed, heartbroken. Li Yu gently patted his back, whispered a few words of comfort, and looked at the cloth tiger in Sibao's hand. It was in pretty bad condition.

Li Yu furtively glanced at Prince Jing. He was also smiling, not upset at all.

Li Yu asked for the toy, pretended to look at it, and softly said, "Don't cry, Sibao. It'll be back how it was once we sew it up."

Sibao blinked his tear-filled eyes, confused.

Li Yu mimed sewing to show him what he meant and opened up the cloth tiger. But as he did, he noticed the words "Pu Liu" embroidered into the tiger's lining.

His heart skipped a beat. Why were there words embroidered inside?

This cloth tiger had been Prince Jing's toy when he was a child, so it couldn't be anything like a love token, but it looked a little like the label on modern clothes! Was the label a name? The person who'd made the cloth tiger?

As Li Yu was thinking, Sibao started getting anxious waiting for him to speak again and pulled on his sleeve. Li Yu returned to his senses and went back to comforting Sibao. Fifteen minutes later, Sibao was asleep in his fish father's arms with tears in his eyelashes. He'd finally quieted down. Li Yu had to strike while the iron was hot and teach the little troublemakers to show love and respect as good brothers should.

Dabao knew he'd misbehaved: he sat ramrod straight, clasping his hands together and asking for forgiveness like an adult. Erbao and Sanbao looked at each other, took off each other's pants, exposing their little butts, and each asked their fish dad to spank the other one.

Li Yu had to hold in a laugh.

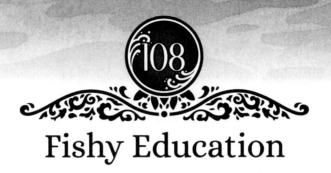

Fishy Education

L I YU PATTED Dabao's head, and he didn't spank Erbao or Sanbao.

Stacking their three soft hands together, he said, "You are all brothers, so you should help and look out for each other, not fight among yourselves. When your brother receives a good thing, you should be happy for him instead of trying to take it. Because—"

Li Yu stopped suddenly. He realized what he was saying and uneasily glanced at Prince Jing. Was it right to teach the children this way? They were children of the royal family, after all...

But they were his children too. If he didn't teach them, who would?

Prince Jing nodded slightly at Li Yu to continue.

Encouraged, Li Yu smiled and continued, "...Because things that are yours will end up in your hands in the end, and things that are not yours will never stay in your hands."

Dabao looked at the cloth tiger, thoughtful. Erbao and Sanbao stopped trying to push the blame onto one another and looked at each other mischievously, both pushing their own butts toward their fish father for a spanking.

Li Yu asked them to put their pants on each other the same way they took them off.

Dabao thought it through. Then he took out the beloved brush that Grandpa had given him, put it next to the sleeping Sibao, and patted Sibao's head, imitating his fish father.

Meanwhile Erbao and Sanbao sat together, trying to put the broken cloth tiger back together again. But the cloth tiger was too damaged for babies to fix it. When Erbao and Sanbao realized this, they lowered their heads, desolate.

At a glance from Prince Jing, Wang Xi brought over a couple of other toys. He usually brought a few toys with him wherever he went these days, and among them was Erbao's favorite cloth duck and Sanbao's favorite rattle drum.

Erbao and Sanbao, following Dabao's example, put the cloth duck and rattle drum in front of Sibao.

When Sibao woke up and looked around, he saw that his brothers were sitting around him and had given him a lot of things. When they saw that he'd woken up, they all came over to kiss him. Sibao loved kisses. He immediately forgot about the cloth tiger and started to play with the toys and join in the kissing game with his brothers.

Li Yu had successfully remedied a little issue between his children and made them forget about it completely afterward.

Prince Jing was listening to him teach the fish children, and he thought that a lot of what Xiaoyu said sounded very sensible. He'd never heard some of these things before—teachers and the Grand Secretaries didn't say things like this. He was used to princes only being polite to each other on the surface, but now he thought the way the fish children had made up was how it should be instead.

Just then, a bright yellow robe briefly came into view outside the palace. Wang Xi, who wasn't far from the door, quickly gave Prince Jing a look. He was afraid that the consort would say something taboo by accident, and he wanted to stop him.

Prince Jing shook his head, stopping Wang Xi from going over. He liked listening to Xiaoyu's reasoning; he didn't think there was an issue.

The emperor heard Li Yu's words from outside. All emperors loved eavesdropping; it had been that way throughout history. Originally, he'd wanted to see what the couple would say in front of Empress Xiaohui, so he followed them secretly and accidentally overheard Li Yu disciplining his children. The emperor didn't quite agree with what Li Yu was saying, so he muttered, "Nonsense," but there was a smile on his face. He watched the children playing together happily for quite a while.

Head Eunuch Luo was with him and privately thought, *Your Majesty said it was nonsense, but you're more excited than ever!*

Prince Jing waited for the emperor to leave before walking over to Li Yu, who had no clue that the emperor's respect for him had grown a little bit. He looked up at the prince inquisitively. Prince Jing smiled and patted his head.

Dabao, Erbao, Sanbao, and Sibao gathered to babble to each other. It turned out that their fish father liked having his head pet too!

Their fish father actually blushed in front of the fish children.

"Oh, right! Your Highness!" Li Yu flipped over the cloth tiger to the side with the embroidered name and showed it to Prince Jing and Wang Xi.

Wang Xi looked at it several times and touched it too. Then he said with certainty, "There is a rule in Changchun Palace that things made by palace servants must be marked in a hidden place. But the 'Pu Liu' embroidered there... Forgive me, but I've never heard of this before. Don't worry, consort. This is most likely a person's name, and I can find out who it is if I check the palace's personnel records."

Li Yu thanked him immediately. He wondered if there would be progress this time, and if it had anything to do with the secret he knew about.

Wang Xi ordered someone to retrieve the personnel records. Soon they came back to report that after Empress Xiaohu's passing, a couple of things had been lost in Changchun Palace, one volume of personnel records among them. Wang Xi took the rest of the volumes and flipped through them, but he didn't find a Pu Liu.

Wang Xi knew that it was a habit in the palace to claim an item was lost when someone couldn't find it, so he was about to start scolding, but Li Yu quickly said, "I was just curious as to who made the cloth tiger, that's all."

On the surface, it seemed that they just weren't able to find it, but it was strange for the singular volume they needed out of several others to go missing.

According to the person responsible for the records, the volume had been lost for a long time now. Those recorded on the volume were from that time and not current servants.

Having hit a dead end, Li Yu decided to go ask Head Eunuch Luo if Prince Jing had other wet nurses, as well as who this Pu Liu was. He was still thinking about the room he saw too. As Prince Jing watched the children play, Li Yu asked him, "Tianchi, can I take a look around?"

Prince Jing agreed, but he didn't ask Wang Xi to follow Li Yu, or have Wang Xi stay behind to watch the children. Instead, he picked up two babies and ordered Wang Xi to carry the other two, and they all followed Li Yu. Li Yu was responsible for looking around, while he was responsible for the children and protecting Li Yu.

Li Yu smiled. He asked a servant to lead the way and started to wander around the rooms.

They finished looking around pretty quickly, but he couldn't find a room that was exactly the same as the one he remembered.

Li Yu had thought before that the rooms in the palace looked very similar to one in the memory, so even if the decorations and furnishings had changed, things like the ceilings and beams should remain the same. Li Yu had hoped that he could use these details to find the room he was looking for, but he was unsuccessful. After circling the place, he found that they'd checked every room.

Li Yu counted the rooms they went through and felt something was off.

Usually, in a palace like this, the rooms would be in pairs—there'd be an even number. That was how it was at Prince Jing's manor. Empress Xiaohui's palace should also follow this rule, but he was certain that they had visited an odd number of rooms.

When Li Yu mentioned it offhandedly, the palace servant knelt in panic and said, "There was another room, but His Majesty sealed it..."

Li Yu was shocked. He had only made a random guess based on Prince Jing's manor, and he'd managed to guess correctly?

The servant peeled back a corner of a heavy curtain, revealing a yellowed seal. The curtain was blocking a room that he hadn't seen yet.

"His Majesty sealed this room when Empress Xiaohui was gravely ill, and forbade us servants from opening it."

The date on the seal confirmed what the servant said. As it had been sealed on the emperor's orders, Li Yu couldn't just casually open it—but since the layout of the rooms in Changchun Palace was symmetrical, Li Yu was able to compare it to the opposite side and concluded that the room he was looking for was probably this one.

The "Pu Liu" embroidered onto the cloth tiger was not necessarily related to the secret, but this room definitely was.

The emperor must be involved with this secret somehow. Why else would he order the room sealed? And he'd done it while Empress Xiaohui was ill, so it would have been a blow to her dignity. Wasn't he afraid of distressing her?

Li Yu was sure that the emperor would usually avoid doing anything to harm Empress Xiaohui. Hiding the existence of this room must have been even more important to him than Empress Xiaohui's dignity.

This secret made him feel like he was surrounded by more questions the closer he got. What kind of secret was this?

"Do you know what's inside?" Li Yu asked the servant.

In his memories, he'd seen the wet nurse ingest a packet of medicine, but he didn't know what had happened next. Could it be that she'd died of poison in this room, and that was why the emperor sealed it?

What a frightening idea. Li Yu felt nauseated just thinking about it.

The servant shook his head. "I came to Changchun Palace afterward, so the room was already sealed when I got here. I'm not sure what's inside either."

Li Yu had expected this. He didn't ask anything else.

Prince Jing noticed that Li Yu had been staring at the room in a daze, and realized something was off. He gave him an inquiring look. *What's wrong?*

Li Yu shook his head. It wouldn't be easy to describe this issue to Prince Jing, mainly because he'd been too young at the time and had no memory of it.

"Your Highness, Consort." Head Eunuch Luo's voice came from outside. "The emperor has brought gifts."

The emperor had been eavesdropping, and after he returned to Qianqing Palace, he had Head Eunuch Luo head over with gifts.

Li Yu was a little embarrassed. They hadn't been away from Qianqing Palace for very long, and the emperor made it seem like one day apart was like three years. But if the emperor had gifts for them, then they couldn't really stop him.

Prince Jing and Li Yu held their children as the gifts were announced.

The emperor had gifted Dabao with a tiny wolf-hair brush—small enough that his little chubby hand could hold it—and gave beautiful zodiac toys to the other three children.

The emperor has already gifted them a lot, Li Yu thought to himself, *so why does he suddenly want to give the children more gifts?*

In any case, it was quite obvious that the emperor favored Dabao. Maybe Dabao was the one who made him feel like one day was akin to three years.

In addition to gifting the children, he also presented a gift for their father, Li Yu. It was a painting by a famous artist of Mencius's mother teaching her child.[16] He felt like the emperor had misunderstood something. He wasn't implying that Li Yu should emulate Mencius's mother and move, right?

"Your Highness, Consort. There's this as well." Head Eunuch Luo had personally brought over two boxes of fish food. "The emperor knows that His Highness likes his pet fish, so he ordered me to bring some fish food. This is jingjiang shredded pork flavored fish food, a variety that the imperial kitchen recently developed."

---

16 Mencius (孟子) is a famous Chinese philosopher, and his mother is known for being a good mother. There is a famous saying "Mencius's mother moved three times" (孟母三迁), recounting how she moved to three different homes in order to find a suitable environment to raise her child in.

As he spoke, Head Eunuch Luo handed the box of fish food to Wang Xi, who immediately took it. Since it was food, he had to open it and inspect it. Wang Xi opened the box and the smell of fish food wafted through the air. Head Eunuch Luo's eyes suddenly blurred as he saw the consort and the four young gongzi staring at the food, unblinking.

Dabao, Erbao, Sanbao, and Sibao were all thinking the same thing: *I haven't had fish food in a long, long time. It smells so good! I want to eat it!*

Li Yu's fishiness was activated, and he really wanted to eat it too, but he knew that he couldn't expose himself in front of everyone. He could control himself, but the children couldn't. Fish food and peach blossom pastries were both foods they'd been pining after since they were babies. But now they'd turned into humans, they were only allowed the pastries—so when they saw the fish food, they couldn't stop staring at it.

Children weren't supposed to like fish food! Ridiculous!

Just as the children were about to start wailing, Li Yu glared at them fiercely. Frightened by their fish dad's scary eyes, none of them, from Dabao to Sibao, dared move or make a peep. Li Yu took the opportunity to slam the fish food box closed and stuff it into his sleeve.

Prince Jing was always paying attention to Xiaoyu. After Li Yu put the box away, Prince Jing cooperated smoothly with him. He took out a few pieces of peach blossom pastry and stuffed them into the fish children's mouths. They immediately forgot about the fish food.

Head Eunuch Luo rubbed his eyes. It seemed he'd been mistaken; how could he think that Prince Jing's children wanted fish food...?

As he was sitting down to have a cup of tea, Li Yu took the opportunity to put his questions to Luo Ruisheng. "Head Eunuch Luo, can I ask you a couple things?" he said in a low voice.

"Of course, Consort." Head Eunuch Luo had a great impression of this consort, so he was willing to answer his questions.

Li Yu asked, "Luo-gonggong, do you know a woman named Pu Liu? She probably used to be a servant in Changchun Palace."

An unnatural expression flashed across Luo-gonggong's face briefly, and Li Yu noticed it. "Consort, why are you asking this?"

Li Yu was cautious. He brought over the ripped cloth tiger and asked Head Eunuch Luo to look at the words embroidered on the lining. Li Yu used this as his excuse. "The children ripped the cloth tiger while playing. I saw this then, and I was curious—apparently, it's someone's name."

"I see..." Head Eunuch Luo smiled. "Consort, you're right. This is the mark used by a wet nurse named Pu Liu who worked for Empress Xiaohui. She had been the eldest and fourth prince's wet nurse, so Empress Xiaohui trusted her a lot. She was Prince Jing's wet nurse as well, but she made a disastrous mistake and couldn't continue. Empress Xiaohui had to cast her out of the palace, and the emperor sealed up her former residence."

Li Yu felt like he'd touched a sliver of light that connected several points of confusion together. If Pu Liu was truly the name of a wet nurse, then her age would be about right. She took care of Prince Jing for a short while, and the emperor sealed her residence...

"Is it the sealed room in Changchun Palace?"

No Outside Fish

"Yes, it's that room," said Head Eunuch Luo. "The emperor sealed the room—Empress Xiaohui was already weak from her sickness; he didn't want her to be upset by seeing it again."

So he did it for the empress...

Li Yu was fairly certain that the sealed room was the one in his memories. If it was Pu Liu's residence, Pu Liu must be the woman in the memory. This wet nurse had been cast from the palace, and even her room was still sealed. It was obvious that her mistake had been catastrophic.

The royal family had a lot of secrets, and Li Yu didn't know if this was something he could ask about. But he was only asking Head Eunuch Luo in private, so it shouldn't be an issue, right?

He kept prodding. "Luo-gonggong, do you know what mistake Pu Liu made?"

Head Eunuch Luo was silent for a moment. "It's been a long time since that incident, so it shouldn't be a problem to tell you, Consort," he said at last. "It was discovered that the wet nurse hadn't taken good care of the newborn Prince Jing, and she caused him to catch a cold. Empress Xiaohui was furious, but taking into consideration that Pu Liu had worked hard as the wet nurse of the late eldest and fourth prince, she showed her some mercy and only cast her from the palace."

"What?!" Why was it completely different from what he had imagined? Li Yu thought her mistake would be related to those drugs, but that was it? "So it happened because she didn't take good care of Prince Jing...?"

Head Eunuch Luo nodded. "I remember it clearly, because it happened right before Empress Xiaohui passed away. Prince Jing was born weak, and...couldn't speak. The imperial physician said that he had to be looked after with great care, but the wet nurse cracked open the window a little and forgot to close it. It was cold at the time, and Prince Jing fell ill soon after. Empress Xiaohui was already doing poorly at the time, and with the added burden of taking care of the newborn Highness, her health worsened."

Li Yu was shocked. "It...happened in that room?"

Pu Liu had been sent out of the palace because she didn't take good enough care of the young Prince Jing. But in the memory, Li Yu had seen that Pu Liu made cloth toys for Prince Jing herself and looked at him with a gaze full of love.

Li Yu had his own sons. He could tell that Pu Liu's love for Prince Jing was genuine.

And someone's personality was not easily changed. Pu Liu was the wet nurse for the eldest and fourth princes, so she wasn't a careless person and knew what she should and shouldn't do. How did she make such a basic mistake when it came to Prince Jing?

And even if the window was open, there was no way he'd catch a cold immediately. The window was far from the bed, and babies were usually swaddled. Cold wind would have to be blowing for quite a while for Prince Jing to get sick; even if Pu Liu momentarily forgot to close the window, wouldn't she have noticed it sooner?

He felt that Pu Liu's actions contradicted the love she held for Prince Jing.

And what did this have to do with the packet of drugs?

Li Yu's mind was mush. He kept chasing this secret, since it seemed to be significant. It couldn't just be a normal scene from Prince Jing's childhood—his wet nurse had argued with someone, then was chased out of the palace soon after.

Li Yu thought of another question. "If Pu Liu was Prince Jing's wet nurse, then why couldn't we find her in Changchun Palace's personnel records?"

"What?" Head Eunuch Luo hadn't expected this. "Impossible. How could she not be in the records?"

Li Yu was surprised too. He'd brought up the missing records deliberately, and Head Eunuch Luo's reaction seemed to be earnest. If even Luo Ruisheng didn't know that the volume was missing from Changchun Palace, it was unlikely that the emperor had ordered Pu Liu's name to be removed.

That made things even stranger. Even if someone was cast out of the palace, there should be records left of them. Why couldn't they find anything on Pu Liu? If the children hadn't damaged the cloth tiger, Li Yu would never have known that there'd been someone named Pu Liu here at all.

Ever since she was cast out of the palace, it was like she'd never existed.

Head Eunuch Luo had answered all of Li Yu's questions. There were still a few weird things about all this, but Li Yu didn't want to ask any more and make a mountain out of a molehill. Pu Liu was simply kicked out of the palace and had her room sealed. It wasn't some crime scene.

Oh, right. Pu Liu wasn't even dead, was she? She must still be alive somewhere, so if Li Yu wanted to know more, he just needed to find her and ask her himself.

But was it really necessary to get to the bottom of an incident that happened and concluded such a long time ago? If he really did find her, how was he going to explain to others how he "saw" and "knew about" Pu Liu taking the drugs?

Maybe it was just medicine for a condition she had?

Not every secret was perfect. Even if the secret wasn't what he thought it was, there was no need to be disappointed.

"Luo-gonggong," Li Yu asked, "where did Pu Liu go after she was cast out?"

"I heard she went back to her hometown," Luo Ruisheng replied.

Li Yu asked Head Eunuch Luo to help him find Pu Liu's residence in her hometown. It was normal enough for a woman who left the palace to return home.

If there were any new discoveries in the future, Li Yu would deal with it then.

Luo Ruisheng excused himself, and Prince Jing and Li Yu returned to the manor with the children.

Thanks to the unexpected situation that had cropped up in Changchun palace, Li Yu decided to start coaching his children.

"Remember, you can't let others find out that you used to be fish," he told them.

This was of the utmost importance. He thought of the amount of effort Prince Jing had put into covering up for them only for the children to almost expose themselves because of a box of fish food. That would have been a disaster.

Li Yu was still fearful. He thought it was time to teach the children how to protect themselves.

Dabao, Erbao, and Sanbao didn't quite get it. It was nice to be a fish. Why couldn't they talk about the time when they were fish?

Under the sparkling gaze of his children, Li Yu felt a little reluctant. He could understand his parents more with each passing day.

He and Prince Jing protected the children well, but they would have to face the world on their own one day. It was necessary for the naive fish children to understand the evil within people's hearts as soon as possible.

"Only you guys and us fathers know about how you used to be fish," the young fish father said sternly. "You absolutely cannot let anyone else know, because they can't turn into fish like us. If they find out, they'll do a lot of scary things to you."

Erbao cocked his head. *Scary?*

Hm...

Li Yu said, "They'll call you strange and lock you all up, and then they won't let you eat anything or see your fathers."

Dabao, Erbao, and Sanbao suddenly sat upright, nodding fiercely. Being locked up, with nothing to eat and not being able to see their fish father...that was truly quite scary.

Li Yu was very satisfied with their reaction. In addition to not letting the fish children reveal their identities, he also had to make sure that they wouldn't be kidnapped by bad guys. Thinking about the latter situation made him a bit emotional.

Touching upon his own experience, he sincerely said, "If something happens to me and I can't be by your side but someone uses my name to call out to you...then they're probably lying to you. Ignore them."

Dabao, Erbao, and Sanbao were all confused again. It was hard to be a secret fish. What did he mean, if Daddy wasn't by their side but someone used his name? The fish children didn't quite understand.

"In any case, remember what Daddy said," Li Yu said. "Ignore everyone unless Daddy says you can trust them."

Dabao, Erbao, and Sanbao understood this, and they nodded. Sibao's hand was propped under his chin. His head nodded too—and then slipped down off his hand.

"Sibao." Li Yu smiled slyly and nudged the little fish awake. "Copy what Daddy just said ten times."

Sibao trembled, feeling sorry for himself. *Sob, I accidentally made Fish Dad angry! His face is so scary! B-but I don't know how to write yet!*

With Dabao's help, Sibao wrote a page full of "Oa," and presented it to his fish father with his soft little hands. Fish Father knew what Dabao's "Oa" meant by now, and he would smile at him whenever he saw it, but when he saw Sibao's "Oa," he wanted to beat someone up.

Li Yu refused to let any of his fish children stay confused about this, so he reminded them whenever he could, and eventually even the slightly slower Sibao remembered his fish father's words.

Before long, Qinghe-junzhu—Ye-shizi and the Princess of Jinjue's daughter—turned one hundred days old, and Ye Qinghuan held a banquet at the Cheng'en Manor. Li Yu had promised to show up with his family and a school of fish. He planned to offer his congratulations first, and after he'd seen the princess and Ye-shizi, he would turn into a fish once he couldn't delay it any longer. Then, he would be a real fish, and the little fish next to him would be plushies. It was hard to tell real from fake, and Prince Jing would be responsible for covering up anything that happened. They would just say that he'd returned to the manor early.

They'd always done things this way, and Prince Jing didn't object. Before they left, Li Yu strung the fish plushies together and was about to put them into the crystal bottle when he saw another bottle, exactly the same as his own, in Prince Jing's hand.

Li Yu felt a little strange. When he looked at the bottle Prince Jing was holding, he saw a gold and silver carp that was very similar in pattern and size to his own fish form...

Why was there another fish butting in on his territory?

Li Yu was alarmed, but Prince Jing put that bottle in his hand, then took out another, slightly smaller bottle from his sleeve, with four small fish inside. He carefully transferred those fish to the bottle he'd handed to Li Yu.

Li Yu realized these new fish were very similar in color to the fish children. Why did Prince Jing have these fish doubles in his possession?

He mulled over it for a bit and finally realized that this was... a stand-in Prince Jing had prepared for him and their fish children.

Always using fish plushies when they went out and having to worry whether or not they'd be found out was quite inconvenient. But if they brought live fish that looked similar to him and the fish children, then what was there to worry about?

Li Yu quickly took the bottle and examined the fish closely.

No two leaves were exactly the same in the world, and likewise, no two fish were exactly the same. The larger fish's patterns were similar to his but had fewer golden scales. If the fish were right next to each other, it would still be easy to tell the difference. But with just one fish, it was almost impossible to tell the difference if you didn't get too close.

Ye Qinghuan and the princess of Jinjue usually saw the fish through the tank or the crystal bottles, so they wouldn't be overly familiar with the fish's patterns. The other fish would be enough to fool *them*, but if it was Prince Jing, it would be a different story.

With this body double, he didn't have to turn into a fish anymore. He could turn into a fish if he really needed to, but the children wouldn't be able to until they were seven years old. Wang Xi had already muttered a couple of times that the little fish in the fish tank were always collectively asleep. Li Yu had made up a random excuse, but he felt that Wang-gonggong was getting suspicious. Prince Jing's new acquisition solved the problem easily.

Li Yu was indescribably happy. "You must have gone to great effort to get these fish." It had to have been difficult if even *he* thought they looked similar.

Prince Jing shook his head; it wasn't that much effort. He'd started looking for them as soon as Xiaoyu revealed his identity. It had taken over a year, and he began to look for substitutes for the fish children as well not too long after. The person he'd charged with this task had said that these things couldn't be forced, but Prince Jing thought that as long as he cast a wide net and kept looking, he would definitely find what he wanted.

Li Yu happily held the bottle and blew a kiss to Prince Jing. What a mess, he used to get jealous of himself (oops), but now that there were fish substitutes and it wasn't him anymore, was Prince Jing going to have to treat the substitute fish the same as his pet fish in front of others?

That might not even be enough. Did he even have to pet that fish as well?

Li Yu realized this and immediately got jealous again. "Tianchi," he blurted out, "you can't have other fish!"

Merman Night Attack

PRINCE JING DIDN'T realize what he meant at first, but Xiaoyu looked like he was facing his archnemesis. Prince Jing shook his head: *I won't.*

Perhaps Xiaoyu didn't want him to get too close to the substitute fish. Prince Jing himself wouldn't even let others touch Xiaoyu, so they shared that in common.

Even after Prince Jing's promise, Li Yu still wasn't fully appeased. Luckily, Prince Jing didn't show the substitute fish very much affection and spent most of the time watching either him or their real fish children.

Li Yu's jealous mind finally calmed down. Now he thought it through, that the substitute fish was just an ordinary koi, not a "yao" like him that could turn into a human. It was completely ridiculous to get jealous of a normal fish.

He felt a bit guilty. He decided to feed the fish well as compensation.

Of course, regardless of what he felt about it, the substitute fish was only there to sit and look pretty. Toward certain humans who were way overthinking things, the substitute fish remained unbothered.

When they arrived at the Cheng'en Manor, Ye Qinghuan and the Princess of Jinjue came out together to welcome them. Li Yu brought the children out first and introduced them one by one.

Dabao and the others were dressed like little immortals in a New Year's painting, each of them wearing bright red robes decorated with gold, with their hair up in little pigtails. The Princess of Jinjue was so happy she couldn't stop smiling and said, almost in disbelief, "My heavens, there really are four!"

In ancient times, it was rare to even see twins, but Li Yu had four at once. The Princess of Jinjue almost didn't want to repeat the process after giving birth to just one child; she felt that Li Yu was practically a deity for birthing four.

"Please, sit." The princess ordered someone to prepare a seat for Li Yu as she served him hot red date tea.[17] Prince Jing, on the other hand, was given biluochun, a green tea. Li Yu took a sip of the sweet tea and noticed that the princess was drinking the same thing. There were a couple of plump red dates at the bottom of the teacup, and Li Yu immediately understood that the princess wanted him to stay healthy.

This was a kindness from the princess. Li Yu thought to himself that he'd had it way too easy when he gave birth. The princess had had to work much harder.

While they were talking, Ye Qinghuan personally brought over Qinghe-junzhu. The little princess was one hundred days old now, and her skin was pale and supple. Her little arms and legs stuck out like lotus root joints—her dewy eyes were like the princess's, but she had Ye Qinghuan's mouth. Around her neck was the lock charm that Li Yu had gifted her.

When the fish children saw the little baby girl, they all widened their eyes, even Sibao, who was usually a beat slower than the others. They'd never seen such a small person. She was even smaller than they were!

---

17   *Red dates are said to help replenish nutrients and blood, and help with circulation, so women often consume it for the health benefits.*

Dabao cried out and reached out to her. Uncle Ye was hugging her—he wanted to hug her too! Erbao, Sanbao, and Sibao followed Dabao's example and started crying out as well. They wanted to play with her!

"No!" Fish Father scolded them.

The children immediately put down their hands, disappointed, still staring at the baby girl. The princess and Ye Qinghuan almost laughed out loud.

"She's still young, so she can't play with you guys yet," Li Yu said sternly. "Remember, you have to protect her in the future."

The children nodded in unison, but they still wanted to see her. The Princess of Jinjue had a cradle brought out, and she put the baby princess inside. The four boys grabbed on to the cradle and gazed at her quietly.

"They're so smart," the Princess of Jinjue exclaimed in surprise.

"The little princess is very beautiful as well." Li Yu couldn't help but admire her.

That seemed to strike a nerve with Ye Qinghuan, whose eyes were glued to his daughter. "Recently, I've been thinking about the fact that in about fifteen years, she'll leave me and marry into another family," he said sadly. "I can't bear to let her go."

Li Yu snorted. In terms of fatherly silliness, Ye Qinghuan really had Prince Jing beat...

"Oh, shut up!" The Princess of Jinjue thought Ye Qinghuan was embarrassing and wanted to throw her teacup at him to shut him up.

But inadvertently, tears welled in her eyes. Even though Jinjue was more open-minded, people there usually liked boys better. When she'd learned from the midwife that she'd given birth to a daughter, she felt a little uneasy, even with her status as a princess.

But to her surprise, Ye Qinghuan and the entire House of Cheng'en doted on the girl very much. Her in-laws visited her every day, asking her about the baby's condition, and often wanted to take care of the baby. It lifted a burden off her shoulders. Originally, she'd wanted to try to have a son as well so they could have one boy and one girl, but her husband, who was usually easygoing, became surprisingly stubborn. He told her that giving birth was hard and that she should recover her health first. There was no rush.

The care her husband and his family showed her made her realize that although the emperor had arranged her marriage, she had married into a good family.

The princess herself still wanted a son—not because she didn't like girls, but because Li Yu's four sons were so lively and clever that it was easy to become envious. The princess couldn't help but look at Ye Qinghuan, and she noticed that Li Yu was also looking at Prince Jing.

The two people, each with their own thoughts, instantly felt a connection. Li Yu scratched his cheek in embarrassment. It was because Qinghe-junzhu was so cute! He wanted one too!

But he couldn't see the baby girl for too long. Soon after, the wet nurse came over and took the little girl back.

Li Yu learned from the Princess of Jinjue that her daughter had caught a chill in the past few days and had only just recovered, so she couldn't stay outside for too long. The princess had been worried for several days because of her daughter's illness, especially since such a young child couldn't take medicine directly yet. Usually, the wet nurse would take the medicine first, wait until the medicine entered the breast milk, and then feed it to the baby.

The four fish children had always been healthy, whether they were young fish or human babies, so Li Yu had never experienced this before. When the princess talked about this process, something tickled at the back of his mind, but he couldn't put his finger on what it was.

With the little girl back in her room, the four children were disappointed that they couldn't see her anymore.

Ye Qinghuan had taken care of these young masters back on the western border, so he knew their personalities well. He smiled and whistled, and Xiongfeng came running in, the hero here to save the day. Xiongfeng recognized Li Yu and wagged his tail excitedly at him.

"Xiongfeng, long time no see." Li Yu squatted down and patted Xiongfeng's head. Xiongfeng tried to lick his hand. Li Yu suddenly felt a chill on his back. He turned around, only to see Prince Jing quickly averting his eyes. Weird.

The children's eyes lit up when they saw the dog, and they finally stopped whining about not seeing Qinghe-junzhu.

"Dogs are good friends with humans! No bullying him!" Li Yu quickly warned the children, but they were still too young and weren't suited for playing with dogs yet. Li Yu carried them and lowered them as much as he could so they could see Xiongfeng clearly.

Xiongfeng had been trained by Ye Qinghuan, so he didn't seem to dare get too close to the children. But he loved children, so he anxiously paced back and forth nearby.

After Li Yu introduced them to the concept of dogs, Dabao, Erbao, and Sanbao moved a bit closer and felt a little afraid of the sharp canine teeth. Only Sibao fearlessly reached out a hand and playfully poked Xiongfeng's nose.

Everyone present—even Xiongfeng, who loved to poke fish— was stunned.

Prince Jing moved slightly, wanting to take Sibao back, but Li Yu stopped him. He saw Xiongfeng tentatively nudge Sibao back gently, and Sibao let out a happy gurgle. Prince Jing finally relaxed.

"Don't worry," Ye Qinghuan comforted them warmly. "Xiongfeng won't bite Sibao."

Li Yu knew it was true; Xiongfeng had never even bitten a fish. Even so, he observed the interactions between Sibao and Xiongfeng nervously. He technically believed in Xiongfeng, but it was impossible for him to completely put his concern to rest.

Dabao, Erbao, and Sanbao were encouraged by Sibao and copied him, poking Xiongfeng with their fingers.

Surrounded by children, Xiongfeng wagged his tail so vigorously that it started to have an afterimage. After wagging his tail for a while, he started to roll around.

"Oh, right." The princess remembered Prince Jing's fish. "Where are the fish?"

She'd been anticipating this for a long time, but she'd forgotten about it for a bit while she watched the children playing with the dog.

Li Yu smiled slightly. In the past, everyone wanted to see the fish as soon as possible, but it really was different after having kids. For the first time, Li Yu showed the crystal bottle without hesitating.

The fish substitute swam around happily with the little fish in tow. The sparkling colors and colorful tail made Li Yu think it was himself for a moment.

The princess smiled and got closer, watched the fish for a bit, and then furrowed her brows.

Was there a flaw?

Li Yu's heart tightened. "What's wrong? Is something wrong?"

"No..." the princess responded. "I just feel like the fish isn't as charming as it used to be."

...I should take that as a compliment, right? Right?

Li Yu smiled and said something deep: "Princess, it's probably because he's the same as me. He became a father, so he's become more mature and steady."

The princess smiled, convinced.

As Ye Qinghuan played easily with the four children, he asked Prince Jing, "Aren't you going to go look at your fish too?"

The princess wasn't aware, but Ye Qinghuan knew exactly how much Prince Jing liked his fish and how unwilling he was to let other people take even a single peek at it. But he'd generously brought his fish to the Cheng'en Manor, and for some reason, Ye Qinghuan felt like Prince Jing was even acting a little cold toward it.

Ye Qinghuan grew more and more confused. Prince Jing had even done something unspeakable to his fish on his wedding night, and Ye Qinghuan still felt sorry for the consort even now. Prince Jing's thoughts were clearly focused on his consort and his children. His cold eyes softened when he looked at Li Yu.

If he was this affectionate, then why had he done that to his fish? Perhaps Prince Jing had just lost his mind for a few days, then realized the error of his ways.

"It's good that you thought it through now," Ye Qinghuan said.

Prince Jing had no clue what his cousin was thinking.

After Qinghe-junzhu's one-hundred-days-old banquet, Prince Jing took Li Yu and his children to visit the former Duke of Cheng'en.

Li Yu knew that today, they'd come not only to attend the banquet, but also to let the former Duke of Cheng'en officially meet his great-grandchildren. Ye Qian was anticipating them and waited for them in the garden with some good wine.

When he saw Prince Jing's four children, the rims of his eyes remained red for a long time.

Perhaps it was fate—the emperor liked Dabao a little more, Prince Jing liked Sibao a little more, and the former Duke of Cheng'en felt more connected to Erbao and Sanbao, the two little rivals. He said that his two children liked to pinch each other when they were younger too.

Who were his two children?

Li Yu and Prince Jing glanced at each other, respect for the former Duke of Cheng'en evident in their eyes.

Since all four children were favorites of different people, Li Yu felt like everything had worked out.

The former Duke of Cheng'en, whose hair and beard had gotten a little grayer since the last time they'd met, held Erbao and Sanbao in his lap as he asked Li Yu to tell him interesting stories from their time in the west. The elderly man was very interested in the duck army, and he'd quite liked the Quanjude roast duck that Ye Qinghuan had brought back. He could eat over half of a duck in one sitting.

They stayed until late into the night, and Prince Jing returned to the manor with a slightly drunk Li Yu. The children had fallen asleep much earlier, and Wang Xi took them to their rooms.

Prince Jing put the dazed Li Yu down on the bed and wrapped him in a brocade quilt embroidered with green aquatic plant patterns. Li Yu suddenly opened his eyes and looked around quizzically. "Tianchi, we're home?"

Prince Jing smiled and patted his head in response. Li Yu's face was burning red, and his mind was dulled from drinking; he couldn't remember what he wanted to do.

Wang Xi knocked gently from outside. If he was this drunk, the consort might have a hangover the next day, so Wang-gonggong came on Prince Jing's orders to deliver sobering tea. Prince Jing was going to go outside to bring in the tea and give Xiaoyu a cup, but Li Yu thought he was leaving and squinted in displeasure.

In desperation, the drunk fish used a skill to keep Prince Jing there. Prince Jing only felt a gust of cold wind before a silver tail speckled with gold swept over and wrapped around his waist.

Heh heh heh. Where do you think you're going?! I'll use my tail to yank you back till the end of time!

The domineering fish tail pulled Prince Jing back forcefully. Prince Jing was afraid of hurting Li Yu, so he complied with the insistent tail and came back to the bed.

Li Yu, seeing Prince Jing "change his mind," chuckled and hugged his neck.

"Tianchi, Qinghe-junzhu is so cute... Dabao and the others really like her...and I like her too. Why don't *we* have a daughter like her? I'd like her even more if she were ours." Li Yu said a bunch of things that would have normally made him blush and wrapped his tail even tighter.

What he meant was that if they didn't do it, Prince Jing couldn't leave.

Prince Jing stopped in place and hugged him back. He would never reject a request from Li Yu, but the request this time was a bit special. He hesitated a little.

"Tianchi, what are you waiting for?" Li Yu scooted over and blew into his ear. "What should I do? My tail is so uncomfortable..."

His tail moved slowly and rubbed around Prince Jing's waist. Prince Jing took a deep breath and picked up this drunken fish that loved to ignite fires.

After they came back from the western border, Prince Jing had made a few changes to their bedroom. Some of the water from the outside pond had been brought in to make a small bathing pool—

it was normally for aesthetics, but it could also be used after Xiaoyu transformed if needed.

Prince Jing embraced his fish tightly and strode over to the pool.

Fishy
Misunderstanding

L I YU TOOK ADVANTAGE of his own drunkenness to ask for it once in an outrageous way, but the system didn't give him any notifications. The fish, eager for a daughter, wouldn't let Prince Jing go, and asked for it again, but there was still no notification. Li Yu was upset. He was determined to make the notification appear.

Was the bathing pool incompatible with a daughter? Then he would change places and try again as a human. He just wanted them to have their own little girl.

Li Yu lost count of how many times they did it. In the end, Prince Jing had to just look at him apologetically. Li Yu poked a trembling finger out, asking for one more try. Prince Jing sighed softly, wrapped his finger in his hand, and put it back under the brocade quilt.

Prince Jing draped some clothes over himself and got up from the bed. Li Yu noticed that his husband's back was still straight, but he was staggering a little. He wanted to laugh, but he was a bit ashamed too.

He'd been too eager. Preparing for pregnancy and other matters like that couldn't be done in such a short amount of time; he couldn't be greedy just because he was a fish with a system. He really did want a daughter, but he had to think of his husband too.

Li Yu opened his mouth to call out to his husband, but his throat was so hoarse that he couldn't make a sound. He wanted to flip over and get up from the bed—but then he realized that while Prince Jing was just walking a little funny, he himself couldn't feel anything below his waist.

This was a battle where they both lost more than they won. Li Yu struggled on the spot for a bit before succumbing to exhaustion.

When he woke up in the middle of the night, he found that he had turned back into a fish and was wrapped in an aquatic plant blanket, lying on his silver stone bed in the crystal fish tank. Prince Jing had probably put him here after his time was up.

His fish form helped him relieve some fatigue. He didn't know how long he'd been sleeping, but at least he didn't feel numb anymore.

Li Yu reluctantly shrugged off the plant blanket and swam to the side of the crystal fish tank to look at his husband. Since he was feeling much better, how was his husband?

The clear, bright moonlight poured in from the window, and the room was silent. But the bed was empty and the person he wanted to see wasn't there.

Huh? Had Prince Jing stepped out?

Li Yu waited a little, but Prince Jing didn't come back. At last Li Yu couldn't wait anymore. He turned into a human to look for Prince Jing.

Last night had been much too intense. His legs were still soft and rubbery when he stepped onto the ground, and he felt like he was floating when he walked. If he wasn't careful, he'd fall.

He supported himself with the surrounding furniture all the way to the door and was about to open it when he heard someone saying quietly, "Your Highness, too much medicine will be harmful to your body. Please think it over again..."

"Yes, this servant understands. I won't say anything, and I won't let the consort know."

Li Yu had already noticed that it was Prince Jing and a servant discussing something outside. Usually, he wouldn't keep listening if it was something he shouldn't be listening to, but suddenly hearing "I won't let the consort know" made him feel a bit awkward.

Deciding not to listen was different from keeping something from him actively. And it seemed like Prince Jing was hiding the fact that he was taking medicine from him—and that he had done so before?

He had to be on his guard a bit.

Li Yu opened the door a crack silently and saw a shocking scene. Prince Jing took a bowl filled with dark liquid from a guard dressed in black and downed it without looking. After he finished, he coughed a couple of times, wiped his lips, and gestured for the guard to leave.

From what the guard said, Li Yu pieced together that Prince Jing was taking medicine, but he didn't know what kind of medicine— and it could harm him if he took too much...

After fighting a lengthy battle, his fish mind was filled with filth. He couldn't help but wonder if it was an aphrodisiac. Could it be that his husband was almost wrung dry and had to use medicine to keep it up?

He and Prince Jing had a great relationship, and their married life was peaceful. They always did it naturally, going with the flow. Could it be that it was actually difficult for Prince Jing and he had to rely on drugs to keep up with him?

Remembering Prince Jing's weak steps just now, Li Yu did think it was a bit suspicious.

He'd heard that when it came to these kinds of men's health issues, outer appearances had no bearing on it. Those who looked fine might still suffer from these problems. From emperors to commoners, this issue seemed to affect everyone equally.

If that was the case, then it was no wonder Prince Jing wanted to hide it from him. After all, men could be incompetent in front of anyone but their spouse—especially this type of incompetence.

Li Yu couldn't keep thinking about this. Prince Jing was about to come back in. He could lie back down on the bed and pretend he didn't know anything, but something like this couldn't be hidden forever. He was more concerned about whether it would cause harm to Prince Jing's body if things went on like this. Would he take more and more medicine, rely on it more and more, and become even more incompetent?

No!

Married life and each other's dignity were important, but his husband's health was also very important. Incompetence in this regard was a condition, and a condition must be treated. If he let it drag on for too long, it might make it even worse.

He couldn't let things go on like this. He intended to try to convince Prince Jing to seek medical help as soon as possible.

Li Yu stood in the doorway without moving. Prince Jing was slightly startled when he pushed the door open and saw him.

From Li Yu's position and his unusually serious expression, Prince Jing seemed to understand something, and his countenance immediately darkened.

"Tianchi, I-I saw everything," Li Yu said nervously. "Don't hide it from me."

He had to come up with a gentle reason to persuade Prince Jing to see the imperial physician.

"It might be hard for you to talk about, but I'm more worried about your health. You—"

Prince Jing looked dejected. Perhaps he'd made preparations in case Li Yu found out. He hesitated for a moment, then reached into his sleeve and handed Li Yu a note. Li Yu knew that this was Prince Jing's explanation. He immediately opened it and read it.

He felt he knew Prince Jing well after being married for over a year, and thought that Prince Jing had most likely taken medicine because of him. He couldn't let Prince Jing think that he was looking down on him in any way.

He'd decided a long time ago that Prince Jing was more important to him than anything else. He had to make Prince Jing understand that the right thing to do was to face it together.

Li Yu already had a plan in mind, but he suddenly stopped when he saw the words on the paper. It was a short line. He read each word carefully, but he still didn't quite understand it.

Because I was born mute.

Huh?

What? Of course he knew that Prince Jing was mute. What did it have to do with taking medicine? Did being mute connect to how he was incompetent in that way? He'd never heard of such a thing.

Li Yu looked back and forth between Prince Jing and the note and asked, confused, "What does this mean?"

Prince Jing's expression changed from embarrassment to surprise.

They both quickly realized something was off. Li Yu quietly whispered his suspicions about Prince Jing being incompetent in that regard, and he couldn't help but reassure him, "It's not a big deal."

Prince Jing rubbed the spot between his brows. He'd assumed Xiaoyu knew what was going on, but Xiaoyu had actually misunderstood... But now that Xiaoyu had already discovered that he was taking medicine, he couldn't keep hiding it.

As if afraid Li Yu would run off, he held his hand tightly in his own. They went to the table together, and Prince Jing wrote something down.

The truth was far from what Li Yu thought was "incompetence." It turned out that the medicine Prince Jing took wasn't to help with "incompetence" or to fix it—but for prevention.

A contraception?

Li Yu suddenly realized this must be the case. He couldn't help but feel angry at being deceived. No wonder there were no results even though he'd been trying so hard for another child. Had he been doing useless work this whole time?

"Why? You know I want a daughter, but why..."

Prince Jing gripped his hand even tighter and glanced at the note.

"Because of this?" Li Yu was so upset that he picked up the note angrily and read it again in front of Prince Jing.

Prince Jing's body shuddered, and when Li Yu read those couple of words, he closed his eyes as if he was in pain. Li Yu's chest felt like it'd been hit. When he returned to his senses, he realized what he was reading.

Because I was born mute.

Born mute...

Born...mute...

The belated epiphany came. Li Yu finally understood.

"Y-you're afraid..." Li Yu let go of the note, trembling, and slowly fell back into a chair.

Prince Jing was born mute. Since he was born that way, it was very likely that it would be passed onto their children. He took contraceptive medicine because he was worried about this.

"But Dabao and the others are fine. You didn't..."

As Li Yu spoke, he realized that Dabao and the others were different. He wasn't aware when he got pregnant, and Prince Jing even less so. Who would have thought that two men could get pregnant?

Naturally they didn't try to prevent it, so he got pregnant and gave birth.

At that time, he took a risk that he didn't even know about—what would he do if Dabao or one of the others had inherited Prince Jing's muteness? That was a possibility that was painful to consider.

Luckily, their four children were fine, but what about in the future?

Prince Jing had taken measures against it, so Li Yu never received any system notifications. He wanted a daughter, but it was impossible to get pregnant.

I'm sorry, Prince Jing wrote. *I asked the imperial physician and Liao Kong as well. The imperial physician said that just because these four children were fine doesn't mean that future ones would be. Liao Kong said that even though you're a carp spirit, the children are also mine.*

Since the children could look like him, there was a possibility that they could be mute as well. Prince Jing had no way to guarantee that their future children wouldn't be mute, so he could only make sure that they had no more children.

He silently wrote, *Not being able to speak is painful.*

Instead of letting a child suffer a painful life after being born... why let a child lead such a painful life in the first place?

Li Yu was stunned and speechless. Just a couple of calm lines revealed the pain Prince Jing had deep in his heart and had never spoken about.

Prince Jing...couldn't speak, and who knew this pain better than he did? He knew it well. He didn't want his children to go through it.

They couldn't take the risk even if there was the slightest possibility, because if Li Yu got pregnant again, they wouldn't give up the child. Not getting pregnant was the only way to cut off all possibilities.

Prince Jing, seeing how Li Yu didn't react, almost couldn't control the panic and anxiety he felt. He started writing more apologies, and Li Yu's vision started to blur as he stared at the ever-increasing line of "sorry"s.

It was disappointing that he couldn't have a cute daughter or any more children in the future, but Prince Jing's concerns were reasonable. He was thinking of the children too. And Prince Jing was an innocent victim. He shouldn't have to apologize like this.

Li Yu stopped his hand and prevented him from writing anymore. He said seriously, "This isn't your fault. Don't think that... Look, Tianchi, four children are enough for us." Li Yu choked. "It's my fault. I didn't know that you were suffering..."

Prince Jing's inability to speak meant he didn't show much emotion. Li Yu had mistakenly assumed that with the protagonist halo and tyrant character setting, he just had a cold temperament and didn't suffer too much from his condition. Li Yu spent so much time with him, and was so accustomed to it, that he would even sometimes forget Prince Jing was mute.

In the novel, it had just been a character trait. Suffering was a type of weakness, and the male protagonist couldn't have that.

But how could the real Prince Jing be emotionless? He was a living person, after all.

Li Yu ached for him. He pushed aside the paper with all the "sorry"s, threw himself into Prince Jing's arms, and burst into sobs. "I'm sorry, it's all my fault. I should have realized sooner..."

Prince Jing hugged him hurriedly, the rims of his eyes red. He wrote in Li Yu's palm, *You're wonderful. With you here, I'm not in pain.*

Li Yu cried so hard that he hiccupped a couple of times, and his legs were still somewhat sore and numb. He sat down on Prince Jing's legs and glared at him fiercely with eyes as red as a white rabbit's.

He wasn't intimidating at all.

"You're not allowed to take medicine secretly anymore," Li Yu started to lecture his husband. "This type of medicine shouldn't be taken so casually! What if you become impotent?"

Actually, Prince Jing had asked his servants who were skilled in medicine to take a look at the prescription, and it was fine. But he would listen to whatever Xiaoyu said. He couldn't become impotent, and he didn't want to either. He nodded in agreement. Since Xiaoyu was in the loop now, they could use other forms of contraception. As long as Xiaoyu didn't mind it.

Li Yu thought about it carefully, and sure enough, he came up with something. His hot lips came close to whisper in Prince Jing's ear. "Tianchi, I have an idea..."

Prince Jing listened, half-amused and half-expectant.

Li Yu chuckled and said, "Why don't you just not come in in the future?"

Not going in at all wasn't an option!

Pet Fish Pet Ducks

AFTER PRINCE JING RETURNED to the capital, the emperor started to rely on him more. Prince Jing was the di son and he'd achieved great feats on the western front, so though he couldn't speak, the court officials didn't say much in opposition.

The sixth prince had had no competition to speak of only a little while ago. But now, having been reprimanded by the emperor for the bribery case, he rarely appeared in public anymore. He chose to keep his head down, which was making several court officials who supported him begin to hesitate.

These officials had originally supported the third prince. When the sixth prince started becoming more prominent, they had even tried to claim that the third prince and the sixth prince were on the same side. Now that the third prince was no longer favored, these officials had never spoken a single sentence more on behalf of the third prince and gone straight to supporting the sixth prince. They were only fence-sitters, after all, so it was typical for them to randomly swap sides.

The sixth prince had his own plans; he couldn't be bothered with appeasing these officials right now. Prince Jing had moved to center stage. Not only did he have political achievements, he'd also gained the emperor's support through his sons. Comparing it to

Lady Liang's pregnancy, the sixth prince could clearly tell that the emperor favored Prince Jing. If he took the initiative to compete with Prince Jing, he would just be following in the third prince's footsteps and make the emperor dislike him. But if he pretended to be weak and bided his time to find Prince Jing's mistakes, so that Prince Jing lost the emperor's favor, then the emperor would naturally turn toward him.

As for Prince Jing's mistakes—he was quite sure he'd already found one. Consort Zhang had found a couple of assistants for him, distant relatives of the Zhang family. The sixth prince could trust them, so he secretly sent one of the more capable ones to verify his suspicions and hopefully gather some evidence. On the outside, the sixth prince looked quiet and obedient, as if Prince Jing becoming more influential was no problem for him. But he was just waiting for confirmation.

Once he had it, he would take him down in one strike.

The wet nurse to the four young children, Madam Qin, had run into some trouble. Her son lost a lot of money in an investment and was chased back to his home by debt collectors. Madam Qin had already given them all of her savings, but it wasn't enough. She'd been looking dejected for the past few days and was inevitably a bit neglectful when taking care of the children. She made a lot of mistakes, and though they weren't huge mistakes, it was enough for Prince Jing.

She knew she had erred, and she knelt to beg Prince Jing to not let her go from the palace. As long as she had this job, the manor would take care of her, and her whole family wouldn't have to worry for the rest of their lives. But if she was chased out, she would have nothing left.

Madam Qin was one of the people serving Li Yu, so Prince Jing looked to Li Yu for his input. Though Li Yu was the consort, he was usually a bit lazy and didn't ask after the manor's affairs. Prince Jing wanted to help Li Yu cultivate some authority and respect, but when he thought of what had happened with Auntie Xu, he didn't think that was a realistic expectation for Li Yu. Prince Jing could essentially guess what Xiaoyu would do, so he might as well let Xiaoyu collect some good karma.

Prince Jing handed the reins over to Li Yu. Li Yu took the olive branch he offered.

The fishy consort didn't really want to manage anything, because power and status often turned couples against one another. Li Yu thought that staying away from power would lengthen their relationship, but the fish-scamming system had given him the quest "Share the Country," so he couldn't just keep loafing around.

Since he couldn't hide, then he should face it bravely. Li Yu took one tiny step in the direction of being the lady of the house, trying it out carefully.

He would start with Madam Qin.

The manor had clear rules, so it was easy to follow them and hard to make mistakes. Li Yu remembered that Madam Qin had a good temper and was quite meticulous, so why did she keep messing up?

"Is something wrong?" Li Yu asked patiently. "Why do you keep making mistakes?"

Madam Qin felt her nose sting. She was just a servant, and the children didn't need her milk anymore. The consort only needed her to help look after and play with the children. In all honesty, she didn't have much work to do every day, even though she was still being paid a wet nurse's salary. The fact that she kept making mistakes in spite of this made her feel extremely ashamed to face the consort.

But not only did the consort not seem to mind, he asked her what was wrong. Even if she lost all her dignity, she couldn't keep it in anymore. She broke down and cried, telling him everything that had happened with her son.

Li Yu asked for the amount, and Madam Qin stated a large sum of money. Li Yu thought for a moment. "There is an easy solution," he decided. "Since you're Dabao and the others' wet nurse, the manor will always support you. We can give you this amount of money right away and deduct a portion of it from your monthly salary."

Li Yu meant that he would lend money to her on behalf of the manor and have her repay some of it every month. He might not have an eye for antiques, but he knew that his husband, who gave him a bunch of priceless gems to play with, was very rich. That amount of money wasn't much to Prince Jing, but to Madam Qin, it was life-saving money. Saving a life was better than honoring someone with a grave after the fact.

And he wasn't giving it to her for nothing; it was essentially an interest-free loan. Since she would pay back some of it every month, Madam Qin had no need to be troubled or feel embarrassed.

Prince Jing had given him the full authority to handle this matter, so it would have been simple enough for him to ask Prince Jing to immediately pay off the debt. However, he felt that now that he was the consort, he had to give it some more thought and consider the case more carefully. Madam Qin had made mistakes, so it wasn't fair or right if he just repaid her debt. What would the other servants think? That they could take advantage of him by making mistakes?

Compared to whom to help and how to help, the manor's authority was still very important.

That was why he chose to lend her money instead. The manor wouldn't lose anything, and Madam Qin would be overcoming this difficulty on her own. Meanwhile, outsiders would see the humanity of Prince Jing's manor.

Madam Qin was overjoyed with this arrangement and wrote a promissory note on the spot. After Li Yu and Prince Jing took a look at it, Li Yu had Wang Xi file it away.

Li Yu glanced at Prince Jing and added, "If others in the manor have similar difficulties, please tell His Highness and he will make the proper arrangements."

Prince Jing unconsciously curled his lips into a smile. He'd wanted to give his consort a chance to cultivate some authority through this incident, but his consort gave the chance to him instead.

Wang Xi felt quite sure that this was for Prince Jing's sake. To the rest of the country, Prince Jing had a reputation for being strict and harsh. It hadn't mattered much in the past, but now that the emperor valued Prince Jing, Wang Xi was afraid that Prince Jing's reputation would be a burden. If they did as the consort said, then his reputation could become a positive one!

Wang Xi expectantly waited for his master's response, and Prince Jing's glance told him: *Do it.*

Wang Xi made arrangements immediately.

Since she'd made mistakes in taking care of the children, Madam Qin still had to be punished to placate the masses. Li Yu had a problem with the manor's "minimum thirty strokes of the board" rule, though, so he wanted to take this opportunity to change that as well. In the past he'd been a lowly pet fish, so the most he could do was act cute. It wasn't particularly useful. Now that he was the consort, he had to take advantage of his new power!

"Tianchi, let's make some small adjustments." Li Yu discussed quietly with Prince Jing. "The first offense will incur ten strokes, while the next one will incur thirty. How does that sound?"

At first he wanted to cut it down to fifteen, but he was afraid that if he directly said fifteen, Prince Jing would think it was too large of a reduction. Li Yu decided to be a bit cunning and started with ten instead.

Prince Jing, of course, guessed exactly what he was thinking. He pursed his lips and wrote, *First offense is fifteen strokes. The next offense is leaving the manor.*

It was reasonable that the punishment for the "next offense" was higher.

Li Yu internally put up a victory sign but externally solemnly agreed.

Madam Qin thanked him profusely and accepted her punishment. After she was struck with the board, she went to accept the money. Wang Xi-gonggong gave her some silver, and she limped out to pay the debt.

When he saw her, the debt collector thought that she must have tried to steal money from her master and ended up punished, so he sneered. "Look at how miserable you are, yet you still can't repay the loan. I have a way for you to get rid of the debt. Do you want to hear it?"

Madam Qin was holding the money that Wang Xi had given her, but she did want to get rid of her debt, so she thought she would hear him out and didn't let him know that she already had the money.

"I know you're the wet nurse at Prince Jing's manor. I want something from there. If you can get it, then I'll forgive your debt."

Madam Qin's heart raced. The debt collector had heard that there were quadruplets in Prince Jing's manor, and he wanted something from the children to be made into amulets to protect a pregnant woman and her child at home.

The country did have such a custom. Things like bracelets or handkerchiefs would be enough, and Madam Qin had quite a number of these things. But while she was pondering whether she should accept, the man specified, "I only want a drop of blood from the eldest young master."

On one hand, she could repay the prince's money honestly, and on the other, she could do what this person said. She had more opportunity than most to get close to the young master, and it was just a drop of blood. It wasn't hard to get it when he was sleeping.

Madam Qin hesitated. When she reached her hand into her robes and felt the money the consort had given her, she gritted her teeth. The consort had been kind enough to help her. How could she hurt the young heir in return?!

She didn't know what this man's intentions were, so she calmed down and decided to delay him. She said that she needed to think about it and then immediately fled back to Prince Jing's manor and knocked on the door to Prince Jing's study.

The candles in the study stayed lit until late night. After she left, Wang Xi went in and didn't leave for a while.

The next day, Madam Qin found the debt collector and said she was at the end of her rope, so she was willing to help. His eyes looked triumphant.

Madam Qin wanted to do it herself, but the debt collector insisted, "Take me to the manor. I'll do it."

She knew he didn't trust her; she had to do as he said. She snuck him in by pretending he was a relative who was just here to ask the manor for a job. After a couple of questions, Wang Xi agreed to let the man enter the manor.

As soon as he entered, he was almost dazzled by all the water in the manor. Madam Qin smiled and said, "His Highness loves fish, and this was prepared for Master Fish."

The man nodded indifferently. It was known in the capital that Prince Jing liked his pet fish.

Prince Jing's manor was heavily guarded, and they were both patted down several times before the man was finally brought into a courtyard.

For some reason, there were two fat ducks in this courtyard, making a racket. As the man stepped in, the two ducks flew toward him and started pecking at him.

The man lifted his hand to hit them, but Madam Qin quickly said, "You can't. This is the consort and the children's pet duck that they brought from the western front. If either are injured, the guards will find out. You'll be beaten if they lose a single feather."

...Pet fish and pet ducks. What kind of weird manor was this?

The two western ducks were powerful. They pecked him until it hurt. But for the sake of his plan, he had to just endure it in silence.

Madam Qin slowed down and led the man into an inner room. There was a child lying on the bed, facing away from them.

She quickly walked in, calling out softly, "Young Master."

The child rolled over, still asleep. From a distance away, the man glanced at the child's face and matched it up mentally with the portrait he'd received. He was confident now. The child was about to wake up, so he quickly asked Madam Qin to lull him back to sleep again.

When the child fell asleep, the man took out a handkerchief from his sleeve and put it over the child's face, holding it there for a bit.

Madam Qin thought he was going to hurt the young heir, so she hurriedly rushed over to save him. The man pushed her aside and removed the handkerchief once it had been there for long enough. The handkerchief wasn't placed tightly over the child's face, so it wasn't dangerous. But there was thorn apple pollen on the handkerchief that would make a person fall unconscious.

Once the man saw that the child was properly asleep, he took out a silver needle and white porcelain bottle from his sleeve. Madam Qin collapsed to the ground, unable to look.

After he'd collected the blood, the man took a silver bracelet from the child's arm and left.

All of this was viewed by everyone waiting in the next room.

Is he gone? Li Yu was holding Dabao in his arms and gestured at Prince Jing.

Prince Jing nodded.

Dabao was sitting in his fish father's arms, afraid to even breathe too loud. He'd just seen what happened, and immediately understood what Fish Father said about people being scary. Dabao knew that he was still too young and couldn't do anything, though, so he simply remembered that man's face and thought he would tell Emperor Grandpa later.

Once Prince Jing made sure it was safe, he rang the jade bell. Wang Xi soon brought Madam Qin in. She stood there, her eyes downcast. Prince Jing ordered Wang Xi to rip up the promissory note as a reward, and she thanked him profusely.

The "child" lying on the bed jumped down and joined them in the room where Prince Jing was waiting, where he took out a bottle of liquid and skillfully wiped his face. The chubby little face that had looked the same as Dabao's suddenly turned into an adult's. Even his voice became an adult's voice.

This was actually a man with dwarfism who was about the size of a child. He was a special guard under Prince Jing's command, and

Prince Jing had called him over to work with Madam Qin and Wang Xi on a particular scheme.

The guard made his greetings and raised his head. Li Yu's eyes shone with respect; he felt like this guard was incredibly skilled. He looked a lot like Dabao, and their differences in figure were impossible to see when he was lying down. It was more than enough to trick a man who'd never seen Dabao before and had to rely on a portrait to identify him.

"Did you change your appearance?" Li Yu asked excitedly. He'd transmigrated, turned into a fish, and even given birth, but he'd never thought he'd be able to witness such skills in his lifetime.

The guard paused and smiled. "I don't know what you mean by change. I just used some makeup—it was nothing but a small trick."

"Even so, that was amazing. How did you do it?" Li Yu couldn't be stopped when he was curious. The guard was going to give him more details, but when he saw Prince Jing's darkened expression next to him, he decided instead to just respectfully clasp his fists together in farewell and take his leave.

The distracted consort focused once again on his husband's big plan. The feeling of plotting against someone with Prince Jing was so satisfying! Especially when the other party thought they had already won since they already had the young heir's blood. In reality, they couldn't have been more wrong.

He didn't even need to think to know who had sent that man. But he was worried the sixth prince would suspect something.

"Your Highness…will he believe this?" Li Yu asked.

Yes. Prince Jing was sure.

The sixth prince was careful and meticulous. If everything went too smoothly, he'd definitely question it. That was why Prince Jing had ordered the guards to check them over multiple times and had even brought out the duck army to guard the family. They had pecked the man dozens of times.

Things felt more "real" when they were more "dangerous."

Prince Jing knew the sixth prince desperately wanted to catch his mistakes, so he'd just hand one over on a silver platter. If the sixth prince rose to prominence again, it would be hard to deal with him. But what if he knew a huge secret of Prince Jing's?

Although the secret was fake, as long as the sixth prince believed it was real, it would work.

Fishy Charging

WHY DID THE SIXTH prince need Dabao's blood? The technology of ancient times was not as good as that of modern times, so what use was blood? Palace novels often included scenes where they used blood to confirm the legitimacy of a child, but as a person from modern times, Li Yu knew that those weren't accurate. What could the sixth prince do with "Dabao's" blood?

Prince Jing tapped Li Yu's forehead lightly and told him a secret of the royal family.

The imperial physicians in the palace had their own secret methods of verifying whether or not someone was a member of the royal family through a few drops of blood. As soon as the sixth prince's lackey mentioned that he wanted to take some blood, Prince Jing knew that the sixth prince probably suspected that his children were illegitimate. Prince Jing had let him take the blood on purpose so that the sixth prince would think he was correct.

Next, the sixth prince would definitely make arrangements to let the emperor know. The crime of sullying the royal bloodline would be more than enough to make the emperor change his attitude.

But at the same time, the crime of slandering a prince was severe enough that the sixth prince would never escape it.

Li Yu and Prince Jing waited patiently for the sixth prince to make a move, but unexpectedly, he retreated again.

As expected of the most patient and slippery boss. Though he'd suffered a lot of losses and faced a lot of mistakes at Prince Jing's hands, he could still keep calm and bide his time until the best moment.

May he bide his time until he turns into a large turtle! Li Yu thought.

Two months later, the annual hunting festival was approaching.

The hunting festival, as the name suggested, was a large-scale hunting event the royal family organized in ancient times.

There was a well-known joke that the founder of a country was good at fighting, while the emperor who maintained it was good at hunting. It went to show how important hunting was in an emperor's career. As a relatively clear-minded monarch, the emperor was quite keen to organize hunting events to show off his prowess, so the hunting festival was created.

This was a grand hunting event, and there was only one rule— regardless of seniority or status, only the results mattered. The emperor usually led a group of royal children in a fierce competition against the civil and military officials for the best prey. Those who ranked highly would receive praise and rewards from the emperor, and those who performed outstandingly would receive promotions, even if they were from a humble background.

The hunting festival was basically a shortcut to success. Everyone knew that if you performed well, the emperor would pay attention to you. Even children as young as seven or eight years old would bravely pick up their bows and arrows to rush to the grounds with everyone else.

But there were some who didn't want to participate in this event that everyone else enjoyed.

Prince Jing rarely went hunting. In the hunting festivals of previous years, he always stayed in his manor instead—usually, Ye Qinghuan would go on Prince Jing's behalf, to just go through the motions. Truthfully, Prince Jing's actions were understandable. After all, what was the point of a prince with a disability making an outstanding showing for himself? Nobody considered it rude that he didn't go; instead, they thought it was how things should be. The emperor never said much about it either.

Though seniority didn't matter in the hunting festival, the emperor still took first place every year.

In the past, second place had usually gone to the second prince, or sometimes the third prince. That wasn't really a surprise. The ranks further down were the ones people fought for.

But the situation had changed drastically this year.

The second prince had gone insane, the third prince was abandoned, and the sixth prince was a dark horse who'd made a breakthrough. Everything seemed to be settled, but then Prince Jing—who was not at all preferred and should never have been an option for crown prince—went to the western front and came back, and things changed again.

As the only prince in the country who had achievements in both politics and military exploits, as well as the noble status of a di son and four lively, healthy gongzi, being born unable to speak was no longer a big deal. Especially as Prince Jing's oldest son was one of the emperor's favorites. Every time Dabao entered the palace, he would sit directly in the emperor's lap. All of these were clear signs of Prince Jing's sudden rise to prominence.

Though there was a saying that princes were not easily given the title of Prince, it wasn't difficult to tell who had lost favor permanently as opposed to a brief fall—it was obvious when you compared him to the Marquis of Ping and the Marquis of An. Prince Jing's title was, perhaps, special, and indicated his place as the emperor's favorite.

Clever people would quietly pay attention to the rankings of this hunting festival, as once the rankings were determined, it might be obvious who was going to become the crown prince.

Even the emperor was looking forward to it. But Prince Jing, who rarely participated, still said that he didn't want to join in this year, and planned to stay in the manor with his consort and play with the children.

The emperor couldn't let things go on like this. He'd seen the battle reports from the western border; he knew that Prince Jing could lead troops and even fight bandits. What was wrong with some hunting?

With a darkened expression, the emperor ordered Head Eunuch Luo to send the message that no matter what, Prince Jing must participate in the hunting festival and was not allowed to shirk that responsibility. Prince Jing had no choice but to head to the hunting grounds with Li Yu.

They were afraid that something would happen to the children if they were left at the manor, so after some discussion they decided to take them all along. There would be imperial guards to keep them safe at the hunting grounds. Prince Jing would also bring enough people to look after the children, and since they couldn't really walk yet, there was no danger of them running around when they got there.

With the children's whereabouts decided, all that was left was to prepare. There were special robes for hunting; Prince Jing made Li Yu a set of white riding robes with gold hems in advance. It was a proper narrow-sleeved, short outfit that looked quite dashing. As soon as he put it on, Li Yu thought he was so handsome that he nagged Prince Jing to wear a matching one. He was drooling at the thought!

A prince and his consort had to wear matching clothes for such an occasion.

At Li Yu's encouragement, Prince Jing didn't just have an outfit made for himself, he also commissioned little riding clothes for the four children.

When the hunting festival rolled around, Prince Jing put on his matching set of black riding robes, with a jasper belt around his waist and a violet gold hairpiece. With his handsome face and upright, attractive figure, he and Li Yu were truly a match made in heaven.

The handsome, attractive riding outfits the adults wore were shrunken down for the four children, making them look round and cute.

Dabao was wearing a little golden riding set and little leather boots. His round body made the clothes bulge, and he wobbled dreadfully with every step, making Li Yu nervous. He could already stumble around on his legs and say a couple of words at a time, slowly but clearly. The imperial physician and the wet nurse both said that boys usually started talking later than this, so the little heir was already doing very well.

Erbao and Sanbao were wearing riding sets of gold mixed with silver. They couldn't walk yet, and they couldn't talk as well as Dabao could either. Dabao held onto the wall and started to move, but Erbao and Sanbao rolled on the ground like two shining balls and clung to Dabao's boots, insisting that he drag them along with him.

Dabao didn't treat the two with disdain. His little face showed a seriousness that was inconsistent with his age, and he raised his stubby legs to step forward with all his might—but he still couldn't move.

Li Yu and Prince Jing both laughed. Sibao, who was wearing a handsome black riding set with silver trim, sat in his fish father's arms and giggled nonstop. But his great joy ended up bringing him sorrow; as he laughed, Li Yu blinked at him and put him down.

Scatterbrained Sibao was the one least interested in his human form, and he felt the same way about walking. Compared to Dabao's seriousness, Sibao put in almost no effort; he let the soles of his feet touch the ground for just a moment and then plopped onto the ground with his butt, reaching his arms out and crying "Aaahhh!" for his fish father to carry him again.

Now that Li Yu had put him down, he wasn't going to pick him back up again.

Sibao stared at him with his eyes that looked like Li Yu's, then copied Erbao and Sanbao by holding onto Dabao's legs.

Dabao had suddenly gained another brother as a pendant...

Li Yu laughed. Wang Xi had already brought the horse over, and Prince Jing put the children in the carriage first. Wang-gonggong was in charge of taking care of them, so when the children were safely in the carriage, Prince Jing, in a good mood, pulled his consort onto his horse and wrapped his arms around him, slowly trotting beside the carriage.

Li Yu kept mumbling that sitting in the front made him look childish, but when the horse started running, he screamed immediately.

When they arrived, Prince Jing and his family first headed to the dragon tent to greet the emperor. The emperor was quite satisfied with how tactful Prince Jing was, and whispered a few sentences to him.

This was the first time Li Yu had participated in such a large-scale event. To avoid any mistakes, he stood politely behind Prince Jing. The emperor gave him a few words of encouragement as well.

He seemed very wise and powerful at the moment. But when he saw the children wearing neat riding sets beside Li Yu's legs, his demeanor changed. He couldn't help but laugh out loud.

"Dabao, are you going to hunt today as well?" The regal emperor transformed into a kind grandpa. He scooped Dabao up with one arm, smiling.

"Grandpa, hunting!" Dabao said crisply.

Once Dabao learned how to talk, Li Yu had tried to teach him the proper way to address the emperor, but "Grandfather" was still difficult for a child to say. The emperor used this as an excuse to permit Dabao to keep calling him "Grandpa." He thought it made them seem closer.

The emperor was happy that Dabao knew to be ambitious at such a young age, and had a thought to teach Dabao archery himself. But such a small child didn't have the arm strength to hold a bow.

The emperor ordered Luo Ruisheng to find a slingshot, and swapped archery for shooting.

Dabao's chubby hands fiddled with the string, not knowing what to do. The emperor stroked his beard and was about to teach him how to use it when he remembered that his son, Prince Jing, was still waiting for him.

Without the emperor's permission, Prince Jing could not move.

"You can go. If you don't place well, don't come back to see me," the emperor ordered, expectantly.

Prince Jing nodded and met Li Yu's gaze.

The emperor's edict for them to participate in the hunting festival had come unexpectedly, and Li Yu didn't know how to ride a horse. Prince Jing gave him a few last-minute lessons, but Li Yu still wasn't very good at it, so it wasn't likely that he would achieve much this time.

And the children had come as well, so one of them had to look after them. They couldn't both hunt.

They'd heard that the sixth prince had arrived before them and had already been at the hunting grounds for an hour. He had gathered a lot of game and was among the highest ranked so far.

"Tianchi, don't worry, go ahead!" Li Yu cheered for his husband, encouraging him on his way out hunting. "Show him what you've got!"

Prince Jing nodded and pulled Li Yu into his arms to rub his head, not caring who was nearby. Li Yu took the chance to be a little lovey-dovey with him, then giddily returned to the tent to sit in a lesser priority position near the emperor.

He listened to the guards' reports: sometimes the sixth prince would catch something, and other times, Prince Jing would. The sixth prince was way ahead at first, but Prince Jing caught up quickly and closed the gap. The first animal Prince Jing caught was a white rabbit. It was still alive, with only the skin on its leg damaged by an arrow.

The emperor's mouth twitched as he looked at it, and he asked Li Yu to take care of it. The children all started to clap.

"Rabbit!" Erbao and Sanbao said, laughing.

Sibao reached for it. "Wabbit!" Sibao was always a little slower, and this was one of the rare moments where he spoke a word clearly.

The children surrounded the snow-white rabbit, clearly enjoying it. Li Yu was suddenly brought back to the time the ducks had entered the house for the first time... Prince Jing must have done it on purpose. What was he supposed to do with such a cutie?

Li Yu happily asked Wang-gonggong to bandage the rabbit's leg. It looked like there'd be another pet to add to the pet fish and pet ducks in the manor.

The results of the hunt wouldn't be available for a while, and the emperor got tired of listening to reports, so he started teaching Dabao how to use a slingshot.

A slingshot needed pellets, since it'd be useless to just pull the string. But the usual pellets were made of either iron or stone, which were too dangerous for children to play with. The emperor, who often heard Prince Jing praise Li Yu, asked Li Yu to think of something.

Li Yu was quite clever. He tore a piece of paper up and scrunched it into a ball. That wouldn't hurt if it hit someone. Pellets acquired, the emperor held Dabao's soft little hand as they both pulled on the string, then let go.

A paper ball flew out and lightly bounced off Head Eunuch Luo, who was trying to inquire for updates. Luo Ruisheng turned around, confused.

The emperor and Dabao both wore perfectly innocent expressions on their faces. *Don't look at me, I didn't do it!*

Li Yu couldn't hold back his giggle. There wasn't anything big going on here with the emperor, so he was mostly preoccupied with Prince Jing.

The guards had come to report several times; the sixth prince was always ahead. At one point Prince Jing almost caught up, but the gap had widened again.

Li Yu couldn't look too anxious in front of the emperor, but he was worried for Prince Jing the entire time. Unthinkingly, he walked to the front of the tent and looked for Prince Jing among the participants.

He found him quickly.

Prince Jing was riding a horse and looked exhausted. He lowered his head and wiped the sweat from his forehead; there was a bunch of prey hanging from the horse's back.

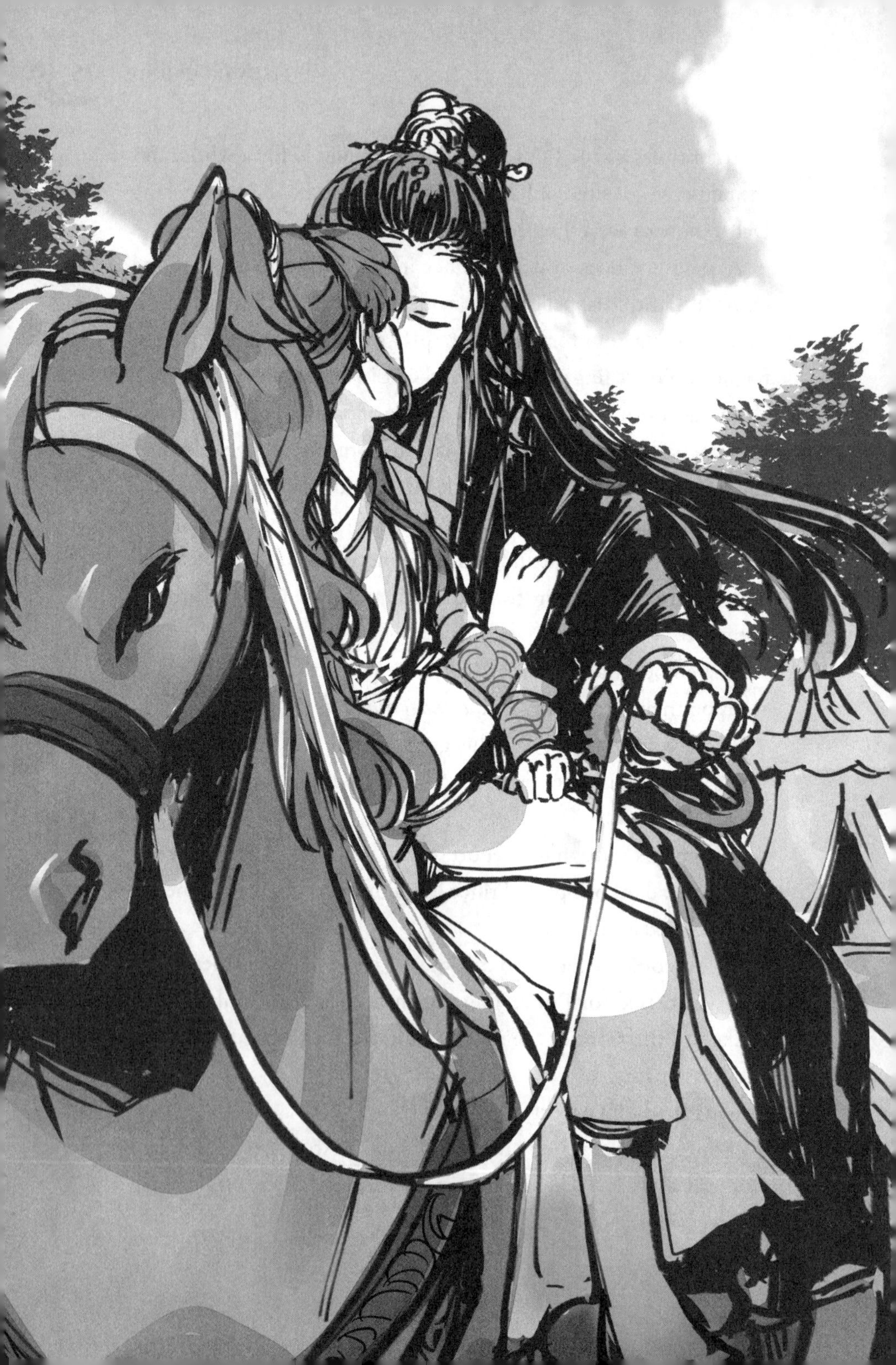

Li Yu felt sorry for him. Because of a single sentence from the emperor, he had to go to such great lengths to prove himself.

Li Yu watched him from a distance. Suddenly, Prince Jing seemed to hear his thoughts and turned his gaze to Li Yu. His lips curved into a smile, and he galloped toward Li Yu, arriving in front of him in an instant. He pulled Li Yu onto the horse, holding the reins with one hand and hugging him tightly with the other. He covered Li Yu's lips with his own, not allowing for any resistance.

Li Yu was instantly surrounded by his hot, familiar breath. Startled, he tried to softly push him away—but it was no use. Instead, he passionately kissed him back.

When the kiss had ended, Prince Jing nuzzled his neck contentedly and put him down. Now, he seemed to be possessed by the god of war. Full of energy, he raised his riding crop in the air, galloping back to the competition.

Seriously... Did he think Li Yu was a battery pack or something?

Feeling invigorated, Li Yu snuck back to his seat quietly, blushing. The emperor was still teaching Dabao how to use the slingshot, and Wang Xi was watching Erbao, Sanbao, and Sibao play with the rabbit. Nobody should have noticed that.

Only a short while later, he heard the guards report that the number of Prince Jing's catches had surpassed the sixth prince's!

Fish Feeding

AFTER THE HUNTING ended, Prince Jing returned along with the sixth prince.

No matter how good the sixth prince usually was at acting, he almost lost control of his expression when he found he'd been beaten by a mute. In the past, when the third prince had been present for events like this, at most he was just the third prince's wingman. He was actually a good hunter, but he'd never dared show off in case the third prince became suspicious. Now he was finally able to show off a little—but, to his surprise, Prince Jing just had to come too.

Most people didn't know that the sixth prince was good at hunting, and the sixth prince didn't know that Prince Jing was skilled either. After all, Prince Jing had never participated in the hunting festival before. To ensure he placed well, the sixth prince had arrived very early and was the first one to rush out when the drums and fanfare started—unlike Prince Jing, who took his time getting to the hunting grounds with his entire family after everyone else had already started ages ago.

There was no rule that said everyone had to start at the same time, just that the total amount of prey taken down determined their ranking. Even if someone arrived late, they could still rank high as long as they were skilled. That was, of course, the ideal situation, but it had never really happened before because arriving late would lose them opportunities and affect their morale.

However, even though Prince Jing started only halfway through the competition...the sixth prince found that any time he relaxed even a little bit, Prince Jing kept catching up.

The sixth prince was already tired, and Prince Jing wasn't in much better condition. Since most of the game had already been caught and Prince Jing had to work harder to find new quarry, his progress slowed down. The sixth prince was sure that his rival wouldn't be able to surpass him. But then, through some unknown means, Prince Jing suddenly started glowing with energy while the sixth prince could barely lift his bow anymore.

Prince Jing caught more game, claiming one target after another.

The sixth prince gave it one last try, but in the final moments of the competition, it was as if Prince Jing had received help from a god—and ended up with more game! Even though the sixth prince had started a full hour earlier!

The sixth prince felt humiliated. It seemed like he wasn't that great at hunting after all.

"Fifth royal brother is truly a latecomer that came out on top and stole the show," the sixth prince said in a strange tone, as he entered the tent.

Prince Jing didn't even look at him as he strode to the emperor to greet him and report his achievements.

The emperor was extremely satisfied with this result—as expected, Prince Jing didn't disappoint him. Even though he had been given a near-impossible mission, he'd surpassed the sixth prince and ranked right below a battle-hardened general.

The emperor realized now that Prince Jing had never been bad at hunting; the reason he'd never joined the hunting festival in previous years was most likely so he could conceal his skills. He wanted to praise him, but he felt some complicated emotions over all this, and he only lightly said, "You can sit."

Prince Jing bowed and returned to Li Yu's side without any arrogance.

Li Yu's lips were red and moist, and his gaze was charming. This couple who had just recharged their batteries still remembered the passionate kiss from before. They couldn't say anything in front of the emperor, though, so they just locked eyes for a moment before Prince Jing smiled and touched Li Yu's hand under their sleeves, intertwining their fingers.

The emperor was sitting on the dragon throne, and from above, he could see Prince Jing and his consort's interactions. He found it both funny and cute.

He turned to the sixth prince and said, "Tianxiao, you did pretty well. Better than I expected."

The emperor wasn't lying. The sixth prince's performance had been impressive; completely different from his previous showings. Unfortunately, though, he still couldn't beat Prince Jing.

The sixth prince's strange attitude immediately vanished when the emperor addressed him. "I'm still a long way behind fifth royal brother," he said humbly. "I'll work harder in the future."

The emperor nodded and told the sixth prince to sit down as well. Next to the sixth prince was his consort, who was pregnant and showing a little bit. She'd been suffering from morning sickness recently, so she was a little tired. When the sixth prince had arrived at the hunting grounds in the morning, he'd handed her off to Consort Zhang and didn't even look back. Lady Liang wasn't feeling well and had been worried about her husband, so she looked even worse for wear. Consort Zhang wasn't the nurturing type. After she'd "looked after" her daughter-in-law for a bit but Lady Liang was still unwell, Consort Zhang assumed that she was just playing it up because she was pregnant, so she didn't really want to pay any more attention to her.

The sixth prince came back, exhausted and upset, only to see a pained expression on his wife's face. He didn't get angry, but he didn't offer her any words of comfort either, so her expression became even gloomier. Though they were seated physically close to each other, that seemed to be the only way they were close.

The emperor was a little annoyed by the sweet demonstrations of love between Prince Jing and his consort, but when he looked at the sixth prince with *his* consort, he felt uncomfortable instead. But the emperor didn't want to interfere with his sons' family affairs, so he ordered his servants to bring in all the game from the hunting festival.

The meat had been roasted by the imperial chef and cut into pieces, waiting on silver plates for the emperor to hand out as rewards.

There was a trick to this. Usually, the festival's participants would offer their first catch to the emperor; if the choice was good, they could earn the emperor's favor, and the emperor would reward the cooked meat back to them.

The general who'd ranked just above Prince Jing had presented a deer, and the sixth prince presented a hawk. Though the sixth prince hadn't beaten Prince Jing, the hawk still gave him bonus points when it was brought to the table.

The emperor rewarded the general with roasted venison and the sixth prince with roasted hawk, but he didn't reward Prince Jing with anything.

Li Yu kept listening, but he didn't hear his husband's name. He wondered what Prince Jing was going to offer. Li Yu wanted to quietly ask him, but then he remembered that Prince Jing's first catch had been a rabbit, the manor's new pet. The rabbit had been reported to the emperor, and the emperor had asked him to handle it.

Other people had deer and hawks, but his husband offered a live rabbit?! Rabbits were so cute! Li Yu didn't think there was anything wrong with presenting a rabbit, but the emperor would definitely look down on it. That was why Prince Jing had been able to give his most significant catch to him and the children to become a pet, right?

Fireworks burst in Li Yu's chest. Just for that, when Head Eunuch Luo brought over a whole roast chicken, Li Yu picked up a huge piece of meat with his chopsticks and put it in Prince Jing's bowl.

Erbao, Sanbao, and Sibao picked up one roasted chicken leg together. Li Yu didn't help them because he wanted to see how they would try to eat it.

The children each only had a single small, white tooth, about the size of a grain of rice. They rubbed their singular tooth back and forth on the chicken leg for a long time without scraping off any meat at all.

"Meat!"

There was good food, but they couldn't eat it—the children were so agitated that they were about to start wailing their heads off. Li Yu took out a small silver knife he had prepared in advance and sliced off pieces of meat from the chicken leg, placing them on a plate.

Li Yu had only sliced off half the meat when Prince Jing took the knife from him and started doing it himself. As expected from the tyrant male protagonist who could hunt successfully in the face of adversity—he sliced much faster than Li Yu did, and in a short while, had a full plate of meat. The three children opened their mouths wide, waiting for Daddy to feed them.

Prince Jing picked up a piece with his chopsticks and was about to feed one of them when Li Yu hurriedly said, "Wait!"

Prince Jing paused for a moment. Blushing, Li Yu copied the children and opened his mouth wide too.

Prince Jing immediately understood. He couldn't help but smile when he saw the adult and three children with blinking eyes and large mouths, like chicks waiting for food. Without any hesitation, he fed Li Yu the meat that was meant for the children.

Li Yu ate the meat off the silver chopsticks and glanced at the three children proudly: *See? He likes me the best.*

...Fish Father took away the fragrant meat. The children were about to cry.

Li Yu was a little embarrassed. He hurriedly stuffed some meat into Erbao's mouth. The tears were still welling up in Erbao's eyes, but his fat, chubby cheeks started moving up and down rapidly. Sanbao and Sibao, seeing that Erbao could eat but they couldn't, became even sadder.

Li Yu and Prince Jing had wanted to feed one each, but Erbao came to a strange conclusion after he ate the meat. Prince Jing gave Fish Daddy meat, and Fish Daddy gave him meat... Shouldn't he give some to Sanbao next?

Erbao liked Sanbao, so he nodded as if he understood. He took out a piece of saliva-covered meat and stuffed it into Sanbao's mouth.

When Sanbao in turn fed another piece of saliva-covered meat to Sibao, Li Yu realized that the children had misunderstood something. He didn't know whether to laugh or cry...but he was happy that the fish children were willing to share.

The children's loving, meat-based game of pass-the-parcel wasn't over yet. As Sibao ate, he thought of Dabao. He started yelling and pointing at him.

Dabao was still sitting on the emperor's knees. When Sibao started wailing, the emperor noticed and waved him forward kindly. Wang Xi picked Sibao up and plopped him over.

Sibao and Dabao met on the emperor's lap. Sibao kept shouting "Aaahhh!" and stuffed the remaining meat into Dabao's mouth.

Understanding slowly dawned in Dabao's eyes...but his brothers had already fed everyone. Who was left for him to feed?

Dabao's eyes lit up. At first, the emperor couldn't hold back his laughter as he watched, but then Dabao suddenly turned around and put the last bit of meat in the emperor's hand. Dabao patted his hand boldly. "Grandpa, eat!"

After the emperor ascended to his position, he had given meat to countless others—but this was the first time someone had given meat to him. Though the meat had been passed around and was covered with different children's saliva, making it inedible, the emperor was quite moved by the children's thoughtfulness.

Prince Jing's children were all good children. In a fit of happiness, the emperor gave them all a huge pot of roasted meat.

They were surrounded by observant people, so as soon as the emperor showed that he liked Prince Jing's sons, these people all started to praise the little gongzi as well. They had practically forgotten that the sixth prince was there too, but the sixth prince just sat there eating his dinner calmly.

At night, Li Yu and Prince Jing stayed in the tent that the emperor had assigned to Prince Jing. Wang Xi and the four children slept in the next tent, only separated from Prince Jing and Li Yu by a curtain.

The outdoors wasn't the place to talk, so Li Yu tried to avoid any confidential topics when he talked to Prince Jing here. They knew each other very well, though, so sometimes they could understand one another with just a gaze.

After they finished getting ready for bed, they met each other's eyes.

They didn't know who started it; their lips pressed together in a fight for dominance. Prince Jing picked Li Yu up and laid him down, letting him lean on his chest as he softly caressed his back.

They'd both expected the sixth prince to make a move during the hunting festival, so Prince Jing had made preparations. But now, thanks to those preparations, they couldn't be intimate with each other yet...

Li Yu lay drowsily on Prince Jing and fell asleep for a little while.

Then, outside the tent there was a small snapping sound. Someone yelled, "Assassin!" and Li Yu immediately opened his eyes, turned over, and got up.

He and Prince Jing were still wearing their robes under the blanket.

They had both been waiting for this moment.

THE STORY CONCLUDES IN
The Disabled Tyrant's Beloved Pet Fish
VOLUME 4

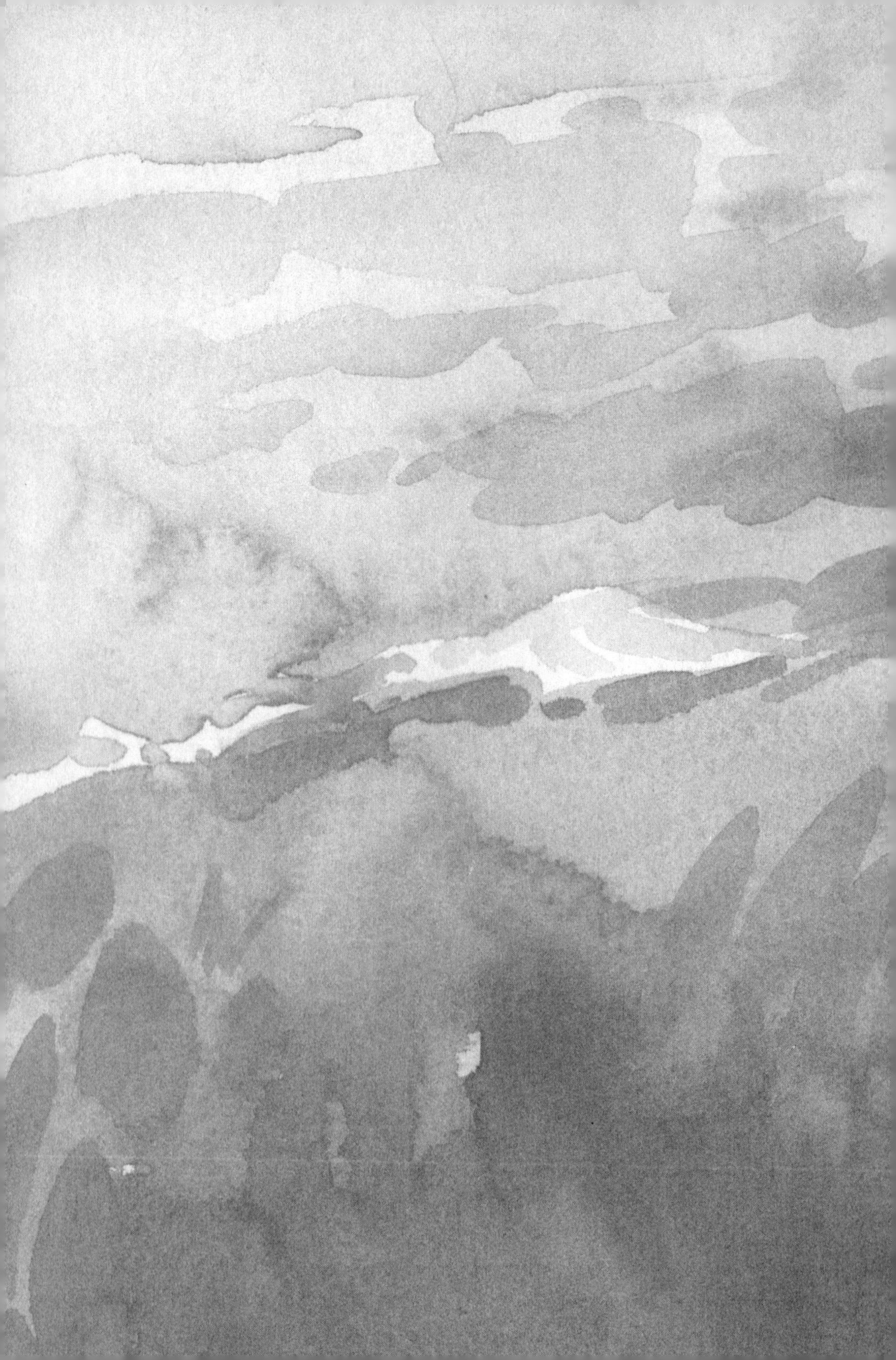

APPENDIX

Characters, Names, and Pronunciations

Characters

MAIN CHARACTERS

LI YU 李鱼: A modern-day webnovel reader who has been transmigrated into a fish.

MU TIANCHI 穆天池: The mute fifth prince, also known as Prince Jing.

THE ROYAL FAMILY

THE EMPEROR: Prince Jing's father.

EMPRESS XIAOHUI: Prince Jing's mother; deceased.

LADY QIU 仇氏: Mother of the second prince, Mu Tianzhao. Previously a noble consort, now banished to the cold palace.

CONSORT QIAN 钱妃: Mother of the third prince, Mu Tianming.

CONSORT ZHANG 张妃: Mother of the sixth prince, Mu Tianxiao.

CHU YANYU 楚燕羽: Prince Jing's love interest in the original webnovel, now one of the emperor's concubines.

SECOND PRINCE MU TIANZHAO 穆天昭: The oldest prince, since demoted to Marquis of An.

THIRD PRINCE MU TIANMING 慕天明: The second prince's rival for the role of crown prince, since demoted to the Marquis of Ping.

SIXTH PRINCE MU TIANXIAO 穆天晓: Pretended to support the third prince while secretly plotting to take over.

LIANG SUYUN 梁素云: The sixth prince's wife.

SEVENTH PRINCE: Unnamed, yet to come of age.

EIGHTH PRINCE: Unnamed, yet to come of age.

LUO RUISHENG: Head eunuch and the emperor's personal servant.

PRINCE JING'S MANOR

WANG XI 王喜: A eunuch; Prince Jing's personal servant.

CHU YANYU 楚燕羽: Prince Jing's love interest in the original webnovel, gifted to Prince Jing by the third prince.

DABAO 大宝: Prince Jing's first son. In fish form he is all gold.

ERBAO 二宝: Princer Jing's second son. In fish form he is gold with flecks of silver.

SANBAO 三宝: Prince Jing's third son. In fish form he is all silver.

SIBAO 四宝: Prince Jing's fourth son. In fish form he is grayish black.

MADAM QIN: The children's wet nurse.

CHENG'EN MANOR

YE QIAN 叶骞: The previous duke of Cheng'en and the current Duke's father. Prince Jing's grandfather.

THE DUKE OF CHENG'EN 承恩公: Ye Qinghuan's father.

YE QINGHUAN 叶清欢: Prince Jing's cousin, heir to the House of Cheng'en.

THE PRINCESS OF JINJUE 金绝公主: Married to Ye Qinghuan.

QINGHE-JUNZU 清河郡主: Ye Qinghuan and the Princess of Jinjue's daughter.

XIONGFENG 叶清欢 ("FIERCE WIND"): Ye Qinghuan's dog.

OTHER

LIAO KONG 了空: A zen master from Huguo Temple, highly trusted by the emperor.

ZHENG JING 郑经: Secretary of the Ministry of Works.

Name Guide

Diminutives, Nicknames, and Name Tags:

A-: Friendly diminutive. Always a prefix. Usually for monosyllabic names, or one syllable out of a two-syllable name.

DOUBLING: Doubling a syllable of a person's name can be a nickname, e.g., "Mangmang"; it has childish or cutesy connotations.

XIAO-: A diminutive meaning "little." Always a prefix.

-ER: An affectionate diminutive added to names, literally "son" or "child." Always a suffix.

Family:

DI/DIDI: Younger brother or a younger male friend.

GE/GEGE/DAGE: Older brother or an older male friend.

JIE/JIEJIE/ZIZI: Older sister or an older female friend.

Other:

GONGZI: Young man from an affluent household.

-GONGGONG: A respectful suffix for eunuchs.

-SHIZI: Denoting the heir to a title.

Pronunciation Guide

Mandarin Chinese is the official state language of mainland China, and pinyin is the official system of romanization in which it is written. As Mandarin is a tonal language, pinyin uses diacritical marks (e.g., ā, á, ǎ, à) to indicate these tonal inflections. Most words use one of four tones, though some are a neutral tone. Furthermore, regional variance can change the way native Chinese speakers pronounce the same word. For those reasons and more, please consider the guide below a simplified introduction to pronunciation of select character names and sounds from the world of *The Disabled Tyrant's Beloved Pet Fish*.

More resources are available at sevenseasdanmei.com

GENERAL CONSONANTS

Some Mandarin Chinese consonants sound very similar, such as z/c/s and zh/ch/sh. Audio samples will provide the best opportunity to learn the difference between them.

- X: somewhere between the **sh** in **sh**eep and **s** in **s**ilk
- Q: a very aspirated **ch** as in **ch**arm
- C: **ts** as in pan**ts**
- Z: **z** as in **z**oom
- S: **s** as in **s**ilk
- CH: **ch** as in **ch**arm
- ZH: **dg** as in do**dge**
- SH: **sh** as in **sh**ave
- G: hard **g** as in **g**raphic

GENERAL VOWELS

The pronunciation of a vowel may depend on its preceding consonant. For example, the "i" in "shi" is distinct from the "i" in "di." Vowel pronunciation may also change depending on where the vowel appears in a word, for example the "i" in "shi" versus the "i" in "ting." Finally, compound vowels are often—though not always—pronounced as conjoined but separate vowels. You'll find a few of the trickier compounds below.

IU: as in **ewe**

IE: **ye** as in **yes**

UO: **war** as in **war**m

CHARACTER NAMES

Lǐ Yú: Li (as in *ly* from merri*ly*), yu (as in you)

Mù Tiānchí: Mu (as in moo), t (as in tea), ian (as in Ian), chi (as in *ch* from *ch*ange)
* *Note:* With chi, the i is not pronounced like ee, the way Li is pronounced. With chi, it is a sort of emphasized ch noise without any vowel sound. This applies to z, c, s, zh, ch, sh, and s.

Yè Qīnghuán: Ye (as in *ye*sterday), qing (as in *ching* from tea*ching*), h (as in *h* from *h*ello), uan (as in one)
* *Note:* The difference between ch and q is that chi is a sound produced more with the front of the teeth with a puckered mouth, while q is a sound produced more at the back, with a wider mouth.

Xióngfēng: Xi (as in *sh* from *sh*eep), ong (like *own* but with the *ng* from ring), feng (as in *fung* from *fung*us)

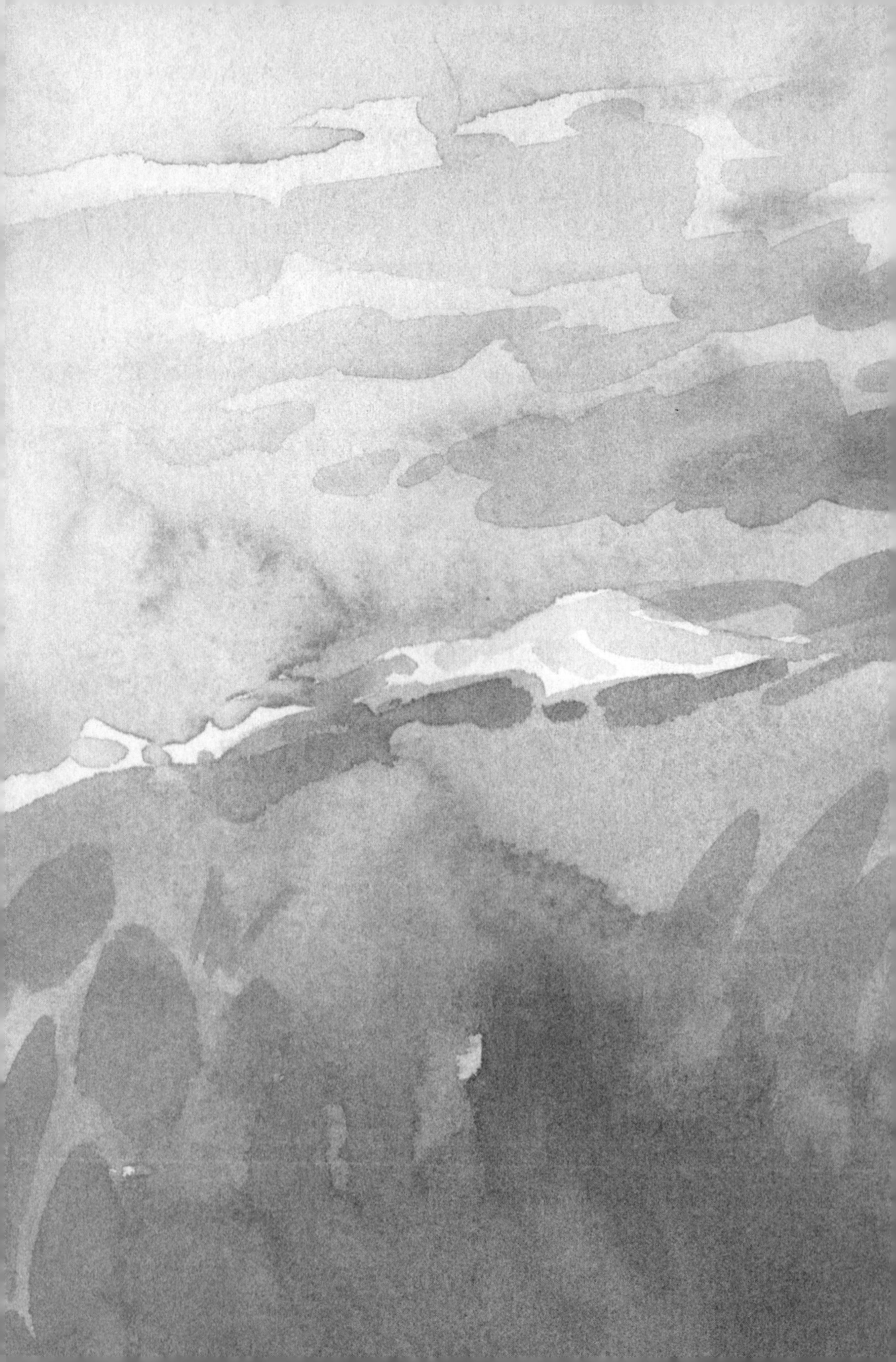

APPENDIX

Glossary

Glossary

CONCUBINES 妻妾: In ancient China, it was common practice for a wealthy man to possess women as concubines (妾) in addition to his wife (妻). They were expected to live with him and bear him children. Generally speaking, a greater number of concubines correlated to higher social status, hence a wealthy merchant might have two or three concubines, while an emperor might have tens or even a hundred.

DI AND SHU HIERARCHY 嫡庶: Upper-class men in ancient China often took multiple wives, though only one would be the official or "di" wife, and her sons would take precedence over the sons of the "shu" wives. "Di" sons were prioritized in matters of inheritance.

ANCIENT CHINESE IMPERIAL HAREM 后宫: Emperors would take multiple wives, and as a whole, they were referred to as the "back palace." This term can also be used to refer to the physical location where the concubines lived, which was the inner half of the palace. The concubines were separated into ranks, and their ranking directly correlated to how well they were treated, how much respect they were afforded, and how much money they were given. The ranks of the concubines changed throughout the dynasties, but these remain fairly consistent and are often used in modern media:

◇ Empress 皇后
◇ Imperial Noble Consort 皇贵妃
◇ Noble Consort 贵妃
◇ Consort 妃
◇ Concubine 嫔
◇ Noble Lady 贵人

ANCIENT CHINESE ARISTOCRACY: It was unusual for a prince to be demoted to a lower rank, but a title like "Marquis" was still a very impressive one. In order, the five highest titles after those of the emperor and princes were as follows:

⋄ Duke 公
⋄ Marquis 侯
⋄ Count 伯
⋄ Viscount 子
⋄ Baron 男

GRAND SECRETARIAT 内阁: The Grand Secretariat was a part of the government responsible for coordinating the rest of the government. Because they controlled communications to and from the emperor, they eventually became more powerful than the Six Ministries. The Grand Secretariat was headed by six Grand Secretaries (大学士).

SIX MINISTRIES 六部: The central government system in ancient China. It consisted of the Ministries of Personnel, Revenue, Rites, War, Justice, and Works. Each of the Ministries was headed by a Minister (尚书) and two Deputy Ministers (侍郎).

IMPERIAL ASTROLOGICAL BUREAU 钦天监: An official branch of the government responsible for things like creating calendars and observing the skies. It was believed that the stars held messages from the heavens, and so the Imperial Astrological Bureau was trusted by the emperor to predict incoming disasters or auspicious events.

TAELS 两: A unit of measurement for weighing gold and silver, used as a standard form of currency.

GOLDEN FINGER 金手指: A protagonist-exclusive overpowered ability or weapon. This can also refer to them being generally OP ("overpowered") and not a specific ability or physical item.